STRANGER STILL

Marilyn Messik

Copyright © 2020 Marilyn Messik
The moral right of the author has been asserted.
Apart from any fair dealing for the purposes of research or private study, or criticism or review, as permitted under the Copyright, Designs and Patents Act 1988, this publication may only be reproduced, stored or transmitted, in any form or by any means, with the prior permission in writing of the publishers, or in the case of reprographic reproduction in accordance with the terms of licences issued by the Copyright Licensing Agency. Enquiries concerning reproduction outside those terms should be sent to the publishers.

Any references to people or places other than those already in the public domain are purely coincidental.

British Library Cataloguing in Publication Data.
A catalogue record for this book is available from the British Library

Satin Publishing
68 West End, Silverstone, Northants NN12 8UY, United Kingdom
Tel: 07803 416159
www.satinpublishing.co.uk
Skype: nicola.fitzmaurice1

ISBN: 9798634927305

for

Dani & Robert

By The Same Author

FICTION
Strange Series
Relatively Strange
Even Stranger
Stranger Still

Witch Series
Witch Dust

* * * *

NON-FICTION
The Little Black Business Books series
Getting It Write. Common Sense Copywriting

HANDS ACROSS THE WATER!

I'm lucky enough to have readers on both sides of the Atlantic, but as you will know there are any number of words which have chosen to 'take sides' and make life difficult for all of us, reader and writer alike. For example, you may be expecting **color** and see **colour** or come across **centre** when you're used to seeing **center**. I know, I know, it's enough to give you a headache, isn't it? For that I can only apologise (apologize!) and send out aspirin when necessary. As you'll see, I've gone with UK spelling throughout the book, simply because that's what I know best, and I'm keeping my fingers crossed it works for everyone.

* * * *

What The People say

What a brilliant unique book. I couldn't put it down ~ **Off-the-Shelf Book Reviews**

A Stephen King-like Dark Tale of Strange Occurrences. ~ **Breakaway Reviewers**

. . . keeps you both on your toes and at the edge of your seat throughout. A must-read. ~ **Elisheva Sokolic. Under Cover**

I spent the first few chapters of this brilliant novel wondering if it really was a crime book, since it seemed to be a very funny description of Stella's mad relatives – then I got swept up in the story, and after I'd finished I couldn't quite see what else it could be. Imagine a John Wyndham character strayed into a McDermid, Kate Brannigan novel, that might give you an idea of this quirky book. If you want to try something a bit different, I'd really recommend this. ~ **Promoting Crime Fiction**

I very rarely recommend books personally (lol) on TBC unless I absolutely LOVE them and Marilyn Messik is, in my opinion, a very underrated author who deserves world fame, adoration, adulation and lots of money. You can thank me later. ~ **Tracy Fenton. The Book Club**

Beautifully written, this book will grab readers on a visceral level. Stella is both heroine, victim and villain, and one of the most compelling characters I have encountered in some time. **For the Love of Books**

I have three of Marilyn's books now, each of them is wonderful. Dark, light, unexpected, comic with real laugh out loud moments and beautifully written. I can't recommend them enough. ~ **Sonia Grimes.**

Marilyn Messik has done it again, I really did enjoy this, hooked throughout. Enjoy, bookworms! ~ **BTP Book Club**

* * * *

Stay In Touch

Twitter: @marilyn_messik
Facebook: marilyn.messik.5
LinkedIn: createcommunication
Instagram: www.instagram.com/createcommunicationuk

WHO'S WHO?

Stella ~ Telepath with attitude.

David ~ Stella's husband.

Laura & Melvyn ~ Stella's in-laws.

Katerina ~ A bolshie Borzoi.

Auntie Kitty ~ Octogenarian office mainstay.

Brenda ~ Office manager.

Ruby, Trudie & Joy ~ Stella's office staff.

Martin ~ Travel agency owner & Stella's landlord.

Hilary ~ Martin's wife

Rachael & Ruth Peacock ~ Telepathic sisters.

Ed ~ Telepath, adopted by the Peacocks.

Glory ~ Telepath, another Peacock protégée.

Sam ~ Telepath adopted by the Peacocks.

Boris ~ Telepath, long-time associate of the Peacock sisters.

Detective Inspector Cornwall ~ Boris's reluctant police contact.

Mrs Millsop ~ Matron

Devlin McCrae ~ Shocked out of a coma by Stella.

* * * *

WHERE'S THE WHALE-SONG?

As the pain began to fade, I heaved a sigh of relief and tried to refocus, although not altogether clear what I should be refocusing on. Having a baby, at the best of times, is a bit of a strain on the nerves, let alone other areas. It didn't help that the stark white walls of the brightly lit room seemed to be moving in on me, then backing off again, it wasn't something walls generally did and I can't say I was thrilled. Had I been drugged or was it simply that recent events had taken more out of me than I'd thought?

One arm was still behind my back, my wrist braceleted by a metal chain looped around the leg of the bed; there was a padlock involved too so I was lying at an uncomfortable sideways angle. I'm not normally a whinger, fully accepting life has its ups and downs, but it was hard not to think of my meticulously packed labour bag back at home, containing such essentials as a natural sponge for cooling my forehead, eau de cologne for my wrists and a whale song cassette, in whose calming qualities David had enormous faith.

I'd realised when the pains started, there was no alternative but to put out another extremely strongly worded mental yell for help, more of a sustained shriek really. I had thought I could cope alone, but had since come to the conclusion that this wasn't working out well. Once I'd admitted that, the possibility of not being able to reach them was a thought too terrible to contemplate.

"You can stop shouting," Rachael's voice, suddenly in my head; loud and clear, crisp and pepperminty. I wanted to sob with relief, but time was of the essence, there were more pressing matters.

"I'm having the baby," I said, although I wasn't even sure whether or not she knew by now there *was* a baby. As usual she had an opinion.

"Well you can't have it now."

"You think?"

"We're on the way, nearly there. Stay exactly where you are." I started to reply along the lines of not having much choice and then it struck me, how could they already be near, then another contraction demanded attention.

"How far apart?" Glory in my head this time.

"What?"

"How long between pains?" I snorted a laugh. I knew if David had been around, he'd have had timings down to the last second.

"Close. Don't know exactly."

"OK," she said, "I'm here now." And she was, suddenly fully in my head with me. She'd never previously taken over quite so completely, although she'd always been able to by-pass my normally strong barriers to find what she wanted to know or to utilise my eyesight: but never previously to this extent. I'd have expected to be horrified instead of which, as I found myself enveloped in the fizzy lemon-sherbet scent of her, I'd never been so relieved in my life.

"Don't know how much time we've got." Glory murmured.

"Can we move her?" Rachael asked. Glory didn't answer, she was assessing. Blind since birth she was using my eyes, taking in the surroundings then running her mind swiftly over the chain that was causing me so much discomfort, passing that information back to Ed; he was much defter at that sort of thing than anybody else. I felt the blissful release of the strain on my arm as he snapped the chain and metal links slithered noisily over the bed frame to coil on the floor.

It was Ed who was driving the vehicle heading my way, and I could feel his intense agitation, which put the wind up me more than anything else could have done. Ed generally maintained a complete block on emotions and I didn't need his panic to fuel mine. Then I stopped thinking as I headed into another contraction. Naturally, David and I had attended NCT classes, and I did have a song ready to belt out as things intensified – apparently it would take my mind off things but,

"Screw the song," muttered Glory, "I've got you." And sure enough, she had. Turns out, 'a trouble shared is a trouble halved,' applies particularly well to labour, who'd have thought? She more or less blocked off what I was feeling, leaving just the residual shadow of sensation. "Got to be able to feel something," she said, "so you'll know what's going on." I was impressed; she could save the NHS a fortune in epidurals, although right now I was prepared to swear the baby was working its way up rather than down, maybe it shared my lousy sense of direction.

"This isn't funny," Glory was a tad snappy; "Only you Stella, could find yourself in a situation like this, I don't know whether you're daft or just plain nuts." I was turning a little grumpy myself and was about to come back in self-defence but Rachael got in first.

"No time to discuss now, we're not far. Ed?" I heard his silent agreement and sighed with relief. I wasn't on my own anymore and I had complete faith in the people coming to get me. But with the comfort of knowing they were near and the easing of pain, panic returned fully fledged.

"Listen," I said urgently, "you need to know…"

Rachael interrupted, "We know."

"It's Ruth."

"I *said* we know." Using elbows rather than hand and wrist still painful from the chain, I eased myself farther up the bed and manoeuvred a couple of pillows to cushion my back against the rigid frame.

"Where is he now?" Rachael asked,

"Upstairs."

"I can't find him."

"No, you wouldn't - he's out for the count. Glory, I used your blanket."

"What blanket? Oh right…" she broke off. She was looking through my eyes at the door which was slowly opening, then sharing my shock and horror at what was heading towards me.

CHAPTER ONE

Not that many people know about me and my peculiarities; and that's all to the good – I hate making anyone nervous. Children though, before they reach the land of logic often sense something, they've no idea what but I've caught many a wide-eyed gaze from a thumb-in-mouth toddler not scared, just aware of something different crossing their path, but it's honestly never been too much of a problem. I've just followed the pragmatic route put in place years ago by my beleaguered, albeit determined parents. They were convinced that some cards are best played close to the chest, and whilst a certain amount of judicious juggling between the ordinary and the not so ordinary has been unavoidable, on the whole it's a policy that's served us well.

Those who know me from way back will know, flying abilities were sadly never again as fool-proof as when I was younger, smaller and lighter, but by far the trickiest issue has always been the often unwelcome, although sometimes indisputably handy ability to read minds. Naturally, I don't deliberately delve - well not unless it's important, but sometimes delving's unnecessary because strong emotions and intentions blast right out and hit you smack dab in the face. From necessity, my blocking tactics are strong and I'm highly skilled at sealing my mental blinds, shutting off the constant inundation and ensuring I'm not always walking around nursing a hell of a headache.

I tend to use all the other stuff on a needs-must basis and yes, I've done a few things in my time which come under the heading of controversial and yes, over the years I have been struck by the odd conscience pang - some sharper than others. I do have some regrets about the range and variety of ridiculously dubious messes I've managed to get myself into, but the fact is, once you're in, you're in and there's never much wiggle room for handling things differently.

* * * *

By the time we were easing out of the 1970's, I was in my mid-twenties and somewhat to my astonishment, had just got married. As chance and luck would have it, I'd happened across someone who, whilst not exactly having the patience of a saint, nevertheless displayed an amazingly high degree of forbearance. When I'd told him the facts I thought he ought to know, he'd have been well within his rights to head shrieking over the horizon and no-one, least of all me, would have blamed him in the slightest. However, displaying stoicism above and beyond, he'd stuck around.

As an added bonus, this newly acquired husband, David, was one of the minority of people I call the blissfully quiet, thoughts neatly compartmentalised, labelled and, unlike a lot of other people's, not ricocheting round his head like over-excited marbles in a pinball machine. I could read him if I really wanted to, but a certain amount of privacy in a marriage is, I think, not a bad thing. Anyway, all of this allowed me to relax and was, as I often told him, just one of the many things about him I appreciated.

Married life hadn't started off as smoothly as I might have wished, although the wedding itself had gone as well as could be expected, albeit with quantities of soggy tissues in evidence. My mother and her sister, Aunt Edna, were sobbing fit to bust because they'd feared they'd never see me walk down the aisle; Laura Gold, my new mother-in-law, was equally emotional because she'd feared she might. She had rather more than the usual number of mother-in-law reservations, and had made it clear to David she felt he could do better, a lot better – and of course, she didn't know the half of it!

There were the usual ups and downs on the big day, and whilst I didn't think I was nervous, my stomach was giving me grief with some uncomfortable twisting. Initially, I put it down to a natural concern that should I at any point turn round too quickly, my rigidly set helmet of hair could knock out a passing relative. It had been so firmly Ellnetted by an over-enthusiastic hairdresser that I suspected it might never move again, at least not in the foreseeable future. Or maybe it wasn't just the hair, maybe unease had snuck in during the fraught period when it was touch and go as to whether we'd get my wedding dress up and over my bottom. Mercifully, my Mother and Aunt were women who rose manfully to a challenge and, with a combination of pushing and clenching they eventually got me in and zipped up, to the relief of all. The dress did, even if I say so myself, give me a pleasing hour-glass figure, the downside being I was only able to breathe in extremely short pants.

Progress down the aisle proved more stilted than stately. My Father, contrary to instruction, had neglected to try on his hired dress suit trousers, so it hadn't come to light until far too late that they were far too long. To avoid tripping and breaking his neck, he had to incorporate a sharp flicking movement of each leg into every step, to get excess material out of the way. I couldn't worry overmuch; I had my own concerns. My breathing, restricted for zip safety's sake, was further complicated by each inhalation pulling in an increasingly soggy section of veil which then had to be unobtrusively blown out again, to avoid death by choking. From under the *chuppah* - the flower-decorated marriage canopy - my Mother, along with Melvyn and Laura my nearly-in-laws, David and the Rabbi watched our progress with varying degrees of apprehension, and there was an audible if restrained sigh of relief when we finally made it.

Aside from the oxygen deprivation and the knotting of my stomach, I was extremely happy, and David and I grinned at each other as he lifted the soggy veil from my face and my mother bustled forward to re-arrange it back over my headdress, although it might have been helpful if she'd wrung it out first.

I am a woman who knows her own mind; always have done, always will and I had no last-minute doubts. Whatever was discombobulating me, it wasn't wedding nerves, at least not mine and I certainly hoped not his. I opened my mental blinds slightly, to see if I could pinpoint anything overtly amiss, but the blast from over 120 people emoting and anticipating - who doesn't love a wedding? - rocked me hard back on my heels and I hastily shut them again. But I'd had enough time to know there didn't seem to be anything untoward occurring and turned my attention back to what we'd actually pitched up to do.

* * * *

The ceremony; the tea dance; the speeches, the cake-cutting and the long-drawn out family farewells all passed in a bit of a whirl and a blur, although throughout, there were concerns about our photographer. Having imbibed more than was probably wise during the reception, he'd started swaying at an early stage. Confidence was further eroded when David pointed out the photos might come out clearer if the lens cap was removed. I'm not overly sentimental myself, so not fixated on photos but I knew how upset my mother would be if she didn't have the requisite album, quite apart from which, he was a tall chap and not on the slim side; keeling over from a sway too far would not only disrupt proceedings but there was every chance we'd never get him up again. I nipped into his head briefly, gave him the equivalent of a hard slap and saw it register as he snapped back to startled attention. Meanwhile Auntie Edna - as always practicality on legs - had organised strong black coffee. Our combined offensive seemed to do the trick and he reverted to the job in hand with a worried expression but less swaying.

As is probably often the case at weddings, I don't think the main man and I exchanged more than a couple of words until we were in the car en route to a hotel for the first night of our honeymoon. Tired though we were, we took the time for a brief discussion on the condition and causes of my stomach discomfort, and I was finally able to identify it for what it was.

"Apprehension," I said and after a pause, "it's Ruth."

"What's Ruth?"

"This feeling; something's wrong, I think something's going to happen."

"Think or know?"

"Not sure."

"Well, even if you're not sure," he said reasonably, "you can't just ignore it, ring and tell her."

Familiar, perhaps too familiar, with all the oddities that make up who and what I am, this feeling was nothing I remotely recognised. It was unpleasant, uncomfortable and nothing I'd experienced before. He was right though; I couldn't keep it to myself.

"We'll stop at the next phone box," I said, "I'll call and tell them. I'll feel fine once I've done that."

CHAPTER TWO

As it turned out we didn't find a phone box, at least not one that worked and by the time we reached the hotel, I'd changed my mind again, this wasn't something I could convey accurately over the phone, it felt too serious. However much I wanted to get it done, dusted and off my conscience, I couldn't ignore the ever-strengthening foreboding. It was Rachael who answered the phone.

"I need to come and see you," I said.

"Didn't you just get married?" I was surprised she knew; the two parts of my life were very separate, which was how I preferred it.

"Yes, but…"

"Why are you phoning me then?" she always sounded as if she was holding the receiver reluctantly and couldn't wait to put it down.

"Told you; want see you, you and Ruth."

"Why?"

"Something and probably nothing, I'll explain when I see you, is Ruth with you?"

"Yes."

"You're at the new place?"

She tutted, impatient with the obvious, "You know I am, haven't you just phoned me here?"

"Right, well can we pop in tomorrow morning?"

"We?"

"David's with me because yes, I did just get married."

"Very well, if you feel it's absolutely necessary, seems an odd start to a honeymoon. You have the address?"

"Yes, should get there about…" but she'd already hung up. I put the phone down slowly. David was working his way through the plate of sandwiches we'd ordered, neither of us had managed to eat much at the party. He raised an eyebrow as he poured a cup of tea and handed it to me.

"Detour definite?"

"D'you mind?"

"Not much choice."

"We don't have to; we can discuss it."

"We already did. Anyway, you're as jumpy as a cat on a hot tin roof, and we both know you won't calm down till you've done whatever it is you have to." He held up a hand as I started to interrupt, "You still feeling it?"

"Maybe," I said. Although that wasn't true, the apprehension was absolute and I had that unpleasant acidy feeling you get when you're hungry, although eating anything right now felt distinctly unappealing.

"We'll go see her, sort it, and then we can head off with an easy mind." He extended the plate with a few sandwiches loitering; I shook my head, so he started in on them himself. "You know," he continued, finishing a mouthful, "it's probably just stuff left over from everything that happened last year." I nodded slowly; it was indeed not that long since I'd been involved in a couple of unsettling encounters featuring obsession, abduction, homicidal rage, a near-death experience and in the last incident, a truly unsettling amount of blood.

"Not having second thoughts, are you?" I asked. David had found himself playing a part in events the previous year, and whilst I'd become accustomed to the hair-raising, he'd leapt in unprepared.

"About?" he was taking things out of his overnight bag which I could see had been packed with his usual precision.

"Me."

"Bit late now," he looked up and grinned.

"You could cite unreasonable behaviour." I floated an unfolded napkin to land fetchingly on his head.

"I'd be laughed out of court," he pulled the white linen off, folded it neatly and put it back on the tray, "more likely to get a psychiatrist than a settlement. Ah, here it is," he pulled out a tattered A-Z, "where did you say this place was?"

* * * *

I had no idea what had governed the Peacock's decision to move; Rachael worked on a strictly need-to-know basis and as far as she was concerned, the fewer people who needed to know anything, the better. Her attitude never struck me as odd – I grew up under the eye of a grandmother who wouldn't tell her left hand what her right was doing, even in an emergency. And, considering the sort of thing in which Rachael and her sister Ruth tended to get involved, it seemed a reasonable precaution.

I'd received a brief communication a few months back, in her distinctive looped hand and purple ink; *'Moving next week. Details below.'* She hadn't signed it, why would she, who else had such a pithy turn of phrase? I called immediately to find out more; luckily it was Ruth who picked up that time.

"You sound tired," I said.

She sighed, "Moving is never easy. We've been a long time in this house and you cannot, Stella dear, for one moment imagine the amount of stuff we have, and you know I hate throwing away anything. Of course, Rachael feels she must conduct things like a military exercise, so exhausting." I laughed, Rachael Peacock in organising mode was a force to be reckoned with, although Ruth was usually adept, probably the only one who was, at keeping her sister in check, but she didn't sound as if she was up to coping with much right now. German not English was her mother tongue and her intonation and the slight disorder of her sentences were more pronounced when she was tired.

"Rachael sent me the phone number," I said, "but not the address."

"Address, ah yes, well we're going to be near the South Downs."

"Bit vague. Any chance of something more specific?"

"Oh, Stella, a lovely place, away from so much traffic, there's space, a lot of space. Ideal for what we need. One moment, I have it here."

I was at my desk in the office and waited while there was a lot of scrabbling at the other end of the phone.

"It's just an hour or two, not too far." Ruth couldn't read me that well over the phone but didn't have to, she knew what I was thinking - I didn't see them that often and when I did, it was usually because I was being hauled into situations I didn't want to be hauled into. But when I needed them, they'd always pitched up, a comfortingly capable cavalry riding to the rescue. I'd felt safer, knowing they were near.

CHAPTER THREE

"This can't be it?" David wound down his window and leaned out, contemplating the closed high gates in front of which we'd pulled up; "you must have taken down the wrong address."

"No, look!" A metal plaque was fixed to one of the broad, high posts, on which the gates were mounted. "This is right; The Oaks." There was a small gap between the post and the almost as high privet hedge which stretched, densely green either side of the gates and as far down the lane as I could see. I peered through to a vast swathe of manicured lawn, fronting an impressively eccentric, red-brick, gabled and towered building. It certainly looked nothing like a private home.

"Their place must be further down this road," David was studying the A-Z, "the name's just a coincidence."

"No," I said, "this is it."

"How can ... ?" I raised an eyebrow at him, "OK, silly me," he muttered as I pulled down hard on the cast iron ring which should raise the bar holding the gates closed. It didn't budge but as I turned, I saw a metal panel beneath the house name. There was a button so I pressed it and this time, the iron ring, warm in my hand from the late September sun moved smoothly downwards. Released, both gates swung silently open, I joined David back in the car and we headed down the drive.

"Blimey!" he said, looking around. He wasn't wrong, my glimpse through the hedge gap hadn't given any indication of the size of the building in front of us. Now, fronted and enclosed by what seemed like acres of flower-edged, neatly mown lawns, much of the red-brick had been taken over by Virginia Creeper at its peak. The ivy blazing in the sun, framed windows of different sizes which in turn were reflecting back the light, so there was plenty of sparkle and glow. Extending to either side of an impressive arched portico; the building seemed to have a surfeit of chimneys as well as, at odd intervals and for no apparent reason several, rounded crenelated towers.

"What *is* this place?" David said, more to himself than me. I actually had no idea but I had no doubts as to who was there; not because of anything I could hear, more because of what I couldn't. In my world, noise is a constant; been so all my life. I have mental blinds to shut out the shouting, but that doesn't switch it off completely, although when a multitude of thoughts are criss-crossing and intertwined, they tend to become just one inaudible hum, unless I focus specifically on an individual. But here, there was genuine silence, powerful shielding. We were so in the right place!

"Must be worth a fortune," said David, "look at these grounds." He nodded his head towards the lawns, sweeping smoothly in wide manicured arcs, before giving way to wooded areas where trees still clung to late autumn splendour. "I thought they were teachers, your Ruth and Rachel, how on earth could they buy something like this?"

"Ruth dabbles on the Stock Exchange," I said, revelling in the silence, reluctant to break it.

"Really?"

"Takes herself out regularly for lunch at City restaurants, the ones popular with financial movers and shakers. Let's just say, she picks up more tips than the waiters."

"Isn't that insider trading – and illegal?"

"Probably, but who's going to worry about a middle-aged lady treating herself to a small sweet sherry whilst delicately dissecting a Dover sole?" She'd taken me with her once, so I knew she was certainly of no concern to any of the raucous traders at surrounding tables; self-congratulating, back-slapping and smugly certain of planned and profitable decisions. By the time they'd made their loud and slightly unsteady way back to their desks to settle in front of figures flowing across monitors, Ruth would have paid her bill, fluttered anxiously with gloves, handbag and umbrella, thanked the waiter for holding the door, found a phone box and suggested to her broker that selling these shares swiftly and buying plenty of those, might be a good move just now.

"And nobody's ever asked questions?" David slid the car to a stop under the elaborately fret-worked and arched carriage porch just in time to avoid the first fat drops of rain that were starting to fall.

"Why would they?" I opened the car door and sighed with pleasure, the silence was so seductive, even the twisting apprehension I'd been feeling, seemed to quieten a little.

"D'you want me to stay in the car?"

"Don't be silly, they'll be glad to see you," I said, although we both had doubts that was true. There'd been a couple of occasions in the recent past when David had found himself involved with Rachel, Ruth and the others, albeit under fraught circumstances. He'd accepted, with admirable equanimity my oddities and theirs, and coped by adopting the attitude of a non-French speaking person stuck in Paris; politely and patiently uncomprehending until someone chose to tell him what was going on.

I utilised the iron door-knocker gripped firmly between the teeth of a lion who could have been snarling; I chose to think he was smiling. After a moment, the door was swung open by a well-upholstered, mid-fifties individual in a spotless nurses cap and an apron so starched it could have answered the door on its own.

"Yes?" she said, and I knew her immediately; large, sensibly rubber-soled feet planted slightly apart, cap immovably anchored with two hair clips, she wasn't snarling, but she wasn't smiling either.

"Mrs Millsop?"

"Matron," she corrected. She looked me up and down and wasn't impressed, "Do I know you?"

"No, no you don't but I know you because of Glory..." I paused. Glory's near-lethal time in the tender care of Dr Dreck was some years ago now, but I'd relived every vivid, hair-raising moment as she later poured the chain of events into my head. Her experiences were unforgettably mine now too.

"You have an appointment? Name please?" This was not a woman who let the grass grow.

"I'm Stella Gold." it was the first time I'd used my married name and I grinned, feeling David doing the same behind me. Mrs Millsop didn't return my smile. As a welcoming committee she was a dead loss. "Actually," I said, "it's Ruth and Rachael I've come to see."

"You mean Miss Peacock and Miss Peacock?." She frowned, obviously not big on informality. "I'll ask again, do you have an appointment?"

"Not exactly but they're expecting us some time this morning." Mrs Millsop paused long enough to let us know who was in charge and that 'some time' didn't really cut it appointment-wise, before stepping back and gesturing us in. She indicated a couple of chairs either side of a console table against the wall, on which was an exuberantly over flower-filled vase

"Would you mind waiting there?" a request in the shape of an order. She saw us seated, at the same time wedging a couple of lush overhanging blooms firmly back down into the vase, the lavishness of the display didn't suit her sense of order. "I'll let them know you're here. Parents are you?"

"Not yet," I said with another grin that she didn't return. "I didn't realise this was a school." I added. She didn't bother answering because a door, farther down the hall was suddenly flung open, crashing noisily back against the wall, where dents and chipped paint bore testimony to similar encounters. Around ten children of assorted size and state of messiness spilled out of the room. Barrelling past at speed, the surge parted automatically either side of Matron Millsop, except for one small boy, owlish in thick-lensed, blue-wired National Health glasses who hit her amidships.

She expelled a pained 'Oof' as he bounced off.

"How many times Iggy?" she stooped to pull him up from the floor where he'd landed, "no running in the corridors." Setting him firmly on his feet, she held on long enough to try and smooth straight brown hair which looked like it'd been dragged through several hedges. He wriggled free, then paused just long enough to put both arms round her – or as far as they could reach - and give her a quick hug.

"Don't you try and soft soap me, m'lad," she snapped, straightening her apron but there was affection behind the snap. I'd opened up as we sat down, but inside the building where there should have been thinking aplenty, the smooth silence told me more. The next minute my head was flooding with peppermint green and Rachael emerged from the room the kids had just left, a battered brown leather portfolio tucked under one arm.

"Thank you Matron," she said, and indicated with a head tilt and no pause in pace that we should follow her.

"Hello to you too!" muttered David behind me, as we headed at speed up a wide staircase at the far end of the hall. She was as angular as ever, in trade-mark crisp white shirt tucked into a belted, below-the-knee pleated skirt, although today she'd pushed the boat out replacing the usual black with a similar number in grey. I was amused as she moved swiftly ahead, to see a small, four-finger mark in blue paint on the shoulder of the shirt. Despite all appearance to the contrary and her peppery, impatient persona, the children she worked with knew instinctively where to turn and I knew, as they did, a brisk, business-like hug from Rachael, for all its brevity and because of its rarity, could ease a great deal of hurt.

At the top of the stairs we followed her along a carpeted landing, then through an open door which took us up a shorter flight to a spacious circular landing, light pouring through an impressive floor to ceiling curved window, overlooking and echoing the curve of the front lawns below. We were in one of the building's round towers and purple-deep lavender told me in which room Ruth waited.

Rachael moved a telephone on the hall table aside, making room to put the portfolio down before she turned to face us. I'd known her over half my life now and at fifty or thereabouts, she hadn't changed much from our initial, indescribably frustrating encounter on the No. 113 bus to Hendon Central, although as she moved forward, light revealed new, bruised shadows beneath her eyes. The uncompromising silver-grey bob cut to just below her ears was as it had always been, widow-peaked and brushed severely back from the pale-skinned high forehead. Over half-moon spectacles, low on an aquiline nose, she looked me up and down for a moment, deep hazel eyes, the only warmth and colour in her thin face.

"Right," she said, "you obviously felt it was important, so I suppose we'd better find out what it is you want to talk about." Crisp, brisk and authoritative, I knew David wouldn't approve the lack of normal pleasantries, the back and forth of mainly meaningless platitudes which normally oil the wheels of communication, but it wasn't necessary for her to ask how I was, she'd swept through my defences immediately, so she knew. Her ability to wade into my head at will had long been a bone of contention between us.

"I wish you wouldn't do that," I said.

"Shield better and I wouldn't be able to. Come along now, quicker you're in, quicker you can be on your way." She led the way down the hall, opened a door, ushered us in and added, "I'm sure you didn't schedule in a visit to us, did you, when making honeymoon plans, er… ?"

"David," I supplied shortly. She knew of course, and she knew I knew she knew, but she was never averse to winding up anyone she could.

CHAPTER FOUR

The circular room we entered was filled with light too; cool autumn sun streaming from skylights set in the double height cathedral ceiling, as well as through French doors leading onto a plant-packed, iron-trellised balcony. A couple of well-worn, red velvet sofas which I recognised from the St. John's Wood house faced each other companionably over a low square table. Their living space, albeit in a different location was so unchanged, I immediately felt at home. The table was smothered with books and papers and semi-supported against the walls were a couple of teetering book piles; volumes which hadn't quite made it onto the packed bookcases. In the shelter of one of these piles was a large chestnut coloured beanbag which may or may not have been offering it some support.

"My dears, you're here." Ruth was bustling towards us, arms outstretched, and I breathed a silent sigh of relief at the sight of her, I don't know what I'd expected but in truth she looked a darn sight better than the last time I'd seen her. She'd regained some of the weight she'd lost so dramatically and her unruly curls, held back with tortoiseshell slides, seemed to have rediscovered their bounce because the slides were fast losing the battle. Her eyes, the striking and only feature she shared with her sister, were back to hazel bright, no trace of the jaundiced dullness I'd found so disturbing when we were last together.

She had on an eye-aching jumper; vivid yellow with black stripes and large bell sleeves, giving her the look of a well-stuffed wasp. Shorter than Rachael, when she folded me into her arms, we were comfortably the same height and I hugged her too, my cheek against hers, breathing in the familiar rich lavender, before she stepped back still holding my arms.

"So," she nodded in approval, "our Stella, a married lady, tell me, is he good to you?"

I laughed, "Bit soon to tell, the wedding was only yesterday," she laughed and turned to David, holding out her arms again. He was surprised, not really ready for a hug, certainly not from a woman he hardly knew and who he'd last encountered during a blood-soaked confrontation with a killer moving a good few degrees past crazy. At the time I'd been badly wounded, as had Auntie Kitty whose heart unfortunately had given up the ghost for a while. This all flashed through his head as he politely moved forward and Ruth chuckled.

"No," she said, "not ideal circumstances were they, but my dear; shall we put that behind us and start afresh?" I don't know what discomfited him more, the hug or the ease with which she'd thrown his thoughts back at him. He knew of course, they were like me but maybe hadn't thought that through enough. Or maybe he'd expected that aspect of things, like a post-meal burp, would be politely smothered in company. Ruth laughed again at that and he smiled sheepishly and shrugged.

"Enough Ruth," Rachael never had a deal of patience with what she considered time-wastage. "Leave the man alone. Now," she turned to me, "what was so urgent it couldn't wait?"

"Oh, for goodness sake," Ruth protested, "give them a minute to breathe." Rachael frowned and they exchanged a flash of thought, so quick even I couldn't catch it. Their minds, as always, were efficiently and effectively shielded so all I got was the familiar, infinitely frustrating smooth grey walls.

Ruth turned back, "Sit, you must be tired, you drove straight down? And after such a big day too. You see Rachael," she said, "this is the sort of thing you do with visitors before you start with an interrogation. I'm going to get us some coffee. No, for David, it's black tea isn't it, one sugar? And cake, I'll bring cake."

David was still standing, "bloody hell," he said. I'd seated myself on one of the sofas and tugged his jacket, I could understand he might not welcome Ruth waltzing into his head willy-nilly, but there was no need to be rude. But it wasn't Ruth that was bothering him.

"What," he said, "is *that?*" and he moved protectively in front of me, bless his heart. Peering around him, I could see the chestnut beanbag was apparently not a beanbag at all because it was now stretching extravagantly, one end high in the air before it started to pad towards us. David backed away a little but couldn't get any further because I was behind him.

"It's Bella," said Rachael, "she won't hurt you." David opened his mouth to declare he wasn't worried, realised how pointless that was and shut it. Bella had a rather glorious, burnished red-brown coat, muscles rippling beneath as she moved. Despite her size, she picked her way delicately over a couple of perilous piles of papers without disturbing a sheet. She stopped in front of David and looked up, not that far, she was a good four feet at the shoulder. She didn't waste time but reared up, placing a paw firmly on each of his shoulders and tilting her head winsomely. He staggered a little.

"She likes you," said Rachael, "alright with dogs are you?" David put one arm around his new friend – simply to steady himself I think, and patted her gingerly on the head. She gave a little moan, I hoped it was pleasure.

"She's not usually good with strangers," said Rachael with interest, she was perched on the wide arm of the sofa opposite and I considered briefly what 'not good' might mean. "Sit," ordered Rachael and Bella and David followed instruction in unison. Years ago, the Peacocks had shown me how to go into an animal's head without causing alarm. Unlike people, animals instantly know you're there, but if you're gentle and as they're not inclined to rationalise, they're generally not that bothered, I was reassured though that this super-sized effort had no harm in her at all right now, although I gained a fair idea of what she could and would do if anything threatened those she felt she was taking care of.

"Hamlet?" I asked, sad because I'd already guessed. The Great Dane, always at the side of one or other of the sisters, had been closely involved in several chapters of my own past history and had saved my bacon a time or two.

Rachael shook her head, "Old age I'm afraid," she said, "he was with us for 15 years, far longer than we could have hoped, old for a Great Dane."

"I'm so sorry."

"Don't be, he was well all his life, and when he was ill and in pain, he was allowed to go. Which is more," she added wryly, "than most of us can hope for." David, next to me, opened his mouth to say something, and Bella on hindquarters next to him, leaned in with interest - I don't know, maybe she was into ethical arguments – causing him to shut it again. He still had major doubts as to whether Bella's intentions were honourable and obviously decided silence was safer.

"She's fine," I said, I put out my hand to pet her and she obligingly moved towards me and did that interrogative head tilt as if waiting for me to say something useful. When I didn't, she settled down, resting heavily against my legs.

"Leonberger, Newfoundland cross," Rachael absently answered David's thought, "some woman bought her from a pet shop to surprise her husband, who was indeed surprised! Stupid woman had no idea how big she'd get and they couldn't cope with her by the time she was only half this size, they took her to Battersea. She'd been there a while by the time we went along. People were cautious about taking her on, but we knew right away she'd be perfect."

"For what?" David said with genuine curiosity.

"The children of course." She rose to open the door for Ruth who'd be coming back with drinks in a moment or two.

"They're not nervous?"

"Why would they be?"

"Right." David, remained unconvinced.

"Some of our children have issues," Rachael explained, Bella gives them confidence to communicate. They'll talk to her, even when they're otherwise completely unable to talk to one of us."

I interrupted, "So, this is what? A school?"

She tilted her head a little; perhaps she'd caught it from Bella, "Yes and no."

"Well, either it is or it isn't." I said.

"Hmm."

"Rachael, we haven't time for riddles."

"Dear girl, it was you who insisted on coming."

"And now I'm here, I have questions."

"As always!"

I ignored that. "The children here?" I left a gap for her to fill, which after a token pause she did;

"…Have a variety of issues other schools can't, or won't cope with. We offer them the sort of freedom they're unlikely to get anywhere else."

"Like Summerhill?" David asked with interest.

She sniffed, "Absolutely not."

"That's near here isn't it?" he said.

"Not that near; but yes, along the coast."

"No compulsory lessons?" he said, "first names for teachers, bit skinny on the rules?" I'd ceased to be surprised at the bits and pieces of knowledge he always seemed to have to hand, but like all journalists, he gathered facts as a matter of habit, filing them with optimum efficiency for when they might be relevant.

"That's not really us," she replied repressively.

"There are others aren't there," he said, "Free schools? Something in Notting Hill?"

"Yes," she was impatient, "but that's *not* how we operate here, so I've no idea why we're talking about them, and I presume this isn't anything to do with why you've come?" I raised a hand to stop the two of them in their tracks; I wasn't the nervous sixteen-year-old who'd perched on the edge of this same sofa several years and some startling experiences ago. Rachael silently answered my pressing question before I'd voiced it, "Not a lot of the children are like us."

"Some?"

"Possibly."

"For goodness sake Rachael!" I exclaimed out loud, for the benefit of David who was head turning between the two of us like someone watching a tennis match without being able to spot the ball. Rachael rolled her eyes, she knew if I was intrigued I wouldn't stop asking, so she sent me what I wanted to know.

Yes, it was a school which had evolved from the Peacock's Practice which was a mix of therapy, tuition and problem solving for children with special needs or behavioural problems. Sometimes, not all that often, those needs arose because they were in some way or another like us. Most often they were traumatised or damaged, defined not by their limitations but by their inexplicable abilities – not understood by the children themselves and certainly not by their parents or the education system.

Cases referred to the Peacocks tended to be those where other avenues had been exhausted. Their professional reputation for dealing with troubled children had grown over the years. Opening the school gave them the facilities to work with more children and on a broader scale, some boarding, others day-students. Some had minor issues, others major ones, a very few didn't fit any recognised parameters. Individual cases received tailor-made solutions that would, in most cases, allow children to move on without the 'disruptive' label. Some of them were sorted in a short time; others would be with the Peacocks for several years.

"There," she said aloud, "satisfied?"

"I'd really like to know what happens to those like us, how they're helped?" But I knew as I spoke, I'd had my lot, I wasn't going to get any more interesting information.

"Ah," Ruth was back with a tray, "you've met Bella?" then taking in Rachael's irritation which was palpable in the room, "as you'll have gathered, a far less snappy individual than my sister." Bella had gone back to her beanbag impression, but raised her head hopefully as Ruth placed filled cups alongside sliced cake and biscuits and re-seated herself. Bella, sighed and put her head down again.

"To see you, Stella dear, so unexpectedly, is wonderful." Ruth like her sister had lived in England for over thirty years – they'd left Germany at the end of the war but sometimes the shaping of a sentence harked back and as she leaned forward to hand a cup to David, the wide sleeve of her jumper fell back from her arm.

"Auschwitz," she said, as she saw him notice the number. She was matter of fact. I knew their history of course, could never forget my hands tightly enfolded in Ruth's – when I first met her and time was short and matters urgent – as she poured into my unwilling head what she needed me to know and understand. How close they'd come to the unspeakable experimentation of the monster Mengele, and why that governed all they'd subsequently done. But in all the years, I'd never once glimpsed that number deep-scored into the skin, she, like her sister, habitually wore sleeves. The shudder that ran through me wasn't shock so much as a visceral response to the malign efficiency governing those tattooed figures.

"You could have it removed?" David was as matter of fact as she, and Ruth answered the why, in the question;

"Some people did, thought it would help. It didn't." She shrugged. I usually could only hear what they were thinking if they chose to let me and then, only what they wanted me to know and no more. Occasionally, as now, I got a swift sense of something flashing between them, a question asked and answered, but before I had a chance to process it, Rachael leaned down and lifted a gift-wrapped parcel from the top of a pile of papers next to the sofa.

"Here," she said, "we were going to post this. We thought you'd appreciate it more than a toaster."

"Goodness," I was a bit stymied; Rachael had given me a gift once before. I was sixteen then, I still had it. The blood stains on the small leather wrist-strap were faded now, the memories weren't. That was the very first time I'd been involved in something the Peacock sisters felt needed to be done.

"That's kind of you," David at least hadn't lost his manners; he nudged me, "Go on, open it." I undid the wrapping carefully, a habit inculcated by my mother's family who considered wrapping paper that hadn't been re-used at least three times, a wicked waste. Revealed was a black, cloth-bound book, gilt lettered on the spine, *Magnolia Street. Louis Golding.*

"Look inside," Rachael said, "it's a first edition." It was indeed, published by Victor Gollancz, 1932 but what spread my smile of pleasure was the inscription on the front end-paper. '*Louis Golding writes this for Christina Foyle in her jade-turquoise frock, now being twenty-one. London 30 Jan 32.*'

"For your collection," Ruth said.

"It's wonderful, thank you both so much," I was touched they'd even remembered my love of vintage books, "that is so thoughtful."

"We thought, um … David might appreciate it too," Rachael added a late attempt at inclusivity. I held the book to my nose – nothing beats the smell of an old book the amalgam of ink, slightly foxed paper and binding glue. The spine was still firm and tight, the gilt lettering only slightly faded as I ran my hand gently over it.

I think then that I must have risen to my feet, the better to get the book away from me. I needed it as far away as possible. I think it hit Rachael on the arm as it hurtled past, I wasn't bothered, I could feel myself swaying, and then gagging. I put my hand over my mouth, I knew it wouldn't be polite to throw up over the coffee table so I had to get away, I turned and stumbled clumsily into an immovable object which turned out to be Bella, who'd stood up too, more than a little confused. David was fast; reaching from behind me, he grabbed both my elbows, the two women were quicker still, didn't hesitate, they were on it, but then they would be, they'd been expecting it. In an instant they'd enfolded my mind, smothering the revulsion and the pain, but not the realisation of what had just happened.

David, pragmatic most of the time, wasn't now, "what in God's name?" he turned me to face him, was holding me tight and my shaking was making him judder too.

"She's fine," Rachael said.

"She's so obviously not!" he snapped.

"No, I'm OK." I sank down onto the sofa because my legs didn't want to hold me anymore. I couldn't catch my breath and as it caught painfully in my chest, my mouth, tongue and, lips twisted away from bitter almonds. "He knew," I muttered, "he knew straight away but it was too late." Ruth had moved swiftly and seated the other side of me had one of my arms, David still retained the other.

"Don't," said Ruth, "you don't have to."

"Don't have to *what*?" David was as appalled as he was angry. I pulled my arms away from both of them, didn't want to be touched.

"I'm fine, honestly. I'm OK." I glanced at Ruth who had the grace to look truly abashed and at Rachael who didn't. "Well," I said coldly, "what was it you wanted to know? How painful a death, how long it lasted, how quickly did he know, what he thought and felt as he died, what effect your little experiment has had on me?"

"Not necessary," Rachael's tone was level, "we know the history of the book. The bookseller who sold it to us, was the one who cleared the house after the wife was arrested. We knew you'd love the book for itself. And..." she added reasonably, "if you hadn't felt anything, it would have been a perfect present!" Beside me, David swore under his breath, we all ignored him.

"Why?" I demanded.

"We..." began Rachael.

"Not me," said Ruth firmly.

Rachael continued, "Very well, just me. I wanted to know."

"Well, now you do. How can you bear to have it in the house?"

Rachael shook her head. "Well, that's what's so interesting, isn't it? We *could* focus hard and get something, but nothing like you just did."

"But I've never had anything like this before – and it's hardly something I wouldn't notice," I said.

"No, it is rare to find it in a younger person, it often only comes to light in middle-age. I just had a feeling about it in relation to you."

"And you didn't think to mention?" in my annoyance I flashed the thought, because that hit harder than words.

"You never asked," she flashed back. Arguments with Rachael tended to be circular affairs, more often than not ending up, near as damn it, where they started. Anyway," she added silently, "wasn't it because of this you wanted to come today, when did you first realise?"

"I didn't, I had no idea about this at all. That's not why I'm here."

David was wearing his Englishman in Paris look. "Words please, can you all use your words." He said.

Rachael nodded, "Stella, I'm assuming, as David is here with you, he knows everything?"

"Of course," I said, then in the interests of honesty added, "more or less," and he raised an eyebrow I chose not to see.

"And is there anything we will speak about today you wouldn't want him to hear?" she continued; I shook my head. "Then," she turned to David, "we'll talk, should we forget to talk, as we sometimes do, feel free to remind us."

"I need to know more about this." I nodded towards the book, now lying open in a corner of the room.

"First things first." Said Rachael.

CHAPTER FIVE

"You said you were worried about Ruth?" Rachael said, "but as you can see," she's perfectly well – probably better than she's been for a long time, nothing to worry about at all."

Ruth was indeed looking far better than the last time I saw her, mind you, as that was when she'd arrived with the others in the middle of a somewhat violent kerfuffle, my powers of observation might not have been up to much. But I also knew what had terrified me - the clear and vivid image of her in the mind of a dying psychopath she'd never seen before. When Jamie had done his level best to murder me and several others, not only was he as far from being in his right mind as it was possible to be, but there was another, far stronger mind, pulling his strings. It was that which had fed and flourished, nurturing, growing and relishing in Jamie's insanity and it was in the midst of Jamie's mess of a mind that I'd seen Ruth.

"I know exactly what you're thinking," she said to me now and smiled at David's involuntary start, "no, not that way my dear, we said, did we not, we were going to stick to talking?" and indeed, the Peacocks were both shuttered tight, as was I now, well at least as tight as I could manage.

Ruth continued ruefully, "There is really no need to worry Stella, we saw off that particular unpleasantness as soon as you made us aware. No, what brought me low was simply glandular fever; ridiculous I know at my age, but it must have been brewing for a while and that accounted for how rotten I felt for so long afterwards. It's notorious for knocking youngsters out for weeks and I'm a youngster no longer. I'm afraid I wasn't much use to anyone for a while but as you see," she patted her not insubstantial yellow and black striped middle, "back to normal now."

"No after-effects?" I asked, but already I was relaxing a little.

Ruth shrugged, "It took a lot out of me and I still get days when all I want to do is sleep – post viral fatigue they call it, it's not uncommon but on the whole, all is well."

"Then what is it I've felt, am still feeling?" my hand hovered at my stomach.

"But you've already put a name to it, haven't you?" said Rachael, "you think it's some kind of precognition?"

"I know that's not possible. Anyway, that's never been…"

She interrupted briskly, "Well, maybe it is now. Things are as they are; you are as you are; you really should learn to keep a more open mind." Ruth moved in, as so often before, pouring oil on potentially stormy waters.

"What my sister's trying to say, Stella dear – in her inimitable fashion – is that it's really nothing at all to worry about."

"You think not? Seeing the future? I reckon that could be a bit of a life changer."

"Always with the drama," sighed Rachael, "you're *not* seeing the future, you're probably *reacting* to something, the way animals and birds anticipate a storm or an earthquake days before it occurs. They're picking up something that's there, it's a reality, just a reality we can't see or sense but they can. Not mysterious, not magical and certainly not always accurate. We don't know how or why. In time we will. It's science, not science fiction. These feelings you're worried about could be due to anything, maybe not even to do with Ruth. I'm afraid this may have been a wasted journey."

David was nodding in agreement and relief at her pragmatism. Work experience when he was younger had him shadowing an old-school investigative reporter, known for sticking a cynical, whisky-reddened nose into places it was neither wanted nor welcomed, but it had opened David's eyes and mind to all sorts of unbelievable. His mentor was on the trail of money thrown - not just by our own government but those of China, Russia and the US - at research and experimentation into all sorts of extra sensory abilities. Roger's career-crowning scoop was going to blow the whole thing open to ridicule and condemnation; until some of the stuff he came across, not only turned his hardened stomach, but also changed his mind.

Now David leaned forward, "Why the book?" he nodded over to where it had landed.

Rachael looked at him over the top of her glasses. "I was interested to see if there was more she could do, things she may not even have realised."

"More?" he queried.

I sat forward crossly, "Hey, I can talk for myself. More?" I asked Rachael.

"I presume," she said, "you'll continue working with Ruth, listening?"

"Well, you presume wrong. I agreed to help when Ruth was out of action, but that didn't turn out too well, did it?"

"Listening was all we asked of you. Why instead of just reporting back, you felt compelled to hurl yourself headlong into a dangerous situation, is a question only you can answer."

Ruth chipped in "True, we did only ask you to pass on anything untoward; no more, no less."

"Naturally," said Rachael with a nod in David's direction, "we understand your circumstances have changed and of course, if your husband doesn't want you to..."

"I make my own decisions," I said sharply, "if I decide to do it, I'll do it."

"Excellent," she said, "knew we could rely on you." She rose from the sofa, while I was still cursing myself, "So, not a wasted trip then. As you see Ruth is stronger every day, although," she added belatedly, "it has been lovely to see you Stella and erm..."

"David," he supplied.

"Indeed, forgive me - my memory." I frowned at her and she had the grace not to meet my eye. Rachael stroppy was nothing new, but I wasn't about to let her get away with fake confusion. "Right," she continued, "we must get on, things to do and I'm sure you want to head off now you have an easier mind, Dorset wasn't it?" she was already holding the door, ushering us out when I turned back.

"My book."

"Don't be daft," David said, "you don't want it."

"I do. If this really is something that's developed, I have to deal with it, learn to switch it on or off. If I don't, I'm going to be having funny turns left right and centre."

Rachael nodded, "Sensible." Rare approval.

On the wide, sun-lit landing, Ruth held out her arms. I hugged her tightly for a good half minute more than was necessary, revelling in the purple deepness, lavender-scented Ruthness of her which almost from the time we'd met had provided a secure harbour. I drew back smiling still holding her, sliding my arms down hers to the familiar, plumply beringed hands and then, just for a fraction of a shocking second I was overwhelmed by a rancidness that smothered me; the unmistakeable offensiveness of something sourly rotting, then it was gone. She returned my smile as we moved apart and turned to say goodbye to David.

Shaken to my core, I did the only thing I could, I hugged Rachael too. Taller than Ruth and not your natural huggy type, she was rigid in my arms as I pulled her close, but I couldn't risk a thought Ruth might hear.

"*It's still there,*" I hissed, "*It's in her.*"

"I know."

"She said it was gone."

"She did."

"*Why?*"

"Because she's not aware of it anymore."

"Don't understand?"

"It's become part of her."

"No, can't be true, she'd know it was still there, she'd read it from you?"

"Can't afford to let her. *Think Stella!* If she knows, *It* will know too. We don't know how to kill it without harming her. Until we do, we can't risk her knowing.

"What can I do?"

"Nothing."

"But…"

"Listen for once will you please. Stay out of it. I hoped you wouldn't be here long enough to find out, we can't trust your shielding."

In the stress of the moment I let that pass, "You can't just leave it like this."

Anguish, frustration and fear was in the clenched hand, momentarily painful on my shoulder,

"This 'thing' has learnt from its experience with Jamie. It's not now draining her as it did him - worse, it's feeding from her. Be assured though we will *not* 'just leave it'." And she put me from her decisively as David moved forward and she pre-empted further physical stuff by putting her hand out to shake his, and I aimed for a normal casual conversational tone.

"Glory's here?" It wasn't really a question, I'd felt her.

Rachael nodded, "Ed too." As she spoke, she was already shepherding us down the stairs, just as Mrs Millsop bustled out of a door further down the wide entrance hall. She was towing a reluctant small girl with plaits and a pained expression who was insisting she was going to be sick.

"Not here, you're not." Mrs Millsop was firm and amazingly swift, whipping open a door and inserting the child into what I presumed was a bathroom. "There you go," she said, "want me to stay? No? Well then, come and fetch me when you're done," she pulled the door to and looked at us, "off now are you?"

There seemed little to add to the obvious and by the time I'd opened my mouth to say something polite, she'd opened the front door. As I passed, I went briefly into her mind. At the forefront were the events of a busy day; the tasks done and dusted, chores to do next, others needing doing as soon as anyone let her have a flipping minute to herself, then there were the few well-chosen words she planned to have with the man from the laundry service on expectations not met. Below the everyday, was acknowledgement of some odd goings on around here that she not only couldn't explain, but didn't even want to think about, and being a strong-minded woman most of the time, didn't. However, sitting comfortably alongside that, was faith in herself. She prided herself on being a good judge of character and rarely got it wrong, (Mr Millsop, the bastard, being the exception to the rule!) and she completely trusted the Peacocks.

CHAPTER SIX

"Right then," David had the car door open for me – lovely manners, my mother commented approvingly every time she saw him do that – "if we get going now, we'll be there in time for a late lunch."

"No."

"Well, we can eat on the way if you want."

"I mean no, I just need a few minutes, d'you mind?" I was already turning, towards the lemon sherbert fizzing in my head and following the path as it rounded the corner of the house to where Glory was seated at one end of a garden bench, face upturned to the autumn sun. As always and wherever she was, at first glance she was somehow as startling as when I'd first seen her, descending the stairs at Newcombe, white stick tap-testing each step. She was only 19 then and now, nearly thirty, didn't look any older. Dark braids, thick and high, glint of gold hooped earring against milk-chocolate skin and one of her silky, vividly coloured kaftans over wide trousers, she looked as if she'd suddenly dropped in from somewhere far more exotic.

I sat next to her, "What are you doing?"

"Grabbing some last-minute warmth."

"About Ruth I mean!"

"Hello there," she said, and I remembered with a guilty start, my new husband, who'd followed me round the corner. I felt Glory's amusement as she continued, "Our paths have crossed before, but I don't think we were properly introduced." They had indeed met previously; having arrived separately on a rescue mission, but as there was a fair amount going on, formalities had gone out the same window David had come in by.

"Well, I'm delighted to meet you properly now," he said. At the same time, he raised an eyebrow at me and tapped his watch.

Glory laughed, "David, you won't get Stella moving until she's good and ready, you should know that by now." I grinned too, however many times it happened, I always enjoyed the fright Glory gave people who knew she was completely blind and thought they knew what to expect.

"She's looking through my eyes," I said.

"Ah. Sorry!" David put the wrist with the watch behind his back, as he took on board that the woman with no eyesight was seeing just fine. I turned back to her,

"Well?" I said. She was, like Ruth and Rachael tightly shielded; I was getting nothing unless she chose to let me.

"You first," she said, "You came because of Ruth, because you're worried?"

"Yes, didn't Rachael tell you?"

"No," she said slowly, "only knew you were here, when you were here."

"And I'm right, there's something very wrong…" she tutted impatiently and shot out one of those strong, deceptively slim-boned hands to take mine. She didn't need to; it was just swifter and stronger that way so in a split second she knew as much as I did. I pulled my hand back, honestly this was a woman who'd been traipsing in and out of my mind for years, you'd have thought I'd have got used to it. I hadn't. I always thought the next time I saw her she'd find I'd strengthened my barriers and she'd just bounce off. Again and again she proved me wrong. David, hands in jean pockets was leaning casually against an ivy-spilling stone urn. I knew the more relaxed he looked; the more intently he was watching. He straightened up and started to say something; Glory raised a finger and shook her head.

"Hang on a minute, I'm thinking, I didn't know about this new stuff Stella's got going on, the touch thing – psychometry,"

"Me neither." I said bitterly.

"Yes, well it's a bit of a nuisance."

"A nuisance?"

"It complicates things, makes you more vulnerable."

"To what and anyway don't we need to be talking about Ruth, not me? I shivered involuntarily as memory of rancidness flowed over me. "Sam?" I said suddenly, "Why isn't Sam here?" Sam, whose ability to diagnose and deal had grown year on year from the time we first met, him a terrified six-year-old, me an equally panicked sixteen. "Sam could get that thing out of her."

"He can't."

"Has he tried?"

"Of course he's tried," she snapped; never strong on patience, our Glory, "but you're not getting it, are you?" David was following the bits of conversation he could, and it suddenly occurred to me, he wouldn't really know what we were talking about, I hadn't had time to fill him in on what I'd felt from Ruth nor what Rachael had said. Glory huffed – she couldn't be bothered wasting words when other things worked so much more quickly, she reached for my hand again and almost instantly, I knew as much as she did – and wished I didn't.

"Oh God," I closed my eyes briefly, assimilating. Glory had spent more time than I had with Ruth, of course she had, so she'd learnt a lot more about the entity that had possessed and driven Jamie to death, exploiting what was already there. It had taken the lust to hurt, hate and violate; magnified and endorsed it, wringing out and relishing every ounce of their shared experience. It was this that was now embedded in Ruth, and as Rachael had said, it had learnt and learnt well, Ruth wasn't to be a short-term option, it was living in her, living off her; a deep malignancy."

"Well that's crazy," I said aloud, "we, all of us together could get rid of it, kill it." I knew this for a fact.

Glory nodded, "Stone dead, no problem, but we'd also kill Ruth, she couldn't survive a concentrated onslaught." I was silent as that sank in and made horrible sense.

"Stella," she said, I've always been honest with you, you trust me, right?" I nodded, there were many things about Glory with which I'd take issue, but honesty wasn't one of them. She went on, "So, trust me when I say we've been exploring all angles and we're not giving up, we'll find a way but it's better and safer if you stay out of it. Right out of it."

"Why?"

She sighed, "Stella, will you just for once, take my word?"

"I want to know why?"

"Because," she said sharply, "you've had more contact with whatever this thing is, more than any of us at a time when you didn't know what you were dealing with. It *knows* you. You're vulnerable and we can't afford vulnerable, this is too serious." She paused, she'd been speaking aloud because she wanted David to know and understand.

"Look, head off on honeymoon, carry on as normal. I know you agreed to continue listening and you'll let Boris know if there's anything to report. But that's it. Don't, and I mean this Stella, don't come here again. We've got this.

I stood up; I was ridiculously hurt at the shutting out, but at the same time, absolutely did not want to become involved again in what might turn out to be life-threatening events, after all I had other loyalties and priorities now. Glory, as might have been expected, paid no attention to my attempted shut down of contact and followed my train of thought. She stood and briefly put her hands on my forearms, smiling a little at my surprise, Glory's general approach to physical contact made Rachael's look positively effusive.

"Off you go," she said and pushed me gently away. David moved from the stone urn. She nodded at him and he, understanding her boundaries, smiled at her. He took my arm, swinging me round to head back towards the car. I didn't look back at Glory, I felt that what had just happened was much more of a goodbye than a see you soon.

* * * *

When we turned out of the drive and picked up speed, the surrounding noise hit me and I realised just how precious had been the artificial silence generated at the school. David was concentrating on the road ahead, allowing me some space and time.

"Are you alright with all of this?" I said after a while. There was a silence, short, but still longer than I'd have preferred. "David?"

"Thinking."

"Taking too long."

"You don't want a knee-jerk response, do you?"

"Maybe."

"Well," he said, "I have to say, this isn't quite how I'd planned to start off but I knew what I was buying into," he sighed theatrically, "any post-purchase issues, I've only myself to blame." I sat back in my seat relieved. I hadn't really expected him to say anything else, but life is full of surprises and I wasn't sure I could deal with any more right now.

"You'll have to fill me in though?" he continued, "I got the gist but there were gaps and we've still got that ruddy book in the boot, shall I stop somewhere and bin it?"

The bibliophile in me was horrified, "You're kidding, right? It was a present."

"More of an experiment."

"I'll sort it," I said, "it was a bit of a shock, that's all... and odd." I wanted to shrug it off, didn't want to talk about it. "Look, I've dealt with this sort of thing all my life, it will sort itself out, *I'll* sort it out. As for the rest..." I paused, there was a fair amount to pass on, but it might not make much sense without its own back history.

I opened my mouth to start, but what with getting married yesterday and all this morning's goings-on, I was pretty much talked out. I'd done my best, told Rachael, and Glory too what I was feeling and been soundly sent about my business, there wasn't much more I could do, but it was only polite to bring David up to speed, I thought I'd take a short cut and put it all straight in his head.

I turned to see if he had any thoughts or questions. He was tight-lipped as he swung into a service station turn-off; bit unnecessary I thought, if our journey wasn't going to be that long. He parked neatly between two large vans, turned off the engine and pulled the handbrake sharply to the max. When he does that, it means if I drive the car afterwards, I can't let it off without two hands and a lot of welly, I started to mention this but he interrupted me.

"Please don't do that again," he said.

"What?"

"That." He touched his head.

"Oh." I paused, "I thought... I'm sorry."

"Just. Don't." I'd never heard that tone before and turned in the seat to face him, I didn't need ESP to know this was not good. I could see I might have overestimated his definition of alright, and underestimated the impact of shoving an information load into the head of someone not expecting it.

"Darling, I'm so sorry..." but he was out of the car before I'd finished.

"I'm going for coffee."

"Shall I come?"

"No. D'you want one?"

"I'm fine thanks," but he'd already gone and I wasn't fine at all. I watched him stride across the crowded car park, he didn't look back. I sighed; this whole married thing might be trickier than I'd imagined.

CHAPTER SEVEN

I returned from honeymoon a wiser woman, although not necessarily in ways I'd have expected. Salutary lessons had been learnt that perhaps should have been studied earlier, but they do say, don't they, every marriage has boundaries and learning curves and whilst ours might have been more off-kilter and steeper than most, we'd talked things over and agreed we weren't going to let that lead to any kind of serious derailment. I appreciated I needed to be a little more judicious and whilst not hiding anything - that wouldn't be right - maybe in future, exercise a certain amount of discretion.

An excellent opportunity to put this into practice had arisen a few days into our week in Dorset. It was later in the year, so not Summer-crowded, and with no particular agenda we simply enjoyed exploring, talking and ambling with plenty of refreshment stops. Mercifully, David proved as lazily disinclined as me to do much more, so whilst there were worthy sights aplenty, and we read up and set out with great enthusiasm, we had a shameful tendency to be distracted and seduced by any number of lovely little tea-shops along the way. By the time we'd got a substantial snack under our belts and strolled around the local craft shops, it was more often than not, time to head back to the hotel and put off the sightseeing for another day.

One such afternoon, we'd set off with good intentions but had found ourselves a couple of hours later emerging happily from a tea-time refreshment stop, arguing whether it had been an unwise decision for us both to go for the coffee walnut cake - should we have boxed clever with one slice of that and one of lemon drizzle and thus doubled the taste benefit? As we walked slowly and contentedly back to where we'd parked the car, evening was drawing in and when we turned a corner; there was a rowdy group of teenagers walking ahead of us. Half a dozen boys and a couple of girls, taking the width of the pavement, were not bothering to move when an older woman with a chocolate-brown miniature poodle on a lead made to pass, she had to step off the pavement into the road, her head down, hurrying, clearly made uneasy by their noise and ostentatious lack of courtesy.

As we moved aside to let her comfortably pass us, I smiled but she didn't notice, too intent on getting home and shutting the door then locking it behind her. She was a maths teacher. She'd taught a couple of the boys in the group for several years, disciplining them as much as she could; watching naughtiness grow into nastiness. In the past, coming across them out of school, she'd have given them a sharpish piece of her mind for loutish behaviour and stood there, tapping an authoritative toe until they parted sheepishly before her. Not now though, things had happened, things had changed. She hoped, in the dusk, none of them had recognised her, they probably wouldn't she reasoned, she had her rain hat on and had kept her head down and she despised herself dreadfully. She was scared of them now; she could be honest with herself, if with no-one else. She knew, once you began to feel like that there was no going back - the children smelt it on you. If she could manage on her pension, she'd have retired already.

As woman and worry moved away, there were laughs and jeers from the boys, and then something else caught their attention, provoking shrieks of shock, horror and encouragement from the girls.

"What are they up to?" David said and increased speed to catch up with them. I pulled back. I knew what they were up to. They were keying parked cars, deep vicious scores cutting along the sides of previously unmarked vehicles; they were three cars in and just starting on a black van.

"Bloody hell, look at that, look what they've just done!" David had stopped at a red Morris Marina, defaced from boot to bonnet. "Oi," he yelled, "you lot, yes you. What the hell d'you think you're doing?" A rhetorical question if ever there was. The group, as one, turned towards us and I felt David's justifiable anger abate a little as they started swaggering back. Individually they were just complexion challenged teenagers, collectively they were something else.

"Oooh, I beg yooour paaardon," one of the two keyers mimicked and David, who was suddenly thinking less public-spiritedly and more along personal safety lines, muttered, "stay behind me, I'll deal with this," and I loved him for that. "Look at the damage you've done," he said, "what's the point, what *is* the point?" He was standing his ground, but if he thought anybody was going to clap hand to mouth in guilt and fear at being brought to book by a mild-mannered, Jewish journalist, he was sorely mistaken.

"Derek, you gonna let 'im talk to you like that?" One of the mini-skirted girls who'd hit the pan stick make-up far too hard – under the just-lit street lights she looked terminally anaemic - moved up alongside and Derek, who hated his name above all things and insisted his mates called him Storm, cursed, curled a lip and let his cigarette drop. He was planning on grinding it out menacingly without looking as per John Thaw on The Sweeney. Inconveniently, the still glowing butt rolled off the pavement into the gutter leaving him nothing to be menacing with and, as a giggle from Pan Stick and her friend confirmed, looking a little silly as he felt around with a winkle-pickered toe.

In my experience, if there's one thing above all else that precipitates violence, it's looking silly, because then there's a lot of lost ground to make up. This occasion was no exception to the rule, and what should and would have stopped with a sneer and some rude words, turned into a move, which I believe surprised the kicker as much as the kicked. He caught David just under the kneecap with one of those viciously toed shoes. David yelped in pain and anger and I got cross.

I moved out from behind my husband and looked at Derek. His eyes widened instantly and he staggered back and shrieked. Pan Stick and company were baffled for only a few seconds, before they too saw what he saw. Not me moving towards them, but a six-foot scarecrow - we'd commented on one in a field earlier that day, hence the inspiration. This scarecrow though had wide, amber flaming eyes, a mouthful of sharpened teeth, a cheerful grin and welcoming arms with extraordinarily large straw hands flexing, stretching, reaching.

It became apparent almost immediately, that nobody was planning on hanging about much longer. Chorusing shrieks and energetically elbowing each other out the way, they turned tail and ran, putting on I guessed, far more speed than had ever been displayed on school sports days. I thought it might be a while before any of them felt like doing damage to anyone else's car - or knee, come to that.

David limped forward and put a protective arm around me, "Don't worry, we're OK, I think I've seen them off."

"Oh, thank goodness." I said, maybe I overdid it because he paused,

"You didn't do anything did you?"

"You told me not to," I said. I like to stick to the truth where possible, "Anyway look," crossing the road and heading our way was the comfortably solid, long arm of the law.

"Evening," he touched forefinger to helmet, "everything all right here, Sir?" he frowned as he saw the damage on the car we were standing by, "yours?"

David shook his head, "No. There was a gang of kids – I scared them off."

"Probably one of them Grundy twins; need a good sound clip round the ear regular, both of 'em." He shook his head, "Bad lot that family, best go round see 'em again." He extracted a notebook, licked the pencil, noted the car number and touching forefinger to helmet again moved off, "Mind how you go now."

"I think we just met Dixon of you know where," I grinned, "and you didn't tell him about your knee."

David shrugged, "No point, anyway that kid's learnt his lesson, scared stiff, you saw the way he made off." I nodded; Derek aka Storm, had indeed been somewhat disconcerted by the turn events had taken. David took my hand and we strolled slowly back to the car.

* * * *

While we were away, we'd discussed and made a few policy decisions regarding Rachael's assumption that I'd carry on 'listening' and reporting on any shrieks for help that came my way. After all, I argued, it wasn't a question of actively *doing* anything, well not really, simply a question of awareness and it was generally only the most fraught of situations which called my attention, and those I wouldn't and couldn't ignore. But, I earnestly assured David, alerting Boris was the extent of my future action plan.

I was still deeply distressed about Ruth, and the same agitated apprehension recurred whenever I thought about her, but I'd been given unmistakeable marching orders. If the combined power of the others was bent on solving a problem of which they were all aware, there was almost certainly little I could contribute, and truth to tell, I so much wanted what I now had, normality. I'd had it up to my eyes with life and death stuff, I wanted my biggest decisions to be whether we could afford to change the tiles in our bathroom.

David had sold his flat which together with savings enabled us to get a two-bedroom, ground floor maisonette in Edgware with which we were delighted, despite some of the unorthodox style decisions of the previous owner, Jonathan 'call me Jonty, everyone does'. I understood on our first visit to view that Jonty, who wouldn't see either fifty or his waist again, still felt he was a charming young scoundrel, living life on the edge which may have influenced his choice of a mirrored ceiling in the bedroom. If I ever wanted to change careers, David pointed out when we'd looked, left and decided to put in an immediate offer, I'd have been a runaway success in the property market because whilst I knew the price Jonty was asking, I also knew to the last pound what he'd be perfectly happy to accept.

We'd taken possession a month before the wedding and plunged into a frenzied decorating exercise to save money. We weren't very good at it. Having purchased some ridiculously expensive, highly fashionable grass paper with a leaf motif, we pasted it enthusiastically onto our lounge walls upside down. Our error didn't come to light until I happened to look at the illustration on one of the wrappings. Still, it looked fine and we agreed that to hang the last roll the correct way would be bolting the stable door after the horse had long gone. We decided nobody would ever notice and if they did, wouldn't be tactless enough to mention. We were wrong; although it actually wasn't the first thing my mother-in-law said when they first came over to see our new home. She was taken aback by the lack of a third bedroom.

"But it would have given you so much more space," she said, I was about to exclaim how silly we'd been not to have thought about that, but David frowned, demonstrating as he sometimes did, an uncanny ability to read my thoughts more easily than I read everyone else's. He put his arm around Laura's shoulder and pointed out that another bedroom would have taken us way over our limited budget.

"Never mind darling," she patted his arm and reached up to remove a blob of wallpaper paste from his cheek, "it's lovely anyway – a delightful little home and I know you'll be happy here," then belatedly remembering, "you too Stella." She smiled at me but I knew she was still deeply puzzled as to how I'd turned so swiftly from driver to daughter-in-law. "Melvyn," she prompted, "new home gift?" My father-in-law, of whom I'd grown very fond, had a tendency to drift away into his own thoughts if he wasn't actually speaking or being spoken to. He came back with a start and handed over an elegant and excitingly wrapped and bowed item which turned out to be an apron, a pair of oven gloves and a toilet brush and holder. "The sort of practical gift, nobody ever thinks to buy you," said Laura as I thanked her enthusiastically, showing my appreciation by immediately placing the toilet brush in situ.

It was Melvyn I'd initially met, when he'd engaged the services of *Simple Solutions* to ferry Laura around. Both she and the car, at that time, were recovering from a 'small prang' and he was uneasy about her getting behind a wheel again until she'd 'calmed down'. Meeting her, I didn't think calming down was likely to occur any time in the near future and nothing I'd seen since had persuaded me otherwise, but I'd been and still was, fascinated by Melvyn's distinctive voice; mellow and smoothly soothing, a shoo-in for a Cadbury's voiceover. It immediately led you to believe that here was a man who could competently deal with anything and everything life might chuck his way, although this turned out, as do so many things, not to be the case at all.

They departed shortly afterwards, earlier than planned because Laura had a 'head' and I was just congratulating myself we'd got away with the wallpaper when she laid a hand on my arm;

"Word to the wise dear," she said, "'next time you want some wallpapering done, perhaps best get a man in, but not to worry, I'm sure nobody will notice."

CHAPTER EIGHT

Although I'd only been out of the office for a couple of weeks, when I went back I was immediately plunged into a bit of a crisis. I'd paused to pull my sleeve over my hand so I could polish up the rather classy brass nameplate I'd had mounted on the wall to the right of the front door: *SIMPLE SOLUTIONS to PRACTICAL PROBLEMS*.

I'd set up the agency nearly three years ago, when I'd come to the conclusion I was never going to make good employee material. Our offices were above a travel agent in Hendon's Brent Street and we'd expanded from our initial two rooms into four, taking over what Martin, our landlord, had previously been using as storage space for brochures, stationery and a vast disassembled model railway he'd years ago inherited from an uncle.

My team had expanded; Aunt Kitty was still doing the bookkeeping and credit control, coming in now on an ad hoc basis - although generally not so much when we needed her, as when she fancied we did, and Brenda had moved with stately precision to take up any slack. Brenda was the first official staff member I'd taken on and I'd done it on the basis of immediate liking, although employing a secretary who hadn't seen hide nor hair of a typewriter in over twenty-five years might have seemed to be overlooking the obvious, but Brenda adapted gleefully to our electric models despite, for the first few months, automatically utilising a brisk left hand for the non-existent carriage return.

There had been, in the early days, something of a power struggle between Brenda and Kitty, who both put in considerable effort when it came to out-bossing and re-organising the other but time, circumstance and some alarming experiences had smoothed any rough edges, and somehow and I've no idea quite how, Brenda had become so much an honorary family member that none of us would have dreamt of not including her in any group gathering. Trudie and Ruby joined us when we took the extra office rooms, although neither Kitty nor Brenda saw eye to eye with me on the new appointees and individually took me aside to voice views which for once, were totally in accord. 'Mark their word' they said, 'those new girls wouldn't last'.

Trudie was a mother of five, given to wearing long, peasant style skirts which were constantly tripping her on the stairs. Trudie, like Brenda hadn't worked for years, not since the children started arriving thick and fast. But it seemed to me that anyone who competently ran a home, husband and five children, must have a mind for logistics, a tendency not to panic in a crisis and a willingness and ability to tackle the totally unexpected.

Ruby had been running the florist shop she'd taken over from her parents for well over twenty years, but with the rent going up and up, it had got to a silly stage and she wasn't prepared to work herself into the ground and not see any money coming into her own pocket. Chatting to her when she came for an interview, and reading between the lines, I saw how she'd worked to keep the shop flourishing and decided if she lavished even half the same care and attention to detail on my business as she always had on hers, I'd have no cause to regret taking her on.

I'd just hissed another breath onto my plaque and was in mid-rub, when the front door opened and Brenda reached out and pulled me inside. She planted a kiss on my cheek, pulled me to her substantial bosom - she was a good six inches taller than me - and encompassed me in the uniquely comforting Brenda essence of freshly ironed white cotton, which was nothing to do with what she was wearing, but everything to do with what she was. A swift hug then she moved me to one side, looked quickly up and down the road and shut the front door.

"Welcome back and we need a word," she hustled me the few paces into what we liked to call 'Reception', although that was probably aggrandising the small counter with its PBX phone system, a small sofa and a couple of low chairs. This was where visitors were greeted and directed through to the travel agency, up to our offices or seated for a while if things were busy. Martin had not viewed the installation of all this with pleasure.

"Bloody ridiculous," he'd said, "who knows from reception? If they've not got the sense to see which office is which, then more fool them!" Hilary, had drawn herself up to full height - she was a good three inches taller than him and he was no short arse himself – blown a disdainful mouthful of cigarette smoke over his head and laid down the law. 'If,' she'd said, 'Martin was not prepared to add an element of class to their operation, then she personally was not prepared to stand around and watch. Off,' she said, 'she would go and find working surroundings which more accurately reflected the superb standard of holiday information she was able to impart.' Martin was a difficult but not stupid man and knew when to beat a retreat, "Have it your own way then, you usually do, just don't come crying to me when it all goes wrong." Quite what dire disaster he expected to result from a small counter and a couple of chairs, was never made clear.

The reception area had originally been staffed by Melanie, straight out of school and beyond thrilled at her first job. She wanted to open her own travel agency one day, although Martin had been heard to mutter if she couldn't tell her arse from her elbow, she'd not be able to tell Tenerife from Timbuctoo. She was perhaps not the sharpest knife in the drawer, but endlessly good-natured and willing to learn, choosing to take Martin's rants as office banter and refusing to be upset. Unfortunately, it proved impossible to wean her off chewing gum. Hilary sat her down for a little talk, gently pointing out it did not give a professional impression, added to which and perhaps more importantly it made her completely incomprehensible when answering the phone. Melanie, cheerfully saw the point and assured us she'd never chew in front of clients again. Having given her word, she stuck to it and all would have been well had it not been for the strategy of storing the wad of gum in her cheek as soon as somebody walked in the door. Unfortunately, this gave her the appearance of a slightly demented hamster and did nothing for clarity of speech. It was risky too; one day she inadvertently swallowed the gum which only got so far down, then stuck. She was turning purple and panicking when Trudie came back in from lunch and without breaking step or sweat, performed a first-class Heimlich manoeuvre, mopped Melanie's sweaty face with a tissue, placed her back in her chair, the gum in the bin and continued upstairs.

"My kids were always choking," she shrugged. In fact Melanie didn't last long after that, perhaps she'd had more of a trauma than we'd imagined because she dashed in one day, shrieked she'd been offered a bar job in Majorca, was leaving immediately and, pausing only to pick up money due and gum from her desk, was out the door.

I persuaded Martin and Hilary to let me sort a replacement and the local paper ad brought in quite a few candidates, although I had no problem choosing. Joy was early thirties, looked twenty, heart-shaped face, bobbed short, blonde hair. She'd been working in the West End, loathed the Northern Line sardine-in-a-tin commute and on the spur of the moment answered our ad. Her surname was Joyful.

"No, not kidding," she said ruefully, "I'm Joy Joyful and yes, I had a terrible time in school but Dad always said it's a name people don't forget; he wasn't wrong and it does break the ice. D'you want to test my shorthand and typing?"

I shook my head, "I'm sure they're fine but I think you'd fit in well with everyone here and that's far more important."

"You mean I've got it?" she bounced in the chair; she was going to rush around the desk and hug me but stopped herself with a mental slap and a reminder to act sensibly. I don't, as I think I've mentioned before, habitually delve but in a job interview a quick scan's not unreasonable, and I was satisfied Joy Joyful was straightforward, uncomplicated, well-intentioned with a strong sense of humour and a pink candy-floss scent. Yes, she'd do nicely.

She slipped into place behind the desk downstairs, as if it had been made for her, even wringing the odd smile from miserable Martin, teasing him gently about his eccentric and colourful wardrobe choices, which were as far from his downbeat personality as it was possible to be, and therefore a mystery to everyone. She and Hilary also unexpectedly bonded over a shared love of knitting, and lunchtime would often see both sat at the small table in the kitchen behind the shop, needles going nineteen to the dozen and a wreath of smoke from Hilary's inevitable cigarette hovering, halo-like above.

At this minute though, Brenda was ushering me firmly through the still dark travel agency and past the kitchen where Hilary was waiting. I opened my mouth to greet her but apparently there wasn't time, Brenda relieved me of briefcase and handbag and pushed me into the toilet, she and Hilary crowding in after me. It was, luckily, a reasonably sized space, although not where I'd normally choose for a chat, but genuine waves of worry were coming off both women, so I shut up. Hilary put the toilet lid down, sat and produced a cigarette from her pocket; Brenda immediately took it away.

"Not now woman, we'll suffocate," then to me "it's Joy."

"What's Joy?"

"There's something wrong," said Brenda,

Hilary nodded, "We didn't want her coming in and hearing, that's why…"

"What if she wants a wee when she comes in?" I asked. They frowned; this obviously hadn't been taken into account.

"We'll be quick," said Brenda.

"I wish you would. What's happened, has she made off with the takings?"

"We think it's Trevor."

"What's Trevor?"

"He's taken to picking her up every night."

"So?"

"And he comes early, so he's sitting there for a good half hour before we close." Hilary put in.

"And?" I prompted, "what's he doing?"

They looked at each other, "That's just it, we don't know," Brenda said, "he's absolutely charming, couldn't be nicer but there's something wrong."

"What sort of wrong?" They looked at each other, they couldn't really say; but these were two bright women, neither of them given to flights of fancy, if they thought something was wrong, something was wrong.

Joy had proved I'd made the perfect choice by living up to her name; she was a pleasure to have around. For a start she was delighted with where she'd landed, losing the commute was, she said, the best decision she'd ever made. She lived in a ground floor flat in Burnt Oak with its own small garden - her pride and joy, and because she wasn't hauling herself in and out of the West End day in and day out, she had so much more time to devote to what she loved doing. She'd started growing her own vegetables and herbs which were obviously flourishing because she often brought in batches for all of us. She was single, but the previous summer had met someone at a friend's party, he'd asked for her number and although she was convinced he wouldn't ring he did, and after a while they'd started seeing each other regularly. She was clearly smitten. She'd always bubbled, but now she glowed, and we were all pleased for her.

Trevor was a solicitor with his own practice, "Really, really clever, really shrewd," she reported, "terribly well thought of apparently." He was taking her to the most wonderful places, lovely restaurants, the theatre twice and on her birthday when they'd only been going out a couple of months, he sent a bouquet of such gigantic proportions it not only filled our reception area, but caused quite a Hilary, Martin rift as every time she passed his desk she muttered,

"Never so much as a daisy, Martin, never so much as a flaming daisy!"

When Joy felt secure enough and stopped thinking every date was their last, she brought him into the office to introduce us, and even under my cynical gaze and some pretty sharp questioning from the serried and suspicious ranks of Brenda, Hilary and Kitty, he didn't put a foot wrong, and was as charming as she'd said. Not that tall, he had a pleasant, open face, fine dark hair and was beautifully spoken with impeccable manners. He appeared as besotted with Joy as she was with him. As they left, Kitty gave her seal of approval - "What's not to love?"

Joy certainly thought so because last January, about five months after they met, she took a week off and returned sporting a wedding ring and a dazzling if dazed smile. She had no family, neither did Trevor and as he'd pointed out, this was such an important time for them, that no one else mattered. So, they'd skipped an engagement, tied the knot in a register office without telling anyone, and then jetted off for an idyllic few days in France. He'd put her flat on the market for her and already received a satisfactory offer, so when they returned from the brief honeymoon, it was to his house in Golders Green.

"All a bit sudden," commented Brenda at the time, "but she knows her own mind, thinks the sun shines out his bottom, so they've as good a chance as anyone." Brenda's cynicism wasn't unjustified; having been comfortably married for twenty-five years with never a cross word, her husband had unexpectedly upped and offed with the local vicar's wife, although not before he'd re-mortgaged the house, sold the car, and cleared their joint bank account.

Now Hilary, from her central position on the toilet said, "Stella, you must have noticed she's changed?" Well yes, of course she'd changed, she was quieter, more settled and whereas previously she'd bounced around the office like the Duracell Bunny on speed, she was calmer, more measured and a little less chatty. I knew the kitchen knit-ins had ceased when she decided she'd work through lunch, so she could leave a little earlier in the evenings but I'd asked her a few times over the months how married life was suiting, and she said she'd never been happier, felt safer or been more cherished. Slipping absent-mindedly into her head, sometimes that can happen, I saw she was telling nothing but the truth. Maybe I'd missed something? Last year had been a busy one in the office, there'd been a run-in with a couple of serial killers – that was a bit of a surprise. Then I'd started working with the police, got engaged, kidnapped, stabbed and watched Auntie Kitty nearly meet her maker. Nevertheless, that was no excuse to let things drop on the personnel front.

"She is quieter," I agreed, "but why's that worrying? She said anything to either of you?" I had a sudden and shockingly vivid memory flash-back to a woman on the floor, turning her head to expel, with the last of her strength, a tooth knocked out by a fist. In that instance, I hadn't done anything until it was nearly too late. "Do you think he's hurting her,? Have you seen anything? Marks, bruises?" both women shook their heads quickly.

"Don't be daft, nothing like that," Brenda drew herself up, "and if I had, d'you think I'd have stood by and done nothing? Told you, it's not anything we can put a finger on."

Hilary nodded and sighed, "Maybe it's nothing. For God's sake don't say anything to her, she'd be mortified we've been talking about her, just thought we ought to say…" she jumped as there was a sudden knocking on the door. I stifled a laugh, as they exchanged panicked looks, I knew it was a tail not a knuckle and sure enough Brenda, unlocking the door was knocked backwards by a surge of cream and brown joining us in what was rapidly becoming a dangerously overcrowded toilet.

CHAPTER NINE

Katerina, the cream and brown blur, was an elegantly elongated bolshie Borzoi I'd sort of inherited. She'd been staying with Brenda while I was away, accompanying her daily into the office and had become bored with waiting on her own upstairs, when she knew very well there were people talking downstairs. She was more elegant than any animal has a right to be, rich, heavy cream with extravagantly lush chocolatey markings although, it has to be said, she leaned heavily towards the neurotic. She'd belonged to and been loved by one of our clients, Doreen who was elderly, eccentric, equally highly strung and now deceased. Doreen's only living relative was a nephew, who lost no time in making it clear his only interest in an aunt he hadn't seen since he was a child, was whether there was anything of value in it for him. I didn't think a tall, slim and nervy canine qualified, and neither did he.

I had no intention of taking on a pet, certainly not one that looked down her long aristocratic nose at me most of the time, but I had agreed to take her while more suitable arrangements were made. Against my better judgement, I became far fonder of her than I would have thought possible. I wasn't sure it was reciprocated, but she seemed to view me as a constant in a scarily changing world and had proved herself astonishingly willing to leap to my defence at difficult times; I owed her.

Right now, she was being uncharacteristically enthusiastic and briefly leant her full weight against my legs, which was the emotional equivalent of being licked to death by a more demonstrative character. Satisfied she was now no longer alone, she allowed us out of the toilet and stalked ahead, sashaying with her usual style up the stairs, confident I'd follow. I turned briefly back to Hilary and Brenda.

"Look, I'll have a chat with Joy, if there's anything to worry about, I'll know." They nodded, both of them had at different times commented I was a great judge of character, both were relieved they'd now shared concerns, and both were pleased there were now three of us on watch.

* * * *

They say there's no such thing as bad publicity, although to be honest, I felt going missing for eight days, a couple of years ago, with my face plastered over every front page and the Metropolitan Police searching high and low for me, didn't show me in a great light. More praiseworthy perhaps was the fact I'd eventually turned up, not-dead, unlike as it transpired a great many other victims who'd spent time in the Hampstead House of Horrors, as the press gleefully labelled it. With a slight re-angling, and because it provided better copy, the papers reporting the story had made my agency seem rather less Practical Solutions and rather more Private Investigations. This had led to an influx of somewhat dubious new clients, most of whom never made it past Brenda, who was frequently to be heard snapping "No, we certainly don't do *that*!" and hanging up sharply.

My original focus when I set up the business had been on collecting, accompanying and safely returning children, the elderly, or pets to dentist, doctor or vet as relevant, as well as organising moves - house or office and supplying secretarial and other office services. But nothing stands still, and we'd gently evolved and expanded into a 'the answer's yes - what's the question?' sort of operation. We knew where, when and how to lay hands on useful people ranging through piano tuners to tree surgeons to theatrical prop suppliers. Along the way we'd also acquired an extraordinary team of redoubtable older ladies, dab hands at anything that could be achieved with a needle and thread. They could design and make a fully appliquéd wedding dress without turning a hair but didn't ever curl their lip at the more mundane - hem turning-up, seam letting-out or zip-putting in and had earned the undying gratitude of many a desperate mother by sewing numerous nametags on school clothes the night before term started.

I arrived upstairs as Katerina was settling herself in her basket in the corner of my office. My desk showed evidence of Brenda; mail neatly placed in 'do now', 'look at later' and 'don't forget!' folders plus a Grodzinski's box of mini Danish to sustain me whilst I went through everything. Slipping into my chair, I reached one hand for the first folder, the other for the pastries and could hear Brenda greeting Kitty, who'd obviously decided today was going to be one of her days and then two pairs of kitten heels tip-tapping up the stairs, heralded the arrival of my Mother and Aunt Edna.

I'd grown the business satisfactorily and liked to think I was responsible for sorting out a lot of problems for a lot of people. What I still hadn't cracked was the all too regular appearances of family members who treated my office as a convenient stop-off or meeting point whenever they felt like it, and they felt like it quite a lot. Whilst this gave us a decidedly convivial ambience, it did nothing to enhance the serious professional attitude I aimed to project. A foot really had to be put down firmly and I appeared at the door of my office ready to do just that, although any pronouncement was immediately swamped by the enthusiasm of people delighted I was back.

Aunt Kitty was in the process of boiling the kettle to make tea for the visitors; Ruby had an open Yellow Pages and was looking something up for them. Auntie Edna was in a chair while Trudie stood behind and gently massaged her temples – Aunt Edna always brought her headaches to Trudie; said she had magic hands. Trudie as usual looked as if she'd drifted into work straight from a Flower Power convention, the polar opposite of Ruby who was invariably as impeccably presented as her floral arrangements would have been when she ran her shop.

I was about to lay down some tough new rules regarding visiting and not visiting, when there were more feet on the stairs; honestly the place was busier than Piccadilly Circus and Joy stuck her head round the door, probably because there wasn't much room to insert herself more fully, she looked worried.

"Stella, hi so glad you're back. There's a couple of men downstairs for you... didn't like to use the phone in front of them. They're um... *Police*. Is everything alright?" I heaved a sigh. No, everything wasn't alright, I had a brief urge to pull a paper bag over my head and send Joy down to say I couldn't see anybody today.

"Nothing to worry about," I said to the concern in the rest of the room, "you know I worked with the police last year, it's probably to do with that." And abandoning tough new rules for the present, I turned back to my office, leaving my door open for the imminent visitation and rather impressed with how that last statement had sounded, although it wasn't so much the police in general, more like one policeman and a reluctant one at that.

The familiar warmth of deep brown silence, tinged with pipe tobacco and aniseed surrounded me well before Boris came in, lowering his head to pass through the doorway. He was followed wheezily by Detective Inspector Cornwall who, in the smallish office, loomed bulkier than ever. When they talk about the 'the thin blue line', they're not thinking about DI Cornwall. From behind my desk, arms folded, I eyed them with disfavour and Katerina growled softly, she was as pleased to see them as I was.

I indicated the chairs with a nod and Cornwall lowered himself, then heaved back up again to get at his pocket and a battered pack of Rothmans. He tapped a cigarette on the back of his hand whilst looking around. He was a man whose solid weight was firmly grounded in reality, but he was no fool either and, despite the fact I couldn't say he and I had taken to each other, I was aware he was a conscientious, clever and ethical officer – at least by his own lights. I also knew his deceptively lazy, hooded gaze had taken in and stored every detail and he could, if required, have given a complete report of what, where and how every single thing in my office could be found – which was certainly more than I could.

He coughed heartily, preparatory to lighting up and the shirt beneath his open jacket strained as belly battled with buttons. Dealing with Boris and me went against every principle Cornwall held dear, with the exception of one – getting as many villains and nutters off the streets and behind bars as was humanly possible before he popped his clogs. And there could be no doubting we'd facilitated some great results for him; it was on the back of these he'd climbed the ladder from Sergeant to Inspector so swiftly.

Boris was fluidly folding his six-foot five thinness into the other chair and turned to the pall of smoke next to him with an almost imperceptible nose wrinkle.

"Stella's recently married,' he remarked, obviously feeling a bit of introductory small talk was called for in the face of my lukewarm welcome, "you met David, I believe?"

Cornwall nodded and said, "Congratulations," thinking, 'poor sod', then regretting it as I frowned at him.

"Thanks," I said. Boris allowed himself a lip twitch; he enjoyed my small exchanges with Cornwall rather more than he should. Early sixties now, his hair had receded a little more since I last saw him, making the shape and boniness of his head, atop his skeletal frame, even more pronounced. He always looked as if he was on day-pass from a medical lecture hall, a life-like, multi-jointed example for study. His mind, as ever, was completely closed and shuttered to me and would remain so until such time as he needed it not to be, although I knew, despite my own defences he, like the Peacocks, thought nothing of strolling into mine whenever he wanted. He wasn't police at all, more as he'd once categorised it, an unofficial type of consultant.

"Well, this is all very nice," I said, "but I'm guessing you're not here for wedding gossip, and this is my first day back in the office. So, to avoid wasting time - mine and yours - can I say I'm really, *really* not getting involved in anything?" Boris crossed one lengthy leg over the other and shook his head reproachfully.

"Stella, so young, yet so cynical, we simply..." he was interrupted by Aunt Kitty who bustled in bearing a tray. Boris courteously stood again as she came in. Into her nineties now and still recovering from a near fatal stabbing, I personally thought a little less bustle might have been sensible, but Kitty had taken it upon herself to organise *Simple Solutions'* hospitality from the get-go and showed no inclination to stop. She'd brought three cups of coffee, sugar and milk served separately and a plate of biscuits. She had enormous respect for the police although, as Cornwall immediately tapped ash into his saucer, I could see that being tested. She whipped away the sullied saucer, wiped and returned it, wordlessly placing the wastepaper bin right next to his chair as she left.

I raised an expectant eyebrow at Boris who in turn looked at Cornwall who developed a sudden fascination with a Bourbon biscuit. I saw clearly how extremely disgruntled he was. His mind was as untidy as his clothes and as stained - with things he'd seen over the years and wouldn't ever un-see. He'd been unexpectedly press-ganged into this unplanned visit, so was being even more unforthcomingly uncooperative than usual because he was uncomfortable. He'd more or less rationalised his association with Boris, but Ruth, with whom he'd had previous dealings made him deeply uneasy, as did I, maybe because he wasn't greatly in favour of women being involved in anything much outside the kitchen. Now, prompted by Boris, he grudgingly reached into the inner recesses of his jacket.

"All we're asking," said Boris, "is can you tell us anything about these? And then we'll leave," Cornwall leaned forward, depositing two small, rough edged scraps of cloth and a smattering of cigarette ash on my desk. When I didn't move, Boris sighed.

"Just pick one up, I assure you, no involvement, just information, not remotely risky." Which only goes to show; nobody ever gets everything right 100% of the time.

CHAPTER TEN

Each piece of cloth, one black one blue, appeared to have been roughly torn from a larger piece of material or garment. I assumed and was unimpressed that Rachael had told Boris about my reaction to her wretched book and like the cloth, I was torn. I wanted to touch it, confirm that what happened with the book was merely an unsettling but passing aberration. I also didn't want to touch it in case it confirmed something else altogether.

"You know, you need to know." Boris said softly in my head, easily following my train of thought. I didn't look at him as I reached for the black cloth. And no, nothing: nada, zilch. I opened my mind, I had to make sure.

I was instantly swamped with Cornwall's discomfort and impatience, then the cacophony of the thoughts of the women in the outer office. Beyond was the babble of people going about their daily business with every now and then, a surge of individual strong emotion, peaking and shrieking high above the surrounding minds. I shook my head, shrugged at Boris.

"Sorry, nothing at all, from this." I said. He nodded and inclined his head towards the blue piece. The sooner I humoured him, the sooner he'd believe me and the sooner he'd go. I picked up the blue material to confirm and get rid, but dropped it immediately in distaste.

"What?" said Boris.

"You *know* what."

"Well, I bloody don't." Cornwall shifted his bulk impatiently, made to grind out his cigarette on his saucer, thought better of it, and utilised the wastepaper bin. "Well?"

"Can you tell us, Stella please, what you got from that?"

"Anger," I said, "bitterness, inferiority mixed with huge conceit, overwhelming hate, quantities of excitement and elation."

"Elation?"

"Yes Boris, elation," I snapped, "because whoever this man is, the first five emotions have combined to produce the last two."

Boris hadn't moved but nevertheless there was a relaxing. He reached into his pocket for a small, white, crumpled paper bag and offered it across the desk.

"Aniseed ball?" I ignored the bag, as did Cornwall. Boris plucked out a sweet and placed it in his mouth, stored it in his cheek and returned bag to pocket. "Man or woman?" he said, looking at the cloth.

"Man."

"Dead or alive?"

"Alive."

"How so certain?" as with Ruth, the fact English wasn't his first language showed very occasionally.

I shrugged. "No idea. I just know," and then silently, because I thought there was probably only so much woo-woo Cornwall could take, I flicked a thought to Boris "Why so interested, you must have come across this before?"

"Naturally," but he was lying. I raised an eyebrow and he added, "although only on its own, not in conjunction with other abilities."

"Great, so even amongst us, I'm strange?"

"You're not unique," he said. I was amused by how much of a *'don't get too up yourself'* tone he was silently able to convey, "Of that I'm certain Stella, just maybe a little… unusual." Cornwall watching was aware something was going on under his nose and didn't like it. He made to speak but Boris absently held up a hand, indicated the piece of cloth and said aloud;

"Do you know who this is?"

"Oh sorry, did I not give a name and address?"

"Sarcasm; lowest form of wit. Do you want to know?"

"No."

Cornwall ran out of the small amount of patience he'd been hanging on to. "Right," he said, hauling himself out of his chair, "we finished here then?" Boris rose too,

"Hang on a moment," I said, "why exactly did you come?"

"I wanted to see for myself whether what Rachael told me was correct." He reached for the material scraps.

"And?" I said.

He handed the material to Cornwall, "Now I've seen."

"The man," I nodded towards where the material was re-concealed about Cornwall's person. "I imagine he's dangerous, it's certainly what he wants to be."

Boris answered indirectly, "Hate, bigotry, violence, it's always there, sliming and simmering beneath the surface, it rises and falls, peaks and troughs." Cornwall snorted in exasperation, obviously not an appreciator of the well-turned phrase. Boris, now well into his stride, continued, "You know, in truth, most of the hate-filled are simply followers but every now and then, every once in a blue moon, from the muck pile there crawls a leader. A leader draws the haters in, gives them direction, furthers motivation, facilitates. If you damage the leader you disable the followers."

"And this is a leader?" I asked though I knew instinctively he was, in the elation that still sang sourly in my head there had been an overweening sense of destiny and entitlement. Boris had followed Cornwall to the door but threw a question over his shoulder,

"What would you say Stella, is the best way of dealing with such a man?" I answered silently, and he shook his head.

"Stella, Stella. Subtlety was never your strong point. No, rather than elimination I'd opt for humiliation. Think about it; elimination makes martyrs; humiliation makes fools." I made to say something but he stopped me with a glance, "Yes, we know you want no involvement, we ask only for a listening role."

"I'd already agreed to that."

"So, you should not worry. We will do what we need to do."

"But..."

"Nothing more you need know right now." As Cornwall opened the door, Boris turned with an afterthought, although I knew him well enough to know any afterthought was planned and timed. "We *can* still rely on you, can we, to continue to listen?"

"I said, I would." He shut the door quietly behind him. Leaving me to ponder, not so much on what he'd said as what he hadn't.

Like Ruth, I had an aptitude for picking up on peaks of emotion, but because fear and anger generally trump laughter and joy, those sorts of peaks were rarely good news for anyone. When Ruth had first been unwell, she'd asked me to work with Boris. All that was required was to report any details and not get further involved. Sometimes that had worked well. Sometimes it hadn't. A visit from Boris always unsettled me. It wasn't that I wanted to know more, in fact, would have preferred to know a whole lot less. I was torn now though, the man that material had been close to, was dangerous. But on the other hand and not to be sneezed at were all my solemn assurances to David on steering clear of risk. I resolutely put Boris and Cornwall to the back of my mind and reverted to what I'd been doing before they arrived, setting out new visiting guidelines for relatives, but when I went out to tell them, they'd already gone.

CHAPTER ELEVEN

I'm ashamed to say I forgot about having a word with Joy until a few days later when I was ushering out a potential who I'd decided wasn't going to graduate to client. I didn't usually see people off the premises, but couldn't wait to see the back of this one. There were clients I loved, some I wasn't so keen on and others I wouldn't touch with a barge pole. This chap fell firmly into the last category.

He'd made an appointment, for which he was forty-five minutes late and with no apology. When he'd been shown into my office and Brenda offered him a cup of coffee, he didn't even bother looking at her, just shook his head and waved her away impatiently. She and I exchanged a look as she shut the door.

"Well now, little lady," he said, leaning back in the chair and spreading his legs wide, "this is your lucky day. Need your tender care and expert services." He wiggled a suggestive eyebrow, "But don't get overexcited, secretarial's what I'm after." I sighed; I'd come across his type before. Fifty, going on twelve, could make the shipping forecast sound smutty, apart from which he'd lost me at little lady.

I smiled politely and started to explain we weren't taking on any more office service clients at present. He spoke over me,

"Listen up, what I want is help with my mail, loads of fan stuff I get. I need you sifting out the nutters, sending photos to the suckers and picking out the few that might do me any good. And don't waste my time playing hard to get." I started to repeat what I'd said, but he was in full, fruity flow, "I know how these things work little lady, you say you can't do it; I'll beg a bit, you agree reluctantly and lump something on top of the going rate because you're doing me a favour. Well, you can skip that part. Chap at the golf club uses you. I know what he's paying and I won't pay over." He paused for breath, allowing me to nip in and assure him he wouldn't be paying over as he wouldn't be paying at all. As I'd explained, we couldn't help.

He was incredulous. "I don't think you know who I bloody am, do you?" he leant forward, hands on spread knees. Broad-shouldered and heavy necked, he used his bulk to intimidate; frequently and successfully.

"I know exactly who you bloody are," I said mildly. He was the straight-talking, near-the-knuckle, cheeky-chappie, micky-taking host of the TV quiz, Loggerheads, "but I'm afraid I still can't help you."

He got to his feet, bonhomie down the drain. "Well, you've wasted my time then haven't you and I don't think much to that. Tell you something for nothing, I'll be spreading a word or two, mark my words, I can make things extremely uncomfortable for you and your oh-too-busy-business." He probably could but I didn't like him, didn't like his tone and wouldn't dream of asking any of the others to work with him.

I watched as he started to experience a certain amount of discomfort in the trouser area. There's always an issue with that isn't there? You can scratch a nose or an ear should the need arise but below stairs? Not so much. Strangely enough he wasn't half as talkative headed out as he was headed in, and he was doing some funny things with his thighs. At the bottom of the stairs and before I said goodbye I alleviated the itch, though not before I'd hooked it in his mind to me and my office. Should he decide to spread a negative word, he'd be the one finding things extremely uncomfortable.

Joy was behind the reception desk as I shut the door decisively behind him. She was sorting holiday brochures into neat piles to go into the stands for Hilary, she made a face;

"Didn't like him, he was all over me when he came in. Offered to give me his autograph, I said no thanks - think that gave him the hump."

I grinned back at her, "Probably, but I didn't take to him either. So," I said, sitting myself on one of the reception chairs, "how's married life?"

"Pretty wonderful actually. You?"

"Bit too soon to tell, but so far so good. How's the house?"

She smiled, "Older than old fashioned at the moment, it was his parents', don't think it'd seen a paintbrush or fresh bit of wallpaper in years. But we're going slowly, having fun choosing, so we can make it our own. Trevor's got really good taste; much better than me at putting all the colours together." While she was talking, I listened to what she was thinking. I wanted to reassure Hilary and Brenda and the truth was, Joy inside seemed as idyllically happy as Joy on the outside.

"If there's so much to do, didn't you think about selling and buying something new?" I asked.

"I suggested that, there's a smashing new estate being built not far from us, all ultra-modern kitchens and bathrooms but Trevor wouldn't hear of it. Anyway, he says I've got no idea about property values and in a few years when we've done it up, we'll be able to sell ours at a much better price, you know, all the original features, fireplaces and that."

I nodded, "Probably sensible. Meant to tell you, I like your hair." She'd abandoned the short golden bob and let it grow past her shoulders. "It's darker too, isn't it?

She nodded, tucking an errant strand behind an ear, "Trevor thought it was too bright before, bit brassy, so I've toned it down a little. Still not sure about growing it though, it's a lot more trouble in the mornings, but he won't hear of me getting it cut."

I smiled, "Isn't that supposed to be the caveman instinct? But it looks lovely, so well worth the extra time."

"Thanks. I'm off for lunch now, Hilary wants me back by 2.00, can I get you anything?"

"No, I'm fine. What's that?" She'd taken a notebook from the side of the switchboard and I thought maybe Hilary had introduced, as was her wont, one of her efficiency-improving schemes which usually turned out to be more bother than they were worth.

Joy glanced up, "Silly really, Trevor likes me to keep a note of when I go out and when I get back, that way when we get home and I tell him about my day, I don't forget things. You know me, mind like a sieve."

I laughed, "Thank goodness, thought it was one of Hilary's strategies." We grinned at each other, and I turned for the stairs, mind already on the limited details I had for my next appointment. "See you later," I said, and she raised a hand as she went out the door.

I thought Brenda and Hilary were definitely mistaken, Joy was deliriously happy, proof of which was she didn't mind falling in with Trevor's thinking on most things. It wouldn't suit me; if David had suggested such a notebook I'd have made a swift counter proposal as to where he might want to store it - but everyone's different and if Joy was worried or unhappy in any way I'd have seen it.

The front door bell rang, the door was unlocked but I turned to go and answer it anyway. As I moved past the reception desk, something Joy had said, bounced back at me - mind like a sieve – well that was rubbish, she was the only one who had the complete office address book in her head, I'd lost count of the times I'd heard Hilary or Martin yell through for a number or name, instantly supplied. I thought I mustn't forget to say that to her, praise where praise is due and all that, but by the time I'd finished with my next appointment, Joy's sieve had been temporarily overtaken.

CHAPTER TWELVE

The mid-forties woman I ushered upstairs and settled in my office was in, what Grandma used to term, 'a right old two and eight'. Well-dressed; black pencil skirt and a grey angora jumper beneath her coat, make-up carefully applied but there was a darker smudge of foundation on her upper cheek which she'd neglected to rub in. It gave her an odd vulnerability, but I felt I didn't know her well enough to point it out. She peeled off a pair of black leather gloves, placed them neatly across her handbag clasp, placed that on the desk, moved it to the floor, then picked it up again to extract a tissue that she didn't use, just held crumpled in her hand. She smoothed subtly highlighted brown hair cut sharply to just below her chin, checking it wasn't wind-blown. It wasn't, so she finally had to answer my 'how can I help?' She started the way most people did; different wording, same worries, hopeful and pessimistic at the same time.

"I honestly don't think there's anything you can do," she said. She was well-spoken, low-toned, "I don't expect it's even something you *would* do, but someone told me..." she tailed off and I reached for my notebook and pen. I rarely took notes, I'd always found whilst busy jotting, something important had been said which I'd missed, and I'd long ago given up my shorthand which had been indecipherable anyway, but the notebook indicated efficiency and attention being paid.

"Let's start with your name?" I suggested.

"Jane."

"Jane?"

"Air," she supplied. I glanced up and saw a woman who'd had far too many years of jokes; "Married name," she said resignedly. "And spelt a-i-r."

I didn't like what I was feeling from her, the external twitchiness was as nothing compared to that within, although she was doing her level best to damp it down. It was impossible to make any sense of her thoughts which were chasing their tails in a frenetically repetitive, viciously disruptive circle over which she had little or no control; no wonder she looked exhausted.

"What is it you think I won't be able to do?" I asked gently. She jumped, as if in that second or two she'd forgotten I was there. She pulled her attention back with an effort and didn't answer directly.

"Actually, it's Dr Air, I'm a Clinical Psychologist. I have a successful practice," she added, "fully paid up member of The British Psychological Society, that's me." She shook her head slightly, "Why am I telling you this?" it wasn't a question that demanded an answer, so I waited. I knew why, did she? "It's because it's important to me that you know who I am..." she stopped and swallowed, an audible click in a dry throat, "or was."

"Let me chase up some tea," I said, getting to my feet, but a brief knock on the door heralded Brenda with what was needed. Depositing the tray, she straightened, smiled then spotted the foundation mark.

"Here," she extracted a tissue from her pocket, "you've got a smudge, my love." She handed it over, indicating where it was needed, nodded as it was dealt with and hurried out again, taking a lot of the tension with her. We laughed and I said,

"My staff really don't know the meaning of boundaries; I am so sorry."

"Don't be, if she hadn't said, I'd have waltzed around all day looking like a lemon!"

"So, Dr Air..."

"Make it Jane." Ashamed, frightened and confused, she'd set out who she was, but that wasn't who she felt like.

"Jane." I agreed, but her attention had drifted again. She was on some kind of medication; it wasn't helping; only adding to the confusion.

I followed in Brenda's gung-ho footsteps, "What are you taking?"

She didn't seem to think it was an outrageous question, "Amitriptyline, anti-depressant. My GP says the way I'm feeling is common at my time of life," she shook her head, "I went to see her for advice, so..."

"Not helping?"

"God no, making it worse."

"Tell me," I suggested. She closed her eyes and I saw the effort she made to put thoughts in recountable order, "Just start with whatever comes into your head, we'll sort it out after." She opened her eyes and for a moment, the woman behind the drugs and worry broke through as she laughed,

"Exactly what I say to my patients."

"Well then, you've seen it work, go for it."

She nodded, "I'm seeing things."

"Anything in particular?"

"Insects… I'm seeing insects and nobody believes me," she paused, "I've had the pest control people in, I've had the house deep-cleaned from top to bottom, same with my car, I've washed and re-washed every piece of clothing I have, and I've had so much dry cleaning done I've had to start using different places, because after a while they start eyeing you suspiciously," she looked up with a wry smile, "you're a kind of last resort."

"Who suggested me?"

"Susan McCrae,"

"She's your GP?"

"No, a friend, we go way back to schooldays. She sort of mentioned you once."

"Sort of?" I asked with trepidation.

"We went out for dinner a few weeks ago, once or twice a year we do that, just the two of us for a catch up, don't talk that much in-between, we're both busy and neither of us is really the chatty type. Anyway, this was ages ago, only a few weeks after Devlin came out of hospital, she was still pretty shaken up, that's when your name came up." A pause for some tea, "Sorry, dry mouth, it's the pills, horrid," she ran her tongue over her lips and continued, "Susan said, and she's one of the most level-headed women I know, she said there was something she couldn't explain about what had happened with Devlin, said she didn't know how, but she thought it was something you did, that got him back."

Young Devlin had got himself knocked down by a car and a devastating head injury had put him in a coma. I hadn't worked miracles, simply gone into his head to see what was what. By pure chance I knew something that had shocked him dreadfully in the past, I used it. I gave him such a terrible fright that his survival instinct kicked right in and yanked him back to consciousness. In truth, he'd saved himself. I shook my head, all my 'keep it under wraps' reflexes to the fore.

"Honestly I can't claim credit, I just happened to be there when he came out of it. Can I ask you a couple of questions?" her face had fallen a little, I'm not sure what she'd expected me to say. From what she'd told me and from what she hadn't, I knew she was a highly intelligent, motivated woman, used to being on top of things. She had a well-managed life, a successful practice and a solid reputation in her own field. The last few weeks had taken her from fear to bewilderment to disbelief to doubting everything she knew. She couldn't believe that now, she was sitting in an Office Services place, above a travel agent, on the vaguest of recommendations. I was indeed, in her mind, the last resort and she was already running through excuses she could use to leave as soon as possible without being rude.

But amidst all of this, nowhere in her head could I find or feel the unmistakeable signs of mental illness. In a lifetime of recognising and steering clear of risk I was usually, not always, but usually able to recognise deviation from the norm. The first sign was a mind either far too hot or way too cold - it wasn't an absolute, but it was an indicator. When the temperature wasn't right, I knew to be wary. In Jane's case, I couldn't feel or see anything other than acute anxiety, panic she was struggling to hold at bay and fear she wouldn't be able to. She took a breath and started talking.

She'd been married, was now divorced - but reasonably so. It was a relationship that had run its course and morphed gently into friendship with little friction, and they met up every few months for a meal or the theatre. All very civilised. There was one daughter, now at University and Jane lived a life tightly under her own control, that's how she liked it. She was a doer, a fixer, the person others brought problems to.

The stupid insect thing had started almost without her noticing. In fact, she was hard pushed to say exactly when. Nobody takes that much notice of the odd couple of autumn wasps near the end of their time, tipsily aimless on rotten fruit and she only recalled them when, a few days later there was an unpleasant cluster of flies wedged in a corner of the window in her consulting room. Probably around half a dozen fat bluebottles, all clumped together buzzing, one or other occasionally rising for a few seconds before returning to the heaving pile. Odd; not ideal, but easily and swiftly scooped out the opened window with a coned newspaper.

At home, later that week or maybe it was the next week, she really couldn't be sure – an exceptionally solid, dark-brown spider squatted comfortably in the middle of the shower tray one morning. She wouldn't have been thrilled to have stepped on it unexpectedly, and obviously that wouldn't have been great for the spider either, so she'd done the business with glass and card, put it out of the window, had her shower and turning to rinse off shampoo, come face to face with it again, this time, at eye level on the inside of the shower door. It gave her a nasty fright, before she ticked herself off – wasn't there a thing about spiders usually being in twos, this almost certainly wasn't the same one come back bearing a grudge. She wasn't keen on spiders and certainly not on such an up close and personal basis, but she wasn't phobic or anything like that it was just a nuisance.

And then her daughter had come home for the weekend, not so much Jane said, for some mother and daughter time, more because she had an obscene amount of washing. Sitting in the garden, enjoying a quick lunch, relishing the last hurrah of an Indian Summer, and a precious if predictably brief chat with Emma, there was suddenly an orderly parade of ants marching briskly over the plate of sandwiches they were sharing. Exclaiming in annoyance, Jane leant forward to brush them off and remove the top layer of sandwiches onto a tissue. Em, stretched back in her chair, tanned legs stretched out and going on forever, asked lazily what she was doing. Jane, tutting and brushing the odd small black straggler off the table, said it was a good thing at least one of them had an eye on lunch or it would all have been spoilt. Em said she hadn't seen any ants and Jane said well, there you are, didn't that just prove her point.

I leaned forward to interrupt and the woman sitting across from me shook her head.

"No, wait, let me finish first." I sat back, and she took another sip of tea, a breath and continued.

The following day, Em was heading back to Bristol, she had a lift with a friend, not a boyfriend she'd insisted, Pete. He came into the house, nice boy, to carry Emma's overfilled case. As he turned to go, clinging to the back of his light green tee-shirt, were several ladybirds. Moving out of a goodbye-Em hug, Jane brushed them off for him. Ladybirds - pretty harmless, right? But not a great fashion statement she'd joked. Pete thanked her and Jane started the usual mother stuff; drive carefully; should they take some Mars bars and apples for the journey; had Em remembered the bits of washing still drying over the radiator in the kitchen? The several ladybirds were now milling around on the hallway floor, vivid red and black on grey-veined stone tiles. Jane moved them gently aside with a sandalled toe, so they didn't get trampled, said she'd get a dustpan and brush in a minute and put them outside. Emma looked down, said she couldn't see any ladybirds and sharp, because she was concerned, turned to Pete for confirmation. Pete embarrassed and unsure of his ground agreed, he couldn't see any either.

"I passed it off with the kids," Jane said, "laughed, told them to ignore me, new glasses probably needed," but I could see Emma was worried. Pete said they'd probably flown away, taken fright when I knocked them off, quoted that old ladybird, ladybird fly away home thing.

"And had they?" I asked.

She shook her head, "Still on the floor, more of them by then; swarming, climbing over each other, little ladybird hillocks of movement. I waved the kids off, shut the door and…" the memory briefly twisted her mouth in distaste, "and I knelt down, put both my hands on them, lots of rigid little bodies squirming; and the smell, there's a particular smell when they're frightened, distinctive, unmistakeable."

"What did you do?"

"I went into the kitchen, poured myself a very large white wine."

"And then?"

"What do you mean?"

"Did you clear them away? From the hall, I mean?" she shook her head, "they weren't there when I went back with a mop."

"And since?"

"Well no more ladybirds, but I have had worms, wasps, silverfish and wood lice."

"And nobody?"

She cut in resignedly, "… sees what I see. Friends, colleagues, my ex, I don't say anything anymore," she sighed, more a sob than a sigh but kept her voice even, "I'm not just losing my mind, I'm losing me."

"And now?" I asked, although I knew. Through her eyes I could see, indeed hear, the buzz of two chunky house flies criss-crossing and cruising a leisurely flight path; hitting the window and circling around and back to hit heftily again.

"Flies; there," she indicated with a nod, I turned to look.

"Don't bother, you won't see them." She was right, I didn't. I turned back to her. She was holding herself together but only just.

"I've taken time off," she said. "A colleague's seeing my patients. These pills are doing nothing other than knocking me out. I don't know what's real and what's not anymore." She leaned forward a little because it was so important to make me understand. "You see, I'm the one who copes, who sorts out everybody else, that's who I am. Except now I'm not. I know my next step has to be a psychiatrist who'll listen to what I'm seeing, and take me down the pharmacology route - heavy duty stuff - no option, it'd be my professional recommendation too, and honestly I don't even know why I've come here." She wound down, refusing to let loose the sob working its way up her throat.

She was telling the truth; I'd felt the unpleasantness of swarming ladybird bodies under my hands. I could see the flies she was seeing. I didn't for one moment think she was delusional and I was prepared to take a guess at what was going on, but not why.

"I don't think you're ill in any way," I said slowly, thinking it through, "just stressed, very! So, if we accept that as true, there has to be some other explanation, however odd."

"You believe me?"

"I believe you believe what you're seeing," I said and saw a fractional easing of her tension. "Are there any current or past patients who might wish you ill, maybe someone felt you hadn't helped them or helped enough?

She frowned, "What on earth could that have to do with this?"

"Probably nothing, humour me," I said. She nodded but I felt her disappointment and resignation. I'd just confirmed what she already thought. I was another dead-end, but she didn't have the strength to argue. She closed her eyes momentarily, and I was delighted to see her going methodically through a filing cabinet kept as immaculately in her head as in her office – gotta love a well-tended filing cabinet. We sat silently for a while, as I went through her records with her. There were a lot of them but in her head, at the forefront, were the very few she felt she hadn't served well, and out of those there were only two she hesitated over.

She looked up, "Only a couple of cases..." she paused, thinking, and nodded briefly, more in reassurance to herself than to me, "I'm good at what I do but look, this is a waste of time. You must know I can't tell you anything – confidentiality, and even if I could, this couldn't possibly just be someone playing a practical joke?" I didn't answer immediately; I was considering the couple she'd pinpointed.

One was a middle-aged man, Civil Service, sudden onset of severe panic attacks. Fighting an immovably stiff upper lip all his life, over a few sessions he clearly saw and acknowledged the pressure cooker he'd created for himself. He was grateful, and then more than that and transference moved to fixation. Confident she could handle it – this wasn't the first time – Jane was wrong. He was out on bail after twice breaking into her house, when he killed himself. So she was right, he wasn't relevant now.

The other was Lucy, eleven, who'd stopped talking. She'd been referred by a school counsellor and challenged Jane's professional detachment because at the time she was the same age as Emma. It took a session or two for Lucy to understand she was in a place of safety and confidentiality. Once she did, the story poured out in one brief, hoarse and traumatic catharsis. Her mother had remarried a few months back; and because the child didn't have the words to name what it was her stepfather was doing to her, she'd stopped using words altogether.

Almost immediately after that session, as Jane was putting into action the next urgent professional steps; Lucy's mother phoned. Lucy, she said, would not be returning, these sessions were doing more harm than good. The level of angry bitterness, buried amidst the bile with which this message was delivered, told its own horror story. The woman knew. The family refused any further contact and moved abroad shortly after. Lucy was the patient Jane felt she'd failed, but I was pretty certain Lucy wasn't who I was looking for.

I stood up, "Look, I've been stuck in this office all day and Katerina needs a walk." Kat, curled and comfortable, looked up aghast, she enjoyed walking about as much as I did, and really only consented to venture outside for calls of nature, and the briefer the better, but this was no time for sensibilities. "Let's get some fresh air while we talk," I said. Jane looked as disconcerted as Katerina and gathered gloves, handbag and jacket with tight lips. She wasn't disappointed she told herself. She'd expected nothing much and nothing much was what she'd got; what a waste of time. On the other hand, once out of the office, it would be less awkward to suddenly remember an appointment, bid a swift farewell with a thanks-for-nothing subtext and beat a rapid retreat.

"We're going for a walk," I said to Brenda's startled face, as our party passed through the outer office, I didn't pause for explanation. I had a hunch and over time, I've learnt to act on them because they get results – not always positive, I should add – but instinct suggested what I had in mind might be the only way right now.

CHAPTER THIRTEEN

As I and my two companions, each as reluctant as the other, strolled down Brent Street, Jane and I were wrapped in her thoughts, and she was giving me the answers to most of the questions I wanted to ask, at the same time as working out when would be the best time to discover she had to dash.

Throughout her training, it had been drummed into her that she wouldn't be able to help everybody; nothing should be considered a failure but rather a learning experience; and she should never cross the line between caring and really caring. But as is often the case, how she was supposed to feel and how she felt, were sometimes not even within shouting distance of each other. The couple of cases she'd highlighted would always bring up guilt and questions - but they took us no further forward with her current crisis.

"Hendon Park's just down the road here," I said.

"Is that a good idea," she said, "won't the dog roll in disgusting things?"

I had to laugh, "Trust me, *I'm* more likely to roll in something than she is, this is one extremely fastidious dog." We entered the park, following the path past the tennis courts and I thought I should test a theory. Bit mean but necessary. Sure enough, Jane swore softly and did a sideways skitter away and around something that wasn't there.

"Sorry," she said.

"What was it?"

"Not sure, something squashed, with maggots, eugh; almost trod in it!" she shuddered, and then looked at me with resignation. "You didn't see it did you?" I shook my head, feeling guilty; I had though confirmed she was exceptionally receptive.

We walked on a little more and I didn't miss her glance back to see how far in we were, so she could make reasonable get-away plans.

"Look," I said, "I'm not sure exactly what's going on, but I might be able to stop it for you." I nodded towards a bench we were approaching and as we sat, I bent to unclip the lead, "Off you go, have a run." Kat gave me the sort of look I'd give anyone who suggested that to me, turned on the spot a couple of times and settled neatly by my feet. I turned to the woman by my side, she was holding her tired face in her hand; the sun mercilessly lighting every line and shadow.

"Do you use hypnotherapy in your practice?"

"I do," she said.

"D'you trust me enough to let me try something similar?"

"What - *here?*"

"It won't take long."

She shrugged, too worn out to disagree and I reached for her reluctant hand. I was about to pull the wool over the eyes of an expert and felt a prop or two wouldn't have gone amiss. In the absence of such, I'd just have to hold her hand.

"Relax," I said, 'fat chance' whipped through her head, but she had the grace to not let it show. "Close your eyes, so you're focusing on the sunlight filtering through your eyelids. Feel the warmth on your face, hear the noises around you; breeze in the trees, birds, children, dogs – now let them go, let them fade gently, hear only my voice, feel only the pressure of my hand on yours.

I paused for breath, in truth I was feeling rather relaxed myself, which obviously wasn't the point. I'd read about the BBC filming Peter Casson at the Alexandra Palace back in the 50's. Putting the volunteers under, he inadvertently mesmerised a couple of cameramen as well as three technicians in the control booth. The BBC, ever caring of the well-being of the nation and its own reputation, dropped the project faster than a hot potato. I pulled my attention back and slipped into her head to briefly black her out. I was going to use something Sam had shown me once, although it was on one of those occasions which came under the heading of dicey - so I hoped I'd paid enough attention to remember correctly.

I visualised shimmering copper threads – they felt like effective barrier material - and I wove those swiftly and carefully into a virtual skull cap inside her head. As I did, as I was in there, I felt something fleetingly familiar, but I had limited time and lacked Sam's abilities. He'd have been able to map her brain and pinpoint precise placement of the protection, I had to opt for a clumsier all-over method, I had to be quick and I couldn't make a mistake.

When I had it where I was pretty certain I wanted it, where I thought it would work best, I was gripped by sudden panic. What if I was wrong? What if the images were being generated by her own brain besieged from a malignancy within, not as I was assuming, from somewhere else? I froze as I thought this through. If I was right, the measures I'd taken should stop the insects. If I was wrong and they continued, then that would be the time to head for a genuinely qualified medical person – and quickly! I examined this logic and my conscience for flaws, found few and withdrew my now extremely sweaty hand from hers, wiped it on my skirt, took a breath and woke her, counting up and clapping my hands sharply, to make everything feel kosher.

When she opened her eyes, the scepticism shone clear. She thought I was a complete and utter nutter, a waste of time and energy. She was cross with Susan for even mentioning me, even crosser with herself for coming. For her to make such an obviously stupid decision, proved beyond doubt she was in an even worse way than she'd previously thought. But she was courteous and thanked me as we walked away from the bench. Said she'd let me know how things went, said please invoice her for the time spent, apologised for having to dash now but had to be somewhere. We shook hands formally and I was amused at how swiftly she'd initiated that shake, just in case I was heading in for a hug. She felt I was well-intentioned and had tried my best, but I was certainly not going on her people-to-keep-in-touch-with list. She, on the other hand, was definitely going on mine; I needed to know how things went.

CHAPTER FOURTEEN

Office life meanwhile chugged along, not always smoothly but generally I felt, in the right direction. Our small team meshed well, although you'd be hard put to imagine a group of women more disparate. Brenda at the helm was ably assisted or as Brenda preferred to put it, interfered with by Aunt Kitty. Trudie was getting happily hippier by the minute, and always looked as if she was going to San Francisco, although beneath the flower power she really wasn't unconventional at all. I knew for a fact, the only trips she ever took were on the stairs and the only pot she used was for her delicious vegetable soup which she often brought in for each of us because she said she had to find a use for all the flipping vacuum flasks, accumulated through years of school trips. She was mid-forties but looked ridiculously young, not much more than a teenager herself. That, combined with fey and flowery invariably led people to underestimate her, but she had a quirkily swift and sharp mind and an instinctive ability to spot new business opportunities.

Ruby, black business-suited, brisk and impeccably manicured - she'd spent a long time with damp, leaf-stained hands and wasn't going there again - was a great front-woman, conveying the impression she'd just hurried out of one board meeting, was on her way to another and ate troublesome clients for breakfast. Truth was, whilst she was indeed excellent at meeting and greeting, she'd worked through years of customer contact in the shop and now was never happier than when left alone with her typewriter and an overflowing tray of manuscripts to be transcribed and transformed from handwritten and unreadable to pristine and presentable. She was building a devoted following of research scientists from the National Institute for Medical Research in Mill Hill, who could never, for the life of them, read back their own notes and were beyond relieved to have found someone who could.

Auntie Kitty, energy only a trifle diminished after the unexpected encounter with the knife-wielding lunatic, oversaw the bookkeeping and, even more importantly, the credit control in a style best described as Mafia Boss. She was also the one best suited to handle our somewhat temperamental alteration ladies who invariably shrieked 'No. No. No. Not possible!' to any suggested deadline, whereupon there would ensue a fiercely hissed exchange of views between them and Kitty, with a fair amount of fee haggling, before matters were settled to mutual satisfaction.

Our Brenda, as we'd all come to call her; sailing magisterially broad beamed, broad bosomed and bossy between our three office rooms, had never been within shouting distance of a management training course but was a natural, a paradigm of perfection when it came to getting everything that needed doing, done by the person best suited to do it, in optimum time with minimal hassle and cordial relationships maintained throughout.

Our odd combination worked well. There were clients who loved Ruby but would have run shrieking from Trudie; others who'd have died of fright faced with Ruby's cutting-edge efficiency. Brenda proved herself time and again to be adept and unrivalled at handling our very young charges as smoothly as those at the other end of the age scale. She dealt out a blend of affectionate discipline, backed by a no-nonsense glint in the eye. 'Boundaries!' she was fond of saying, 'that way everyone knows where they are.' She could smell 'playing up' from a mile away, but always recognised genuine distress or confusion and knew when a schedule needed tearing up in favour of a bit of time and a listening ear. Our team of intelligent, motivated women, each recognised and respected the same qualities in the others, resulting in great working relationships, genuine affection and for me, the feeling of being supported by a well-upholstered army.

I was, as promised, keeping an eye on Joy – I think we all were. She was a little more subdued than she'd been, but there was no doubt in my mind – or in hers, because I checked – that she was idyllically happy. She'd taken to wearing an Alice band to hold back her now much longer hair. She'd also eliminated her fringe; Trevor said it suited her better without. I didn't think it did and the toothed plastic of the band, pulling hair hard back from her forehead, made her look both younger and more vulnerable, but that was just my opinion. She'd changed her signature red lipstick for a paler shade. Trevor, she told me, loved her new look, said it was far more modern and the other lipstick made her look a bit like a nineteen-forties film-star.

She loved it, she confided, that he took such an interest in her appearance, even went clothes shopping with her which meant she ended up spending far more than she'd ever have done on her own. I told her David also had a great fashion sense - he could sense whenever we veered near any shop where he might be required to sit and wait while I tried something on, and had developed the ability to change direction faster than you could say, 'it won't take long.' We laughed and I collected the mail I'd come down for. As I moved away, I was caught in the genuine warmth of her affection and appreciation of Trevor.

Her notebook was still much in evidence and she was industrious in recording the ins and outs of her day, but she didn't feel it was any kind of imposition. I'd made sure I was in reception on several occasions when Trevor came to pick her up. He and Joy were clearly delighted to be back in each other's company, but he took time to greet me warmly, ask after David and have a brief chat about business, his and mine. I had no compunction in mentally checking him out, but there could be no doubt his feelings were absolutely genuine; in Joy, he felt he'd found his perfect woman. As he helped her on with her coat, insisted on carrying her shopping bag and announced no cooking for her tonight, he'd booked a surprise table; I could only hear and feel good things in his head. As they left, he had a protective arm round her shoulders and I thought, if this was a cartoon, they'd have walked down the street, framed in a big pink heart.

*****

A much-needed coat of paint was due to be applied downstairs in the travel agency, because Hilary said the place was becoming off-putting. How the heck, she demanded, could Martin expect clients to imagine and book their five-star luxury holiday if they were sitting in two-star shabbiness? Martin had reluctantly agreed, but when I seized the moment to say we needed to make sure all the offices downstairs and up, were well-maintained, he was predictably as far from keen as he could be. So I had a word with Hilary.

The next thing I heard was that Martin definitely felt upstairs could do with a freshen-up too. Hilary was a shining example of a woman who knew her own mind, and conviction combined with non-negotiable determination usually wins the day. Thus, it came to pass that normal chaos was augmented by masses of dust sheets, tools, pots of paint, mugs of tea and ladders over which we and clients had to climb. The project was in the tender charge of Mr Pegneddy, who'd come to us highly recommended by my Mother-in-law, apparently he'd been 'doing them' for years. I thought if he was good enough for Laura, whose house looked permanently staged for an Ideal Home photo shoot, he was almost certainly up to our standards, and he'd since also done jobs for a couple of our clients who were delighted.

When he originally came to meet me at the office, he wasn't the artistic Italian artisan I'd been expecting, but a bow-legged, elderly chap who didn't look as if he'd have the strength to partner a paintbrush, let alone a roller. He was shiny-topped bald but with an incongruously lush grey ponytail gathered at the back. He chuckled wheezily and nudged his companion when I greeted him by name.

"Got it wrong love, everyone does. I'm Mr Peg see, this 'ere's Eddy." Eddy, as tall and silent as Mr Peg was small and chatty, ducked his head in awkward acknowledgement, "Daft as a bucket of brushes he is, don't say much neither," Mr Peg gave him a fond shove with a shoulder that just about came up to Eddy's elbow, "but best bloody worker I've ever 'ad. Fifteen years we been together, Mr Peg 'n Eddy see?"

Whilst I had things running smoothly in the office, I was aware a little more effort needed to be put in on the home front. David had been wonderfully accepting of most of my idiosyncrasies but as we all know, going out together is one thing, living together quite another.

At home, with my parents and Dawn, there wasn't really a line between what was normal and what didn't come under that heading at all and nobody batted much of an eyelid at anything that went on. Obviously that was a completely reversed when I was out and about, but married life fell betwixt and between and I didn't want to repeat the fright I'd given David the first time I needed the carving knife for the roast chicken. Yes, it did whip across the room at speed and indeed it did pass him at nose height, but honestly it wasn't as close a shave as he made out. We laughed about it afterwards, although I felt he wasn't quite as amused as he could have been, and I promised to be a little more circumspect in the future.

CHAPTER FIFTEEN

My new touchy-feely ability that had developed whilst I wasn't looking was a bit of a nuisance and I can't say I was thrilled; it felt way too woo-woo for my liking, but as with anything, once you stop being surprised, you have to adjust. Initially, I was unexpectedly swamped with a bucket-full of emotion-laden information several times a day, without any kind of warning, but then I found it seemed to work like static electricity and I got used to treating unknown objects with the same caution you use on a metal doorknob when you've just walked across a nylon carpet – that swift fingertip touch to get any shock out of the way before proceeding. I don't think anyone noticed or if they did, they didn't say anything, and it wasn't as if all objects were a problem, most weren't. It did put paid though to enjoyable meanderings around the antique market in Hampstead. Perhaps not surprisingly, the majority of items there carried emotional history, usually several histories, and these were never neatly layered, more of a mishmush of sensation. Finding I could look, but best not touch took a lot of the pleasure away. On the plus side it meant I didn't spend as much and retired a lot earlier for hot chocolate at the Coffee Cup across the road, an establishment that had been going for so long their crockery was probably older than most of the goodies in the antique market.

* * * *

The cloud on my horizon was still Ruth. The initial pain and pulling in my middle regions had, thank goodness, faded a little but every time I thought about her the sickly, heavy discomfort returned. I'd phoned a couple of times, to find out how things were. I spoke to Rachael the first time, which meant I didn't get a straight answer to anything. The second time I rang, Mrs Millsop answered and had to be persuaded to find Glory for me.

"Not part of any job I took on," she grumbled "running all over the shop, looking for people." But I persisted and after a long wait,

Glory came to the phone, although I could hear Mrs M holding forth in the background on nobody in the place ever being where they said they were going to be, when they were supposed to be there. Glory wasn't over-communicative and sensing her unease, only increased my own. Things were pretty much the same she said, then turned away for a moment to ask an obviously hovering Mrs M, if she wouldn't mind just checking on the children Glory had briefly left on their own.

Turning back to the phone she said, "Nothing's happened, nothing's changed. Health wise, she's better than she's been for ages."

"It's gone?"

"We keep thinking maybe it has and then there's just a little something that isn't right, isn't Ruth and then we know we're wrong. We have to be ultra-careful, daren't probe."

"Couldn't you though? Without her knowing?" I realised as I said it, that just wasn't possible and Glory, didn't even dignify it with an answer. "Who's down there with you?" I asked, I knew so little about the new set-up and for an instant felt a ridiculous, not-been-invited-to-the-party pang of exclusion but only briefly, it was a world away from my far more mundane day-to-day, and that was what I'd wanted.

"Ed's here."

"How is he?"

I heard her affectionate smile, "Same."

I smiled too, "And Sam?"

"Not living here, but visiting a lot, he's not that far."

"What's he doing?"

"Thought you knew; Oxford Uni Med School."

No, I hadn't known, "How's he getting on?" another stupid question. Sam had tried to kill me when we first met, but you can't hold that against someone, certainly not a frightened, near feral six-year-old. Anyway, since then he'd more than made amends. There was a breakthrough technique I'd read about recently, magnetic resonance imagery, apparently it was going to revolutionise diagnostics because of the internal images it produced, but Sam had always been able to do that, no machine necessary.

"Enjoying it?" I asked.

"No, not really. Hugely frustrated he has to do it and obviously he's younger than everyone else and treated as a bit of a prodigy which never makes for popularity, but he knows it's necessary."

"Give him my love?"

"Course." I was surprised, usually any hint of sentiment brought forth an acerbic response, she was distracted though and as worried as I was, maybe more - Ruth and Rachael had taken her in, more or less brought her up, they were family.

"I'd better let you go or Mrs M will have your guts for garters." I was reluctant to cut the connection because of the flipping push-me-pull-you feelings I had. "Talk soon?" Reporting the conversation to David later, he wanted to know why I'd phoned,

"Couldn't you just… you know?"

"Over a distance it would have to be urgent – and loud, sort of a scream and you don't scream the place down just to say hello, how are you."

* * * *

Closer to home I was doing my best with the Mother-in-Law; I wanted her to like me but as I've said, she had a tendency towards the unpredictable, and even before I'd complicated things by marrying her son, it was always difficult to know quite where you were with her.

Melvyn made a point of reminding me often how badly Laura suffered with her nerves; as if I could forget, but he thought if he kept mentioning it, he could provide cover for the slight chill in the air when she was near me. I knew it was on his mind, because when worried he'd slide his glasses up onto his forehead to massage his eyes with thumb and fourth finger, but as he invariably had a lit cigarette between the forefingers of the same hand, it made me pretty worried too, although I could only assume, if he was going to put an eye out it would've happened by now.

Laura was elegant in the extreme; slim and with deportment that owed everything to the Lucie Clayton Charm School and a lot of walking around with a pile of books on your head. That same head, weekly highlighted and coiffed was often briefly angled when she spoke - as if she'd just become aware of an odour beneath her finely arched nostrils and wasn't quite sure what it might be. She was courteous if chilly, invariably beautifully turned out - I don't think she'd have recognised a track suit if it bit her on the bottom - and on a constant diet, goodness knows why, I never spotted an inch of flesh she could spare. Nevertheless, she was inclined to wave food away, murmuring she couldn't possibly, and had been known to toy with a slice of chicken and three petit pois for far longer than they deserved, before declaring herself absolutely stuffed. The woman was indeed a slave to her nerves, not to mention everyone else's and when stressed, which happened often, would delve into her handbag for a 'migraine' pill. These took effect mighty quick, leading to Laura grabbing your hand, resting her head on your shoulder and murmuring how very, very fond of you she was. In the driving-around days it had made things problematic, changing gear with someone glued to your side was always a challenge. On the plus side though, there was never a chance of her sneaking up on you unexpectedly, preceded as she invariably was by a knock-out waft of heavy-duty perfume and the well-bred clink of chunky jewellery.

When David and I got engaged she slipped into pink pill mode, and stayed there for quite a while, so I'd spent a lot of time with her firmly attached, muttering she couldn't be more thrilled, no honestly, really, really truly thrilled. I think she was probably drifting in and out for a good couple of weeks because she was thereafter a little hazy on the details of anything that occurred during that time, including our conversation about what I should call her. With a magnanimous wave of the arm that wasn't wrapped round my waist, she'd said anything I liked, which I couldn't help but think was taking a bit of a risk. But when I later tried a tentative 'Mum' she was aghast, and a flash of thought which I couldn't help but catch, indicated she'd really rather I stuck to Mrs Gold, but she smiled tightly and said maybe we'd just go with Laura.

She was though, extremely helpful whenever they came to visit, and was able to give me a variety of tips as to how David liked this, didn't like that and mightn't it be a good idea, as I was so busy, to do a little dusting every day, rather than let it accumulate for the weekend? I always thanked her enthusiastically, avoiding the amused eye of my husband and the worried one of my Father-in-Law. She and Katerina, also had a way to go with their relationship. Laura was invariably startled whenever she saw her and because she jumped, Katerina who could match her, nerve for nerve, jumped too.

"Oh," Laura would exclaim in the same tone of amazement each time, "it's the dog!" whereupon both she and Kat would toss their heads and look pointedly in the opposite direction.

CHAPTER SIXTEEN

Over the course of time, I'd come to realise that the 'listening' with which I'd been tasked, was misnamed. It was more 'hearing' and I wasn't thrilled about it, but as far as it's ever possible to be sure of anything, I was sure Boris was on the side of the angels and worked to a strict moral code albeit uniquely his own. And there could be no disputing the outcomes of some of my alerts, so my conscience wouldn't let me stop listening.

There was the teenager walking home from school who was snatched from the street, then snatched back a wonderfully short time later. She'd initially been too shocked to scream, but I'd heard her anyway and acted. Boris never contacted me after the raised alarm, but sometimes I picked up things from the press. Apparently, in the brief time it took the nearest Panda car to get there, a white van had already been stopped in its tracks by a car diagonally and inexplicably blocking the road. The elderly driver could give no explanation as to exactly how that had happened, but by then there were screams for help coming from inside the van and the hysterical girl was helped out by passers-by. In no time at all, the grubby van driver had been hauled out of his grubby van and was face-down in the road with a bloody nose. He was being ungently restrained by a couple of hefty builders who were of the thump-now-ask-questions-later school of thought. Evidence in the van implicated the driver in at least two other recent appalling cases that hadn't ended in recovery. He was currently awaiting trial.

Another time there were ten girls from the Philippines who thought they were coming to Britain as au pairs. Crammed together and locked in the back of the lorry that had picked them up, one of them nursing a swelling eye where the man she'd questioned had hit her, the girls had come to the rapid conclusion this wasn't what they'd signed up for. Fear and panic as realisation set in, multiplied by ten hit me like a brick to the head. The lorry was intercepted.

A few weeks after that, there was a man who'd spent an evening in the pub nursing beer and grudges who'd come to the irrefutable conclusion that his ex-girlfriend needed teaching a lesson and that there was no time like the present. He'd been waiting by her front door when she came home from a night out and she knew as she saw him, what he'd come for. Her terror jerked me awake, and I amplified it and immediately shot it through to Boris. I only had a rough location, but the sound of sirens blaring up and down nearby roads paralysed him just long enough for her to kick him where it mattered, and run.

None of the above was pleasant but it was worse when it was too late. When the bomb at the Ideal Home Exhibition went off in March of '76, I was still living at home and was knocked off my feet in the kitchen by the combined emotional charge from the injured and the fleeing – but too late to do anything to help. Then in August, when things kicked off at the Notting Hill Carnival, there was the same broadcast of shock and fear as revellers tried to get away from violence that suddenly erupted around them. It had boiled over, fuelled by levels of anger and resentment simply not comprehended by the majority of men, women and children there to have a good time. The fight would have flared up and died down quickly were it not for the iron determination of a group of fascists, also there to have a good time. Their vitriol of hate and excitement peaked and surged above everything else. The police acted immediately, but damage was done; over 300 injuries on both sides, along with a major loss of trust. It was months later that Boris and Cornwall dropped in on me, but I instantly recognised what it was that seeped out from the material they gave me to hold; bile-coloured viciousness, I'd felt it before. I had no idea whether it was the same person, but it was the same hate.

In the first few months of that year and newly married, I made an attempt to recalibrate, change my settings a bit. I'd become used to the wave of discomfort whenever Ruth came to mind, that was one thing, the 'hearing' was another, but I felt the touch thing was an oddity too far and cherished hopes it would vanish as unexpectedly as it had arrived. In the meantime, I had to deal with it by trial and error; some things were more problematic than others. Books were dreadful.

Hendon Public Library had been heaven and haven to me from the time I was old enough to make my own way but now, gathering an armful of books became an exercise far more fraught. Sometimes, I was aware before I even slipped it off the shelf that a book was going to give me grief and I had to steer clear; others gave no warning until I had them in my hands. This ability had entirely its own logic; a book held for a long period of time allowed emotion to be absorbed and retained whereas a book swiftly read, not so much – unless the emotion at that particular time was overwhelming. I often wondered, would the emotion remain as long as the book existed, or dilute and dissipate over time possibly unknowingly absorbed by subsequent readers? Of a couple of things I was certain; negative stuff lingered longer, whilst joy was depressingly less evident and all this had made my once peaceful pleasure a darn sight less so, although I presumed my hesitant shelf-progress simply made me look like a woman who couldn't make up her mind.

What with running the business, the discomfort connected to Ruth, the try-not-to-touch rule, an ear open for anything I should tell Boris and an eye on what I shouldn't tell David, there was a lot to think about, but it was Mac Fisheries that truly gave me pause for thought.

CHAPTER SEVENTEEN

I've never been keen on fish – sneaky small bones, undiscovered until they're in your mouth, eugh – unfortunately, my daily route to work, having parked the car, took me past our local Mac Fisheries, which even from the other side of the road wasn't great, but one sunny day in April, as the smell from the fully stocked slabs outside the shop hit me, I gagged. For a sweaty few seconds, I was sure I was going to throw up under the critical gaze of all those dead fish-eyes.

I thought I'd stood stock still but maybe I was swaying; either way I must have looked odd because Michele, who ran Young's Haberdashery down the road stopped in concern, which was equally odd. Hilary, who spent a lot of time in the shop lusting over trimmings, often commented Michele wasn't a natural people person and her successful business wasn't down to customer service so much as no competition.

"What's up?" she said sharply, pausing alongside me. I nearly said; my breakfast but even the thought made me feel worse, so I shook my head. She already regretted stopping but having done so was stuck.

"Well," she said, "you'd best get along to your office then." I wasn't ready to open my mouth yet, so nodded slightly but must have swayed a bit more because Michele and I could feel her intense reluctance, put out a hand to hold my arm, this was not a woman comfortable with contact, but luckily she had initiative. She shot out the arm that wasn't holding me up and grabbed a passing young man.

"Here, this lady's come over funny. I'll take her bag and the dog, you hang on to her," she said, "it's only up the road." She removed bag handle and lead from my cold and clammy hand, "What're you waiting for?" she demanded of him, "not got all day." By sheer good luck, she'd happened to hijack a chap well used to bossy women, he lived with a mum and four sisters, so was more or less pre-programmed to obedience for a quiet life. Before

I had a chance to insist I was fine, he'd looped an arm round my waist and we were hastening after Michele's sensible brown brogues. The door of the agency was open, and my conscripted hero hung on manfully until he'd deposited me on the reception sofa.

"No sweat," he waved away my thanks, "likely something you ate eh?" And he departed before he could be roped into anything else. Michele's relief at having seen me safely delivered was palpable, even more so as just then Brenda and Hilary arrived and she handed over bag, lead and responsibility.

"Taken bad," she said, jerking her head at me "walked her up the road, leave her with you, alright?" and she was off. Brenda, who came gloriously into her own at times like these, headed for the kitchen at speed and instructed Hilary to get my head between my knees. Hilary advanced purposefully, lit cigarette clamped in place to leave both hands free.

I moved back on the sofa hastily, "No, I'm better." Accustomed as I was to the smoke wreath which generally hovered murkily above Hilary's head, it bothered me more than usual, and I turned my head away.

"Sorry pet," she said amiably, exhaling in the opposite direction. Head to knee action avoided, I rested it on the back of the sofa, then heard with astonishment what Hilary was thinking, as Brenda the Capable bustled back with a glass of water, tea, a damp cloth and a big smile.

"We wondered when you were going to say anything."

"No," I said, "honestly, it was just the fish." She raised an eyebrow then seeing I meant it, moved a pile of papers to one side, perched a substantial tweed hip on the reception desk and handed me the water and the cloth.

"On your forehead, it'll help."

Hilary, blowing smoke considerately in the other direction, patted my knee.

"I was the same," she said, "put on right away," she nodded at my stomach whilst I had a quick think about dates.

"Here," said Brenda, "drink the tea and look, couple of Ginger Snaps, they'll settle your tum."

Obediently sipping and chewing, I felt a right idiot. I made to say something but Hilary shushed me;

"No talking, it'll pass sooner," and then Joy turned up, flushed and breathless, doing a double-take as she saw us assembled.

"Whoa! Welcoming committee?" then looking at the wall clock, "not late am I? Sorry, tried to clear up before I left."

I felt her anxiety and shook my head, "You're fine." She knew we weren't clock-watchers, there was always someone to take over the reception desk if needed, and it wasn't as if hordes were hurtling in at any one time. I felt if one of us needed to do something and got in a bit late or left a bit early, what did it matter, but Joy said;

"It's important I'm not late. Trevor says, 'not on time; not on the ball'!" I saw Hilary and Brenda exchange a swift, expressionless look.

"You're fine," I repeated. She smiled back uncertainly. What I appreciated about Joy was she'd never been a 'what should I do next?' kind of a girl but like the rest of the team, made and took day-to-day decisions completely in her stride without consulting anyone and rarely put a foot wrong. Initiative is worth its weight in gold – it oils the wheels, but recently there had been a fading of that confidence, I felt a stab of guilt. It wasn't that I hadn't noticed but I hadn't raised it with her and I should have done, I could have reassured her.

Kat who'd been sitting quietly by my feet, waiting for the talking to stop so she could head up to her basket for a morning sleep, stirred, shook herself in an elegantly understated manner and sashayed over to greet Joy, who to Kat's surprise, recoiled. As an office favourite, this was not the reaction she expected. I knew when I had to go out and Kat got bored with Brenda, she'd descend to settle herself comfortably at Joy's feet, which had the advantage of allowing her to greet me with a reproachful face whenever I came back. Joy always said she liked Kat there, made her feel guarded at which we all laughed, nobody felt genteel Kat was likely to strike the fear of anything into anybody.

Now Joy shrugged apologetically, and reached out a couple of fingers to pat Kat's head. "Sorry, sorry, but..." she stopped, embarrassed.

"What?" said Brenda.

"It's just... well, Trevor's said sometimes when I get home, I sometimes smell... you know... a bit doggy." Katerina tossed her head, turned her back and settled down to a bit of intimate grooming which broke any tension in the air. Brenda and Hilary were uneasy; I was appalled.

What Brenda and Hilary couldn't know was a short shower, in Trevor's opinion, wasn't sufficient to deal with this sort of olfactory issue. At least twenty full minutes were necessary. He'd pointed out, with affection and a cute wrinkle of his nose, that sometimes the individual concerned was the last to notice a shortfall in personal hygiene. He'd bought Joy a timer she could set. Her overriding emotion, emerging from the shower flushed with embarrassment, hot water and the rough loofah Trevor favoured, was guilt. Guilt she hadn't known there was a problem, guilt that Trevor had put up with it for so long without mentioning, and huge gratitude that he finally had. He'd put it off because he hated to upset her and often now, when she emerged, wrapped her tenderly in one of their big bath towels and reassured her again that you get so used to smells on yourself, you simply don't notice them the way other people do.

"Well, can't stand here gossiping, all day can we?" Brenda was picking up her hastily discarded coat and bag, "Come on; all the upstairs lot - upstairs." And the brief awkwardness was covered up, smoothed over, an ugly little spot covered by concealer, although concealer never really works, does it? As we went upstairs, I glanced back at Joy - pale lipstick, Alice-banded, no-longer-bright-blonde hair, high collared blouse, mid-calf Sandra Dee flared skirt. She looked lovely; she just didn't look like Joy.

But she was happy. I couldn't get round that fact. She was only feeling anxious this morning because she'd thought she was late. She'd never had a job she enjoyed more than this one. She loved the camaraderie in the office and she took pride in her own efficiency, although work, as Trevor was always pointing out, was only a small part of her life now, certainly not the most important part and she could stop whenever she wanted. She didn't want to but it was rather wonderful to know how much he cared. Never in her life had she felt so special, so happy, so cared for, so lucky.

As our upstairs office door shut behind us, Brenda turned to me, "Well?"

"Well what?"

"Something's not right, can't you see?"

"She's happy Brenda, she's madly in love with him, I know she's changed and we may not like those changes, but it's not really our business is it, as long as she's happy.

"Well I don't know how you can be so sure." she snapped back in a very unlike Brenda way. I couldn't of course answer that truthfully and I couldn't ignore what she was saying, but neither could I deny what Joy was feeling. It was all a bit Catch 22, on top of which it seemed I was pregnant. Some days just don't go the way you expect them to.

CHAPTER EIGHTEEN

I had consulted my Mother far more than I'd expected to on the surprisingly complicated business of running a house, planning meals and dealing with a quantity of washing that I refused to believe was generated by just two people. It wasn't just the cooking which, to be honest, was all still a bit of a mystery to me, but the forward thinking and shopping. On top of that were such puzzles as *Evelyn Rose* laying down one cooking temperature, when the ladies of *Way to a Man's Heart* dictated a different one altogether. Now however, I needed input of a different nature and considering my Mother had spent years dealing with Agony Aunt questions, freelancing efficiently and sometimes concurrently for *Woman*, *Woman's Realm* and *Woman's Mirror*, she seemed the obvious place to start.

She listened to what I had to say with no surprise. Yes, she was watching Joy too; Hilary and Brenda had spoken to her. She told me what she'd told them - it was a familiar story.

"Shouldn't I do something?" I said, "It's…" I paused for thought, "It's like he's erasing her, rubbing her out little by little."

"But you know she's happy?" There was no need to dissemble here; we both knew how I knew.

"Never been happier."

"Well there's your answer then." My mother was pragmatic, although beyond that I saw levels of frustration and anger accumulated over many years, over similar issues. "Listen to me, sweetheart, there's nothing, *nothing* you can do. The marriage may last and work and work well, because that's what she chooses. Or there may come a time when she stops being happy - next month, next year, twenty years from now, but it's her choice. You have no rights here."

"But…"

"No buts. If Joy came to me and wanted my opinion, I'd tell her what concerns me but until such time you, me, Hilary, Brenda, all of us can scream blue murder, it won't make any difference."

That conversation didn't make me feel better, but as long as Joy was happy, I was helpless. The only comfort was that I had her under my eye almost daily, I would know the minute that changed.

* * * *

I had heard they were developing something in America that could be used to confirm a pregnancy in your own home, but over here we were still reliant on the GP. We hadn't yet joined a new practice, so I took myself back to Hendon to Dr Woodside, who was getting on a bit but was at least familiar. He wasn't exactly a ray of sunshine, probably because he was totally unsuited to do what he did, his dislike of touching people having grown with the years; there wasn't a day that passed he didn't curse himself for not going into psychiatry. He preferred to hear about symptoms as opposed to actually having to look at anything, but he'd become a little hard of hearing. This meant that those in the waiting room often became rather more familiar with your intimate issues than was comfortable for anyone.

I gave him facts, dates and a sample, but he said he probably ought to check; neither of us was keen but it seemed needs must. Yes, he said, probably coming up for three months but he'd send the sample just for certainty. I should book into the hospital for a first visit, and then see the midwife monthly here at the surgery. Early days though, he said, lot of things could and often did go wrong but try not to worry. I exited the surgery to a lot of congratulatory smiles and nods from those nearest the Doctor's door and decided that as a lot of Hendon now knew, I probably ought to share with those more closely involved.

David hadn't been able to come with me, he'd been commissioned by the Telegraph to do a series of articles for a science section they were running on genetics, one of the innovators was over here from Switzerland and there was a press conference that couldn't be missed, but in fact he got home before I did. I was pleased, because for no apparent reason I'd been crying all the way back.

"Are you nervous?" I asked once the news had been imparted and we'd both calmed down slightly.

"About?"

"The baby."

"Why?"

"It might take after me?" He paused; the thought obviously hadn't occurred to him, then he shrugged and hugged me.

"Nobody else in your family is like you. No reason to think the baby will be."

"And if it is?" I said.

He grinned. "We'll have our hands full, won't we?" Which made me cry some more. I could only hope I wasn't going to be this soggy for the duration.

* * * *

My parents and sister were as excited as might have been expected, although unfortunately, our visit coincided with Dawn being collected for a date with a nice boy who, caught up by default in the kissing, crying and congratulations, developed a look of incipient panic and after that evening was never seen again.

"Can you feel anything?" my Mother asked.

"Don't be silly," said my Father, suddenly an expert on all things ante-natal, "Far too early."

"No, I mean *feel* anything?" and she made the gesture she used to indicate oddities – a bit similar to the Queen's circular wave. I shook my head; I was in no way sure whether I did or didn't want to 'feel' anything.

The news went down less well at the in-laws, which might have had something to do with David saying, "Hello Granny," when his mother opened the door. Melvyn kept saying he couldn't believe it, just couldn't believe it, which seemed silly as presumably he knew how this sort of thing happened, but he grabbed me for a bear hug, then touched my cheek gently – I just wished he'd put down the cigarette.

My Mother-in-Law rallied bravely, said she couldn't believe it either but kissed us, said she'd do anything and everything she could to help, all the while thinking, she wasn't ready for this, and in the general kerfuffle I forgot myself completely and replied I wasn't either, but I don't think anybody noticed.

After the initial excitement, things settled down as they usually do and I duly booked in for my first hospital visit, on my own, because David was seeing an eccentric geneticist who could only be interviewed on a Tuesday because he didn't speak to people the rest of the week.

"You mean journalists?"

David shook his head, "No, anyone; his family, his team at the University, no-one."

"So how…?"

"Notes. He passes them notes. Apparently, feels he can say all he wants on a Tuesday, and not wasting energy on vocalising means more productivity the rest of the time. Thing is, what he's working on, is so out there, people are prepared to put up with whatever he wants to do. Getting him to agree to see me hasn't been easy." I assured him I didn't mind, this first visit was only going to be lots of form filling, blood tests and passing out – I'm not good with needles. I'd probably be unconscious a lot of the time so he really shouldn't worry.

I didn't immediately take to the midwife I saw. I wanted her to be warm and friendly, instead she was cool and business-like and kept calling me Mum. I told her, before she took my blood that I usually fainted, and she said 'well, she was sure I wouldn't this time' and then took the fact that I did as a personal insult. As she hauled me off the floor and propped me back up in the chair, she told me we were running over time and I must remember other Mums needed seeing. I was suitably chastened whilst at the same time quite perky with relief at the blood test being out of the way.

She felt my tummy then listened through a Pinard horn which put us uncomfortably close for a while. Baby, she said, was good size for dates – strong heartbeat, all was well. I believed her, but couldn't help double checking and was reassured to see there was no dreadful truth she was hiding. I also saw she felt she'd drawn the short straw this particular morning. She was tired, her feet ached, and her back too after a late night with a patient on the ward a good few hours after her shift had ended. She'd overslept this morning so hadn't had breakfast and to top it all, here she was having to handle a fainter.

I was instantly ashamed, and when she handed me my pregnancy booklet - to keep on me at all times mind; I thanked her sincerely, apologised for passing out, said I was grateful for the way she'd put me at my ease. She initially thought I was taking the mickey, then realised I wasn't and patted my hand. Mum, she said, should just stop worrying; we didn't want a stressed baby did we. I agreed we certainly didn't and we parted on good terms.

CHAPTER NINETEEN

There was an incident that made some of the papers around that time, it wasn't huge news and probably only gained column space because it was a good filler and allowed some amusing copy lines. *The Eagle has Landed* was showing on a Saturday night to a sold-out cinema in Finchley, and whilst Michael Caine and Donald Sutherland were doing their stuff onscreen, a rat joined the audience.

It was apparently minding its own business, making its way along a row in the middle of the auditorium, and had gone completely unnoticed in the dark until it was brought to general attention by a woman whose foot it happened to climb over. She looked down, leapt up, tried to climb onto the back of her now upended seat and screamed. A lot.

A few people in the immediate vicinity started looking around to see if they could relocate seats, making a phlegmatic British assumption that she was drunk, drugged or a bit funny in the head, and a cinema official would be along shortly to deal with her. Her companion, an older woman, was struggling to pull her down, hush her up and understand what had happened; when she did, she started shrieking too. She was a little more coherent. "Rat," she hollered, "bloody great rat!"

At this point, a lot of people took the decision that maybe the rest of the film wasn't worth hanging around for, especially as the message, as messages often do, had mutated to "Rats!" A surge of highly motivated humanity made for exit doors which were never designed for everyone to try and get through at once. Panic feeds panic and there were a lot of minor injuries as well as one broken leg, a fractured wrist and two asthma attacks.

A specialist pest control company were rushed in to do what they were good at, although by then any self-respecting rat would have been as panicked as everybody else and long gone. Traps were laid, poison spread, the whole building checked from top to bottom and lots of ticket money refunded. The theory was it must have come in through one of the service doors backing on to the bins, probably left that way too, sensibly avoiding the stampede for the main doors. The story hung around for a day or two, people shivered in empathy, rats in the dark not being anyone's idea of a good night out. There were lots of James Cagney jokes and then it all died down and everyone –apart from those who'd been there – forgot about it.

A month or so later, at Her Majesty's, Godspell was in full noisy flow, and a minor disruption at the back of the auditorium didn't immediately register until the panic ripple widened. As large sections of the audience started jumping up, brushing themselves down, shaking their heads, yelling, stamping and wriggling it became evident that something was 'not right'. By the time the curtain was hurriedly brought down and lights equally swiftly put up, order had been abandoned. There were injuries again, some minor, several more serious. The theatre manager swore blind, every kind of safety procedure was in place for evacuation, all the staff knew what to do to get people out safely, but - and here he shrugged while furry-monster mics shoved him in the chin and cameras jostled in his face – people had panicked unnecessarily. He was right, the majority of the audience had arrived breathless and frightened on the pavement, with not the faintest idea why they were there.

Apparently, it was ants. Not your everyday ants – although even those wouldn't have gone down well, but according to one witness 'socking enormous, bloody great things, size of my fist.' And whilst there might have been a certain amount of exaggeration, there did seem to be a consensus from all who'd actually seen, or shaken some off, they were ants – but not as we know them.

The theatre and surrounding area was blocked off and Environmental Health alarming in full decontamination gear, moved in. Reassuring statements were put out and several entomologists got more exposure in a few days than they'd dreamt of in a lifetime. They said it was simply a swarming, earlier than usual because of unseasonably warm weather. Earlier and longer breeding periods meant increased numbers and insects larger than the norm. However no-one, not Environmental Health nor insect experts were prepared to be pinned down precisely, because by the time they'd got in, the insects had got out and the question of how they were there in the first place was also left open to speculation and further joyous copywriting opportunity was seized, with lots of different riffs on 'antybodies'. It was odd though that so many insects, causing so much disturbance to so many people, could disappear so completely. Surely, it was argued, there should have been at least a few squashed ex-ants left for the experts to examine.

The mass panics had been distressing for me because something that strong can't be shut out altogether, and I'd had a stonking headache on both occasions, but there seemed little point in contacting Boris, I had nothing helpful to tell him. My headaches, of course, were nothing compared to those of cinemas and theatres all over London, who suffered a hit in the pocket. They rallied manfully - ticket prices were slashed, free refreshments thrown in for good measure and human nature being what it is, those who hadn't actually had the fright of their lives, muttered about storms in teacups, mountains out of molehills and lightening not striking twice and within a short time, things returned to normal.

As it transpired, fans of stage and screen were correct to be unconcerned because the next time there was a huge panic - you'll remember this one - was at Madame Tussauds, packed to the gunnels with tourists, families and school outings.

It started, aptly enough in the Chamber of Horrors, and because there were the usual patient queues around the block waiting to get in, when people started flooding out screaming, those waiting outside panicked too. It was only a few months back, in January, that the IRA had triggered thirteen bombs in Oxford Street, setting fire to Selfridges, and a scant three years before that there'd been the explosion in Madame Tussauds itself. Amidst the panic and confusion, parents were separated from children, teachers from students and tour leaders from tours. The emergency services turned out mob-handed and a major part of the West End went into lockdown. There were quite a lot of people hurt that time, mainly crush injuries, and tragically, two deaths; a terrified Japanese couple fleeing from they knew not what, knocked down and killed by a taxi.

It was assumed the bomb or bombs had been made safe, there was no explosion, but the security services clamped down on the press and there was pretty nearly a complete news blackout. I called Boris.

"Do you have anything?" he said.

"No, as usual, all the emotional stuff afterwards, nothing before, but I wanted…"

He cut across me, "I was waiting to hear from you. This time might have been different."

"Why?" I was pacing back and forth as far as the phone cord would let me; I was both distressed and frustrated that I was never able to do anything constructive when it came to attacks like this. Experience had shown those responsible for planting devices designed to kill and maim, were not much troubled by an excess of emotion, I didn't hear them because there was nothing to hear.

"It wasn't a bomb," he said.

"But I thought…"

"Well, it wasn't."

"What was it?"

"Butterflies."

"*Butterflies?*"

"A lot of them."

"You're kidding!"

"You know me better than that."

"But *butterflies*, that's ridiculous - more Disney than disaster - why such panic?"

"People are primed to react to each other, rather than to the cause itself."

"Well, where did they come from?"

"No idea."

"There's been nothing on the news," I said.

"No," he paused, "it sounds laughable, but it turned lethal. Let me know if you hear anything?"

There was something at the back of my mind which, even after the call was over, niggled and wriggled. Something Boris had said, not today, some time ago, about cause and effect; I just couldn't remember what, or why it might be important and it kept slipping away before I could find a connection.

And then one weekend, five or six weeks later, there was a whole hoo-ha when mice invaded the restaurant of a well-known five-star hotel, just reading the details made you want to stand on your chair and scream. It was one of those places where none of the menus had prices, implying if you needed to know the cost, you shouldn't be there in the first place. It was always in the papers with a stream of film stars, royalty and other upper echelons going in or coming out, so there was definitely an element of schadenfreude about the mice infestation. There'd been another crowd exodus, this one however, more controlled, due to the number of security people already in attendance, and the only thing injured was the reputation of the hotel. All in all, it had a certain schoolboy prankish feel and, it was rumoured, had possibly been staged by a rival chef.

Driving to work that Monday, the connection I'd been trying to remember suddenly came back to me clear as day. It clicked into place like one Lego brick into another, but made no sense. The incidents certainly matched Devlin's idea of humour, but that couldn't be the answer.

When I met Devlin McCrae he was ten. Big blue eyes, a lip built for quivering and the face of cherub; he was the picture of innocence When I arrived to meet his mum prior to undertaking some errands for the family, Celine, the au pair was sobbing in the kitchen. Devlin had a forensic fascination in seeing just how hysterical he could get her and that day had slipped a large, realistically flexible, black rubber spider into her cup when her back was turned. Enjoying her coffee, she'd almost drained the cup before finding herself up close and personal with the realistically moving insect, legs drifting lazily in the liquid. She hadn't stopped screaming for a full five minutes. Of course that could have no bearing on what had been going on. Nevertheless, when I got to the office, I dumped bag and dog and went out again.

Jane Air was not the least bit pleased to see me. In fact, what went through her head was could she shut the door in my face and pretend she wasn't in, which was a bit silly. She opted instead for the old, 'gosh, so sorry, just on my way out,' which I countered with the old 'my fault for dropping by without calling first.'

"Perhaps though," I added, "a quick word, just while you change out of your slippers?" she looked down and had the grace to smile. She led me through to an immaculate pink and grey living room and indicated one of the chairs either side of a fireplace where a tall vase displayed a few tastefully chosen grasses.

"Goodness, this looks interior designed," I said and she laughed.

"It was. I'm hopeless at this sort of thing; I gave her a budget and free rein."

"Well, it's lovely."

"Thank you." There was an awkward pause and in the absence of any more small-talk, good manners prevailed, "Can I offer you coffee, a cold drink?"

"Just water would be lovely, if you've got time?" I followed her into the kitchen, which was far more lived in and a lot less store window display. She filled a glass silently and I saw it wasn't me she disliked so much, as what had happened between us. Actually, she wasn't at all sure what *had* happened but whatever it was, it did not fit her professionally perceived order of things. She'd come to me in desperation; not herself, not thinking straight and only on the vaguest of suggestions from Susan. After that, everything had settled down, complete coincidence. If she'd just held on a little longer, it would have all stopped anyway. She wanted to forget what had happened, didn't want to think about our stroll in the park yet now here I was, in her kitchen.

"How have you been?" I asked.

"Fine thank you." she smiled politely. She didn't want to talk about the insect thing, then decided if she pre-empted, she'd get it out of the way quicker.

"That other silly stuff – all sorted. It was simply stress and probably hormones too. And an overactive imagination. Whatever it was, worked its way though. Should have let you know but..." she gestured to indicate busy, busy life.

"Great," I said, while she fought a brief battle between wanting to know what it was I'd done and not wanting to know at all. I helped her out; "That's not what I've come about. You remember we chatted a little about what you do?" she nodded, although she'd been so befuddled by panic and pills she didn't really remember.

"Well, I wondered," I said, "if you'd see someone as a patient – wasn't sure though whether they had to have a GP referral to you first?" she looked puzzled, as well she might, I wasn't quite sure which way this was going either.

"With a phobia you mean?"

"Exactly," I said, gratefully, "In fact, more than one, she's barely able to leave the house." Jane took a card from her handbag on the kitchen counter.

"Certainly, if she gives me a call, I'd be happy to see her," she paused, "but... can't you help her?"

I shook my head over the poor fictitious phobic, "Goodness no, far too close; she wouldn't take me seriously. Jane, I'm so grateful, really," and I pulled her into an enthusiastic hug. If you're holding someone tightly enough, it's tricky for them to shake you off, however reluctant and astonished they are. I had what I needed to know almost immediately, but for a good few seconds longer I held on, for my own comfort, because the confirmation of what I'd suspected, was devastating.

CHAPTER TWENTY

"You're sure?" Boris's even tone was consistent, whether a matter was momentous or mundane and together with the impenetrability of his mind, made him impossible to read, especially over the phone.

"I am, but I don't understand how it's even possible. Is it? Possible I mean, and if it is, then it's all my fault."

"If it is, then it wasn't anything you did deliberately, right? Pointless to speculate."

"So, what do I do now?"

"Nothing," he said, "stay out of it."

"But..."

"No buts."

"Will you tell me?"

"When I know," and with typical lack of sign-off he was gone. I put the receiver down slowly. He was right, there was no point in wondering. If Boris knew, Boris would handle but that didn't stop me feeling sick to my stomach, and this time I couldn't blame the baby. The fleeting familiarity, the trace of something I'd felt in Jane's mind when I first met her, but hadn't stopped to identify, was Devlin McCrae. When I went back and held her, that was confirmed. It was completely impossible yet absolutely unmistakeable.

My history with Devlin wasn't great; I could still recall he and I locked together in his mind, shrieking in shock, horror and fear. Subsequently and not surprisingly, he hadn't wanted anything to do with me and I didn't blame him in the least. But what I was, what I could do wasn't like the measles, it wasn't the sort of thing someone could 'catch' but now, nearly three years down the line, I didn't know what to think. But I'd been told to keep out, and for once I had no urge to ignore that.

* * * *

Boris turned up one afternoon a week or so later, mob handed. When he appeared at the door of my office, he was with Glory and Ed. Any one of them on their own would have attracted a sideways glance, as a group they were a little overpowering. Brenda had met all three on different occasions but Ruby and Trudie hadn't and I could feel their astonishment reverberating.

"What?" I said standing; the better to bear any bad news, "what's happened? Something's happened?" Glory moved fluidly into the room ahead of the two men, with Brenda thoughtfully holding her elbow to steer her to a chair. She needn't have worried; Glory was using Ed's eyes but Brenda wouldn't know and Glory thanked her warmly as Brenda took the white stick to prop it carefully against the wall.

"Calm down Stella." Boris folded into a chair.

Glory said, "You're pregnant." I wasn't showing yet, but it wasn't a question.

"Yes, I know," I said as I hit two blank grey walls in the heads of Boris and Glory and a third one in Ed's, although in his as usual, there was some very pleasant easy listening music – could have been Dean Martin.

Brenda brought in another chair for Ed who, still looming in the doorway, was cutting off much of the natural light. Six foot five, built like a fridge on steroids, he took up a lot of space. Taking the chair from Brenda, he nodded thanks. No smile, Moebius Syndrome rendered him expressionless, but he handled it effortlessly now, and recognising Brenda's slight uneasiness sent through a warmth that made her relax. He only did that if he took to someone; everyone else just had to deal with it. He positioned the chair carefully a little way back and between those of Glory and Boris and sat gingerly. He always sat gingerly, because some chairs simply weren't up to the job, luckily this one was pretty solid, a hand-me-down of Aunt Edna and Uncle Monty's and they always bought quality.

I was still standing, fists on the desk, leaning forward, torn as always between a certain amount of pleasure at seeing them and a far larger amount of anxiety as to why they were here.

"The crowd panic thing - was it something to do with Devlin?" I asked with apprehension. Boris nodded.

"*How?*"

"We're not sure yet."

"But it's not…"

He raised a hand in a stop signal, I could have throttled him, he quirked a lip at my thought and I felt anger rising to mix with guilt and worry. Glory, who knew me better than Boris intervened sharply,

"Stop it Boris, you're being deliberately cryptic and Stella, we haven't time for you to fly off the handle." I opened my mouth to protest, "Shush." She said, "all you need to know is, yes you were right and yes Devlin has been taken care of."

I gasped, "You don't mean?"

She chuckled, "Don't be so melodramatic; I mean he's being taken care of and you don't need to worry, but you also don't need to know anything more at the moment. No," she held up a halting hand too – must have caught it from Boris, "That's not why we're here." As per usual, Glory hadn't dressed to blend in; flared cobalt silk trousers were topped by a multi-coloured kaftan. I sighed; I knew if neither of them was prepared to say anything else on the subject then nothing else would be said. There was so much more I thought I should be told, but I wasn't going to waste my breath. I sat down.

"We've come about something else," Boris said, then almost to himself, "didn't know about the baby."

"Well, now you do, and actually the usual way to go is 'congratulations' or maybe, 'what lovely news' even perhaps 'how exciting'. You pick." I caught Ed's eye, knew if he could, he'd be grinning. Glory shifted impatiently.

"Don't be so silly, you know everything we wish you. But I don't think you should call and tell Ruth and Rachael, not yet." I raised an eyebrow, but she wouldn't be drawn. "Look, we'll go into all that another time, for now, just do as I say."

Boris spoke before I'd had a chance to take issue, "We're here to ask for your help."

Here we go again, I thought. "No," I said, "I've made it absolutely clear; I will listen and report, I will *not* get involved further than that, especially now, I have different obligations."

He nodded, "You do, but perhaps to more than just your immediate family."

"In any case, you haven't heard what we want." Glory pointed out.

"Don't need to, not interested, not getting involved, nothing more to say."

"Oh, for goodness sake," she snapped, and behind that I picked up something I didn't want to. I don't think she was aware of it, and it wasn't because I was able to get through her shielding, I'd never been able to do that unless she let me. But Glory; self-contained, self-controlled, competent and composed for as long as I'd known her; now wasn't. Her shielding was as strong as ever, but something was seeping out. It was an unpleasant shock. Glory was a rock, a constant; she'd sorted, supported and saved me from the consequences of my own foolish actions on so many occasions. I didn't expect and certainly wasn't ready for her to have a wobble and I also knew, if there was something scaring Glory, it sure as hell would scare me more.

"Alright, tell me," I said to Boris, "you're here so I'll listen. But only listen," he nodded; he'd had few doubts. I'd spoken to him, but remained looking at Glory, not liking what I saw. Heavy, black hair was piled high, fastened and held in place with the usual two long gold pins and hooped gold earrings swung against cheekbones other women would kill for. The gold, the black, the vivid colours combined and fooled the eye, so you didn't immediately note the paleness of her usually rich, coffee-coloured skin and the shadows below her eyes. Her breathing was swift and shallow and slim unadorned fingers, usually elegantly resting in her lap were clenched into fists. Ed was watching me watching her, read my concern and nodded fractionally - I wasn't wrong, I was right to worry. With an effort, I tuned back in to Boris who apparently was waiting for me to answer a question I hadn't heard.

"Sorry I wasn't listening properly."

"I said, have you heard of the National Front?" I nodded, who hadn't? The group with the avowed intention of turning the Union Jack from patriotic symbol to danger signal had been hitting the headlines a fair bit recently. Any mention in the papers or on the radio provoked a curled lip from Aunt Kitty and *'mamzars'* spat out under her breath and you didn't have to understand Yiddish to catch the sentiment.

My grandmother and her sisters had been in Cable Street back in 1936. They never spoke about it to me but as a child, I knew a firmly shut door meant something I wasn't supposed to hear. Well naturally, that didn't work! It was back when Mosley and his home-grown fascists were at their bullying, black-shirted busiest, forerunning what would shortly, in Germany, become efficiently industrialised on a grand scale. Ideology licensing violence: violence enabling ideology, and what better place for a mob to march than the East End of London with its high immigrant population.

Grandma and her sisters, with their husbands, had moved out of the area, but along with so many others, they went back. There was a major police presence to prevent trouble but in Whitechapel, people had decided they 'weren't having it!' and a surge of determination built effective barricades. Sharing my Grandmother's memories, I knew she'd been scared witless at the time, but that wasn't going to stop her yelling defiance along with everyone else.

Armed with brooms, mops, heavy iron saucepans, utilising anything and everything that could be thrown, dislodged or poured out of windows, the East End made its point clear. English, Jewish, Irish, West Indian, Socialist and Communist stood shoulder to determined shoulder and forced back the Police who were protecting Mosley's right to free speech. He'd been determined that what he had to say and the triumphant march to go with it, would go down in history, and it did – although not the way he wanted.

"Stella!" Boris was looking at me expectantly, "what do you think?"

"About what?"

Glory huffed impatiently and rather than wait for Boris to repeat, just pushed it into my head. I laughed, although it wasn't funny, they'd got me involved in some pretty crazy things but this took the biscuit.

"You want Glory and me to take on the National Front?" nobody else was smiling. Well, Ed couldn't but the other two should have been.

"Not take them on," Boris, moved an aniseed ball from one cheek to the other, goodness but I did not like the smell of those sweets, "merely insert a spanner into the works."

"Us and who else's army?"

"Sarcasm," said Boris, "and I believe Stella, I've mentioned this on more than one occasion, is never helpful."

"For Pete's bloody sake," Glory didn't do shilly-shallying, "either you'll do it or you won't but we have to get a move on." she stood up.

"What *now?*" I said, "you want me to do something *now?*" Boris stood too but I was looking at Glory again, the quality of stillness and focus that was such an integral element of who she was, was notably absent right now. Ed put out a hand and touched hers briefly, he knew as did I, if there'd been room in my small office, she'd have been pacing. She made an effort to compose herself.

"You're frightened," I said. She didn't answer; she was slipping on the cream coloured trench coat she'd folded over the back of her chair, tying the belt decisively.

I looked at Boris, "How risky?"

"Ed and I will be there, no real risk."

"And I am not frightened," Glory said.

I nodded and reached for my own coat, "OK. Let's go." Glory was telling the truth, it wasn't this proposed outing that was so distressing her, it was something else entirely but if I couldn't stand by Glory when she wasn't her best, then what use was I? As we moved out of the room a warm, extremely large hand engulfed mine and squeezed gently. It was about as effusive as Ed got but all the more appreciated for that.

I'll be honest, I wasn't thrilled with the way things were going. As I'd seen them walk through the door, I had determined there'd be no budging, yet here I was – budged. My conscience was and always had been an ongoing liability, and frankly a flipping nuisance. I was far crosser about that than about anything they wanted me to do. I wasn't really worried about risk, the last couple of times I'd got into a spot of bother, I'd been on my own, but I'd coped – more or less. Whatever was going down this time, I'd be with Glory, and Ed and Boris were there as back up. What could possibly go wrong? As we filed out, Brenda turned in surprise.

"Everything alright?" Our Brenda was more attuned than she knew. I briefly balanced truth against peace of mind and also marital harmony. Peace and harmony won hands down.

"Brenda, David won't be home just yet, but be a love and leave him an answerphone message, so he won't worry. Let him know I'm meeting some people, but I won't be too late." Not an outright lie, just sparing on detail, best for all really.

As we went down the stairs, I felt a small bubble-bursting sensation in my stomach, I'd felt it earlier in the day too, it wasn't remotely similar to the apprehensive twisting I'd become so used to in connection with Ruth, but neither did it feel like a kick.

"Yes, it's a kick." Glory was behind me, using my sight to negotiate the stairs, so was in my head and had felt it too.

"Really?" I stopped and she bumped into me. I hadn't expected to feel anything for a few weeks yet, but maybe the baby had more common sense than I did and was registering a protest at the current outing. "It didn't feel like a kick."

I glanced back at her and she smiled briefly, "I don't think it does at first and look where you're going for God's sake, or we'll both fall and break our necks."

CHAPTER TWENTY-ONE

They'd arrived in a rather shabby, once-green van which wasn't at all the sort of thing Ed usually drove but apparently was less likely to attract attention. Shabby it may have been on the outside but inside was a different and pristine story. Boris sat in the front with Ed, Glory and I moved to the seats behind. As Boris made to slide the door closed, it turned out there was an additional passenger. I thought she was asleep in her basket and knew Brenda would have taken her home for the night, but Katerina apparently had her own ideas. She gave Boris the look you give someone who's just nearly shut you in the door, and stepped up and into the van, seating herself next to me.

"Not worth taking her back up," Boris said, "she can stay in the van while you're inside."

"Inside where?" I wanted to know, a little clarification wouldn't go amiss, but as was often the case, an answer from Boris veered all around the houses.

"For every group there is a leader and there are followers. Correct? And what is it a leader has to have?" he paused, and I understood input was expected, I looked at Glory, she didn't say anything, I shrugged. Boris gave up on us as a bad job and continued. "Respect. A leader must command respect. Sometimes that comes from charisma, sometimes fear, more often a combination. Lose that, lose status, lose control. Correct?"

"Get to the point," I muttered.

"That is the point. You and Glory are going for a drink in a public house. A room at the back has been hired for a meeting of this group which," he glanced at the clock on the dashboard, "should be starting round about now. When they've finished working themselves up, they will close the meeting and come to the bar for a drink. This is their habit. The leader of this group is a man called Alfred Beeton, his closest associate and ally is a man called Vernon Sloop. You will make both these men look like fools."

"And that's going to put a stop to the far right?" I wasn't impressed, "you're telling me, if Hitler had slipped on a banana skin, things would have gone differently?"

"You can chop down a tree in one go," Boris was annoyingly enigmatic, "But a constant eroding of its roots, is a far more effective way of weakening it. Erosion is probably all anyone can do - small steps."

Ed was negotiating us smoothly through the traffic, but it was rush hour and the going was slow. Lulled by the stop starts, I may have dozed for a while, as did Kat, I blamed the baby, don't know what Kat's excuse was. I woke when we stopped.

"Here?"

"The Royal Oak." Boris got out, held out a hand to me as I climbed down followed by Glory. He kept his hand on the open door.

"Aren't you coming in with us?"

"I'll be there," he said, "in due course, although, you might not notice." Boris was the ultimate blender-in; I'd never quite worked out how he did it even though I'd watched carefully. If he didn't want people to see him, they didn't; they looked over, around or even directly at, just didn't see. It wasn't anything I or the others could do.

"Ed?" I asked.

"When you need me..." He was a man of few words.

Glory had put on a pair of dark glasses, tuned into my sight and Boris handed her the white stick. She glanced back briefly at Ed and they exchanged a thought, too quick for me to catch. Before Boris had a chance to forestall, Katerina had followed us out and I rested my hand briefly on her head, which came conveniently to waist height – or at least it did when I'd had a waist - then pushed her gently back towards the van.

Boris stopped me, "No, take her," he flashed through what he was seeing. Glory; small, slim, exotic and blind and me; way behind in the exotic stakes, still at the tubby stage rather than plainly pregnant, and Kat; a dog who looked as if she was only passing the time till her next fashion shoot. Oh, we were so going to fit in at the Royal Oak.

CHAPTER TWENTY-TWO

You know the sort of entrance John Wayne used to make, in the old Westerns? Pushing through those swing doors; a long, slow survey of the room to an indrawn communal gasp from the drinkers, followed by complete silence. The hitch of a gun holster and a slow stroll to the bar, a single nod at the barman who pours a whisky, slides it along the wood, then dives for cover.

Well, maybe that's not quite how it went, but it was a scenario I played in our heads, that made us both laugh so we headed in with a grin on our faces. It wasn't crowded; a couple of elderly chaps settled like fixtures and fittings at a table in the corner. I don't think they moved a muscle the whole time we were there.

There was a younger man in a paint-spattered coverall staring morosely into his beer at one end of the bar, and a middle-aged man staring morosely at the jukebox choices at the other end. On the other side of the room, near an empty fireplace, there was a group of six older women of assorted shapes and sizes, all knitting. Glory was holding my arm for effect and I walked her carefully over to a table not far from the women, and then went to get a couple of drinks, leaving Kat to do her best impression of an alert guide dog.

The decor had seen better days, quite a lot of them, as indeed had the barmaid. Diana Ross on the jukebox was throwing herself into *Ain't No Mountain High Enough,* but the joint wasn't exactly jumping. I rested my hand on the bar's wooden surface, it was pitted, scratched and sticky enough to make me hastily remove it. I smiled at the barmaid who didn't smile back; she wasn't happy, she wasn't the barmaid either, she owned the place and had taken one look at us as we crossed the floor, and with the sure instinct of someone who's spent a lifetime pulling pints, knew trouble when she saw it. Bad enough, she was thinking to herself, that the bloody knitting club had turned up as usual, despite her phoning Doreen to say would they mind coming in another day. It wasn't as if she made any money on them – a milk stout each and a couple of packets of salt and vinegar between them, and sat there the whole evening. She swiftly poured the fruit juices I ordered, hoping we'd drink up quickly and bugger off before that lot came in from the back.

As it happened, we wouldn't have been quick enough anyway, because the meeting broke up just then and a crowd of men and a good few women, surged in. They were hyped by hate, rhetoric and being part of a tribe. They all headed for the bar at the same time. I knew Beeton immediately. Boris had shown us a photo but I didn't need that; the dank, bleak sourness of him was what had seeped into the scrap of material Boris had used to test me. He sauntered in after everybody else and the crowd parted to let him through. He walked with the chip-on-the-shoulder strut of a small man, and a swift glance confirmed an extra couple of inches provided by Cuban-heeled boots, which must have brought him up to about five seven but he was very sure of himself, turning a bullet-shaped shaved head from side to side surveying his people. He was in charge here. He knew it and they knew it.

I doubt I'd have been keen on any of this lot as individuals; as a crowd they were toxic. With the night being warm, there was an awful lot of tattooed flesh on display - and none of it was hearts and flowers. I didn't want to go into any of the heads in front of me, didn't have to, what they were thinking and feeling was coming off them in waves.

The excitement in the room was feverishly palpable, Beeton was a good speaker, and he said exactly what they wanted to hear, putting into words precisely what they felt. He'd whipped them up into a fighting frenzy; good thing there was the march in a couple of days. The simmering anticipation of violence and disruption was lighting them up like Roman candles, and they were oozing the courage of a crowd - aggressively jokey, chummy jostling, shoulder slapping, boxing feints, bouncing and swivelling on the balls of their feet in combat boots which creaked and squealed protest against the wooden floor. None of them wanted to stand still; they were a poisonous powder keg waiting to go off.

As glasses were drained, refilled and drained again, noise and jittery movement increased exponentially, an excess of energy looking for an outlet. I momentarily caught the eye of the woman behind the bar, she jerked her head slightly at me; get out. I knew she meant well. I ignored her. Our table was just beyond that of the knitters but nobody had taken any notice of us, then I realised the knitting women had all shifted their chairs, just enough to shield Glory from sight.

Beeton had his back to us, leaning on the bar with one boot on the foot rail, holding court. A taller, broader guy stood next to him. Looking around the room from his higher vantage point he suddenly spotted us, stared in astonishment then gave Beeton a nudge that made him swing round. Pale blue eyes in a surprisingly youthful face moved over us slowly with nothing short of delight. He wiped some beer foam from his mouth with an arm; this was a chap who felt a good many of his Christmases had arrived at once.

"Here we go," Glory murmured in my head, "me or you?"

"Let me," I said. A sense of something happening filtered through and quietened the crowd; people were turning to see what it was. From the jukebox, Dusty Springfield told us *She Just Didn't Know What To Do With Herself* and Beeton set his glass down gently on the bar. Then, sure and certain every eye was on him, and that everyone had clocked Glory, he started to stroll across the room and I pulled his left foot forward and up; his other foot followed as feet tend to do and he went down flat on his back with a thump which startled dust from the hard wood floor. If it was as sticky as the bar, he wouldn't be getting up that quickly.

"Oh dear, what's happened?" Glory, clutching my arm in alarm and best blind mode, broke the horrified silence, her voice ringing across the room. I patted her hand comfortingly.

"Nothing to worry about, a gentleman here has just had a bit of a fall, must have been something slippery on the floor." I leaned forward all compassion and concern, "Sir, are you hurt?" He'd given his back a teeth-jarring blow, but it was his ego that was badly bruised. I tutted sympathetically, "You went down terribly hard, didn't you?" I leaned my head a little closer to Glory, putting my hand over my mouth for an aside which unfortunately was audible to all.

"The way he kicked his legs up there – thought he was doing the Can Can."

"Ooh shoosh," said Glory, "he'll hear." Vernon Sloop was trying to hoist Beeton to his feet but that darn slipperiness on the floor must have still been there, because as soon as Beeton got to a certain point, his foot just plain slid away from under him and he was back on his backside. There was an awful lot of effing and blinding and then, friend Vern must have stood on the self-same slippery something, though his landing wasn't quite so painful because he landed face first on top of Beeton, an embarrassing juxtaposition.

"Oops a daisy, Maisie!" someone called out cheerfully and somewhere in the room, someone else smothered a laugh.

"Perhaps," I suggested helpfully, "if you and your friend just shimmied on over a teeny-weeny bit, it might not be so slippery there." Pale blue eyes fixed on me and turned to ice as he and Vernon disentangled and finally, clinging to each other, regained their feet and sprang apart. At any time, this was a man ripe and ready for violence, unhinged, unbalanced and right now, extremely unhappy. There were veins standing rope-like on his bull neck, another one pulsing at his temple.

"Is he alright?" enquired Glory loudly, "only I keep hearing people falling down." Ice blue swivelled from me to her and he reacted completely instinctively with a torrent of verbal diarrhoea covering what she could do, where she should go and what he wanted to happen to her. He was just getting into his stride and advancing towards us, when someone gave him the most enormous whack round the head with a bag full of knitting. It was the unexpectedness I think, that got him.

It was a good many years since Ethel Mount, a stalwart of the knitting club, had felt the need to pull someone up this way and, truth to tell, she'd quite forgotten how good she was at it.

"You shut that filthy gob right now, Alfie Beeton," she yelled, "I won't have you talk like that in front of decent people, I won't have it, you hear me?" Beeton, stunned into temporary silence, opened his mouth, but Ethel wasn't finished, "I've wiped your dirty arse more'n once and your snotty nose too. I've taken your mum in when your low-life dad went too far with fists – thrown 'im down our stairs more'n once. Wouldn't put up with his filthy mouth and I'll not put up with yours neither." She swung decisively on a sensible heel with a 'that's him told' expression and walked back to where knitting had been temporarily suspended.

There were perhaps fifteen seconds when things hung in the balance; he'd been dead scared of Auntie Ethel when he was a kid, she told you to do something, you did it or you got one of her right handers, nobody round here crossed Ethel. But then, over her shoulder, she added, "You leave them girls alone, they done nothing to you. Sit down and shut up and I don't want any of your tantrums." And that tipped the scales, the wrong way.

CHAPTER TWENTY-THREE

Beeton let out something between a growl and a roar, strode the few paces after her and placed two hands under the table she was about to sit down at. It was long, wooden and heavy but he heaved it up as if it weighed nothing. The five women still sitting scattered. Two fell in their haste, bottles, glasses and balls of wool flew to shatter or unroll, and Beeton told Ethel, one hand now at her throat, in extremely graphic detail where exactly she could shove her effing wool and stick her bleeding needles, interfering old cow.

Well, this was all just too much for knitting club founder, Doreen. Fifteen years they'd been going; every Tuesday, 8.00 sharp, regular as clockwork and an annual outing Christmastime for which they all put a weekly pound in the pot and records meticulously kept of who'd paid and who owed, and never a cross word. Doreen had, on occasion, wondered whether Ethel was a little bit on the rough side for the group, she certainly had a mouth and a half on her, but it takes all sorts and rough or not, Ethel was one of her Knitting Girls and Doreen had responsibilities.

She bent clumsily, knees not what they were, picked up an empty pint glass from the floor and swinging full circle for maximum momentum, brought the chunky glass down on the swastika tattooed in blue on the back of Beeton's shaved head.

"Get off 'er you dirty bugger," she yelled. She didn't knock him out. She did though divert his attention.

This whole evening wasn't going the way Beeton had envisaged. His speech had gone down a treat, the group's determination to make this march matter was brilliant, they were on fire and he'd been ready to bask in a bit of the admiration he so richly deserved. When he came into the bar they were queuing up to buy him a drink, then somehow it had all gone to hell in a handcart. Bloody Ethel giving him what for in front of everyone, and now some crazy old bat, he'd never seen in his life before, bashing his brains in, well, she was going to feel the back of his hand that was for sure, he drew his arm back and Glory froze it in mid-air.

"Don't do that," she said conversationally and sent him flying sideways. He landed a safe distance away and Glory sent Vernon after him for good measure, whereupon a brief misunderstanding arose, each man thinking he'd been punched across the room by the other.

Attention momentarily diverted; the landlady took action. She wasn't a woman who had the wind put up her easily, all sorts she'd had in here in her time, bodily thrown out a good many too but she could see the way this was going and 999 was now on the cards. First though, she swooped on the knitters, gathered them up like a mother hen and chivvied them rapidly into the back room. She grabbed Glory's arm as well, Glory shook her off, good-naturedly.

"I'm fine," she said, "really. Go on, lock the door, make that call, then make everyone a cuppa, and a drop of brandy in it, wouldn't hurt." Both Glory and I were a little astonished at the swift turn things had taken and we really hadn't had to do that much, it seemed more a question of light the blue touch paper and step away.

Back at the bar, the crowd had divided into factions, the majority were ready to wade in and sort out whoever was giving Alf grief, although at the moment he only seemed under attack by a couple of old birds and Vernon. There were though, out of the thirty or forty gathered, two or three who were grinning and nudging each other. Cocky little bastard was Alf, thought he was the big I am and now look at him, maybe he'd had his time. Let someone else take charge; someone who could handle himself.

Whilst still puzzled at the way things had gone down, Alfie Beeton was sure of one thing, authority needed to be reasserted and reasserted pronto. He knew only too well which of those in the crowd behind were champing at the bit to take over and was thrilled to the tips of their bovver boots at his humiliation. He'd show 'em. He swung on his heel and came straight for us spitting blood, in more ways than one, owing to Vernon's head having at some point made contact causing damage to lip and tongue. He knew it was violence that inspired loyalty, and if they weren't shit scared of him and his temper, he'd lost the upper hand. As he charged, Glory rose slowly holding her white stick crossways before her face, a hand at each end. The move was unexpected, her positioning accurate and the sound the bridge of his nose made as he ran straight into it wasn't pleasant.

"Hey, Alfie boy, need a hand?" someone sniggered. Someone else told him to belt up, another someone threw a punch and then all hell broke loose. It was mayhem, but oddly familiar, although I hadn't actually been in the middle of a pub brawl before, but we've seen them on screen, fist hitting flesh, inarticulate yells of fury and pain, people thrown over tables, others bashed on the head with a chair, although so far nobody had crashed out through the front window. In the background, some ready wit had put another coin in the jukebox and the New Seekers, when they could be heard, wanted *To Teach the World to Sing In Perfect Harmony*. Looking around, I wished them luck with that.

I thought this might be a good moment to start winding things down from our end as everyone seemed to be doing very well on their own. Glory nodded and we stood, but with a weirdly rising howl of fury, Beeton was on us bearing a grudge, and then some. He wanted to inflict on us the maximum amount of damage he could, in the shortest possible time; his fury carrying him way past the restrictions of repercussion and he leapt for Glory first.

Kat, who disliked unpleasantness of any kind, had stayed under my chair till now but as she emerged, he trod heavily on her paw and she went for his leg. As he'd no idea there was a dog in the picture, this came as a surprise, but not enough to change his plans – he was so far gone I shouldn't think the pain penetrated anyway. Glory and I moved back a couple of swift steps, exchanged a flash of thought and did together what we felt was necessary.

We took the bitterly corrosive, all-encompassing hate, fear, ignorance and aggression of a bigot and reflected it right back at him. It stopped him dead in his tracks. For a moment he remained standing, then as it permeated body and mind, his legs folded bonelessly and he sank heavily to his knees. What we'd done hadn't been pleasant, although as Glory silently pointed out, we'd simply reflected back what he owned. Even so, I think we were both taken aback at the potency of the sour hatred which moved through him like acid. Quite how powerful was evidenced by the reaction of the battling masses who stopped beating the hell out of each other for a good few minutes. They weren't the most sensitive bunch but they must have shared briefly, an echo of what he was feeling, a sort of bitter, smelly psychic belch and it created a brief hiatus. Unfortunately, we were only halfway across the room when that discomfort was dismissed and they pulled themselves together. They didn't know quite what had transpired but they it had something if not everything to do with us.

In that instant, reunited, they became a mob with a single-minded mob mentality. With a roar as if from a single throat, they charged towards us led by a shrieking woman who'd smashed a bottle and, with it lethally jagged and pointing, was making good speed. We swung round to face them. Kat, sensibly retreating behind us, and Glory reached for my hand, the physical connection strengthening whatever we were going to do, although at that point I wasn't quite sure what that was. Would we be crossing a moral line, if we turned a whole roomful of people, however unpleasant, into dribbling idiots?

"Up?" she said, "That'll throw them – quickly now." I had a moment's doubt, not having done it for ages, I could be a bit rusty but no, back came the old skill, smooth as silk and up we shot. The crowd headed by lethally-broken bottle lady were naturally surprised. As they skidded to a cartoon-like halt, practically beneath us, there were a lot of upturned faces where aggression had rapidly changed to gob-smacked.

"Now the tattoos."

As we hovered, I don't know whether Glory shouted or just thought loudly, it didn't matter, working smoothly together, we simultaneously lasered in on inked flesh; on swastika and skull, words and symbols, all the declarations of hate people had happily chosen to be indelible on their skin. There was a lot of ink involved, so it was easy to focus and heat. It took a few seconds for them to become aware of various portions of anatomy mysteriously heating up, and then the heat increased and there was a great deal of hollering, turning in circles and grabbing at inexplicably painful parts. Bit harsh? It probably only hurt as much as when originally done, and maybe it would make them consider the wisdom of having anything similar done in the future. Anyway, by the time the ink was really hot, we'd stopped doing anything and were drifting slowly downwards, though nobody was paying attention, being somewhat involved in their own affairs.

A warm, extremely large hand descended gently on my shoulder, another on Glory's. Ed was behind us and we both automatically backed closer to his reassuring bulk. He hated this sort of thing even more than Kat, and he had none of Glory's combative nature. He disliked violence of any kind and his misfortune had always been that his size and dead-pan reaction made so many want to 'have a go'. He was more than able to take care of himself, just hated doing it. Nevertheless, he was one of the bravest people I knew. Even scared rigid, he'd waded in, time and again, to save one or other of us.

Boris was moving forward now, from the side of the room. I'd no idea whether he'd been there the whole time, I hadn't seen him, hadn't sensed him, but he was here now and I was relieved, I was starting to feel tired and my legs were aching.

"Your Attention Please!" he'd added, a pleasingly magnifying, megaphone echo and depth to his voice, so attention was gained quickly. "Please drop anything you are holding," and such was the authority and expectation of obedience, they complied and there was a clatter as bottles, broken and unbroken hit the floor, along with an assortment of vicious looking knives and a range of knuckle dusters. "And now, if you have anything in your pockets that I wouldn't like, please empty them." The unprotesting crowd seemed to have gained a fair old grasp of what Boris would or wouldn't like, and a lot more unpleasant items were extracted and

added to individual piles. There was a brief pause, "And the rest," he said. I couldn't believe there was more to come – but there was.

"Ed, if you wouldn't mind?" he said without looking round, and the little piles of vicious intent which had accumulated next to nearly every individual began to move; slowly at first then gathering speed, scraping and bouncing as they shot across the floor to form one extremely solid, jaggedly high metallic heap. "Now, face down, on the floor, arms stretched in front. *All of you. Now!*"

This was an exceedingly bewildered branch of the National Front. One minute they'd been rallying behind a sterling chap, part of a triumphal movement - nothing illegal, free speech, England and St. George and all that. Next they were flat on the floor, nursing painful burns in unexpected places, cut and bruised from fighting – nobody was quite sure what that had been about, the sterling chap was crying in the corner - and to cap it all two crazy women had played some kind of weird magic trick on them.

Not one of the gathered assembly could say precisely what had happened but they were clear, from the sound of fast approaching sirens what was going to happen next. It had been that sort of an evening.

By the time we were on our way out, the police were on their way in; pleased, if startled to find the troublemakers ready and awaiting collection. There was an older man, not in uniform who seemed in charge, as he and Boris passed each other he sketched a salute, Boris nodded briefly in return and we headed back to the van. A short way down the road, an enormous wave of tiredness hit me. Ed felt it and didn't say anything but swept me up easily in his arms for the last bit.

You might remember seeing it in the papers, around 10th August it would have been: **Knitting Club Sorts Out National Front** was the header in The Times. The Mail went with **National Front Get the Needle**, The Guardian opted for **Wool Pulled Over Eyes of National Front** and I think it was the Sun that put out ***Alfie Beeton Beaten!*** The reporters who'd pitched up shortly after the police, had been faced with a tricky decision, pick up on the scraps of unlikely information about two women or go with something fractionally more believable. They went for the latter, after all it was a gift of a story, and Doreen and Ethel arm in indomitable arm, united in righteousness, slid into celebrity as if to the manner born - dozens of interviews and appearances in the same week on both Russell Harty and Michael Parkinson.

I suppose there may have been an issue as to whether the sort of interference we'd staged was a mistake, because publicity is lifeblood to any organisation, but then again, it rather depends on the type of publicity. The group we'd come across was a small part of an unpleasant whole but the ridicule surrounding them, went a long way!

The right-wing march went ahead in Lewisham on 13th as planned, they had a big turnout, but there was an equal mass of people who, as Doreen might have said, 'just weren't having it!' The marchers found they weren't only vastly outnumbered by counter demonstrators, but that lots had taken the trouble to bring along knitting needles and wool. The Police ensured streets were efficiently cordoned off and marchers found themselves corralled and chivvied in groups down empty side roads. There was still plenty of hate spewed, the inevitable nasty clashes and some injuries before the march was over, but it certainly wasn't the triumph it was supposed to be. It's awfully difficult to inspire hate and fear when so many people are laughing at you.

CHAPTER TWENTY-FOUR

I didn't feel it was necessary to trouble David with my evening at the Royal Oak. I'm all for honesty, but sometimes a bit of mystery in a marriage isn't a bad thing, and I hated to upset him. I do know though that once you start with complicated lies, things can go seriously pear-shaped, especially if you can't quite remember what it was you said. So, I kept it simple, told him I'd met Ed and Glory, we had a snack out; and no, no idea quite where because Ed drove, and yes it was lovely to see them again and no there wasn't really any news, only that everyone was still worried about Ruth.

I was seeing the midwife on a monthly basis now and our relationship had moved forward. She said I could call her Mavis and I said could she stop calling me Mum. She had adapted and was dealing good-naturedly with my routine of fainting at blood tests, keeping me on the couch so she didn't have to keep picking me up. When I apologised the last time I came round, she patted my arm kindly and said not to worry, she was grateful for those few minutes because they allowed her to catch up with paperwork. I was getting regularly baby-kicked now and Mavis said she was happy, everything was normal and baby was thriving but of course, she always added, if there was anything at all worrying me - I shouldn't hesitate to pop in and see her. As the main thing worrying me was whether I'd suddenly hear my baby talk to me, I wasn't sure this was anything she could help me with, but thanked her anyway.

We went on a shopping trip, with my Mother for advice and David for carrying. At Mothercare, we bought several maternity smocks which I felt didn't so much hide the bump, but made me look ten times the size I really was. The lady serving us chuckled heartily at this, because apparently everyone said the same thing, which made me wonder why they didn't do something about it. But as I couldn't get into my normal clothes, had already had more than enough shopping for one day, and couldn't now think much further than the next toilet stop, there seemed little choice.

Hilary had made it her mission to knit everything and anything I'd need for the baby and was, to Martin's irritation, constantly nipping down the road for technical discussion with Michele Young at the wool shop. I was a little startled at the growing pile of hectically multi-coloured babygros she was producing, I hadn't come across knitted ones before, wasn't sure how practical they'd be, and could only trust the baby wouldn't have a great colour sense. Nevertheless, I appreciated enormously the affection behind the gesture and regretted I'd probably never have the chance to introduce Hilary to Doreen, kindred souls if ever there were.

All newly-weds have their ups, downs and adjustments; ours were simpler in some ways, more complicated in others.

"Nice evening," David would comment noncommittally on the way home from a dinner party.

"Mmm."

"You look lovely in that dress."

"I look enormous."

"That'll be the baby."

"I did wonder."

Short pause, "You didn't take to that Annabelle, did you?"

"Not really."

"Seemed nice enough."

"She flirted with you."

"She didn't after the bowl of chocolate mousse fell into her lap."

"Mmm, unfortunate?"

At other times, things could get little terse. "That's the last quiz supper we're going to Stella."

"Why?"

"You know darn well!"

"We came top, didn't we?"

"Only because you got most of the answers before I had a chance to open my mouth."

"Not my fault – the quiz-master guy was looking at the answers before he'd even finished giving the question."

"You shouldn't have been listening!"

"He was thinking loudly."

* * * *

I wasn't feeling comfortable, and that wasn't just because I was looking increasingly like a small tent in motion. There was an underlying unease, I didn't know whether it was just to do with worry about Ruth, or whether there was something else but it was a discomfort that wouldn't go; sitting like a small hard stone in my stomach, unmoving yet causing sick-making ripples. I kept harking back to what had been said on the way back from our evening out at the Royal Oak.

When we'd climbed back in the van, Glory had briefly wiped one hand against the other, brushing away the taint of what we'd felt in there. For most of the way, nobody had much to say and as always, it was a wonderful silence, a blanketing from the rest of the world. Glory broke it after about twenty minutes, sighing and turning in the front seat. I was seated behind Ed with Boris on my left so she didn't have to twist too far or uncomfortably, but I could feel her reluctance.

"Will you remember not to say anything to Rachael or Ruth about the baby?"

"I should think they already know?"

Glory shook her head, "They haven't said anything and I think they would," she looked at Boris who nodded agreement. "For obvious reasons then," she said, "we don't think you should visit."

"Why is that obvious?" I hadn't planned a visit but being told I mustn't, was a different thing altogether.

"It might be better if they know nothing about the baby for now." I waited for an explanation and after a pause she added, "Look, I wouldn't say it if I didn't need to. Don't ask questions." There was an unspoken couple of words at the end of that which chilled me, what she meant but hadn't said was 'it's safer'. She turned back to the front again, gazing sightlessly out of the window. She did that sometimes, didn't use anyone else's eyes; simply retreated into her blindness.

Nobody else spoke and after a while I must have dozed, not waking till we stopped when I found I'd been snoring against the shoulder of a slightly disconcerted Boris. I gathered he hadn't had much to do with pregnant women who dropped off anytime they had the chance. Glory got out, pulling down the front seat and holding on to my hand because I was still half-asleep and had managed to get tangled up with Katerina, who chose to exit at exactly the same time. Glory unwound the lead from my legs and Katerina, who generally did effusive about as much as Ed, gave her an affectionate nudge on the hip with her head, then started pulling towards our front door, she'd had enough for one evening. Glory, put her hand gently on my stomach for a few seconds and answered the unasked question.

"No," she said, "nothing odd." And I suppose it was because I was relieved that I stupidly forgot to ask Boris to please keep me and my conscience up to date with what was happening about Devlin.

CHAPTER TWENTY-FIVE

"That girl," said Brenda, "is going to pieces in front of us, what're we going to do?" she was standing in the doorway of my office where I'd just landed thankfully in my chair - getting into work was getting no easier, whichever way I walked to try and avoid it, the fishy goings-on at Mac Fisheries was still getting to me. I held up an unhappy hand, breathing slowly in and out, which Midwife Mavis said would help, but didn't really.

"Sorry, just…"

"I know," she said sympathetically, "Mac…"

"… don't even say it." Everyone said the sickness stopped after three months but my body hadn't got the memo and here I was, three months further on and still wobbly with it. Katerina was circling uneasily; I'd like to think in concern but in reality it was because the cleaner had moved her basket - only a few inches - but Kat liked everything just so. I moved it with my foot and she inclined her head graciously and settled in.

As the sickness started to recede, I sat up straighter and smiled my thanks to Trudie, who'd slipped through the small space Brenda left in the doorway, with a cup of tea and a plain biscuit, she put her arm round my shoulders and gave a squeeze. As a mother of five, she'd taken it upon herself to give hugs whenever I was near enough. At the beginning I hadn't been keen, but she meant so well I couldn't hurt her feelings, and after a while I got used to it and found it oddly comforting, although I did have to ask her to hold back if clients were there; it just didn't look professional.

"You mean Joy?" I said to Brenda.

"Of course," Brenda came fully into the room and Aunt Kitty, who'd just turned up, although I couldn't think why, this was another one of not-her-days, followed her in, parking her trolley-on-wheels in the doorway where someone else was bound to fall over it.

"She's right, you know." Kitty, standing next to Brenda usually made me grin. Brenda, a tall woman shaped as she put it 'for comfort over speed', towered above Kitty who'd only been five foot in her heyday and was certainly shorter now. I wasn't smiling now though, because they were right, there was something very wrong with Joy.

When she'd joined us, nearly three years ago now - blonde bobbed, red lipsticked, and a distinctive, pink candy-floss scent – life spilled out of her. Despite mock-cursing her late parents for their name choice, it couldn't have suited her better, but it was more than just her name that had changed over the last months and yet I *knew* she was happy.

"How can you say that?" queried Brenda, "You can't ever know what's really going on in someone's head?"

I shrugged, "Just a feeling I suppose." But it wasn't a feeling, it was a certainty, I'd stake my life on it. I don't like to take liberties, but in Joy's case I made an exception and automatically checked her whenever our paths crossed. It had become a habit of which I wasn't proud but the result was I knew how she was, at any given time of the day.

"But you've only got to look at her," Brenda was saying now, her voice low, aware Joy could nip up from downstairs at any time. "It *can't* be right."

It wasn't. Joy was shrinking in every possible way, inches, attitude, confidence. She'd always made most of her own clothes – she had a great figure, innate taste and style and knew what suited. Changes in how she now dressed had been gradual, not immediately noticeable. I knew Trevor enjoyed taking her shopping, said he didn't want his wife sitting at a sewing machine when she could buy whatever she wanted. Apparently he'd scoop up an armful of items in a store, bringing them all for her to try on, one after the other, until she didn't know where she was and he'd tell her not to worry about choosing, why not take them all? The assistants, busy wrapping, would tell her she didn't know how lucky she was, and she'd laugh and tell them that actually she did.

Maybe it wasn't surprising how, over time, his taste and preferences were reflected a little more than her own and perhaps suited her slightly less.

Trevor had said he'd love to see her hair a softer colour, maybe she'd even grow it a bit? Then he wondered if that softer colour didn't call for a whole new range of make-up. They'd gone up to Harrods one Saturday afternoon and, sitting on a high stool she'd been thoroughly Mary Quanted; quite a pale look but apparently very 'now' and Trevor loved it, said he couldn't get over how gorgeous she looked. There was a pile of stuff they'd used on her face; moisturiser, toner and goodness knows what else and that, she'd said, was before they'd even started with the actual make-up. Trevor had winked at the Quant lady and said they'd better take it all or he'd never hear the last of it. Joy had laughingly protested; said she honestly didn't need all that and when on earth would she find time to put it on? But Trevor had jokingly put his hand across her lips, told the saleswomen to take no notice of her, told Joy he'd never had anyone to spoil before and that if she loved him, she'd let him.

Trevor thought it was wonderful that she'd started a patch in their garden to grow herbs and vegetables the way she'd done before they were married. He did worry though about her getting earth right up under her nails, there were infections you could pick up from soil, he said, and after all, you never knew quite where next door's cat was doing her business. Joy didn't want him worried, so took to gardening when he was out, but inevitably there was less and less time for it and it was true, her hands did benefit and he'd pointed that out, said her nails were growing beautifully and she must start having a weekly manicure – but he was also terribly concerned she may be missing out on something she loved, so he went straight to the newsagent to arrange for three different, glossy gardening magazines to be delivered every month. That way, she had the best of both worlds, elegant hands and not missing out on the pleasures of gardening.

It was Hilary, delving for a sneaky snack one morning who discovered Joy had emptied her desk of its previously always-to-be-counted-on stock of Walnut Whips. Joy came downstairs, just in time to catch Hilary's displeasure, laughed and said not to worry, she'd get Hilary some for her own desk. Apparently, Hilary told us later, Trevor hadn't said anything, but Joy could tell he was concerned about something and eventually got it out of him. He was worried she might be getting just the teeniest bit stout – sure sign of a happy marriage, he said, but if they were going to start a family of their own, she wouldn't want to spoil their chances in any way, would she?

There was no disputing; Joy felt Trevor was the most wonderful husband any girl could have had the luck to find. At the same time there was no doubt she was looking, sounding and acting like a completely different woman. But a completely happy woman. We had no right to comment, let alone interfere in any way. Although that didn't mean I wasn't going to keep checking. And that was what I told Brenda.

* * * *

I wasn't sleeping well, so neither was David. He said it was like being in bed with a family of squirrels fighting over breakfast, an odd analogy I thought, but not one I had the energy to question. Not only couldn't I get comfortable in bed, but during the day my head felt muzzy and lazy a lot of the time. That lasted until I climbed into bed, whereupon all hell broke loose and I was on full red alert.

My concentration wasn't what it had been either. I did silly things like floating a basket of washing ahead of me down the stairs, forgetting what I'd done and tripping over it. Another day I'd lifted a box of Sugar Puffs from the larder because I couldn't be bothered to get up from the table. Halfway across the room, I must have been distracted for a second or two, it was a nearly full box with contents not easy to clean up due to stickiness and we were treading on strays for days.

I was missing Ruth and Rachael dreadfully, which was plain silly. If it was a chat you wanted, Rachael was never going to be your woman and Ruth, on the odd occasion I tried, never seemed to be there. After Glory's warning-off, I was also acutely aware I shouldn't say too much, so it was ages since we'd spoken. I was dreaming a lot, tangible stuff - sounds, smells, tastes, colours, it was like sitting in the front row of a crowded cinema for several showings and all rather exhausting. I could never remember them clearly when I woke, only the uncomfortably unpleasant after-taste they left, along with a background headache from sitting too close to the screen. And the whole time there was a rhyme going round and round and up and down in my head. I didn't have the words, just the rhythm and I didn't know whether it was a nursery rhyme or a song I'd heard, but it was driving me nuts.

I'd woken David and Kat a few times by screaming loudly. He said I wasn't properly awake and was babbling about 'the smiley one'. When it happened for the fourth night in a row, he muttered something about me making about as much sense asleep as awake, which I felt was unnecessarily snarky and uncalled for.

We'd originally discussed and decided against having Kat sleep in our room and David purchased a splendid, purple cushioned basket for her. He brought this out nightly with great ceremony and placed it temptingly in the hall, next to the radiator, exclaiming loudly - he read that if you enthuse, your dog will pick up on that and want a bit of whatever you're enthusing about. Kat must have missed that article because she paused only to briefly sniff the basket on her way to the bedroom.

David thought she just needed training. For a few days he picked her up, no easy task and placed her gently in the basket where I softly stroked her head and murmured soothingly for a minute or two, before a mad dash was made for the bedroom. There should only have been two dashing, in fact it was three, and one of us always got there first, dived under the dressing table and refused to come out. After a while we gave up and gave in and the purple basket was moved to a corner of the living room where it took up service as an unorthodox and not very efficient magazine rack.

CHAPTER TWENTY-SIX

I'd settled nicely into my routine visits to Midwife Mavis, although however hard I tried, I always seemed to turn up late and that never went down well. 'Only person round here allowed to be late is Baby!' she was fond of stating.

That day, when I left for my appointment. Joy was on the phone at the front desk. She was in a brown and grey check pinafore dress over a high-necked cream blouse with a pussycat bow. Her hair was pulled tightly back from her face and combined with the pale, off-white lipstick she'd adopted, made her look a little drained. She smiled up at me without interrupting the long-winded holiday query that was going on. I mimed I was off to the surgery and she thumbs-upped me. In days gone by, she'd have whipped open her desk drawer to offer me sustenance on the way, although it was probably better for the general health of all that she was on her diet.

Quite apart from what she kept in her drawer; Joy used to be sugar-sweet scented; pink candy-floss textured but there was only the merest hint of that now. I'd never come across anything like it before. It felt to me as if she was in an imperceptibly shrinking space; walls, ceiling, floor, fractionally yet inexorably closing in. The impact of that impression was so strong I stopped. She put her hand over the mouthpiece.

"Stella, you OK?"

"Fine," I said, "thought I'd forgotten something, but I haven't, just baby-brain!" she smiled and turned her attention back to the call. They were busy in the travel agency, despite Martin wandering around exuding doom and gloom and muttering 'this was their worst year ever'. Hilary said ignore him, he said the same thing annually. Today both Hilary and Martin had clients at their desks, currently in that state of blissful anticipatory sun-kissed stupor brought on by glossy brochures. Hilary spotted me and beckoned me over.

"Stella, do me a favour? Passing Michele's?" I nodded and she burrowed briefly, apologising to the couple in front of her as she handed me a paper bag, "promised I'd get these back to her, d'you mind awfully?" Young's was a few doors up the road. It was, Martin said unkindly, the place buttons went to die but the fact Hilary spent far too much time and money there, probably accounted for the cynicism.

Michele was behind the counter telling a customer that if she thought zig-zag trim would go with that jacket, she needed her eyes testing. Michele was never slow in coming forward with an opinion and most customers didn't seem to mind. She maintained those that did mind needn't bother coming back, which I suppose was one approach to customer service.

Having come to my rescue outside Mac Fisheries early on in my pregnancy, Michele always looked slightly anxious when she saw me. She wasn't a hands-on sort of a woman and preferred a counter's distance between her and anyone else.

"You heard about last week, I suppose?" she said pursing her lips, "shocking fuss with your women." Michele ran a continuing war of attrition with our group of temperamental and often irascible clothes-alteration ladies, who were even more opinionated than she was. I wished she wouldn't keep calling them my women - made it sound like I was running a brothel.

Our 'alterations department' were five ladies who met by chance, attending weekly English conversation classes at the Town Hall. Amongst a lot of men and younger people, they'd formed their own little clique. Their English, at the end of the course was no better than at the beginning, but they had established a mutual understanding and a great friendship. Two were Polish, one Russian, another hailed from India and the last of the gang was French. None could speak the language of the others, apart from the two Poles, naturally, but by coincidence each had been, back home, a skilled seamstress and it turned out there was nothing they couldn't design; make, alter, embroider or bead.

Kitty came across them when treating herself to tea and a chocolate slice at the Florence Lounge in Hendon. They were all of a similar vintage and they'd invited her to join them. With broken English supplemented by Hindi, Yiddish, Russian, Polish and French; a lot of miming and much hilarity, they explained what they did; she told them what she did and then she brought them to see me, which was how *Simple Solutions* came to have the best design and dressmaking team this side of Chanel! Every commission was, it has to be said, accompanied by obligatory haggling over rates and deadlines and often greeted with head shakes and hysteria before being impeccably completed. The amount of business we gave them was growing and as a consequence, so were their dealings with Michele, who'd found to her annoyance that her opinion was neither wanted, needed nor listened to. Last week's stand-off apparently was over specially ordered pearl buttons which were found wanting. Multilingual heated recriminations were exchanged and apparently insults and a lot of buttons had been thrown before resolution was reached.

"I did hear," I said, "And I know they can get excitable."

"Excitable's not what I'd call it," Michele arched her neck like an offended swan, but I could see she wasn't that bothered, she felt there was nothing like a good argument to get the energy flowing. I left her to further castigation of the zig-zag trim lady, and made my way to where I'd parked the car.

David had taken it upon himself to make a car change and one day with maximum drama and a blindfold had presented me with a surprise waiting in the road. It was enormous.

"What do you think?" he asked. I thought I'd never be able to climb up into the driving seat; I thought even if I did, I stood no chance of seeing over the steering wheel; I thought I wouldn't be able to park it in a month of Sundays; I wondered if the garage would take it back and I thought wasn't it good thing David couldn't read my mind. I plumped for honesty.

"I'm pretty speechless."

"Quite something, isn't it?" he said patting it proprietorially.

"It is indeed quite something."

"It's a Rancho. Lots of room for a carrycot in the back and I've had straps put in, so the baby won't fall off the seat.

"Thoughtful."

"And look, there are fold down seats at the back, we could probably get as many as ten people in."

"Good to know."

Unsurprisingly, David was in no way open to the idea of taking it back, even when he suggested I took it for a spin and climbing in proved as problematic as I'd feared, and was only finally achieved by a two-handed heave to my rear end. Once in, with the seat cranked high, I could in fact see over the steering wheel – just. The vehicle had the widest tyres I'd ever seen, other than on an armoured tank, so any manoeuvre was enough to make a strong man weep, let alone an eight-month pregnant woman. When we were together, David drove, and when I was on my own, provided no-one was watching, I had to elevate myself, bump and all, drift sideways into the seat and add a little extra something to the wheel turning – my own version of power steering.

Now, aware I was running late for Mavis, I made good time to the clinic car park and was relieved to find and fit into a parking space. I was having my usual battle of wills with the steering lock which had a bloody mindedness all of its own, when there was a sudden sharp metallic rapping on the window, right by my ear. I jumped. The woman who'd used her car keys to noisy effect was shouting and gesticulating, I thought maybe she was in trouble of some kind and wound the window down hastily. Turned out she was just angry.

"That's my parking space," she yelled.

"I'm sorry?" I wondered if she was one of the doctors who had allocated places, although if she was, I didn't think much of her bedside manner. "Actually I didn't see it was reserved."

She glared at me, "S'not reserved, you snooty cow, I saw it first, then you drove in and took it."

I really didn't need this. "I'm so sorry," I said, I know how annoying that can be, but it was an empty space, perhaps you could go to that other one, look just over there."

"Why should I? You go." This was getting silly and I didn't have time for silly. I opened the door, forcing her to move back, I could see she had problems, the least of which was the parking space issue. In her head there were an awful lot of grudges, I was just the latest. She raised a threatening fist with the sharp key protruding between her clenched fingers, I don't think she actually planned to hit me but I lifted her up and shifted her sharply out of my the way, setting her down by her car, which had stopped askew behind mine with the door hanging open. A toddler was standing in the front seat watching solemnly.

"Don't you bloody shove *me*" she snarled.

"You're not setting a very good example are you?" I pointed out, looking at the kid in the car and she spat out an instruction as to what I should do next, which I probably deserved. The child had now climbed down from the car and was crying.

"*Shuddup!*" she whirled and bent to give him a swift, stinging slap on the back of his legs. Now that wasn't necessary, it wasn't his fault. She was tightless and there was a lot of pale, goose-pimpled flesh showing below a mini-skirt, so I showed her just how painful that sort of slap could be on a bare leg. She swung round baffled, but of course there was no-one behind her.

"Hurts, doesn't it?" I said, moving past and because I wasn't just late, I was cross as well, I linked that memory. Every time she slapped that child, she'd feel it too. I left her trying to work out what the hell had just happened and trotted into the clinic. Mercifully Mavis was running late herself, so by the time she called me in I'd had time to grab a waiting-room chair and look as if I'd been there for ages.

"Any problems?" she wanted to know as she measured, blood pressured and palpated. There were in fact plenty of problems but nothing I could trouble her with. I was getting clumsier by the day. Last week I'd broken two plates on their way from cupboard to table. Bearing in mind the Great Sugar Puff Disaster, I'd held them extra firmly, but midway just sort of lost them and they crashed and smashed. I knew brain fog was normal, but in my case it meant my mental blinds started flipping open at unexpected times, so in the middle of a conversation I'd suddenly be hearing half a dozen others, criss-crossing and tangling in my head. It was like hearing several radios on different stations simultaneously. Sometimes I just had to stop talking, put my head in my hands and let it all fade and flow away. That brought its own problems, giving people enough of a fright to get busy with wet towels for the back of my neck, tiger balm for my forehead and a sweet drink for blood sugar, it was all a bit tiresome.

"Well?" Mavis, washing her hands at the sink, looked over her shoulder,

"Sorry?" I'd forgotten what she'd asked.

"Cotton wool in your ears? Anything bothering you?" I shook my head, "what are you hoping for?" she said, drying briskly. Actually, I couldn't make up my mind, strange like me or not like me? I was trying not to come down on either side, but remain flexible. Apart from a lot of kicking and squirming, the small being inside, didn't seem to have anything to say, so for the moment I was thinking normal.

"Right," said Mavis, "well Baby's happy enough, Mum just needs to relax more. See, on the top there," she pointed as she handed me my records to put away, "phone number. Any questions ring me. If I'm not on, one of the others'll see to you," she tutted at my upended tortoise impression as I struggled to sit up, "now, what have we said? Over on our side, first." I'd become quite fond of midwife Mavis, bossy as she was, she reminded me of Rachael, I hoped she'd be on duty for the birth. I obediently rolled my hefty self over on my side and she looped her arm below mine to help me slide off the couch. As usual, most of the couch's paper covering came with me.

"Oops, sorry," I apologised, laughed and looked up. Looking back at me was a chalk-white face with a frenziedly fixed grin and achingly empty eye sockets.

CHAPTER TWENTY-SEVEN

The baby must have felt the shock as much as I did, the adrenaline would have shot through her too, and how odd in that moment, I didn't doubt the bump was a she. Midwife Mavis put her head to one side above the crisp blue uniform, tilting the rigid whiteness as if listening then, arm still looped through mine, moved closer as if to impart a secret. Behind the horror of the impassivity, was a strange intensity of concentration, curiosity and intent.

I was acutely aware of my baby, unusually still within me, whilst all around, unnaturally amplified were the familiar sounds, smells and bustle of the clinic; antiseptic, anticipation and apprehension, for me, swiftly shifting shades of metallically scented silver. Mavis was still there, I could hear her running a pre-eclampsia checklist in her head because I'd mentioned headaches - blood pressure, ankles urine all checked. I reached out with my fingers, moving smoothly through the white to warm skin beneath; she took a step back. Midwives touch patients, patients don't touch midwives.

"Sorry," I said, "bit dizzy."

"Baby pressing on blood vessels I expect; nothing to worry about." Brisk behind the mask she didn't know was there, Mavis helped me off the couch, "Pop onto that chair for me, here - sip of water." The blank-eyed blazing grin bent to look into my face, "hmm, let's get that head down," a hand on the back of my neck, "that's it, arms on your knees, can't have you falling off. It'll pass, just stay where you are while I finish your notes." And Mavis, with the not-Mavis face, sat to briskly fill in blanks with a biro.

I was over the initial fright but baffled; I couldn't feel or sense anything at all that would account for what I was seeing.

"How we doing?" I knew she had a roomful of women to see after me, and had surreptitiously checked her watch, she was anxious to move on, but wouldn't let me go until she was certain I was OK. I got to my feet, reached for coat and bag.

"I'm fine now, really. Sorry."

"No problem," she said, "here, Stella dear, your notes," but that wasn't Mavis speaking, the hint of an accent, the intonation, the affection and for a second or two, the unmistakeably rich, purple-deep lavender overwhelming other scents and senses. I wanted only to let go, to lean into the warmth and familiarity. Then cynicism and baby kicked in at the same time. The voice and scent were as false as the face, and with the thought lavender faded fast, leaving only a rancid aftertaste. And as Mavis ushered me out of the door, the mask was already dissipating, the effect oddly more chilling, because for a moment she was neither one nor the other.

"Let's have you looking a lot less pale next time." she said. I nodded, with remaining traces of white I could have said exactly the same to her. "Now, what on earth have you done there, silly girl? Here," she handed me a plaster. I must have been grasping my notes too tightly, a semi-open staple had pierced my finger and now she'd pointed it out, it hurt disproportionately, the way those small injuries do, there was blood on my records now, it felt portentous.

Sometimes there's something you have to think about; it's important but disturbing, so you have to find a time when there's energy to take it on and until you do, it's not anything you can discuss. So, when David wanted to know if all had gone well at the clinic I said yes, and when he raised an eyebrow at a brown stain on my white t-shirt, and drew his own conclusions, I let him.

"What was it then, Flake? Mars Bar?" he said. I looked sheepish. I wasn't keeping things from him, but if I wasn't clear what had happened, how on earth could I explain it to him?

It was no surprise that I had a nightmare that night, although it gave David and Kat a terrible fright; apparently I sat up, singing.

"Singing?" I asked, when he finally managed to wake me, "*Singing?*"

"And you're even more tuneless asleep than awake."

"What was I singing?"

"Hard to say, nothing that'll trouble the hit parade anytime soon," he saw I wasn't laughing with him, "some kind of nursery rhyme I think, hey Sweetie, you've had these before – well, not the singing – but nothing to worry about," he heroically hauled himself out of bed, "I'll make you a hot milk." As he left the room, Kat settled down again with a martyred sigh.

"You wanted to sleep here fur-face; you'll have to take the rough with the smooth!" I told her. I was stone tone deaf; never sang and no idea why I'd started now. Sipping the welcome hot milk and with David asleep again beside me I desperately wanted to talk to one of the others, but Glory had been insistent I shouldn't phone the school, she wouldn't have said it without good reason. I'd have to fall back on Boris.

* * * *

This proved easier said than done, which had never happened before. I tried him unsuccessfully at regular intervals over the next couple of days and left increasingly terse messages on his answer machine, adding sourly that it was a good thing this wasn't a flipping emergency!

When I did get him, it was a startlingly unsatisfactory call. I gave him a quick precis, mask and all and he listened carefully, said 'hmm' in some places, 'ahh' in others and I could almost smell the aniseed ball I knew he had in one cheek. I did not feel I had his full attention and thought I might scream, if he blamed it on the baby.

"You know," he said, "the body does odd things to the mind and you are due to give birth soon." I clenched the phone receiver with which I'd have liked to bash him – perhaps we could have chuckled over that bashing and put it down to the pregnancy as well. Instead I opted for a more grown-up approach.

"This is me, Boris," I said, "I know what's real and what's not," and then because I felt I hadn't imparted properly the full fright of the happening, I sent him the face. It's never easy to do over the phone but I didn't expect the reaction I got.

"It's Comedy."

"Well, I'm not laughing" I snapped, then realised he was right.

"Exactly," he'd picked up that thought well enough, "the Greeks used masks because amphitheatres were so big, most of the audience weren't going to hear a word of the play, at least this way they'd know if they were watching a comedy or a tragedy and…"

"Boris," I broke in, "you're missing the point. I realise *what* it is, I want to know *why* I was seeing it?" he heaved a sigh that sounded almost as long-suffering as one of Kat's.

"Stella, it's something you see all the time in theatre ads and television. It is a symbol, something so familiar; you probably don't even notice it. You were lying down and the midwife warned you, the weight of the baby can restrict your breathing. Your brain plucked a random image from memory to alarm you, you reacted, you moved, oxygen problem resolved."

"So, just my imagination then?"

"No, your brain reacting to risk."

"Where was the other one then?"

"Other one?"

"Tragedy," I said, and put the phone down.

* * * *

I won't lie, and I'm not proud, but, after putting the phone down, I sulked. Boris hadn't been rude, customary courtesy was all in place but I couldn't get over his disinterest. I felt I'd gone overnight from valued colleague to hysterical nuisance. Then I realised, I hadn't even asked about Ruth or Devlin, but I was damned if I'd ring back, however much I wanted to know. One thing I did know for sure was I wasn't going to get much work done for the rest of the afternoon. I decided to pull rank and leave early.

Brenda eyed me as I told her I was off, "Should think so too, you look awful," she never pulled punches, "go on. Get your feet up, all under control here." I thanked her with a smile, called bye to Ruby and Trudie and with Kat on my heels, headed downstairs; literally as it turned out because the next thing I knew, I was flat out on the floor at the bottom surrounded by a lot of people talking at once in deliberately calm voices, and there was something wet on my face. It was all rather unexpected, I must say, and I was tempted to simply stay there with my eyes closed while I tried to work out what had happened. I realised that wouldn't be fair so I opened one cautiously.

"She's coming round."

"Don't move her."

"Stella, can you hear me?"

"Of course, I can hear you," I turned to look at Trudie but couldn't. I hoped it didn't mean I'd broken my neck, but it turned out that Joy, behind me, had my head in an iron grip. I thought I'd hear a lot better if she took both hands off my ears and told her so.

"Have to keep your head still." she said, "St John Ambulance."

"I don't need an ambulance."

"No, I did a course."

"That's for us to decide," said Brenda.

"What? Whether Joy did or didn't do a course?" I asked, everyone wisely ignored me, probably not the best time for jokes.

"This is silly, I'm calling 999." Hilary grabbed the phone on the reception desk.

"No, *don't,*" I said. "I'm not hurt. I don't want a fuss." then I chuckled; I was lying at the foot of our stairs, circled by Trudie, Ruby, Brenda, Hilary and Joy plus Kat at my right shoulder, who'd taken it upon herself to supply intermittent licks, supplementing the wet cloth someone had put on my forehead. Behind Hilary, Martin was hovering anxiously, no change there then, but so were two other people I'd never seen in my life before. Presumably they'd popped in to book a holiday and were now in the middle of a crisis. 'No fuss' didn't seem to be the order of the day. I stifled a laugh because I could see giggling was only going to further agitate everyone. I shut my eyes briefly because a ceiling light above my head was shining directly into my eyes.

"Uh oh, she's going again, I'm ringing," said Hilary.

"I am not going," I said sharply, "just give me a minute." It wasn't easy to concentrate, even when everyone stopped talking, there were all sorts of medical scenarios running through different minds. It was like watching an episode of Dr Kildare with the sound turned up and was distracting while I was attempting to do a 'Sam'.

When I'd been stabbed a year or so ago and he was sorting me out, he'd made it seem so simple. It wasn't necessary, he said, to create the 3D body image he automatically did, because injury usually gives off heat as the body tries to help itself; if you looked, you couldn't miss it. I'd never tried to follow up on that, there was enough hypochondria in the family already and I felt developing diagnostic abilities would help no-one, but now I did a quick survey and was pretty sure, there wasn't anything going on that shouldn't have been.

"Joy," I said, "let go my head, I haven't broken anything."

"What about the baby?" Brenda asked.

"No, don't think I broke the baby either."

"Kicking?" Trudie put a hand on my stomach and after a moment smiled, "kicking." A concerted sigh of relief went up followed by a chorus of consternation when I insisted I just wanted to go home.

We compromised by the team hauling me to my feet and sitting me on a chair with Hilary and Brenda stationed either side in case I toppled and Joy conjuring up tea and biscuits for everyone – well, we'd all had a shock – whilst decisions were made as to next steps because nobody would hear of me driving myself.

I didn't remember falling and I thought I'd know if I'd tripped. I didn't think I'd passed out either, I'd done enough of that at recent blood tests to recognise a faint when I saw one coming on, so no, I hadn't fainted. Ruby who could see the stairs from her desk said I'd stood at the top of the stairs for a moment, then went down like a sack of potatoes.

"Legs just folded," she reported, "you didn't even try and hold on to stop yourself. That's why drunks and babies don't usually get hurt when they fall - they don't realise what's happening." I wasn't really listening to her, I had no memory of falling but I remembered very well what had happened just before I fell.

Someone was chanting, I couldn't remember the words but I recognised their rhythm.

CHAPTER TWENTY-EIGHT

Confabs had been going on over my head; it didn't appear I had a vote. It was decided Joy would drive me home. If we were short staffed she was sometimes roped in to pick up or drop someone, so was insured on my car. Brenda nominated herself to ride shotgun and stay until David got home. Joy went off at a trot to get the car, and we walked out to meet her at the kerb; Brenda holding my arm, Ruby taking Kat's lead, Trudie carrying my bag and other stuff and Hilary in a supervisory and door-holding role. I was remonstrating that I was fine and honestly didn't need all this, when Trevor pitched up to collect Joy and the day got just a little bit more awkward.

"Everything alright?" he enquired with concern, as our procession advanced. It was a while since I'd seen him; he was as urbane as ever and with impeccable manners, immediately relieved Trudie of bag and files. I'd rather gone off him because I didn't like the changes in Joy, even though he made her so happy. I knew that was irrational, unfair and none of my business, I ought to make an effort to be less judgemental.

"We'll drive you home," he said.

"No, really, thanks, it's…"

He interrupted, "I insist," he made to take my other arm but Brenda nodded to where Joy was neatly sliding the Rancho into a conveniently vacated spot, just behind where he'd parked his car.

"Your lovely wife's been co-opted," she said, "that way Stella will have her car at home." Trevor was standing in front of us and Brenda made to walk round him. He didn't immediately move but looked briefly back over his shoulder at Joy, who'd got out to open the back door to let Kat jump in.

"I'm really not happy about Joy driving a strange car," he said, adding with a small inclination of the head, towards me, "certainly not with such a precious cargo."

I might not like what was in his head, which at a quick glance showed not only his assessment of Joy's abilities but the need, as always, to sort out the misguided and impulsive decisions women tend to make if left to their own devices. This was a man genuinely striving to do the right thing, even if underlying that was a slight air of martyrdom; it wasn't easy every day, keeping an eye on the girls in his office, ensuring they didn't do anything stupid and now here he was again, having to sort things out.

"Don't be so silly!" Brenda wasn't a woman who welcomed instruction and she'd taken against him long before I had. She'd had a terrible shock with my stair dive, so didn't need, didn't want and didn't intend, to stand on the pavement arguing. "It's not a strange car." She said, "Joy's driven it a lot."

Trevor swung on his heel. "Joy?" he said. She was back in the driver's seat and lowered the window.

"Hi Darling, actually well yes, I have."

"Don't remember you mentioning."

"Oh for goodness sake!" snapped Brenda, "she's driven the car before; she's driving it again. Follow if you want, but I'd like to get Stella home and resting," and she moved us decisively past him, settled me in the front, got in the back and pulled the door sharply shut behind her.

Joy hated to upset Trevor, he never deserved it and he was only making a fuss because he was over-protective, but right now she had her priorities, he had to understand that. She'd said she'd drive me home and that's what she was going to do, she smiled at him.

"Sweetheart, I didn't tell you, because I know how you worry, but honestly it's fine. Look, you go straight home, pop dinner in the oven for us, it's all ready. I'll catch a cab so I won't be in long after you. All sorted."

Actually it wasn't all sorted. Trevor wasn't angry, of course he wasn't, but he'd found the best way to deal with the fairer sex, bless their hearts, was to remain calm but firm, clearly explaining the reasoning behind any decision. This time though, that ruddy Brenda woman had interfered, she was a bad influence on his Joy. No matter, he reassured himself, in a loving relationship, self-control was essential so he'd follow that ridiculously cumbersome car, full of misguided women. Then he'd take Joy home and they'd talk things over. Their marriage worked so well because they did have rules and agreements. Once any of those went by the board, the order of things was disrupted, and disruption, like anger, did no-one any good in the long run.

In my car, heading for home, all three of us were quiet but for me with my current diminished control over my mental shutters, quiet didn't equate to silence. On the contrary, Brenda was loudly going through the list of things she'd do; starting with getting me into bed, whether I liked it or not. She wasn't sure what time David got in, but she'd not leave until he did, meantime should she ring my Mother? She didn't want to give her a fright. She also wanted to check, without alarming me in any way, that my hospital bag was packed, just in case the fall had set anything off.

Joy was concentrating on the driving; it was something she enjoyed and she was good at. She'd lost a certain amount of confidence because she wasn't doing it as often as previously. When they went out, Trevor insisted on taking the wheel, a man's job he'd said with a loving kiss on the forehead, her job was to relax, look lovely and watch the world go by. She hoped he wasn't too upset; Brenda could be a bit bossy and Trevor hated bossy, but perhaps she herself hadn't handled it as well as she could, but then Trevor always told her laughingly, she'd not been around when they were handing out tact. On the other hand, if she'd not done her bit in getting me home and something went wrong with the baby, she'd never have forgiven herself. She'd apologise to him properly when she got in and make custard to go with dessert, Trevor loved home-made custard.

"This turning Stella?" she asked.

"Yes, it's number 1, but it's right down at the end, near the park. Thanks so much for this Joy." She took her hand off the gear stick and gave my knee a companionable squeeze.

"Don't be daft. Just don't give us another fright like that."

"Too right," Brenda chipped in from the back, "nerves won't take it; I'll end up like your Mother-in-law." We laughed, Laura had a tendency to start violently at the slightest unexpected noise, this made everyone else jump too – bit like a disjointed Mexican wave going round the room.

David wasn't home when we got there and Brenda, after a brief but spirited discussion about bed, gave in and let me stretch out on the sofa instead, insisting on a blanket over my legs which I accepted in a spirit of compromise. As she headed for the kitchen, I said I honestly didn't think I could drink more tea, but she said she was going to make it anyway, then perhaps we'd phone my mother, keep her up to speed. She added casually, we might as well also go through the stuff I'd packed for hospital, check I had everything there, not that it'd be needed yet but it never hurts to be ahead of yourself. I said I hadn't packed yet and she sucked in a small breath and said well now was as good a time as any, wasn't it?

I knew when I was beaten and in truth, wasn't feeling too clever. I didn't think anything was wrong baby-wise, it was more the inundation of thought I was having trouble shutting out. As if that wasn't enough, amidst the cacophony were some lines I must have heard somewhere, they were circling round and round in my head and giving me a headache. I put both hands over my ears, which of course achieved nothing, other than alarming Joy.

"Stella?" she said and Brenda was out of the kitchen in a flash.

"Just a bit of a headache," I said.

"What sort of headache?" Brenda wanted to know.

"Nothing to worry about, honestly, I often get them. The midwife said if they're really bad, I can take a couple of paracetamol tablets, but I'll wait and see, sometimes it goes on its own."

The doorbell rang and Joy went to get it, accompanied by Kat, who liked to keep an eye on comings and goings. It was Trevor, and we heard him insisting he wouldn't leave until he'd checked there wasn't anything he could do for me.

"You drove very well dear," he said to Joy, as they came into the room. She smiled with pleasure; she knew she had but it was nice to have him say it. I hoped Brenda would keep her mouth shut, should have known better.

"She's an excellent driver."

Trevor smiled warmly, "Indeed she is - when she concentrates and doesn't get distracted by pretty things in shop windows," he laughed and put his arm round her, "isn't that right darling?" Brenda caught my eye; I shook my head slightly and she busied herself tidying some magazines on the table. The tension between Brenda and Trevor was palpable; these were two people who did not like each other one little bit, although her thoughts were a lot less complicated than his. She'd come across his type time and again, could chew him up and spit him out without missing a beat, saw and hated what he was doing to Joy and itched to do something about it.

He knew her type too and usually steered well clear. It wasn't that he couldn't give as good as he got, it was the pointlessness of having to. Why waste his valuable time on a stupid woman who thought she knew better than he did? Joy was fond of her but then Joy was a soft touch for anyone who gave her a smile, and sometimes needed a word here and there, to keep her on the right track.

He turned to me, "Stella, is there anything more we can do before we head off?" I smiled and shook my head, but his last thought had annoyed me. I spoke to Joy and yes I did it deliberately and no, I shouldn't have.

"Thanks so much Joy for stepping in and getting me home. You know, I'm not going to fit behind that wheel much longer, you might be doing lots more toing and froing, will that be alright?" she moved away from Trevor's arm and bent to give me a swift hug.

"You know it will; whatever you need."

I raised my arm to hold her too. "We all throw a lot of stuff in your lap, but you do know we couldn't manage without you?"

"Oh shut up will you, all those hormones are making you sloshy," she laughed, but she was pleased. Trevor took a step forward to take her elbow.

"I'm a lucky man," he said fondly, "don't think I don't know it. Now best be heading off," he paused, "did you give Stella the car keys back?"

Joy nodded, "On the hall table."

"Are you sure darling? Didn't see them when I came in?"

"I'll get them Stella, so you know exactly where they are."

Trevor smiled indulgently, "Forget her head if it wasn't screwed on." Joy was back in an instant, worried.

"I swear I put them there."

"Not to worry," I said, "can't be far." Too right they weren't. I knew exactly where they were, how they got there and why.

Trevor, who did indeed deeply love his wife and consider himself a lucky man, nevertheless felt for her own good, the occasional misstep was not a bad thing. In the same way exercise was good for the heart, exercise was good for the mind; brain-training he called it, the occasional harmless manoeuvre strengthened efficiency and taught people to check and double check and thus avoid similar happenings. He used this often in the office, worked wonders for some of the daft girls he'd had working for him over the years. The best thing was he never had to plan it; opportunities just arose. Now he shook his head gently.

"I bet you automatically slipped them in your handbag, silly bean."

Joy frowned, "Of course not, why..."

"Humour me Joy, I expect Stella wants us out of her hair now. Now, where's your handbag?

"Outside in the hall."

"No, it's not, look it's here. Honestly my darling, what are you like?" he picked it up from the floor beside the sofa and handed it to her. The keys should have been lying near the top, where he'd put them as he brought the bag in unnoticed. They weren't, because I'd lifted them out and put them on the floor under the hall table.

"Brenda," I said, "be a love, pop your head out, if Joy put them on the table, they most likely got knocked off when we dumped those files." Brenda was back in a few seconds with the keys.

"Mystery solved," she said. Joy relieved, stopped rummaging through her bag.

"And you did leave your bag in the hall," I said, "I picked it up and brought it in here, thought it was mine, it's me who's the daft one." I smiled warmly at Trevor, 'put that,' I thought, 'in your brain and train it!' But smug didn't last long. It never does.

It seemed that what was sauce for the goose wasn't so great for the gander. Trevor knew he'd put the keys in the handbag and because his confidence had never been eroded by anyone, he had no doubts. He therefore jumped to the only possible conclusion; it couldn't have been me because I'd been on the sofa the whole time, it was that that bloody Brenda. Must've spotted him with the bag and taken the keys out. That there was precious little logic, and even less likelihood in that, didn't seem to strike him but in his head, behind the smile and gentle joshing, something stirred.

Brenda didn't know quite what had been going on, but she saw and sensed his discomfiture and couldn't resist.

"*Now* who's a silly Bean?" she enquired cheerfully, and Joy laughed. From behind the rigid day-to-day control in Trevor's head because, after all, control of himself as much as others was what he was all about, something was seeping. I felt it, wasn't sure what it meant, did know it was my inability to leave well alone that had possibly prompted it. With a swift apology to the baby, who'd had quite a day of it, I rolled gently off the sofa which was luckily quite low.

CHAPTER TWENTY-NINE

Distraction is always effective and in the general fuss and consternation - getting me off the floor, back on the sofa, re-covered with the blanket and renewed ambulance discussions, the tension in the room and in Trevor dissipated. Then my parents arrived, Brenda having called and whilst they were having events fully explained, David arrived home.

If he was surprised to find our small living room busier than Piccadilly Circus on a Saturday night, he adapted swiftly, took charge and proposed a compromise. As I was insisting I didn't want to head off anywhere in an ambulance, he phoned the number Mavis had given me and although she herself wasn't on duty, one of the other midwives was reassuringly unbothered.

"Easy to misjudge size and weight of tummies at this stage so it is, she probably lost balance for the minute. But you know, Baby's ever so well cushioned in there, won't have felt a thing." Nudged urgently from either side by Brenda and my Mother, David asked about hospital.

"Not at all, only if something's going on," she said.

"Anything going on?" he repeated looking over at me, I shook my head, presuming she meant with the baby, as opposed to all the other complicated areas of my life.

"There you are then pet," she said comfortably when the news was relayed, "bed, warm drink, feet on a hottie, good night's sleep, right as rain by morning." It seemed the emergency wasn't too much of an emergency after all. I'd been planning to stop work within the next week or two anyway, I could still do quite a bit from home, but once again there were people busy talking over my head, and the general consensus was for the sake of everyone's nerves, maternity leave should start sooner rather than later.

I was watching and listening to Joy and Trevor as they said their goodbyes. If I'd been disturbed at the changes in Joy, having now seen them together, I was even more worried. I shouldn't have done what I did with the keys, there was no doubt that together,

Brenda and I had poked the bear, which as anyone with common sense knows is not a clever idea, but I understood a lot more now.

They were in balance as a couple, if it stayed that way and both were content, it was nothing to do with anyone else. There was no doubt Joy adored him. She was an intelligent woman who'd made decisions; he had his funny ways, but who didn't? And if keeping him happy meant following those routes and rules he preferred, that didn't bother her overmuch. Trevor indisputably loved her too, it was his pleasure to spoil her with gifts, surround her with little luxuries, guide her when he thought she needed guidance. He was pleased and proud of the way he was shaping her to be the best person she could be in every possible way. It was a happy, relationship which would last - as long as the status quo did, but it was built on a fragile foundation.

Earlier, searching for the keys because Trevor naturally assumed if something silly had been done, it was she who'd done it – Joy had felt humiliated, shown up in front of me and Brenda. She hadn't liked that, especially as it turned out not to have been her fault at all. Trevor wasn't always right! And with that thought, and from behind the barriers we all put up to channel our thinking along routes we want, there was irritation. If I felt concerned about Joy before, it was nothing to what I felt now and what made it worse was worry that I'd allowed my view of right and wrong to colour hers?

That wasn't the only thing playing on my mind; sipping yet more tea on the sofa with all sorts going on above and around me, I was still mulling over why I fell. I wasn't much the wiser for thinking, but what had come back to me was what I'd heard, not that it clarified anything. It was that ruddy bloody rhyme, the rhythm of which churned continuously in my head, but now I had some words too, '*I wish, I wish, I wish I knew, exactly what to do with you?*' Could it be that I was just rehearsing rhymes for the possibly choppy waters of parenting, or was this something else altogether?

* * * *

The new regime, or as everyone persisted in calling it, maternity leave, started immediately even though we were only halfway through November and nothing was due to happen for four or five weeks. Despite being constantly in touch with the office and having lots of work to do at home, I'd wondered whether I'd feel a bit cut off but as it transpired, that was the least of my worries because the nearest and dearest wasted no time in setting up an informal rota, which pleased David no end. It meant people were always popping in unexpectedly, bearing chicken soup, smoked salmon sandwiches with the crusts cut off, pastries or similar goodies and more often than not, someone forgot the exact time they should be 'popping in', which meant two or three people arrived at more or less the same time and the sort of well-catered, convivial atmosphere that had always prevailed in the office, simply continued at my home.

I wasn't worried how well *Simple Solutions* would function without me; Aunt Kitty had an eagle eye on the accounts and on the odd occasion credit chasing was needed, seized the moment with delight. Brenda had an equally fierce focus on work coming in and work going out and after all, I was only at the other end of the phone should I be required - or as I came to realise - every time it occurred to one of them that they should call with a query, to reassure me I wasn't now superfluous to requirements, which was really very thoughtful.

I was still having bad dreams, couldn't really remember them when I woke but knew they hadn't been fun. They left me drained and apprehensive, adding to the background discomfort I still felt when I thought about Ruth and as with a sore tooth, I thought about her a lot. That wretched two-line rhyme was also still doing the rounds in my head and that made me uneasy too. Apparently the best thing to counter an earworm is another earworm, so I went with *'I do not like thee Dr Fell, though why that is I cannot tell.'* It was from way back, when my Mother used to walk me to school, and needed to divert my mind and keep me grounded - flying would have got me there quicker, but might have caused consternation at the school gates, so we adopted Dr Fell and took turns chanting as we walked. I thought he'd helped then, maybe he'd help now.

* * * *

I left it a couple of weeks, before I spoke to Boris again, I wasn't thrilled with how our last chat had gone, apart from which it wasn't easy to find a time when I was on my own. In the meantime, I'd been scouring the daily delivered paper and was relieved to find no odd happenings were reported - well, at least nothing I felt might be Devlin related. When I did get hold of Boris, he waded in with questions before I had a chance to voice any of mine.

"How are you?" he said.

"Fine thanks."

"Any changes?" Did he, I wondered aloud, mean the swollen ankles I couldn't see anymore, or the industrial size bump which was why I couldn't see them?

"I meant," he said patiently, "have you heard anything from the baby?"

"Nope, no call, no letter, not even a lousy postcard - kids huh?" Boris was unamused, and I remembered I wasn't just phoning for a bit of light banter.

"What happened about Devlin?"

"You don't have to worry; the matter is sorted."

"Well? Was it him? Was it my fault?" I asked with trepidation.

"It would seem that waking him the way you did..."

"I had no choice."

"I'm not criticising, it was a last ditch try and it worked, I believe you saved his life," he paused.

"There's a 'but' coming isn't there?" I said.

"Indeed. It appears you may have inadvertently kick-started something in him which might otherwise have stayed dormant."

"I didn't know that was possible," I said.

There was another brief pause; Boris liked to choose words carefully. "It isn't something we've come across before, so we are a little in the dark. That said, it is not something with which we could ever experiment."

"Dreck did." I said. Over the years, Dr Karl Dreck had never diminished in memory. He'd overseen an ambitious, government-funded social study on the hunt for ESP, but had taken the project a great many unorthodox and chilling steps further.

"So it was Devlin? Why?"

"Because he could, because he had no concept of consequences. Trust me, he is being taken care of," I flinched, he caught the thought and barked a laugh, "Don't be ridiculous."

"Should I go and see him, where is he anyway? What about his mother, the family, what do they think?" I felt dreadful, "do they know it was me?"

"Stop firing questions, this is not a good time."

"Why?"

"What did I just say, no more questions. Ah Stella, I'm afraid you'll have to excuse me, there is my doorbell ringing." I put the phone down convinced of two things; they were definitely keeping me away from something I was sure I ought not to be kept away from, and Boris was never going to be up for a best actor Oscar.

It was around that time that something else started up. At least I think it was then, it may have been earlier, but because initially it was in the background, woven in with my Ruth anxiety and the Devlin stuff, I couldn't be sure. This though, when I took the time to think about it, was different and not great! It was low keening, a soft grieving, and what all that was about I couldn't begin to fathom. It certainly wasn't the sort of alarm shriek that necessitated a call to Boris, it wasn't even there constantly but drifted in and drifted out and whenever I tried to focus, it slipped through my fingers like fog. It was a sadness wrapped in guilt and grief. I hoped to God it wasn't the baby and was briefly chilled to the core, before acknowledging that was plain stupid, these emotions were adult and complex and coming from much farther away.

There were plenty of issues on which to brood during my enforced resting time at home. Would I ever get into normal clothes again? Why couldn't I talk to Ruth and Rachael? Would any of us ever understand why Billie Joe McAllister jumped off the Tallahatchie Bridge?

Closer to home; why could I not grasp the NCT different breathing levels? How many more pots of chicken soup and casseroles could we fit in the fridge and if one more person said, 'enjoy doing nothing now, you'll miss it when the baby comes.' could I avoid throwing something that wouldn't just be a tantrum?

CHAPTER THIRTY

With the 'keep an eye on Stella' rota at full strength, you might have thought the house couldn't get any more crowded, but then we had to factor in Mr Pegneddy, called in to help finish off the nursery. David had spent a lot of time sweating and swearing over the gorgeous paper we'd bought. It turned out that unless each panel was lined up with scientific precision on the wall, cute elephants, pigs and ducks became detached from trunks, trotters and beaks. This made for a rather ghastly hodgepodge and not a great way to introduce the infant to the world of nature.

I felt I should contribute to the decorating and David and I had a brief but brisk exchange of views. He said I should put my feet up and I said I'd been doing that all week, but it turned out to be a bitter victory. No sooner had I taken up my assistant decorator role than I misjudged the flight of a tin of paint I wanted. It crash-landed on my foot and I was forced to retire in disarray and agony. I was instantly demoted to refreshments and despite my foot swelling to gargantuan proportions, felt obliged to put on a brave face and insist it didn't hurt in the least.

By the time the paper was finally up, it did look lovely, although I had some concerns about one top corner of the room, where it hadn't stuck perfectly. David tired, but alpha male triumphant, assured me it just needed a touch more paste. Unfortunately, the following morning when he popped his head round the door to admire his handiwork, almost every single strip had peeled gently off the walls and come to rest, concertina-like on the skirting board. Mr Pegneddy, blue-lighted in, surveyed the catastrophe with an experienced eye.

"Well, you've gone and got your bloody paste wrong 'aven't you?"

David conceded this could be so, "Can you fix it?"

Mr Peg sniffed "Mebbe," he said. "Eddy?" Eddy glanced at my stomach and muttered;

"Probbly, best be quickish."

* * * *

Hilary appeared in the kitchen one morning as I was making the first couple of strong teas for the decorating team. I raised an eyebrow at her.

"I used Brenda's key," she said, waving it at me, "don't mind do you, said I was going to pop in and she gave it to me before she left; said you might be asleep." She gave me a kiss on the cheek, and shivered, "Freezing out there, I'm not stopping, Martin's outside in the car, I brought this." Hilary's needles had not been idle in recent months; she was producing on a grand scale. This time though, it wasn't one of her knitted efforts which tended towards the chunky, but an exquisitely detailed and decorated white cot quilt.

"From the Sewing Ladies," she laid it on the kitchen counter, having first given a precautionary wipe with the sleeve of her coat, and smiled at my pleasure, "Smashing isn't it? They wanted it brought now, just in case they said, but they'll be round to see you soon. Oh, for goodness sake!" she reached behind me for a tissue from the box, "here, it's only hormones Petal."

"I know," I sobbed,

"These for inside?" she picked up the two cups and I could hear her exchanging pleasantries with Mr Peg and Eddy before she popped her head back round the door again.

"I'm off now, you alright?" I nodded, blew my nose and we laughed. I walked with her to the door, waved to Martin in the car and was turning to go back inside when Brenda's scream reached me, actually not so much a scream, more a battle cry. It was so sudden and so loud, my knees buckled and I fell against the wall. I must have made a sound because Hilary turned and hurried back and Mr Peg shot out of the nursery.

"Funny turn?" he said, "Not to worry, my Mrs had lots of 'em."

I grabbed Hilary's arm, tighter than I thought because she flinched, "You said 'before Brenda left', where is she, where'd she go?" Hilary gawped at me; I shook the arm I was holding, "Where. Is. She?"

"Joy's."

"Why?"

"She hasn't been in this week Joy, I mean – flu."

"And Brenda's gone over?"

"Said, didn't I? Just to see how she is. Look, come and sit down and when she gets back..."

"Got the address?"

"Brenda's?"

"*No,* Joy's. D'you know where she lives?"

"Course I do."

"Come on," I pulled her towards the car. Martin was standing with the driver's door open, trying to work out what was going on. Behind us Mr. Peg was taking all this in capable stride.

"Carry on then, shall we?" he asked mildly, I waved backwards in assent, and then saw Katerina peering from behind his leg. "Hold on to Kat for me? D'you mind?"

"Don't you worry yourself, my little love," he nodded amiably and shut the door. I got into the back seat of the car, faster than I'd have thought possible, and yelled at Martin.

"Get in, drive."

"Hospital? Right-you-are!" Martin was surprised but in control, and Hilary who'd leapt into the passenger seat was jerked back as he hit the accelerator and we took off, in his head, he had flashing lights and a siren.

"No, not the hospital, Joy's." I yelled, leaning forward between the seats.

"Why's Joy coming?" Martin yelled back. He'd hit the A41, and was straight into the fast lane. Hilary turned; she'd no idea what was going on but had a good grasp of what wasn't.

"It's not the baby?"

"No."

"Good thing," she muttered, "we forgot your hospital bag. Martin go to Joy's."

"But…"

"Martin," Hilary snapped, "*Joy's.*" Martin said something under his breath, but so used was he to following Hilary's instruction, especially when hissed, that he did an immediate, immaculate U-turn and slammed his foot down.

Martin, wasn't one of the most sensitive people I'd come across, but he'd picked up the urgency and drove like a bat out of hell, hunched over the wheel and swearing at drivers who didn't get out his way quick enough. I had my eyes closed, listening for Brenda; but there was nothing. I was holding tightly to the back of Martin's seat as if I could will us there faster. When I opened my eyes, Hilary's scared gaze met mine. She was clutching the strap above the passenger door, didn't understand what was going on but knew it wasn't good.

Martin did a sideways swoop across a wide tree-lined road, skidded a little and screeched to a halt outside a large detached house. I was out of the car first, Hilary caught up with me halfway down the path and breathless and panicky we reached the door together. There was no answer to the bell and even Hilary heavily wielding the knocker didn't bring a response. Inside the house though, everything was under control, Trevor's control.

CHAPTER THIRTY-ONE

Hilary took in my anguished face and said, "We have to break the door down."

"Don't be daft," Martin had caught up with us. While they exchanged glares, I did my best to imitate Ed and deal with what turned out to be several locks. I had to be quick and it wasn't pretty, but;

"Look, it's not locked," I said, pushing it open.

"We can't just walk in!" but Martin protested to empty air; I was halfway up the stairs with Hilary on my heels.

Life in the Hamilton household had not been sailing in calm waters for a good couple of weeks now, and the disruption arose directly from that day when everyone made such a God-damn ridiculous fuss about a silly fall. Trevor couldn't comprehend precisely what it was that had caused the current difficulty, but he wasn't a man to shy away from whatever had to be done to get things back on track. He was very well aware you had to take charge of an issue, before an issue took charge of you.

He must have heard us downstairs at the front door but knew we couldn't get in, triple locks and a bolt. You could never be too hot on security nowadays, crimes day and night and after that bloody woman Brenda had turned up on the doorstep that morning, he'd been scrupulous in locking up after her. When Hilary and I burst breathlessly shoulder to shoulder into the bedroom, it came as a surprise, but he thought he hid it well, greeted us politely and apologised for the bit of a state things were in.

Joy was on the unmade bed, one arm extended above her head. One leg of a pair of tights was knotted so tightly round her wrist that her dangling hand was pale and bloodless. The other leg of the tights, had been wound several times around an ornate wooden finial on the headboard and securely knotted. Joy wasn't completely conscious, her eyelids drooping shut for far too long with every blink and when she did open them, her gaze was dazed and unfocused. She was struggling to make sense of what she was seeing and wanted to ask someone what was going on but couldn't, owing to the wide brown expanse of shiny duct tape covering her mouth, puckering the skin of her face in an extended stretch.

Across the room, Brenda lay spread-eagled on the busy brown and green flowered carpet. Her head was at an acutely unnatural angle, jammed against the base of a looming, mahogany wardrobe. There was a long rip in the skin of her face, running raggedly from the outer edge of her right eye, down across her cheek bone to the corner of her mouth, it was bleeding quite heavily and because of the angle at which she was lying blood had dribbled over the bridge of her nose and ribboned down the other side of her face. Trevor had pulled up the bench type, dressing-table stool, so he was sitting close to Brenda; he hoped, he said, we'd forgive him for not getting up.

It was a lot to take in. Hilary, by my side gave a low hoarse cry and froze momentarily because she couldn't decide which of the women she should rush to first. Martin behind me simply froze. Shock petrifies, holds you rigid and for several beats I was with Martin, for which I had no excuse, it wasn't as if I hadn't known more or less what we'd find.

At Hilary's cry, Joy turned her head, eyes widening as she saw us, crowded close in the doorway and then Hilary was at her side, reaching to untie the tights.

"No," Trevor spoke quietly, but firmly, "Hilary, not now, if you wouldn't mind. Please move away from the bed." Hilary, without pausing, told him succinctly what she thought of his suggestion and what he could do with himself, and I didn't disagree, luckily she wasn't party to what was going on in Trevor's head; mind you, he wasn't either.

Currently, his mind was working on three entirely different levels, so I could see why he was having a problem. On the surface, temporarily in charge, he was cool, calm and courteous. Below that but surfacing with increasing frequency, was a rich vein of justifiable anger and righteous indignation. 'What had he done to deserve this?' it wanted to know, 'Only given Joy everybloodything a woman could ask for,' it answered. 'And,' it added, 'look at the patience and care spent in helping her become the exceptional person she could be; although of course she still had a way to go.'

And beneath calm and controlling, below anger and indignation, there was a whole other layer which, whilst unexpected, couldn't be denied. It was that layer that was registering the tremendous amount of pleasure he was deriving from actions he'd been forced to take.

All in all, It hadn't been a great morning. Joy was still getting mileage out of this flu bug she'd had - high temperature, sneezing, aches and pains, etc. but he did feel, after two days in bed she should start pulling herself together. She hadn't got up when he did, said she still felt dreadful, and then she'd been yammering on about something, all the while he was getting dressed. It irritated him.

They'd discussed this fault of hers several times before. It was quite simple. If she asked a question and he answered, all well and good. If she asked a question and he didn't answer, that indicated he didn't want to. Finished. End of. It was a concept she hadn't really grasped. This morning, he jokingly said, if she didn't stop going on, he'd have to tape her mouth. He had the roll of tape in his bedside table, it was something he'd done before - but only in fun, it had made things quite a bit more exciting one night after a couple of glasses of wine each, and she hadn't minded.

But this morning, when he'd taken the tape out of the drawer and placed it pointedly on the bed, she'd gone mad; sat up, started telling him off for no reason at all. He'd been at a bit of a loss; this wasn't the Joy he knew and loved and before he could decide the best way to handle it, she was climbing out of bed and then she swore at him, which was crazy - Joy never got cross, certainly never swore. He was enormously relieved when he suddenly realised what was going on. His poor girl: her temperature must have shot up, she was delirious, didn't know what she was saying and now she'd dragged a suitcase from the bottom of the wardrobe and was opening drawers and putting clothes in at random.

When he wrestled her back to the bed, she didn't seem to understand he was doing it for her own good and struggled like a wild thing under his hands. Seeing her like that was extremely unpleasant and distressing and in trying to loosen his hold, she succeeded only in giving her head an almighty crack on the headboard. Thankfully, she was dazed and silent for the minutes it took him to grab the first thing to hand - a pair of tights she'd taken from the drawer - and secure her to the bed. He was stroking her hair back from her face, explaining he was going to get her a couple of aspirin to bring down that rotten temperature and then he'd fetch a nice cup of tea. But when she opened her eyes she clearly hadn't listened to a word he'd said, didn't understand it was for her own good and when he tried to go over it again, she was making so much noise, he had to put the tape over her mouth, it was just going to be on long enough for him to explain about the fever. Then the doorbell rang, and on the doorstep was the pain in the arse from the office.

He said how lovely it was to see her but explained Joy was still poorly and not up to seeing anyone. And she said, she always had an answer, that was exactly why she'd come; she'd brought soup or some such ridiculousness. He'd thanked her nicely, held out his hand to take the container, said he knew Joy would be touched and he mustn't keep her from the office, but no, that wasn't good enough for her. She moved forward and she was a big woman, so he had to step back and before he knew it, she was halfway up the stairs, saying she'd just pop her head round the door, wish Joy well, see if she needed anything else.

He started after her, because of course he needed to explain what she was going to see, but had to turn back to lock and bolt the door and by the time he'd got up the stairs, it was too late for explanation. As he came through the bedroom door, she flew at him like some sort of a she-devil, letting out what could only be described as a war cry, it was truly alarming. Clearly the woman was dangerously deranged and he reacted instinctively. His clenched fist hit bone and his signet ring scored deeply across her face as she was knocked back against the wardrobe which luckily was as solidly built as she was. She slid awkwardly downwards, her bottom hit the carpet, and she toppled sideways and lay still. He hadn't intended to hit her that hard but after all, he had to defend himself and Joy too, and people really should keep their noses out of other people's business.

Behind him, Joy was now getting herself in a proper state, throwing herself about and that was only going to make her temperature worse, and even with the tape on she was making such a noise he could feel the first creepings of a headache. He decided if anyone was going to get aspirin and a cup of tea, it ought to be him first, he honestly couldn't remember when he'd last had such a stressful morning. He popped to the bathroom for aspirin, came back and peered down at Brenda. She really was bloody Brenda now; he chuckled; one of his major attributes he felt was the ability to find the humour in most things. Then he went downstairs to make tea. No point in making for the women yet; Joy was in too much of a lather and Brenda was spark out.

The aspirin saw off the headache, he phoned the office to say he'd been detained, finished his tea and went back upstairs to have a think about what to do next, and then the ruddy doorbell went again and despite the fact that nobody could possibly get in, the room was suddenly full of people. More noses in his business, and when he'd politely asked the Hilary woman, who always smelt like a stale ashtray to please not interfere, she was unnecessarily offensive. She was jolly lucky he was a reasonable man.

CHAPTER THIRTY-TWO

He was not going to descend to Hilary's level of vulgarity, but he felt he needed to indicate this was no laughing matter. Still seated on the stool, he leaned down to one side and picked up something. It was heavy, an effort to lift from his sitting position but he didn't want to stand, standing he felt was more aggressive and he didn't want things to escalate.

"This," he said reasonably, showing them what he was holding with both hands, "is a cast iron doorstop, shaped like a tortoise, d'you see? The parents bought it years ago." He leaned forward, an elbow resting along each knee so the doorstop was now poised above Brenda's head. "If," he said, "you all turn right around and go, we'll say no more," he paused. "If you persist in interfering in what really is nothing to do with you, I will drop this onto her head. Now what's it to be?"

Normally, in an awkward situation I would have assessed, decided and implemented whatever needed to be done. Implementation isn't always right, but it's usually better than hanging around to see how things go. Now though, it felt as if everything was happening too quickly and I hadn't caught up, in fact the room seemed to be tilting slightly and I felt the need to hold tightly to the door jamb next to me. There was some kind of interference coming from somewhere or someone, it was blurring both my reasoning and my balance and then I felt the faint beginnings of a not-quite-comfortable tightening around the baby, increasing to not-so-comfortable-at-all. It was familiar, nothing to worry about, a Braxton Hicks, my body rehearsing for when the time was right, but oddly enough it counteracted the interference in my head.

I straightened up; Brenda wasn't dead, which had been my initial horror, I could see her chest rising and falling but I didn't know how badly she was hurt and was pretty sure a cast iron item on her head wasn't going to improve things. I lifted it out of his hands; he was right it was heavy, and sent it swiftly across the room. It struck the opposite wall with a dull thud and made a dent before hitting the floor.

Trevor stood abruptly, he wasn't sure exactly what had happened there, he hadn't planned to throw the doorstop, but in his head violence was fast superseding control, although righteous indignation was struggling for position too. The current circumstance was directly and incontrovertibly the fault of all these interfering, jibber-jabbering women. Lessons needed teaching. He pulled his foot back to kick Brenda in the ribs and I knocked him flying in the opposite direction. He landed clumsily, crashing hard against the wall, slipping sideways then out of sight on the far side of the bed. On the bedside table sat an ornate wrought-iron lamp base up which, three seriously over-fed cherubs were climbing towards a faded pink, tassel-trimmed shade. He must have hit the table corner on his way down because it tipped slightly, the lamp slid and from the emitted 'ooof', must have been nearly as heavy as the tortoise. From Joy, I registered a fleeting shaft of pleasure, she loathed that lamp, it'd belonged to his mother and he wouldn't hear of changing it, then I think she passed out again. I hoped she didn't have concussion.

Hilary was still having trouble with the tights; I had a go at ripping them but couldn't, so I burnt through them. As they split, Joy's arm flopped loose, still tightly braceleted and Hilary suddenly remembered she had scissors on her. Whipping them from her coat pocket she cut away the material to reveal and relieve the sore wrist beneath. I thought, when we had a moment, I must tell her it wasn't sensible to carry scissors like that, what if she fell? Someone nudged me and I jumped. Martin was behind me.

"Called Police," he mouthed, jerking his head slightly to a phone on a landing table, then his eyes widened and he took a precautionary step back as Trevor made a sudden reappearance, surging up from the far side of the bed like a demented Jack-in-the-Box. He staggered to his feet, then flopped down next to Joy who was just coming round again. She saw him and shrank back against Hilary, who put both arms round her and hissed at him - an entirely instinctive, animal response, and all the more effective for that. Trevor, jerked back a little but his need to put the truth out there was stronger than anything.

"Listen," he said, struggling to sit up, "this isn't how it looks, Joy, tell them," he suddenly leaned over and ripped the tape fiercely from her face. She screamed as it came away, taking a lot of skin with it. Hilary, leaning over her, had tried to bat him away but wasn't in the right position to reach him so I knocked him unconscious. Caught off balance on one elbow, his eyes rolled up and he toppled slowly back off the bed and out of sight again. I assume he landed on the lamp. I wasn't sorry.

There were a few seconds while those of us still conscious took a breath, then Martin cautiously stepped to the end of the bed, peered, then white with fright turned back.

"I think you've killed him Hilary. For Christ's sake, how hard did you hit him?" Hilary, having charged in like Boadicea spotting a Roman, was now starting to crumple a little at the edges, she clutched Joy even tighter.

"I didn't touch him," she said, "I couldn't reach."

"Don't talk daft," I said, "of course he's not dead, just knocked out, nothing you did Hilary, he overbalanced." She relaxed a little and Martin, now Trevor was out the way, let his better nature take over and moved to help her sit Joy up. Hilary was using her hanky to try and blot away some of the blood blooming across Joy's face. Nobody questioned what I'd said, people don't when circumstances are on the fraught side and memory's the most unreliable of all our senses.

I let go of the door jamb, although not without an effort. I didn't feel too brilliant and whatever was messing with my head, was still at it. I took Trevor's place on the dressing table stool and bent to feel Brenda's pulse; I felt her neck, just below her chin as Rachael had instructed me years ago in a not dissimilar situation. The pulse was strong and the ugly cut across her face had stopped bleeding. I abandoned the stool to kneel clumsily, and in the absence of anything else, tried to dab away some of the blood with the edge of my maternity smock.

"Ouch," she said loudly, I jumped and she opened her eyes, "what're you *doing*?" she swatted smock and hand away.

"Don't move," I said, pushing her down gently.

"She OK?" Hilary called over.

"'Course I'm bloody OK. Where's that bastard, I'll teach him to hit me."

"Seems to be back to normal." I reported back to Hilary, as Brenda clambered unsteadily to her feet and I grabbed her hand. I wanted to stand too, but that wasn't going to happen without help. She pulled me up next to her and we swayed a bit, holding each other for balance before Martin took action again – he was turning into a proper power-house. He tried to sit us both back on the stool but it was instantly clear that wasn't going to work without one of us falling off the end, so he led Brenda to the end of the bed. She sat heavily and turned, the first time she and Joy got a proper look at each other and both were shocked into silence. I felt lightheaded, mainly from the noise in my head and put it into my hands for a moment or two to see if that helped.

"'M'alright." I muttered, to reassure Hilary whose anxiety was thrumming across the room. Then there was the shocking sound of the front door slamming back hard against the wall, and what sounded like an army storming the stairs yelling "Police."

"Oh, dear God," said Hilary, "I'm in Z Cars," and slid off the side of the bed in a dead faint, at least I hoped it was just that, although I felt a bit peeved she'd got in first. It wasn't an army, just two reassuringly bulky policemen who took in the scene and had to be dissuaded from cuffing Martin who was slapping Hilary's face to bring her round. Behind and almost obscured by larger colleagues and high helmets, was a smaller man who looked thoroughly cheesed off. If there was one thing he hated, it was a domestic. In his time, he'd seen too many people battered black and blue, still insisting they'd walked into a cupboard door. Time wasted and no arrest to go on the sheet. And then he caught sight of me and became even less thrilled.

"I know you, don't I?" he said accusingly, I knew him too, Detective Sergeant Mousegood, who could forget a name like that? He'd taken my statement after the Lowbell fiasco, he'd had a nasty cold then, his small pointed nose, red raw from handkerchief action and I saw he was sniffing now, maybe not a cold, perhaps hay fever? From a pocket he extracted hanky and notepad and I admitted that yes, he did know me.

"Those nutters in Hampstead, wasn't it? He said surveying the room with a jaundiced eye, "What is it with you and trouble? Hobby is it?"

I could see the telling of what had transpired was going to fall to me as Martin was busy protesting his innocence, Hilary was spark out and Brenda and Joy didn't seem to have a coherent word to share between them. I started, but was stopped by one of the uniforms who'd removed his helmet and immediately looked less intimidating.

"Hang on hen," fifties, with a head of thick silver hair and eyes which had seen too much over the years. He'd identified himself as PC Macleish, and when not yelling 'Police' with the intention of putting the fear of God in you, was softly spoken. "Still in the house is he?"

"Trevor?"

"He the scrote who's done this?"

I indicated, "Other side of the bed," I said, "he fell off."

"Fell off did he, how'd that come about then?"

"Overbalanced?" I suggested. He looked over at the bloodied faces of Joy and Brenda and his lips tightened. He'd grown up with a father whose regular end-of-week celebration was a skin-full, followed by what he called a wee cuddle. On the occasions the wife didn't cuddle with enough enthusiasm, a slap or two was in order, just so's she'd know better next time. The slap or two had never produced the hoped for level of compliance in PC Macleish's Mother, and over time there were more black eyes than hot dinners, a twice-dislocated jaw, loss of hearing in one ear and dead of a heart attack before she touched 60. Not long after, the howlin auld bugger's liver gave up and gave in; he died swiftly, unmourned. Years ago it was now but time hadn't healed. He moved over to peer down at Trevor, tightened his lip further and turned back to Mousegood.

"Out cold," he reported. Mousegood had it in mind to further explore, how a fall off the bed had knocked someone out quite so thoroughly, so I put my hands on my bump and winced a little to refocus his mind and he took a step back, nobody wants to upset a pregnant lady. He sneezed and nodded at the other PC.

"Sanders?" the other uniform was checking Joy with brisk efficiency and innate kindness, "you're not bloody Florence Nightingale you know, just get an ambulance, man, that's what they're for."

I was indescribably relieved that people who knew what they were doing were here now, but the noise in my head had ramped up and I was having terrible trouble shutting it out. My attention was caught and held by a small black and white dog I hadn't noticed before. It was sleeping on its side in a corner of the room, breathing deeply and evenly, and that was odd because it had a silver zip running all the way from tummy to throat. Trevor bought it for Joy last year, gave it to her in the office, to 'keep your jim-jams in.' I remember Hilary and I had exchanged a look, now the pyjama case turned its head slowly and opened one sleepy plastic eye to look at me. I must have exclaimed because a hand took my elbow.

"Hey," Macleish was moving me back to the stool to sit again, "not going to faint on us too?" I shook my head; Hilary had played that card, nevertheless the solidity of the hand was welcome, I glanced up to thank him. Bending solicitously over me was a porcelain-headed, laughing policeman; wide-mouthed with mirth as he leaned in further, tilting his head in a parody of concern. Eyeless he watched me, tongueless he chanted. I knew the chant and my mind chanted with him; *'Oh, I wish, I wish, I wish I knew, exactly what to do with you.'* And I was completely swamped, suddenly and unexpectedly by the bitter intensity of a wave of anger and in that instant I knew the thing I wanted most in the world, was to take the blue serge arm against which I was leaning, and break it. I knew precisely the three weakest break points on the bones, the ones which would inflict maximum pain and permanent damage. I readied myself to turn and act, I had to be swift, needed to take him by surprise.

"*NO!*" I said aloud and loudly - no time for pussyfooting around, "*Not* my circus, *Not* my monkeys!"

"Is it the bairn?" concern was broadening his accent, but at least he had his head back..

"Not unless it's Rosemary's Bairn," I said grimly and used the strength of the blue serge arm to lever myself up from the stool, I needed to stand and stand strong. The arm's owner was worried, although not half as much as he'd have been if he knew what I'd had in mind a few seconds earlier. One thing I was certain of though, whatever I'd just experienced, it wasn't anything to do with the baby, this was an old and knowing anger and bitterness.

"Easy pet, you're shaking. Is... y' know, anything happening at the minute... downstairs?"

"Only cramp in my leg."

He chuckled in relief, "Aye, it'll be on your nerves. Wife always says, on your nerves when they're inside, on your nerves when they're out! Here, let's get you over to the bed, make you more comfortable."

"Thank you Constable, that'll do." DS Mousegood, in the face of labour being imminent had backed off, but now he'd statements to take; just his luck he thought, that he'd been saddled with Sanders and Macleish, molly-coddlers both of them.

The bed was getting more crowded by the minute, lucky it was a good size. Joy was sitting up, Brenda had an arm around her, while Hilary perched on the side with Martin patting her hand, was apologising for being so silly. I found myself a space at the foot and prepared to give a slightly expurgated version of events. PC

Macleish was right I was shaking, fine tremors travelling up and down my body, I wasn't cold, more feverishly hot and louder now, on the extreme edge of my perception, the soft, grieving keening was rising and falling.

As Mousegood appropriated the stool, dragged it nearer, sneezed and prepared to take details. I was aware that from somewhere, something had watched this whole episode with curiosity and delight and was still watching.

CHAPTER THIRTY-THREE

David was not best pleased. He'd phoned home mid-morning and been informed by Mr Peg that I'd gone off in a proper rush. Jumping immediately to the wrong conclusion he'd driven back from Oxford, where he'd been doing research at the Bodleian. At Formula 1 speeds, he'd made good time and headed straight to the Royal Free Hospital where, as luck would have it, he arrived around the same time as we did. He was surprised to find that far from breathing in short pants in Maternity, I was part of a procession of anxious, bloodied people being escorted into A&E. Martin, holding on to Hilary, Brenda and Joy holding on to each other and Trevor, stretchered and unconscious shepherded by a couple of large policemen, one of whom put a firm flat hand on David's chest as he rushed towards me, and demanded to know who he thought he was.

Having identified himself and had it confirmed by me that he was indeed my husband, he was obviously interested in an explanation. This took some time because there were several people doing it and as I expected, the others had noted nothing attributable to me that struck them as any odder than everything else that was going on at the time.

Brenda needed a substantial number of stitches while the rest of us were bathed and bandaged; correctly counted the number of fingers held up; said what day of the week it was and told them who was Prime Minister and after not too long a wait, were pronounced good to go.

David who had been despatched to phone the office, came back to report all was well. Not only had Aunt Kitty, Ruby and Trudie taken over and held the fort, upstairs and downstairs like the troupers they were, but Kitty, who'd never been out the country in her life, sold two expensive Italian holidays on the strength of her wonderful memories of Sorrento, and another family was coming back the next day to hear all about Torremolinos.

PCs Macleish and Sanders stayed long enough to see us given the all-clear, which was above and beyond and very much appreciated. Joy, white and rigid had reconfirmed there'd never been any physical violence prior to today, she definitely didn't want to press charges and Brenda, tight-lipped, stitches and bruising livid on her face, acceded to Joy and followed suit. Macleish knew this wouldn't be the end of it, not by a country mile. Experience, professional and personal, had taught him once violence comes out, it's well-nigh impossible to lock it up again. He told us all to take care now, patted a shoulder or two, and wished me best of luck with the bairn then high-helmeted once more, departed.

Trevor had suffered a stroke. I didn't know whether it was my fault or not. He'd regained consciousness we were told; they were taking him up to the ward now, Mens' General, visiting hours on the noticeboard. As the doctor nodded to us and hurried off I followed, cornering him before he could dash into another cubicle. He didn't hide his irritation, pointing out stiffly that as I wasn't related to the patient, he could give no further details. He made to move around me, but I was a bulky blockage and assuming that shoving me to one side might well go against the 'do no harm' principle, I didn't budge. I said I understood but could a stroke be caused by a knock on the head? I've found in the face of a direct question, relevant information usually snaps unavoidably into place. As he repeated firmly he could tell me nothing, I read that Trevor had already been on medication for high blood pressure, a problem they felt was certainly a major contributory factor.

"'Was permanent damage likely" I asked, and read that I was one of the most annoyingly obstinate and obtuse women he'd had the misfortune to come across, and the stroke was mild, reflexes good, no impairment of movement or speech. I stepped back and with a frown he hurried past.

In my brief absence, arrangements had been made. Hilary and Martin were taking Joy and Brenda to Brenda's flat, where Joy would stay for a couple of days and, under the generalship of my Mother and Aunt Kitty, three teams had been mustered. The first;

Ruby and three of the Sewing Ladies were even now on their way to Joy's house on a clean and clear up mission, and would pack clothes and other necessities for her. The second; Trudie with the rest of the Sewing gang, were at Brenda's because her neighbour luckily had a spare key. They would make up the spare bed, prepare a hot meal and wait to welcome the wounded. Kitty had been left in charge back at base and was manfully handling everything at the office whilst team three, my Mother and Aunt Edna, had already dropped off a three course hot meal at Hilary and Martin's and were even now en route to ours with more food and no doubt the odd word or two about the sort of things you shouldn't be doing when you're nine months pregnant.

* * * *

It was no surprise the 'keep-an-eye-on-Stella' regime and rota turned positively draconian after that, and if I'm honest, I wasn't all that sorry. Recent events had unnerved me more than a little. I wasn't usually so jumpy - I blamed the baby! I did feel bad though that whilst everyone was rallying around, I was in no way jolly company. I was uneasy on so many different levels, my brain felt fogged, and I wasn't sure what, on my worry list, I should be focusing on first.

I worried about the baby; was she healthy? Could she be damaged by stress? Was she normal? I worried about Joy because Trevor was due out of hospital soon and she kept insisting he was a changed man, she was certainly a changed woman who seemed to be looking at things from a rather different angle, and I had no idea how well that was going to go down. I worried about Devlin. Had things been sorted. If yes, how? If not, why? The icing on the cake was Boris ignoring phone calls, not returning messages and when I sent out a hefty mental yell, I got nothing back and my stomach was still twisting, whenever Ruth came to mind.

There were other problems too business-wise, maybe not quite on the same scale but concerning nevertheless.. When a bride and her mother at a final fitting, changed their minds and wanted the sleeves removed from a nearly completed wedding dress, Marie-Claire, Zofia and Elizaveta flatly refused to ruin the balance of the gown or unlock the door until agreement had been reached? Marie-Claire, pre-war had been with Madeleine Vionnet, and apparently Parisian couture houses don't subscribe to the Customer Always Right code. Mercifully, I didn't hear about this particular skirmish until it was done and dusted, by which time, bride and mother had been convinced of the grave error of their ways and indeed were tearful with gratitude for being forced to see those.

And talking of tearful, would the soft crying in my head ever stop and give me either a break or a clue?

CHAPTER THIRTY-FOUR

I was never sure whether Laura's stints on the Stella rota were voluntary or press-ganged, but she was doing her fair share of 'popping in'. I felt we'd made progress in our relationship – at least now when she saw David and I together, she didn't look as if she hadn't the vaguest idea who I might be. She failed though to understand why I hadn't given up work, 'It wasn't as if', I heard her thinking, 'it was a nice little secretarial job'. Running your own business, to her mind, came under the heading of plain wilful and honestly, some of the people I got involved with seemed to be more than a little odd; luckily she didn't know the half of it.

I wanted her to like me – I felt anything more than that might be pushing it, but I knew the way to a mother's heart was through her son, so first step was a clean home and if I fell short, next best, was the illusion of one; this could be easily achieved by spraying some furniture polish into the air when I saw her coming down the path then answering the door a little breathlessly, complaining that dust gets everywhere, doesn't it? Don't judge me!

* * * *

Laura 'popped in because she was passing', on a freezing Wednesday afternoon, mid-December.

"Shame, you've just missed Auntie Kitty," I said, "she popped in too." I felt dreadfully guilty at the time everyone was spending with me, and kept assuring anyone who'd listen that I really would stay out of trouble long enough to have this baby. Nobody seemed convinced.

"I'm glad to see you though," I added. I knew for her it was more of an effort than it was for the others. She wasn't comfortable with the sheer physicality of pregnancy, never had been, couldn't wait for her own to be over, and perhaps was still making it up to the baby. She never had a second, and once in casual conversation, when David said, 'did you ever want another one Ma?' it was lucky he hadn't been able to read her internal shudder.

I also knew, the further we got, the more scared she was of something 'happening' whilst she was there and her relief whenever she left without having had to deal with a daughter-in-law in labour was palpable. I gave her a clumsy hug; it wasn't easy getting close to anyone these days and I made it brief because I could feel her holding back from contact with the bump.

"You're freezing," I said, "go on in, sit down, I was going to make a cup of tea and then *It's A Wonderful Life* is on."

"Oo lovely," she said, with the enthusiasm of Marie Antoinette promised an outing to see a cutting-edge gadget "you're the one should be sitting down though, I'll make tea." I let her, I knew it would make her feel better and if the tea didn't, a pill might. Years ago, a helpful GP when she complained of panic attacks, not sleeping, feeling boiling hot then freezing cold, had handed her a prescription.

"These'll sort you out m'dear, ladies of your age, prone to this sort of thing; next time you get into a lather; one of these'll relax you." She'd been relaxing a great deal ever since. When I first started driving her, I popped into the Library reference section and checked out the name on the box of the pills, I understood she shouldn't be taking them so frequently, but also, if she wanted to stop, it wouldn't be easy. My conscience wouldn't let me keep quiet but when I brought the subject up, she didn't want to know, said did I really think I knew more than her doctor? Now, as she did the necessary in the kitchen, I didn't have to listen hard to follow her train of thought. She was worried I looked terribly on edge. She herself had just swallowed a pill; more for my benefit than hers because someone needed to remain calm, I knew this meant she'd shortly evolve into Laura Two and sure enough, when she brought in tea and a sliced swiss roll, she sank down close to me on the sofa.

"I'll be Mother, shall I?" she said. Katerina, ensconced in an armchair, blending beautifully with the cushion, raised her head and uttered a soft whoof. Laura jumped, "Oh, the dog! Didn't see her there, does she eat cake?" I said Kat would probably eat anything if it was presented nicely enough, but on balance, best not. We lapsed into companionable silence with Laura every now and then patting my arm and murmuring how very, very, very fond of me she was, very fond. I patted her back, said I was very fond of her too and before James Stewart had even tried to jump off the bridge, she was dozing.

The curtains were drawn, holding in the warmth against the dark, the soft snores of Kat and Laura intermingled and backgrounded the familiar story onscreen. I'd had a couple of slices of cake, justified as one for me, one for the baby and had drained the last of my tea, when I started to feel a little peculiar and then quite a lot more peculiar. I didn't think it was to do with the baby but she had gone very still. Too still? I jiggled a little, and was rewarded with a healthy thump. It was probably nothing. I should just relax.

I must have relaxed more enthusiastically than I thought, because when I next looked at the tv, they were smack-bang in the middle of the bank rush. I wasn't concerned, I knew James Stewart would win the day. My head felt stuffed to bursting point with soft cotton wool, in which were wrapped various thoughts, but every time I tried to grasp one, it slipped away. Perhaps a glass of water? I manoeuvred myself to the edge of the couch, stood up and rapidly sat down again, both legs felt like well-cooked spaghetti. I had another go, wobbled cautiously to the kitchen, had a glass of water, sat on a kitchen chair and promptly fell asleep again, jolting awake only when I nearly fell off and the truth dawned.

My Mother-in-law had given me one of her bloody pills. I was beyond livid, what was she *thinking*? Could it hurt the baby? How long would it take to wear off? Would it count as self-defence if I throttled her? I opened my mouth to call, then shut it again, couldn't remember her name; now that was worrying; I searched in and around the cotton wool but nope, nothing. Obviously I'd have to go in and ask her, then I could tell her what I thought of her and by that time, maybe effects would have worn off.

Hauling myself up, full of righteous indignation and holding on to the back of the chair prior to launching myself in the direction of the door, there was an awful ringing in my ears. I paused to let it pass but that didn't happen because it turned out to be the phone. Perhaps it would stop if unanswered but no, this was one determined caller. Handing myself from one chair back to the other, I hoped it wasn't somebody just ringing for a chat, I didn't think I was up for small talk. I managed to get the receiver to my ear, then had to stop and turn it the right way up. It transpired it wasn't small talk at all.

CHAPTER THIRTY-FIVE

Propped unsteadily against the wall, I shut my eyes, all the better to concentrate and make sense of who it was and what they wanted.

"Stella, *Stella?*" the woman on the other end was sobbing. I opened my eyes and admitted it was me. I'd no idea who she was, though as I couldn't name my own Mother-in-Law, I wasn't surprised.

"It's me, *Susan*," she said and through the distress, must have realised she wasn't getting a coherent response, "Stella, can you hear me? *Please*, *please*, it's Devlin, it's really bad."

"Susan?"

"Yes, yes, Susan McCrae. Stella, you have to come, we're at the Royal Free, Devlin's… oh God!" she choked on a sob.

"What's happ…"

She cut in, "… I'm sending a minicab, please, please come." Then she was gone.

I replaced the receiver and tried to think, I understood the urgency, knew I should be galvanised into action, just wasn't sure how much galvanising I had in me. I was scared that what I was feeling might get worse before it got better, my brain didn't deal lightly with pharmaceutical interference, great word pharmaceutical, I rolled it round my tongue for a bit before realising I might be drifting; and I was still propped against the kitchen wall. With an effort I stood upright and for a moment the mists cleared and I edged a little closer to sensible. I'd go straight to the hospital in the cab, by the time I got there, even if not fully functioning, I might be able to do something to help and I was increasingly afraid that whatever had happened to Devlin, had happened because of me.

I'd leave quietly, wouldn't disturb Laura – Ah, *that's* who she was. I thought I ought to take a few things with me but drew a blank as to what those might be. Perhaps best to travel light. I got myself to the front door and struggled to get it open, it tended to stick in wet weather and required a particular technique, the intricacies of which seemed to have slipped my mind. When I finally cracked it, a blast of icy air slapped me hard in the face and the sickly yellow street lighting, highlighted thin, icy drizzle.

I shivered, which made me think a coat might be in order. Luckily the coat rack was handy; handy to hold on to as well. I lifted down a coat, had a bit of a struggle getting into it then couldn't understand why it reached the ground and I couldn't find my hands, but at that point a car drew up, flashed its lights and I had to hurry. The path was wet and slippery, so I walked gingerly, arms out for better balance, then realised I was not alone. Katerina, who loathed the wet almost as much as the cold was welded to my left leg. Well, that wouldn't do. I appreciated the gesture but obviously couldn't take her, I turned her round gave her a shove in the right direction and a sharp mental command. As so often, she took not a blind bit of notice. I calculated - the slippery distance to the cab was now less than the slippery distance back to the front door. I didn't want to take chances and didn't have time to argue, I'd just have to call from the hospital, get someone to come and collect her, or maybe she could sit in reception and with that muddled reasoning, I reached the cab. As we tumbled clumsily into the back and I pulled the door shut three things struck me as troubling; I was wearing David's coat; I still had my slippers on; and how did Susan know my address?

****

Mulling over the last and possibly most concerning question, I had no idea how long we drove for, or maybe I'd gone to sleep again – ruddy pill! When the car stopped I rubbed a gap in the steamed-up window and peered out. Drizzle had turned to snow, but not so heavily I couldn't immediately spot this wasn't the Royal Free Hospital.

"Excuse me," I leaned forward, always good to be polite, even if you're fast coming to the conclusion that something, somewhere is definitely not kosher. He didn't turn, so I touched him lightly, whipping my hand back quickly. This was one frightened shoulder; terror he'd felt and was still feeling, leapt from him to me.

He turned very slowly. I was befuddled, but not so far gone that I couldn't read what was in his head, had there been anything to read, but there wasn't, only a fear-flavoured blank with an occasional free-floating tendril of half-formed thought floating by. This wasn't good, not least from a road-safety point of view. Something had broken this man's mind.

"Fare's paid," he said tonelessly, looking at, but not seeing me. "Get out."

"Where are we?" I knew as I said it, it was a waste of breath; he had no more idea than I did. I opened the door and paused; my facetious thought wasn't so facetious at all. I didn't know who he was, who'd done this to him or what was going to happen next, but I couldn't in good conscience let him drive off, so I knocked him out. He slumped awkwardly and there was an aborted beep as the side of his face slid past the horn. He came to a stop, draped over the handbrake. He didn't look comfortable but was probably safer there than behind the wheel. I switched on the hazard lights, strobing orange couldn't easily be missed in a wide road with no streetlamps and on the upside, he wouldn't be unconscious forever by which time I might well be out again and could take over and drive. There was a brief moment when I thought, why not just do that now? But then Susan's desperation rang in my head again, so I couldn't. There was a rug on the passenger seat and I covered and tucked him in, it was the least I could do. It was now snowing in earnest, too dark to make anything out easily, but from the absence of nearby house lights, I assumed we were in a road where neighbours weren't within screaming distance. Was that a good or a bad thing?

Something nudged my arm and I jumped convulsively, Kat looked at me reproachfully, well I wasn't having that,

"You insisted on coming," I told her as I opened the latch on a black wooden-strutted gate and crunched unsteadily over gravel, heading for not-the-Royal Free and reflecting whoever had thought small stones as a walking surface was a good idea, deserved to be shot.

The house was set a way back from the road, double-fronted and built on a small rise, with several steps to the front door and light from a couple of windows. I wasn't nervous, I was well able to take care of myself, but I wasn't thrilled either and as David's coat, trailing the ground was doing a grand job of snow clearing, he was another one who wasn't going to be pleased. My slippers, unsurprisingly, had not held up well, I was chilled and shivering and willing to bet this little jaunt wouldn't be on Mavis the Midwife's list of things Mum should be doing.

There was a square of thickly distorting, swirled glass set two thirds of the way up a glossy black painted front door. It was reflecting back a weak beam from an overhead porch light, presumably there so visitors could see this was number 20. There were a lot of things running through my mind and something that wasn't, although so accustomed to the soft grieving had I become, I didn't immediately pinpoint its absence.

I couldn't see a doorbell, but actually it's easier to express your annoyance with a doorknocker, although on this occasion, at first knock, the door swung wide. I wanted to laugh. The only thing missing was a sinister hinge squeal, some ominous music and lots of people yelling *'Don't go in!'*

I went in.

CHAPTER THIRTY-SIX

The front door opened into a rectangular lobby area with coat hooks, shoe rack and a couple of past-saving potted plants. From the lobby a frosted glass door opened into a spacious hall, a couple of doors either side, a staircase to the left at the end. The carpet was brown with a hectic orange swirl motif that could have done with a lot less repeating. The house was still and stale, the smell of recently burnt toast overlying memories of other meals gone by; it didn't seem to be a place where windows were flung open often.

I called hello to no response then getting crosser by the minute, yelled for Susan, although by then I knew this was none of her doing – at least not voluntarily. Hoisting David's coat which had become heavier and harder to handle the wetter it got, I hiked across to the first room on the right, opening the door onto more orange swirling, it really was the sort of carpet that makes you want to step back and go somewhere quieter.

The room was large. A solid Chesterfield sofa in buttoned, dark green leather faced a tiled fireplace with matching armchairs either side and welcome heat blasting from a three-bar electric fire standing in the fireplace. A couple of dim-bulbed standard lamps with shades heavy on the pom-poms, were doing their best to add something to the feeble light from a central ceiling fitting. An upright piano with a metronome and some loose music sheets notionally separated the two areas of the long room with the far end given over to a dark wood dining table centre-pieced by an over-large china vase. Taking up space at the fireplaced end were more occasional tables than any self-respecting room has a right to, and on every flat surface – of which there were plenty - stood china figures on lace doilies, whilst gilt-framed paintings did for the walls, what the china was doing for the tables; overpopulated was one way of describing it.

None of this was doing my cotton-wool stuffed head any good and I knew I still wasn't thinking properly. I shut my eyes briefly, just to give them a rest. The cab was still outside, hazard lights strobing through the window, highlighting the carpet which was the last thing it needed. This was a fool's errand and the idiot was me. Time to call it a day.

"Ghastly, isn't it? Not my taste." He'd come silently into the room behind me, though I'd recognised what and who he was before I'd reached the front door. The incongruity of dull brown trousers and dark green buttoned cardigan topped by the white impassivity, rictus grin and gaping eyes of the mask should have looked ridiculous but didn't, and when he chanted softly, it came as no surprise.

"*I wish, I wish, I wish I knew, exactly what to do with you.*" Hearing it now, aloud, I understood it was less a question than pleasurable review of possibilities. Still, I wasn't going to fall down on the social front, I came right back with my old favourite of mine,

"*I do not like thee Dr Fell, The reason why I cannot tell.*" He chuckled, with genuine amusement – it didn't make him any more likeable.

"Why the mask?" I said.

"Oh, you mustn't mind that, bit of fun; theatrical self-indulgence you might say." He took it off, not letting the elastic at the back mess with his hair carefully parted to the right. "Didn't alarm you, did it?"

"No." I said, but then he knew as well as I, real-life monsters don't need to look frightening. Mid-sixties or thereabouts, he epitomised average; height, build, hair, green buttoned cardigan, he'd be hell to spot if he sat on the sofa. A single memorable feature was his mouth - exceptionally full and clearly defined lips pushed into a pink pout by slightly buck teeth, he'd hated those lips all his life. Every now and then his tongue flicked out to do a circuit, perhaps checking to see if they'd grown any less obvious. He looked me up and down, humming softly to himself and then smiled.

"Let's get that wet coat off you."

"I'm not staying. You conned me into coming and I have the cab outside waiting."

"So, I believe," he said, "good luck with that," he glanced at the electric fire, "warm enough for you in here is it? It's on full, but that wind gets through all the cracks; and we have snow I understand," he shook his head, "they're saying two to three inches tonight, country'll grind to a halt as per; put money on it." He straightened an embroidered cat cushion on the sofa and patted invitingly, "Sit yourself down," then spotted Katerina, who'd remained firmly behind me, "ah, you've brought a friend." He stretched out a hand for her to smell, but she'd taken his measure and growled long and low in her throat.

"Shy," he said, "she'll settle," I didn't think she would. He moved in a murky brown miasma, his scent the musty staleness of fabric left damp for too long, it was overlaid by the artificial sweetness of Brut Aftershave which he must have splashed on all over, it didn't help. I could feel him probing, trying to get into my head but anger and distaste are great barrier enhancers. Despite the cotton-wool and shaky balance I knew my own strength and had assessed his. He wasn't that strong; he could be handled but that was beside the point. I'd been suckered into whatever twisted little game he thought he was playing and I wasn't pleased. Neither was I happy that he knew enough about me to use Devlin as bait. He picked up on that, slipped into a pitch perfect imitation of Susan McCrae, voice breaking on a sob.

"Please, oh please Stella, get here quickly!" then in normal tone, "I'm rather good at that sort of thing, even if I say so myself."

My displeasure was growing in direct proportion to the pill wearing off; and I'd already set aside an extremely sharp piece of my mind for Laura on the morality of drugging pregnant daughters-in-law. Prior to that though, I needed to deal with Obnoxious; make it clear, however great he was at imitations and whatever fun he'd been having with putting the masks in my mind, it stopped here and now. I needed to get home; I knew for a fact, none of this would come under David's definition of taking it easy.

"Tea?" he asked.

"Don't be stupid. Why am I here?" he chuckled again, sat down in one of the armchairs, leaning back and undoing a couple of cardigan buttons to allow paunch room.

"I won't be stupid," he said, "if you'll stop being grumpy."

"*Really*? We're going to play Mr Men? Say whatever it is you think you've got to say, but I honestly don't think you know what you're dealing with." I glanced over at the mantelpiece where a chunky shepherdess, was shading her eyes and checking for sheep. I lifted her in a leisurely way, broke her into two pieces which I let go so they hit the carpet swiftly. He didn't move. Watched her go up, watched her come down and smiled.

"Told you," he said mildly "all this," he waved an encompassing hand, "not my taste, not that bothered. Smash away, you'll do us both a favour."

I was running low on whatever patience I'd started with. "If you want to tell me why you went to the trouble of getting me here," I said, "do it now, then I'm off."

Obnoxious rose from the chair. I wasn't prepared to take chances; I took action instead and pushed him firmly backwards,

He said, "Oof" and sat heavily.,

"I warned you," I moved past, Kat hard on my heels, "you really don't know what you're dealing with."

He licked his lips, "And neither," he said, "do you."

CHAPTER THIRTY-SEVEN

He wasn't that strong, certainly not a match for me, even with Laura's pill on board. Turned out he didn't have to be. My head was suddenly flooded with agony; not mine, but the pain of others - a tsunami of sensation which barrelled and smashed straight through my barriers and I understood instantly. It was a numbers game. I don't know exactly how many were there; ten, twenty, more? It was impossible to tell, and when I thought it couldn't get worse, it did. From the midst of those minds united with mine in unsought intimacy and anguish, the ultimate horror was in the one I knew almost as well as my own; rich lavender - Ruth. Fury rose in me, fuelled by outrage clean-cutting through the pain..

I must have hit the floor at some point because I was on all fours, hands either side of me. I got to my feet, letting the heavy wet coat slide off my shoulders, not an elegant rise, but it did the job. Inside, the baby had gone very still, what he'd done had affected her too. My baby and Ruth - there were no words to express the depth of what I felt but what was surging to the surface was far more powerful than words and way more dangerous. I'd spent my entire life learning control, but this level of malevolence demanded response and retribution. It was sparking lethally from my fingertips and I raised my hand. He smiled, he thought it was amusing.

"Oh, I wouldn't," he said, "that would be foolish indeed." His tone was neutral, he knew what I could do to him but wasn't in the least bit worried because then, shrill and discordant, above the cacophony of the others, Ruth screamed in shock and pain.

"There now," he said placidly, "you see why you need to behave nicely. I can make life awfully uncomfortable for my friends – and yours. You hurt me, I hurt them - a little or a lot, it rather depends on how difficult you're being."

What was in me had to go somewhere, it had gathered too much momentum to pull back; I turned away from him as figurines flew, met in mid-air, smashed and crashed. A picture ripped from the wall taking a chunk of plaster with it; the piano lid slammed, an ornate side table was cleared of framed photos in a clean sweep, two of its legs snapped and it hunkered down wounded. The chandelier above the dining table was swinging and jerking, dusty crystal glass drops trembling – perhaps they knew what was coming next. I breathed in and took back some control but the chandelier was already on its way, it wrenched free of the ceiling and headed for the large vase below. The impact of one on the other was phenomenally ear-jarring and followed by a long-winded pitter-patter of glass and china flying up before raining down. I don't know whether I'd frightened him, I'd certainly scared the hell out of me.

"Better?" he tilted his head politely.

"It'll do for now," I said and utilised a cushion to brush broken china off the sofa then sat carefully, in case I'd missed a bit. Kat, who'd made the mistake of taking cover beneath the dining table, made her shaken way back, stepping delicately over assorted obstacles and leant heavily against my leg.

He did a mock turn-down of the mouth, which didn't sit well with the pout, "You know, I only heated this room up for you, I never use it, please don't worry about clearing up."

"What do you want?" I said flatly.

He nodded towards my stomach, "That."

I kept my expression neutral. My blinds were firmly back in place and I didn't think there was any way he could get in, but I was aware with my habitual leap-first-look-later confidence in my own abilities, I'd put myself and imminent offspring in a situation we certainly hadn't covered in NCT classes. There were a number of priorities right now; Ruth and the unknown others; the logistical issues of getting out of here; how I was going to be able to explain this to David, and how essential it was to keep my guard up because I certainly wasn't prepared to join his pain club anytime soon. All in all, and whilst I hate looking on the black side, right now it would seem I wasn't in a great place, in any sense of the word.

"Shall we just run through just a couple of things, then I'll show you your room." He interrupted my thought.

"My room?"

"You didn't think I'd expect you to sleep on the sofa? I think you'll be pleased with what I've laid on, but first - the phone?" I followed his glance. The receiver had come off and lay on its side, beneath a doily and next to an upended table. "Out of order, I'm afraid, I pulled out the wires, so 999's off the menu, and if you're thinking of getting in touch the other way," he touched his head briefly, then shook it, "I wouldn't, you've seen how painful that is for others. Now, are we clear?" when he smiled, he looked like Bugs Bunny turned feral.

"What's to stop me just leaving?"

"Don't be tiresome. I can't stop you, but they can." Pink lips pouted and for a few seconds voices shrieked in my head. He nodded as he saw me react, "There you go, you've got it! Good girl. I taught you know, for many years. Found students learnt better and quicker when shown not told, d'you see?" he took silence as assent and stood, neatly re-buttoning the cardigan. "Righty ho then, upward and onward."

Either I'd misjudged the height of the sofa when I sat, or I was wearier than I thought, because when it came to get up again, I couldn't. Rather than struggle on the slippery leather, I shifted my bottom sideways to reach and gain leverage from the high arm. I must have placed my hand where hers had so often rested, and she hit me like a ten-ton truck.

***

Alison Olivia, that's who she was, never just Alison because Mummy loved the rhythm of the two together. Addressed as Alison only, was a sure sign she was in trouble – as indeed she often was. She was a post-war baby who became an intelligent, opinionated child. There were no siblings, so included in and absorbing adult conversation, she was articulate and blessed with a decisiveness that defined her. School reports regularly spoke of her 'knowing her own mind', clear code for rarely doing as she was told. Mummy and Daddy made it clear from the beginning; this was not a Good Thing, but she was well aware they actually thought it wasn't a Bad Thing either. The way they framed it was knowing your own mind at six could be problematical but later, making your way in the world it would never be less than an asset.

She knew they were proud of and impressed by the individual they'd produced and if they ever had a disagreement, not an argument, arguments never did anyone any good, but a difference of opinion; anything from choice of wallpaper to a day's outing, they'd settle it with, 'We'll ask Alison Olivia, she won't be dithery-dathery,' and indeed, she never was. Daddy once, ruffling her hair affectionately said something about the sum of two parts being greater... and she knew how much she was loved; not so much from what he said, but from the soft warmth that filled his head when he said it.

They were a tight-knit unit of three and content with that; there was no extended family to speak of, neither parent having siblings and they didn't have a wide circle of friends but she understood that was choice not circumstance.

When she was six and a half, they'd gone to Cliftonville for a holiday; a cab, a train and another cab to get there, all very posh and the sea right in front of the bedroom window. One day Mummy didn't feel well, she had a bad tummy-ache. Alison Olivia got the milk of magnesia from the bag in which were packed all such remedies — you never knew when you went away whether you'd be able to lay hands on what you wanted — but when it turned out the tummy-ache was bad enough to call in a doctor, she put the blue tinted bottle neatly back in the bag.

By the time the doctor arrived and was on his way up to their room, it was actually supper time and Daddy said, 'did she think she could go down to the hotel dining room herself?' The nice waitress would take her to their usual table, and she could choose her own supper from the menu. He was awfully anxious, which was a bit silly because she knew exactly where to go and she took her book with her, so she'd have something to do while she was waiting. She had pineapple juice to start, then some roast chicken with potatoes and carrots, she knew all about rationing of course, but that had been when she was a baby, so she didn't remember much; it was over now and she saw the pleasure her parents took in the hotel menu. For afters she had fruit jelly with a portion of vanilla ice-cream even though it was a choice of one or the other on the menu, but the waitress said Alison Olivia was the best behaved guest she'd ever served - probably a bit of an exaggeration, thought Alison Olivia, but no-one looks a gift horse, or in this case an ice cream scoop in the mouth.

When she got back upstairs the doctor had gone and Mummy was in bed looking pale and a bit weepy. She held out her arms to Alison Olivia, gave her a cuddle and said not to worry; everything was fine although it was clear it wasn't. Alison Olivia understood Mummy had been upset by someone called Miss Carridge, but then Daddy said time for bed and in the morning Mummy might have a bit of a lie-in, but he and his best girl would go down to the beach anyway. She'd made a favourable impression with her solo supper and next evening, when coffee for the grown-ups was served after dinner, the Manager came over with some chocolate truffles, compliments of the kitchen, and several other guests stopped her parents to say how well brought up she was; so mature for her age; beautifully behaved. Alison Olivia didn't know why it was so clever to go and have supper, but Mummy and Daddy who'd been a bit down in the mouth all day were pleased, so she was pleased too.

Daddy's work was high up in the Home Office. She thought for years, and fairly logically, when he left for the station, he went to another house, where he worked upstairs, before returning promptly at 6.30 every evening. She liked to watch for him from the window, his gait unmistakeable, a propulsion from the heel, which drove him forward swiftly, his rolled-up umbrella deployed meticulously in time with each step. Mummy always told him off, well not really telling off, just fake cross, because his shoes had to be re-heeled so often. She once asked Mummy whether he had lots of friends at his home office, but she said not really, it wasn't encouraged; colleagues yes, some of them nice chaps but because of the nature of the work, most kept themselves to themselves. From this conversation she took away the firm impression he worked with animals and plants, until one day she asked about it and the silly mistake came out - 'nature of' apparently not meaning what she'd thought, but after they'd all stopped laughing, Mummy said Alison Olivia really should know how important Daddy's work was, and she could be very proud of him because he'd done a lot in the War and had to sign something called the Official Secrets Act, which showed how high up he was.

Alison Olivia knew from friends at school, not everyone's home life was as ordered or as comfortable as hers and the years blended and passed so smoothly, she didn't ever want it to change; Alison Olivia wasn't keen on anything new and untried.

Around the time she left secondary school, Father retired. He'd been saying for ages he couldn't wait and Mother said she couldn't either. Although the big day, when it came, came quietly with no fanfare, just one Friday night, instead of leaving his briefcase on top of the shoe cupboard in the hall, he put it in the cupboard under the stairs.

"Well," he said, "that's that then," and over supper he opened a bottle of wine – unheard of except at Christmas – and Mother said it was a whole new life ahead. But it wasn't, because two weeks later he had a heart attack, and although the ambulance came quickly and they were all so kind, it was too late. They said it would have been quick; he wouldn't have known what was happening.

They'd never been a family who'd gone overboard on emotion, 'stiff upper' had been a favoured expression, and as Mother pointed out, nothing could be changed, so talking over and over was wasting good breath. They should instead be thankful he'd left them comfortable. House paid for, pension coming in, savings in the bank - they'd always been sensible, never stinted themselves but never been silly either - the sooner the two of them got back into a routine, the better it would be for both of them.

Except they didn't get back into a routine, because Mother started forgetting things, not the usual sort of things like keys or glasses, but how to boil an egg which, with nicely buttered soldiers had been a staple of Saturday morning breakfast for as far back as could be remembered.

'Nothing to worry about,' said their doctor cheerfully after examining Mother, bereavement does this, only to be expected; it would pass; three good meals a day, no stress or over-excitement, maybe a day or two at the seaside and she'd be right as rain. Alison Olivia reflected as they left the surgery arm in arm; other than Father's heart attack, stress hadn't factored majorly in their lives to date, neither come to think had over-excitement, so steering clear of both shouldn't be a problem. What she genuinely couldn't understand was why Dr Akerton with so much experience in assessing people, couldn't see that inside Mother's head, things weren't right at all, her thoughts were every which way and consequently getting caught up in each other, tangling and knotting dreadfully.

When she'd pointed this out, during the consultation, he'd placed an avuncular hand, hot on her knee; said she'd always had too much imagination than was good for her. She should get out more, find herself a nice young man; and because she was distracted and tired, she forgot her manners and muttered as she helped Mother to her feet, "Like you have?" she suspected that she and Mother might have to find a new doctor.

Whatever was going wrong in Mother's head went wrong swiftly. Alison Olivia knew it was more than grief, and deferred her place at Teacher Training College for a year. In the event, Mother passed away the following March, a neat seven months after Father, and then it was nineteen-year-old Alison Olivia. Alone.

* * * *

"Well?" Obnoxious was tapping an impatient foot, "we haven't got all night?" I was still on the sofa, still had my hand on the arm to pull myself up. I must have frozen as I absorbed everything; the essence, personality and memories of Alison Olivia who'd sat so often where I was sitting. As I got up, he pursed those lips;

"You've tired yourself out haven't you, all that showing off, I expect. Let's get you down to your room, have to take good care of you?"

CHAPTER THIRTY-EIGHT

I thought he'd made a mistake, slip of the tongue but he hadn't, instead of heading up the hectically carpeted stairs, he went to a door at the far end of the hall under the stairs. Maye he was going to lock me in a cupboard, although he'd have a job cramming something of my size in with the usual Hoover, ironing board and other stuff. It turned out the far wall of the crowded cupboard wasn't a wall at all; it was another door. Was I heading for Narnia? Had Laura's pill not worn off? Was this all an unfortunate hallucination? But hallucinations don't smell. As the door swung smoothly and silently outward onto a landing, strip lighting sprang to life, and there must have been some sort of fan because the under-stairs staleness was replaced with something else, the unmistakeable smell of every hospital or clinic I'd ever been in, and that's when I really knew I was really in trouble.

With Kat welded to my leg it was a dicey descent down a spiral staircase and she whined softly all the way. I felt much the same. The stairs took us to the centre of a wide, well-lit circular space with as many as half a dozen doors set at intervals, harsh lighting made brighter by being reflected back from large glassed panels, one adjacent to each of the doors. I knew an observation window when I saw one and my blood ran a little colder. A couple of the windows had blinds down.

"I expect," he said, waving a smug arm, "you're wondering how I've achieved all this." Actually, that was the last thing on my mind, but he told me anyway. Apparently there had always been a substantial wine cellar running beneath the house and this had been converted and extended. Looking around it was obvious this was no D.I.Y. job, this had been planned and built by people who knew what they were doing and the stark utilitarian contrast with upstairs' outdated suburbia was disorientating. He picked up the thought.

"Astonishing, isn't it? And clever, nobody ever has, nor would ever suspect, what goes on down here." I wasn't really listening but tuned back in when my attention was caught by a phrase at the end of a sentence.

"… fully equipped medical facility and laboratory."

"You're a Doctor?"

He grunted, "You don't listen do you? I said before; Scientist," he straightened his cardigan, raised his chin, "several extremely well-thought of papers to my name, way ahead in my field. He bent to pick up a piece of fluff which had settled on the grey, soft tiled flooring, but the swell of bile that scented his last statement indicated clearly, if he was ahead of anything, he was the only one who thought so. He wasn't a multi-tasker either, so whilst he was directing my attention to various points of pride and interest, I learnt a lot more.

Years earlier, as a student, he'd volunteered on a research project; he needed the money. The study was on Chance and Probability, and the whole thing was as boring as anticipated. It was only by chance – oh the irony – that one of the research assistants, strictly against protocol, told him his scores were interestingly high; shapes, numbers, colours he'd guessed correctly. put him into the tiny percentage of the population who could do that. He was delighted; nobody in his life to date had seen or mentioned evidence of extraordinary, although he'd always suspected that was an oversight on their part. Unfortunately, whilst a high score was gratifying, it offered no clear direction as to how it might be used to his own advantage.

He went into teaching. The students he worked with bored him as much as he bored them. He didn't like them, they didn't like him; he did the minimum necessary to hold his post and every student he taught, knew and resented that. He wasn't a man you'd call happy in his vocation, but hours and holidays enabled him to spend time doing his own research, and what had started as a reluctant interest, grew over time and slid into obsession.

After all he reasoned, if exercise created muscle, wouldn't the same principle apply to the brain? Logically there were then possibilities to be explored. For example, if this type of ability could be exercise-enhanced in an adult; how much more powerful might such a regime prove at earlier stages of brain development? Was an inherent ability genetic? If so, was it possible two people with ability would produce a third whose talent was doubled?

He religiously exercised his own limited ability, researched, theorised and for years rose above numerous rejections from scientific and medical journals; 'no thank you very much,' they said to submitted papers, 'not quite what we're looking for,' or 'not science, science-fiction!' and from one editor unafraid to speak his mind 'too much of a whiff of eugenics, old chap, not touching with a bargepole!' He despised them for their lack of vision, was furious that none of them saw what he did and livid he'd never received, and probably never would, the accolades which were his due. And in all that time he hadn't stumbled on where his own brilliance really lay.

It wasn't always career-enhancing or expedient to be a bachelor – people made assumptions past a certain age, aside from which, by the time he hit 40 he decided he was entitled to his share of domestic comforts. He was bored with his own cooking and tired of paying a cleaner. He needed a wife; he met someone a suitable five years younger and because he'd learnt to mimic those emotions he didn't feel, he wooed and won her.

Even then he'd have been none the wiser if, six months into the marriage, a single event hadn't piqued his interest the way she never had. They'd had a row, something trivial, she irritated him almost beyond bearing sometimes and looking at her white neck, he imagined his fingers squeezing, squeezing. Of course, he wouldn't have done it, she wasn't worth the risk; it was just a thought, a bit of pleasurable imagining, but she reacted. Both hands flew to her throat, her eyes widened and her breath caught. The scientist in him was riveted.

The argument was smoothed over, and in the following weeks and months, experiments with or without her knowledge were conducted and irrefutable conclusions drawn. She became ever easier to manipulate and by the time she realised what was happening it was already too late, because by then she could be easily brought to heel, pain being a great influencer of behaviour. Following the logic of the methodologies he himself taught, he calculated and concluded that statistically, if he could do what he could do and she was what she was, there would be many others too, only undiscovered because nobody had bothered before to look. He now knew not only exactly who he was looking for, but how to control them. He began to hunt.

* * * *

"This is you," he said now, calling back my attention by opening one of the doors, "I think you'll find I've thought of most things you'll need for now and… " he smiled, "for later." I stopped in the doorway of a larger than expected room and ran through my options, of which there weren't many. I wasn't thinking as clearly as I should, perhaps I was more unnerved than I wanted to admit. I'd been in sticky situations before, but then it had just been me, this was different, I had responsibilities. Surveying the room, not really taking anything in, I knew I could overpower him, deal with any locks and leave. He caught the thought, shook his head a little and in my head just a few people screamed. To hell with it, I turned towards him to lash back. I left it too late because by then he'd plunged a needle into my arm.

"Just a little prick," he said.

I had just enough left in me to mutter bitterly, "…can say that again!" before things started to go black. The pink, Bugs Bunny pout was the last thing I saw before my eyelids came down.

CHAPTER THIRTY-NINE

When I came round, I spent the first minute eyes still closed, patting David's side of the bed to see if he was there. He wasn't. Maybe – and a girl can only hope – he'd got up to make me a cup of tea. My mouth was impossibly dry and my tongue, just hanging around in the middle wasn't doing anything constructive, I moved it experimentally but any hint of moisture seemed to have gone. Then I remembered where I was, why I'd come and how much bother I was in.

I opened one eye cautiously, snapping it swiftly shut as it was assaulted by stark white fluorescent lighting bounced off stark white-tiled walls – this was a room that might have benefitted from a bit of interior design. Something cold touched my face and I pulled back briefly before I recognised the heavy breathing. Opening both eyes, I was shocked to find I could still only see out of the original and thought I'd gone blind in the other, before realising it was due to me being awkwardly draped across the bed, face-down on a soft pillow. I raised my head the necessary few inches to an elegantly elongated and worried face inches from mine; Kat was obviously waiting for someone responsible to take charge, which was a shame, because so was I.

"Well, this isn't going to get the baby bathed," I muttered and as if to emphasise the point, got a sharp kick, although if the baby had any sense, right now she'd be looking up adoption options. Goodness only knows what he'd shot me full of. Whatever it was had packed a hell of a punch and I don't suppose Laura's pill beforehand had helped much. I ached all over, my arm was sore where I'd been jabbed and each limb weighed a ton. I wasn't sure I'd ever want or be able to move again, then I spotted a jug of water and a glass and my priorities changed. I tried to sit up but that didn't go well. Turned out I was wearing a thick metal chain round my wrist. The other end was anchored around the metal bed leg and secured with a padlock. I wasn't pleased. I lifted the jug and poured water, and then floated the glass over so I could use my movable hand and drink which made me feel marginally better. There were a couple of sandwiches on a plate next to the jug, I got those too, then took stock.

The room was spacious enough but without that much in it. As well as the bed and hospital-style bedside cabinet, there were a couple of pale blue plastic-covered easy chairs that looked anything but relaxing, and what was probably a drugs cabinet on the wall. The top of a hospital type trolley parked along the opposite wall had a cloth covering what might be medical instruments, nothing I was ready to deal with yet. There were two doors, one we'd come in by, the other I assumed to a bathroom, which brought up another issue; it wasn't yet urgent but soon would be.

There was a small fridge humming in the corner, fluorescent lighting humming in the ceiling, some kind of air vent humming on the wall and yes, I wasn't mistaken, someone humming in my head, that was an awful lot of humming. I was still wearing what I'd left home in and could see my worse-for-wear slippers loitering beneath one of the chairs. There was no natural light in the room and no clock so I'd no idea how long I'd been unconscious, or indeed what time or even day it was, and I had pins and needles in the chained hand – a highly unsatisfactory state of affairs all round.

Now I'm not daft - opinionated maybe, misguided from time to time certainly and possibly far too quick to leap before looking - but not daft. I needed to call in some heavy duty help and the sooner the better, but I couldn't mentally yell without alerting Obnoxious and he'd made it clear how he'd demonstrate his displeasure. I couldn't protect the many who'd be shrieking in agony, but did I have what it took to stand by while they did? There was something, something that might just be useful niggling at the back of my mind, I thought it may have been something Glory once told me, but it was on memory's edge just out of reach, making me want to do a bit of shrieking on my own account. I wasn't helping myself - breathing fast, tense from top to toe and the more desperate I was, the less likely it would drift back.

I made a conscious effort to relax and think, Kat was resting her chin on the edge of the bed and I suddenly knew what might help. I reached for her collar and drew her closer, putting my arm round her neck and sensing her astonishment; we didn't have that sort of relationship. She was loyal and fond of me in her way, she just wasn't a demonstrative sort of a dog, but it only took a few seconds for her to understand what was needed and she laid the warmth of her fine boned head against mine. My breathing adjusted to hers, I buried my face in the silkiness of her hair and let her simpler energy move in, pushing the complicated tangle of mine back, clearing my head. In the space created and because I'd stopped trying, I remembered. I told her she was wonderful, which she knew anyway and she moved away with relief, staying close, just not that close.

Glory spent her first years in a children's home during the Blitz. The numbers of orphaned, injured and irreparably damaged children taken into care stretched the home's facilities and staff to breaking point, and night-time when terrors ran wild, were the worst. It was discovered purely by chance when five-year-old Glory slept in a dormitory, even the most disturbed and distressed children settled, she was far more effective than the strongest sedatives. They had no idea why and would never in a million years have guessed a truth that Glory herself didn't know. All she knew was the crying of the children hurt her ears and their nightmares ripped her mind, but if she placed soft blankets in troubled heads and smothered the horrors, everyone had a better night. She'd used it in self-defence, could I turn it around; protect others by smothering Obnoxious for a while? It wouldn't be long-term, but might last long enough to get help without causing harm. I settled more comfortably on the bed, well as comfortable as is possible with a chained wrist, and focused on Obnoxious. He was upstairs in suburbia; in a room towards the back of the house.

"Let me help." For a few bewildered seconds I thought it was the baby. It wasn't. It was Alison Olivia, previous resident of this house and apparently, still here.

CHAPTER FORTY

I don't know which of us was more startled; she that I knew her or me that she was locked in a room just doors away. And I did know her, not only her past but also her present; the sadness, the soft mourning at the back of my mind for so long. Why on earth though had I not been able to pinpoint who and where she was as I'd done with so many others? I should have been able to locate her, let Boris get her out. Nothing seemed to make sense and for a few moments our thoughts and questions clashed, criss-crossed and knotted. Usually I like to take control but maybe I was more shaken than I thought, because it was she who pulled back first.

"Wait! No time. I'll help, but then you have to stop me."

"Stop you?"

"You have to," she said, "I can't do it myself; I've tried, he always knows, won't let me." I thought I'd misunderstood, so she laid it all out for me with a lightning swift information dump, a whirling blur of facts, comprehension, conclusions and choices. I put all of that in order as quickly as I could, infected by her urgency and pieces of the puzzle clicked dreadfully into place.

* * * *

It was Alison Olivia he'd met and married; it was her limited psychic ability that unleashed his. She'd never given much thought to it, no reason to think she was different from anyone else, assumed everyone had similar occasional mental intrusions and dealt with it in ways that best suited.

And it was never all the time, just came and went, often with months or years between, no big deal. She could turn it down, tune it out more or less completely and the only time it intruded was under some kind of emotional overload. By the time she married, she barely remembered it was there, and by the time she realised the marriage had been a terrible mistake, if she thought about the ability at all, she thought it was the least of her problems. She couldn't have been more wrong.

When Obnoxious, whose name turned out to be far more prosaically Phillip, accidentally stumbled across what she saw as a liability, he saw it as heaven-sent. He couldn't believe his luck. He'd been researching for a long time and here was what he'd been looking for - right under his nose. He turned the full, cold focus of his resentment, frustration and thwarted ambition onto the woman he'd married.

Her telepathic ability proved disappointingly limited, but that didn't matter, because by then he'd found she was something else altogether.

She was an amplifier, an energy source, an enabler; powerful in a way that had fate not thrown them together, would almost certainly never have come to light. Her uniqueness led him to his own; enabled him to grow into something he always knew he was destined to be. His talent was locating and latching on and into others.

He could utilise their combined talents, his and hers, to worm into the mind of anyone, but normals weren't in any way as rewarding as those with even the slightest psi abilities. And naturally it followed that the cream of the crop, the delicious and most fulfilling fruit at the top of the tree were those possessed of powerful extra sensory perceptions – rare, but oh so rewarding.

His ability was to crawl in and infiltrate, put down roots. By the time a host became aware, and they didn't always, he was in too deep to dislodge, embedded in such a way that causing his destruction would precipitate theirs.

Sometimes he went in and stayed deliberately dormant, content to gently suck experience, emotion and energy. Other times he preferred to play puppet master, actively manipulating individual and events to create whatever he happened to be hungry for. It transpired that drugs, sex, and violence were none the less enjoyable if experienced vicariously; and all the better for there being no risk, no danger, only an ever-growing greediness for more.

He was a natural parasite, she thought of him as a multi-tentacled octopus, each tentacle buried deep in an individual mind. No limit to tentacles, no limit to victims. Over the years he'd learnt and evolved as all successful creatures must. There'd been mistakes of course; some people weren't able to tolerate the intrusion, it killed them. Others had their minds completely blown but could still be useful, like the unfortunate cab driver. He, Phillip, liked to say 'Life is a learning curve', apart from which there was always more prey and he relished the hunt as much as the infiltration.

She was different, possibly unique, probably irreplaceable. He'd looked, naturally because it's always sensible to have a back-up, but without success. So she was treasured, cherished, something so precious has to be kept safe. Safe and obedient.

Everything that arrived full blown in my head rang horribly true and tallied with what I knew; I'd been an unwilling witness to the fall of Jamie and in the maelstrom of his mind, even as it was being sucked out of him, even as he'd died, I'd understood what was happening if not who was doing it, and I'd known that claws were in Ruth too. This was all somewhat of a tricky situation. A thought occurred.

"Is there anybody else down here, the other rooms?"

There was a pause then, "Not anymore."

"What happened?"

"You don't want to know." She was right; there was only so much I felt up to, right now. I changed direction.

"How long have you been here?"

"A while." What she wasn't saying chilled me, she was a post-war baby like me, we were a similar age give or take.

"Will you do what I've asked?" she interrupted. I hadn't misunderstood what she was asking. She better than anyone knew what he was, knew he had to be stopped and saw her own death as the necessary first step.

"Absolutely," I agreed. I didn't have time to argue, I'd explore options other than elimination later. "But I need you first." I caught a sense of her absolute exhaustion, physical and emotional, together with the vast corrosive guilt she carried. Imparting so much information had drained her.

"I'm assuming he can't hear us?" I said, a little late to ask but I had no sense of him, so didn't think he could. I picked up her assent then showed her what I had in mind. She understood instantly and, clumsily at first as we each adjusted to the rhythm of the other, then faster as we did, we constructed something thick and soft, heavy and smothering. Two of us had it ready far quicker than if I'd attempted it on my own, and it was stronger for the dual input. Then I took a deep breath; I was only going to ask because it was so important and I wasn't feeling 100% but she was there before me.

"Of course," she opened up and feeling that strength unleashed, powering through me, made me understand more clearly than anything else how it had been possible for him to do what he was doing. It felt as if a searchlight had gone on in my head, I instinctively, if pointlessly, shut my eyes against the brightness. Then I took what she was lending me, added my own energy and threw it to where, pink lips pursed in concentration, he'd just put down his pen. This might be our only chance; failure wasn't an option.

We swiftly draped our blanket round his mind and then I knocked him out, although even as he went under, he tried to lash out, punish me with the pain of others. But we'd succeeded, he was too well wrapped - snug as a bug in a rug - and he slid off the chair and hit the ground.

"Just one more thing, then you can rest," I said to her. I heard nothing and froze, had I inadvertently done what she'd asked and finished her off? Then she surged back, and with her power behind mine I sent out a yell for help that I hoped would be heard. If it wasn't, I'd have to try and get us both out on my own.

"Sleep now," I said to her.

"Will you... ?"

"When you're asleep," I told her and felt her drift away. 'Not on my watch,' I thought as I felt her let go and then belatedly realised while she was still with me, I should have used her help to cut the chain, but I didn't have the heart to wake her. I'd do it myself. I twisted on the bed to better see the chain and as I did, felt a distinct tightening in the bump area.

"Not to worry," I muttered to the baby, who was obviously being squeezed, didn't like it and had gone very still, "Braxton Hicks," I said, and then after a moment or two, "or maybe not."

CHAPTER FORTY-ONE

As the pain faded, I tried to refocus, although not that clear what I was refocusing on. I was cross, this was extremely bad timing and perhaps earlier exertions had tired me more than I'd thought because the stark white-tiled walls of the brightly lit room seemed to be moving in, then backing off again. It wasn't the way you want walls to behave.

One arm was still behind my back, I'd got distracted before I could break the chain holding it there, so was still lying at an uncomfortable sideways angle. I'm not normally a whinger, I know life has its ups and downs, but it was hard not to think longingly of my meticulously packed labour bag back at home, packed to the gunnels with essentials such as natural sponges to cool my forehead and dampen my lips, eau de cologne for my wrists and a whale song cassette in whose calming qualities David had great faith.

I'd realised when the pains kicked off, there was no alternative but to put out an additional yelp for help, more of a sustained mental shriek really and that was without input from my new friend. Having once taken the decision that I had to get assistance, the possibility of that not happening was a thought too alarming to contemplate.

"You can stop shouting now," Rachael was suddenly sharp in my head, peppermint green and snappy. I was tempted to sob with relief but time was of the essence, so I dealt with the pressing issue.

"I'm having the baby," I said, although still wasn't sure whether or not she even knew there was a baby; if she didn't, then this whole thing would be a double surprise.

As usual she had an opinion. "Well, you can't have it now."

"You think?"

"We're already on the way, won't be too long. Stay exactly where you are." I was going to say not having much choice, then it struck me, how could they already be on the way? But another contraction demanded my attention.

"How far apart?" Glory in my head this time.

"What?"

"How long between pains?" she said, and I snorted a laugh, I knew if David had been around, he'd have had timings down to the second.

"Close. Don't know exactly."

"OK," she said, "I'm here now," and she was, suddenly fully in my head with me. She'd never previously taken over quite so completely; I'd have expected to be horrified instead of which, as I found myself enveloped in the fizzy lemon-sherbet essence of her, I'd never been so relieved in my life.

"Hmm, not sure how much time we've got."

"Can we move her?" Rachael asked. Glory didn't answer, she was assessing and running her mind over the chain that was causing me so much discomfort and passing information back to Ed; he was much defter at that sort of thing than anybody else. I felt the blissful release of the strain on my arm as he neatly snapped it and metal chain slithered noisily over metal bed frame to coil on the floor.

It was Ed driving the vehicle heading my way and I could feel his intense agitation, which put the wind up me more than anything else. Ed generally maintained a complete block on his emotions and I didn't need his panic to fuel mine. Then I stopped thinking as I headed into another contraction. Naturally, David and I had attended NCT classes, and I did have a song ready to belt out as things intensified – we'd been told it would take our minds off any discomfort but;

"Screw the song," muttered Glory, "I've got you," and sure enough, she had. Turns out, 'a trouble shared is a trouble halved,' applies particularly well to labour, who'd have thought? She'd more or less blocked off what I was feeling, leaving just the residual shadow of sensation, "Got to be able to feel something," she said, "so you'll know what's going on." I was impressed; she could save the NHS a fortune in epidurals, although right now I was prepared to swear the baby was working its way up, rather than down; maybe it shared my lousy sense of direction.

"This isn't funny," Glory grumbled, "only you could find yourself in a situation like this; don't know whether you're daft or just plain nuts." I was turning a little grumpy myself and was about to come back in self-defence but Rachael got in first,

"No time to discuss. We're not far. Ed?" I heard his silent agreement, and sighed with relief, I wasn't on my own anymore and I had complete faith in the people coming to get me, but with the comfort of knowing and the easing of pain, panic returned fully fledged.

"Listen," I said urgently, "you need to know…"

Rachael interrupted, "We know."

"But it's Ruth."

"I *said*, we know."

Using elbows rather than a hand and wrist still painful from the chain, I eased myself farther up the bed and manoeuvred a couple of pillows to cushion my back against the rigid bedhead.

"Where is he?" Rachael asked.

"Upstairs."

"Can't find him," she said.

"No, well, he's out for the count, I used the blanket."

"Blanket?" said Glory, "oh right…" she broke off. She was looking through my eyes at the door to my room which was slowly opening, and then she was sharing my shock and horror at what was coming in.

CHAPTER FORTY-TWO

From the doorway she said quietly, "You didn't do as I asked."

"I didn't," I agreed. I was trying to rationalise what I was seeing with what I knew, but it didn't make any sense and there was no way of hiding my reaction. She was upright only with the aid of a wheeled walking frame, because matchstick legs below a mid-length, shapeless cotton dress would never have supported her. Her arms, thin and scarred, were taut and shaking on the frame, they were taking what weight she had, although didn't look as if they could do so for much longer. There was a sound and she glanced towards the stairs with apprehension,

"Still out?" she asked.

"Like a light," I said.

"Still in here though," she raised one thin arm to her head, anticipating the pain.

"Even if he comes round," I said, "he won't be able to hurt you, the blanket will hold."

She nodded, not reassured and I understood how much courage it had taken for her to leave her room. Pain and worse, the anticipation of pain, isn't easy to shake off.

She was almost completely bald with only a few thin white tufts clinging obstinately to a bone white scalp. Her eyes in the skull of a folded and hollowed face were blue and bright with awareness; she knew what she looked like.

"I don't know how I can help," she said as she moved forward slowly, but I can at least be with you until your friends arrive."

"Thank you," I said and meant it. Glory, in my head was still and silent, I don't think she knew what to say either and even the baby seemed to have temporarily stalled. Instinctively, I put my hand out and after a moment's hesitation she moved to take it, lowering herself carefully into the bedside chair. She hadn't felt human contact in a long time, had forgotten the warmth of another hand. She closed her eyes savouring that as she regained her breath, then she said,

"You got the wrong war," and for a moment I didn't understand and then I did, but that wasn't possible.

"I'm afraid it is," she said.

"But I thought…"

"I know what you thought. You were wrong."

I inadvertently squeezed the thin hand in mine and she flinched.

"Sorry," I loosened my grip, but knew she didn't want me to let go.

"You didn't tell me," I said.

"You wouldn't have believed it; sometimes you have to see something to know it's true."

"Then you're…" I was trying to calculate based on what I knew.

"Coming up for 60. Born 1920, I was indeed a post-war baby, just a different war. She paused and coughed over a voice dry from disuse, I gestured at the glass of water on the cabinet, she used the hand not in mine, drank a little, went on "This is the house I was brought up in."

"I know." I said. She nodded, registered no surprise, she'd already been in my head.

"I was 35 when I met him, on the shelf but very comfortably so." Regret and loathing seeped through our joined hands, "We both taught you see. He took a job at my school; 1955 that would have been. He was nice to me. We married quickly; we weren't youngsters, a long engagement would have been foolish. Naturally he moved in, house all paid for, silly not to." She took another drink, replaced the glass.

"We were never love's young dream, but we suited. I stopped work when we married and, as is said, you never know what goes on behind closed doors. Behind ours, the first months weren't too bad and I'd never expected bliss anyway. Things changed when he found I wasn't such a consolation prize after all. Actually, he felt he'd hit the jackpot and for a brief while I revelled in that. Whilst I was busy revelling, he crawled into my head; hooked into my mind; learnt the power of pain and how to calibrate it. Too little didn't keep me in check as much as he wanted; too much and…" she paused, memory still raw, "Once he knocked me out for three whole days, by the time I came round, he was frantic and I could remember nothing, nothing at all! Oh, it came back slowly; everything came back, maybe it would have been better if it hadn't. He realised he could kill me and obviously that was the last thing he wanted; you don't kill a golden goose. By the time I'd fully come back to myself, I understood I wasn't able to get away, but I had to try and stop him; I tried all sorts of things."

As a necessity, because of the time constraint, her story was a swift mix of speech, thought and emotion. She was optimistic, ingenious and imaginative in the ways she tried to eliminate him, but as time went on, optimism faded and died. She came to the inevitable conclusion the only way to stop him 'gathering' – that's what he called it every time he added a new mind to his growing collection – was to take herself out of the equation, but it's well-nigh impossible to go behind someone's back when they're in in your head and plotting, however devious proved no match for pain.

"Brain-washed," she said, "in a shockingly short time, you're brain-washed, conditioned. You learn as a cow learns to fear the cattle prod, and the agony of anticipation is as bad as the reality because anticipation goes on for much longer."

"And you've been down here all the time?"

"Goodness no, upstairs for many years, cooking cleaning, the usual sort of stuff."

"But when you went out, couldn't you have just run?"

"Didn't go out; he shopped, told anyone who asked I was agoraphobic, unable to leave the house. Then," she paused to think, "1969 or 1970, I think it was, he decided it might be better if I was out of the picture completely. Heart attack: very sudden, very sad, although by then there weren't many people he needed to tell – the postman, the milkman, a teaching colleague I'd vaguely kept in touch with.

He'd been converting the original wine cellar for years; kept getting different people in, so most of them never got the whole picture of what it was he was building."

"Must have cost a fortune." I said.

"It did," she agreed, "mine! When it was finally finished and fully equipped, he decided I should stay down here." She countered my gasp.

"It hasn't really felt as long as it's been. I sleep a lot, he puts something in the supplies he brings me. I don't really mind that."

Gravelly with disuse, her voice was going again and she drank. She'd kept her tone pragmatic, but I was holding her hand which told me so much more. I understood he was scrupulous in his care, ensured enough to eat, drink, occupy her mind. She was precious, but he'd long ago stopped thinking of her as a person; she was a power-source and like any piece of equipment needed to be kept in the best condition, because he used her often.

"What's happening with the baby?" she asked suddenly.

I was startled. "Oh, well the contractions seem to have stopped." I felt bad, I'd rather forgotten about the baby, that didn't bode well for the future. "Glory?" I said.

"It happens." Glory had been taking everything in, but Alison Olivia jumped convulsively and I realised I hadn't done any introductions – how rude. As she pulled back I realised for her, the addition of another mind meant only more fear more pain, more guilt.

"Ten minutes, we're only about ten minutes away," Glory, aware of the other woman's distress had cut down on the usual briskness, "would have been quicker but the snow's pretty bad you know."

Alison Olivia grabbed my arm with her other hand, "Please, will you do it now? End me. You can, you've done it before haven't you?"

"Don't," said Rachael.

"Of course not," I said.

"But you *promised*," Alison Olivia wailed, twisting away from me in panic and desperation, "you gave me your word, you said…"

"Stop that. Right away please." Rachael who'd been listening too, wasn't going to waste time with hellos, nor did she seem to feel a gentler approach might help. She'd gone straight into Alison Olivia's head. She was used to being obeyed and Alison Olivia was used to obeying, she swallowed a sob.

"And none of that." Rachael instructed. I did sometimes wonder whether she'd missed her vocation with the Samaritans. "Alison Olivia, no… I'm sorry, can't be doing with that, too long. Going forward, you're Alison. Can you work with that?" The newly named was as stunned as Rachael intended, but there was still a small spark left.

"Look, I don't know who you are and I don't give a damn what you call me, but you have no idea what I've done."

"Own free will?" asked Rachael.

"No."

"Well then."

"No, *no* - you don't get it. He can't do what he does without me, my death's the way to stop him - my revenge, his payback. But… "

"He's implanted something, made sure you can't. So you want us to. You want to wash your hands of damaged minds in his menagerie and check out. Right? Nobody packed an emotional punch quite like Rachael.

"What else I can do?"

"Don't know yet. But you're no use to anyone if you're dead. Anyway, we're here now, make your mind up."

CHAPTER FORTY-THREE

Events had leant towards the surreal from the moment Laura had slipped that pill into my drink and they simply carried on in that direction. I was now aware of muffled activity upstairs but could hear nothing clearly.

"Soundproofing," murmured Alison, "if there's screaming down here, it can't be heard upstairs." Up till that point I'd been keeping an inward eye and ear on the blanket wrapped around the unpleasantness upstairs, and felt huge relief as Ed's mind joined mine, took over and I knew I could let go. Alison felt a shift too and automatically tensed to receive the pain.

"No," I said, "we've still got him." She relaxed, then tensed again as the room suddenly got extremely crowded. David bowled in first and I wasn't sure I believed my eyes.

"What are *you* doing here?" I said.

"No Stella, what are *you* doing here?" David rarely yelled, but as it was only righteous indignation that was holding back huge anxiety, I wasn't judgmental; he was probably in the right and I owed him an apology. His hair was standing on end where he'd raked fingers through and he definitely didn't have the cool, calm demeanour the NCT preferred in a birth partner. I could see I had bridges to mend, but I had questions,.

"How did you know where to find me?"

"I didn't know where to find you, nobody did. Then I thought maybe you'd gone down to the school, I couldn't get them on the phone, lines down in the snow, so I drove there.",

"The *school*? Why on *earth* would I go there?"

"Well I don't know, do I? Who knows what goes on in that crazy head of yours?" I glared at him, honestly, did he think I'd dashed out on a dark snowy December eve just for fun, and indeed since I'd been here, fun was the last thing I'd been having. I started setting this out for him but didn't get far.

"Not now," Rachael hurried in which was worrying, I don't think I'd ever seen her hurry before.

"Where are we?" she asked,

"Well *I* don't know," I said, "I came in a cab…"

"With the baby?" she snapped. Glory who'd followed them in and was still in my head, snorted a brief laugh and answered.

"Contractions seem to have stopped."

"Because it's not safe, she doesn't feel safe," the renamed Alison said softly. She wasn't used to putting forward a viewpoint. David, who'd taken my hand, suddenly focused on who had my other one and was unable to hide his shock. I felt that go right through her but she continued evenly.

"It's fact, if an animal is in danger; labour often stops until it can find a safer place." I gave her hand another small squeeze. Considering this was a woman who hadn't encountered a stranger for probably the last fifteen years, she was not only coping well with the influx of three of them, but attempting to hold up her end of the conversation as well.

Glory nodded, "She's right," then to Kat who'd been undecided at whether she should be repelling boarders or welcoming allies said, "Hello, you here too?"

"Really Stella?" Rachael said, "Did you really have to bring the dog?" I started to explain what had happened but didn't have a chance to finish. "Come along, we have to go." I obediently if cautiously swung my legs over the side of the bed.

"Go?" David was indignant, "are you crazy? Go where? She needs an ambulance."

"David," said Rachael, "There's one room upstairs looks as if it's been hit by a bomb, another where there's a deeply unconscious man, and this lady…" she nodded at Alison, "would like us to kill her, before we go." Rachael, now on one side of me with Glory on the other, hadn't quite finished. "It's complicated, police will be involved and goodness only knows who else. No. We need to go. Stella, shoes?" I nodded at my sorry pair of slippers under the chair.

"Those are all I've got."

"Oh for goodness sake!" Rachael said, as Glory chuckled and flew them over for me to put on. They'd dried but I doubted become any more weatherproof. "Here, hold her." David thus instructed and momentarily silenced, put an arm round my middle and didn't even flinch as Glory floated me above the ground to make the going easier.

I was coming down a little from the euphoria evoked by the appearance of Rachael and Glory and grateful to feel I was no longer in sole charge of the complicated mess I'd got myself into. Truthfully all I wanted was to be sitting up somewhere in the pink frilly bed-jacket my Mother had bought, holding my baby and smiling graciously as more flowers were delivered.

As we reached the foot of the stairs Ed was heavily descending to see how we were doing, and Rachael shot him a question.

"*No*," I said as I intercepted; "Absolutely not.. You cannot bring him,"

"Who?" David was looking from Rachael to me, but Alison had picked up, so knew exactly what was being discussed and I felt her horror.

"I'm sorry," said Rachael to both of us, "No choice," and she showed us how she'd last seen Ruth; deeply and unreachably unconscious, Sam anguished and watchful by her side. For a few seconds, deep purple lavender surrounded us and Alison swallowed a sob as she caught and recognised it.

Rachael answered her unasked question, "My sister. Now, what's it to be, will you try and help us, or shall we simply help you?"

****

I don't remember too much about that journey, I was focused inwards, so don't suppose I was great company. They'd come in the large smooth-running vehicle, more of a mini-bus really. It accommodated a lot of people in three rows of luxuriously leathered seating onto to which I gratefully collapsed. Kat had made a unilateral but firm decision not to go on the floor, so was wedged firmly on one side of me with David was on the other. I felt Kat's positioning was more for her own comfort as opposed to compassion for my condition, but she felt pleasantly warm and solid at a time when not much else did.

Rachael and Glory were in the row behind us, either side of a totally traumatised, erstwhile Alison Olivia. Rachael, no stranger to the effectiveness of emotional blackmail had persuaded her to briefly postpone annihilation, but even as mentally and physically wrecked as she was, exhausted by incarceration, pain and loss of hope, there was still room for fear and she'd shrieked in shock at the sight of Ed advancing across the room to carry her upstairs. Poor Ed, truth be told, he was as terrified as she; convinced if she struggled she might snap one of those sad stick arms or legs. As a precaution, he briefly nudged her into unconsciousness, and by the time she drifted back she was safely in the van. Also in the van, locked securely in the back, dead to the world and staying that way courtesy of Ed and Rachael, was our additional and extremely unwelcome passenger.

As we'd left the warmth of the house I'd been relieved to see the cab had gone, my conscience was a bit overburdened at the moment and I wasn't sure I could take responsibility for him too so opted for an out of sight out of mind attitude.

The weather had worsened considerably but drivers don't come much better than Ed and the van was well able to cope with icy conditions, even so, there were a couple of times when we all felt the loss of grip and there was a communal indrawn breath at the resulting smooth, never-ending sideways slide, not released until Ed regained control.

I'd assumed, as had David that we were headed for the nearest hospital. This alarmingly proved not to be the case, although I think I realised before he did. A silent but terse query to Rachael confirmed we were going back to the school. I wasn't in the least bit happy about that and dreaded to think what David would say when he knew. I wasn't even reassured to learn Mrs Millsop was a qualified midwife.

"Why not hospital?" I wanted to know.

"Can't risk it. Safer with more of us together."

"But…"

"Better safe than sorry."

"Of course, but…"

"I assure you if things go wrong, we will get you to hospital."

"Gee thanks," she ignored any sarcasm and I think then I must have dozed against David's shoulder for a while before something woke me.

"Oooh," I said.

David anxious, and who could blame him said, "What's happening?"

"Contraction," I muttered and Glory, who'd gone off duty, bustled back into my head to help.

"No, no, no. No contractions yet," said David, "hang on a bit, try and relax." I didn't have breath to respond but on the whole, I was getting pretty fed up with people telling me when I could or could not have contractions, whose womb was it anyway?

"Hang on a minute," David said, this time to no-one in particular, "shouldn't we be there by now?" He wiped away some of the condensation on the window at which point he suddenly realised what he would have realised a lot earlier if he hadn't been so overwrought. His voice rose in protest, "Where are we going?"

Rachael said from behind us, "Private Clinic." David turned to face her and I chose to zone out of the hissed and heated exchange that followed. I had more than enough on my plate and wanted only to lie down somewhere quiet. I very much hoped the baby had enough energy left to do what needed to be done, I didn't think I'd be much help. Then David recognised the high gates opening before us and finally understood where we were, and as Ed skimmed through and we headed down the drive, there was another frank exchange of views.

As we drew to a smooth halt beneath the over-ornamented portico, the heavy front door was flung wide and light surged out along with Mrs Millsop; a starched and capped Boadicea, primed for battle.

"How far apart?" she barked,

"Just under two minutes." David was on it as I'd known he would be. Glory and I exchanged brief amusement.

"Since when?"

"They stopped for ages, started up again fifteen minutes ago."

"Right. Problems I should know about?"

I giggled, "Don't get me started!" Everyone ignored me whilst David whipped from a coat pocket my meticulously maintained record book, slapping it into Mrs Millsop's waiting hand with military precision. At the same time, Ed passed him my hospital bag, my meticulously packed hospital bag, even in all the panic he'd remembered to bring it, what a husband!

"No time to dilly-dally," Mrs Millsop was in her element and as the only one present with practical experience automatically took charge. Behind us, I was aware of Rachael trying to persuade a reluctant Alison to leave the safety of the van and let Ed carry her inside, but poor Alison, having made it this far had reached the end of a tether pretty worn in the first place. Her breathing was fast and shallow and she was whimpering. Ed and Rachael in a swift exchange of thought were about to gently put her under again when Mrs Millsop, currently mistress of all she surveyed, spun on her heel, took the few paces back to the van, produced from somewhere about her person a brown paper bag and clamped it firmly over Alison's mouth and nose.

"Panic attack," she said briefly, "Breathe in… aaannndout, that's good. And again for me." Focused briefly on the drama behind, I was unexpectedly engulfed in a heady waft of Yves Saint Laurent – Opium, if I wasn't mistaken.

I turned my head slowly. Surely not? But yes, "*Laura?*"

"Stella," she said and tried to take me in her arms. We were more or less the same height, but there was an awful lot of tummy between, she settled for holding both my arms. "Stella, darling, poor David's been so worried, well we all have. You do know, you'll have to be more thoughtful once the baby's here."

I looked at David who shrugged helplessly, "She was at home when I got there, insisted on coming, didn't have time to argue."

Laura laughed lightly, "Silly boy, I do have a stake in this." but beneath the brittleness I read her guilt, her fear of what David would think and her agony of anxiety about what I was going to say next.

"Well, I'm very glad to see you," I said and couldn't help a grin at this blatant untruth. Surprisingly she grinned back, genuine amusement lighting her face in the way her usual social smile never did. She held me tightly for a few seconds longer, squeezing briefly, before letting go, then started and looked down.

"Oh!" she said, "the dog!" but neither she nor Kat seemed to have energy or inclination to do so much as a head toss and just stayed where they were. Laura was both relieved and grateful, she was also completely out of her comfort zone and baffled by my peculiar set of friends, none of whom she'd ever met nor heard about before. Behind us, Mrs Millsop removed the paper bag and said with satisfaction;

"There, that's the ticket!" and stepped back, getting her first look at Alison and not skirting the issue; "dear oh dear, look at the state of you."

Alison let out a sob strangled by a chuckle, "Haven't looked in a mirror for years," she said.

"Probably best," said Mrs Millsop firmly and without a trace of irony, just someone seeing a problem which needed dealing with. "We'll get you sorted, Matron's word, rely on it! Come along then Ed, get her inside, chop chop." As she spoke, she moved Laura aside, retook my arm and marched us into the warmth. I just knew, had there been a sword to hand, she'd have been holding it triumphantly aloft. Propelled briskly forward, I was reflecting on how the carefully maintained, distinctly separate areas of my life had so suddenly merged, it was all a bit much; the sooner they laid me down with some whale song, the better.

CHAPTER FORTY-FOUR

The baby obviously felt there'd been enough hanging around, and waited just long enough for me to be ensconced in a side-room off Mrs Millsop's spacious clinic - better equipped than most hospitals - before making her imminent presence felt. I promptly lost a fair bit of self-control and NCT teachings, swore roundly at David, informed Mrs Millsop in no uncertain terms that I didn't want her telling me what to do, and yelled for Glory.

Glory and the baby in fact arrived at the same time, both in a rush but with no undue fuss, although when Mrs Millsop, who'd had enough experience to ignore my instruction to get lost, swaddled her tightly and moved to hand the small parcel to David, he was spark out on the floor and not one of us had seen him go.

"Should be shot," grumbled Mrs Millsop under her breath, handing the baby to Glory, and unceremoniously hauling him out of her way, before plumping my pillows with a few punches and settling me more comfortably on the bed.

"Bit harsh," Glory was jiggling the baby gently.

"Not him! Whichever idiot it was, thought it'd be a good idea to have Fathers in the room."

"Is he OK?" I leaned over to look; he was indeed out for the count.

"He'll live," said Mrs Millsop with scant sympathy, "best out our way for now."

I held out my arms and Glory, who was more emotional than either she or I had expected, passed the parcel and I looked into the eyes and mind of my daughter. Other than a wave of protectiveness that had I been standing would have knocked me flat, I couldn't feel anything at all to worry about. I glanced at Glory.

"A normal baby girl," she agreed silently. We both looked at the small being in my arms who stared back, in the wide-eyed, startled-owl way babies have.

"Rightiho." I understood Mrs Millsop's default position was long-suffering and put-upon, and she was having a tough time right now, concealing how much she was enjoying herself. "This isn't going to get the baby bathed, is it? And God only knows what you've been up to tonight - I certainly don't want to – but let's clean you up a bit, then you need to rest. Give me Baby."

"No." said Glory and I together. I knew why I didn't want to let her go, but Glory's response was a little worrying. Mrs Millsop bristled but recognised a brick wall when she ran into it.

"Few minutes longer then," she said, "and I suppose you'll both be wanting a hot cup of tea?" she was straightening the bed around me and moved Glory out of the way so she could tuck me in even tighter. "As for you Glory-girl, you'll need to make yourself scarce soon, let Stella get some rest." Glory turned to give her a quick, one-armed hug and was batted away impatiently, "Get off, silly so and so." But I saw and was surprised by the deep affection between the two.

As soon as Matron's comfortable rear end disappeared out the door, Glory drew a chair to the side of the bed; I put out my hand and she took it. There was information needed exchanging and we didn't have much time.

"Ruth?" I asked and instantly saw her as Glory had, earlier; deeply unconscious, an almost imperceptible slow rise and fall of her chest the single sign of life. To say she was a shadow of her former self didn't cover it. Flesh had fallen shockingly away from cheekbones that now stood stark; her lips were colourless, sunk inwards. She had her arms above the blanket covering her and once-plump fingers with painted nails, one of her small vanities, denuded of varnish and rings, were clawed and clenched.

"How long?" I meant, how long had she been this way.

Glory chose to misinterpret, "Not much longer. Sam says it's eating away at her, sucking her dry and she'll simply move to a level where her organs will shut down one by one. Like your Alison said, he hooks on, crawls in and embeds." Glory's self-reproach drenched me, the guilt she shared with the others that they hadn't immediately known, and that perhaps if recognised at an earlier stage they could have done something but,

"We weren't sure for such a long time, he was so well hidden."

"But last year, when she was so unwell?"

"We think he overestimated how much he could take; when he realised what was happening to her he eased off almost completely," in a chilling echo of Alison's words earlier, she added, "no one kills the golden goose."

"Why? Why her?"

"We believe he stumbled across her by accident, he'd probably never found anyone anywhere nearly as strong, and then…" she stopped.

Our hands still joined, I drew back to look at her, "And then?"

"He found you."

"*Me?*"

She sighed, "That confrontation at Jamie's – we came to get you – we'd no idea it could be anything remotely connected to our worries about Ruth, but you knew, didn't you? You saw what had happened to Jamie, what had driven him insane; you saw the link to Ruth?" she paused again then continued, "When you recognised what he was, he also saw and recognised what you were." Shock zipped through me, as I started to see the whole horrible picture – and my role in it.

Ruth and Jamie were both random victims; but *I* was the one who'd tuned into Jamie's nightmares and followed them up. It was because *I* got in too deep and needed help that two random victims of the same predator were brought together. I'd seen the link but I'd also been the link.

In her mind, Glory had assembled a sort of crime-investigation board, and I was the string, the common factor, connecting Ruth and Jamie, both tied to and infected by the ghastliness of Phillip. Glory waited for me to understand something else, to catch up – and I did.

The twisting apprehension, the masks, the chant, the constant crying in my head. I had been carrying the connection, the infection with me, just hadn't recognised it for what it was. I felt Glory's distress, knew she had no reassurance to offer.

"It didn't occur to us at first either," she said, "Jamie was right out of the picture by then, and we thought if we kept you completely away from Ruth, he was unlikely to find you, and in the meantime the rest of us were all trying to locate him. You did insist on coming down after the wedding but other than that, we've done pretty well keeping you away."

"And Ruth couldn't know…"

"…about the baby. If she knew, he'd know too and that would put you even more at risk. Your level of ability plus a brand-new baby. Getting hands on you would be like winning the lottery twice over, and all the time we thought we had you covered…"

"…he was already in and knew everything. 'Come into my parlour said the spider to the fly' and I bloody well did!" And then Mrs Millsop arrived back with tea.

CHAPTER FORTY-FIVE

David was mortified; and not helped by Mrs Millsop making it clear, in her opinion Fathers who insisted on being present, were probably best off on the floor and not getting in the way of other people with a job to do. Luckily, none of this was enough to wipe the smile off his face as he cuddled the baby and Mrs Millsop, having applied a witch hazel saturated cloth to the egg-shaped bump on his forehead, was tactfully removed by Glory to give us some time alone.

As is so often the case in life, these long anticipated early moments with the baby weren't quite as I'd imagined they'd be. David was, understandably, still not on board with the fact that not only were we not as planned in Edgware General Hospital Maternity Unit, but that nine months pregnant, I'd thought it a good idea to head out in blizzard conditions omitting to tell a soul where I was going. This decision had, he pointed out, resulted in him driving all over the country (I felt this was an exaggeration) through snow and ice, accompanied by his hysterically, guilt-ridden Mother, who insisted it was all her fault but refused to go into details, and without his coat, which someone had borrowed. It had all been, he said, a bit stressful.

That I'd then had to be rescued from a cellar in which some maniac had locked me was worrying and even more worrying was instead of handing said maniac over to the police, we'd brought him home with us.

I had to admit, looked at from David's point of view – indeed from anybody's point of view, I hadn't handled this well. On a positive note he was so nerve-frayed with all the above that he didn't have the energy to give me the piece of his mind I deserved. This was a good thing, because I was tired in a way that knocked all previous tirednesses right out of court. So much so, every time I blinked, my eyelids showed an iron determination to not re-open for business any time soon. The baby, who might have expected to be the focus of all attention, seemed to be fairly philosophical that she wasn't, and kept dropping off against whoever was holding her. We'd discussed names, despite Aunt Kitty insisting it was bad luck to choose a name before the baby arrived, and we'd lined up three for a girl as I was so certain. We said we'd finalise once we saw who turned up and that wasn't hard. She looked like a Sara.

What with Glory's recent input and its ramifications rocketing around my head, and trying to present David with some kind of rational explanation for recent events, I wasn't sorry when Mrs Millsop re-appeared. She was, she said, putting her foot down.

"We'll feed Baby, then sleep." I said I had to talk to Glory again but she wasn't having any of it. "I'm the one who says what happens or doesn't happen in my clinic."

"But I want…"

"Well if wishing and wanting were doing and making, we'd all be a lot better off, wouldn't we?" she said, and I could see resistance was futile. The quicker I did what I was told, the sooner I could do what I wanted, and I wasn't going to be much use to anyone if I couldn't keep my eyes open for longer than two minutes at a time. I fed Sara, not without a fair amount of misgiving once I felt the strength of those small jaws, and David went off to check on what was happening with his Mother, who'd had a bit of a funny turn on being presented with her new granddaughter. Her complete 'overwhelm' was two halves of a whole, one half thrilled and thankful the baby had arrived safely, the other completely unable to deal with Mrs Millsop's, "Nana will have to get used to nappy changing again." Under no circumstances did Laura plan to be a Nana; a Grandma possibly, but she wasn't even sure about that, and she certainly didn't intend to get involved in the mucky side of things. She felt she was far, far too young for any of this and all of a sudden, came over tearful. She was going to go to bed she said, she needed time to "Get over everything!"

I flatly refused to let Mrs Millsop take Sara away while I slept. She wasn't impressed.

"That's plain silly. Don't come grumbling if you don't get a wink because Baby's crying." I assured her I wouldn't and she brought in a cunningly converted plastic crate which she'd lined with layers of blankets and placed on one of her trolleys, so I could pull it close to the bed.

Given it was now past midnight and had been an eventful day, I expected to go out like the light Mrs Millsop clicked off as she left. Instead of which I was wide-eyed and wakeful. David was just across the hall in another clinic room, said if I needed anything to call, and when Sara cried, he'd get up and change her, but as I heard him snoring as soon as his head hit the pillow, I wasn't setting too much store by that.

I desperately wanted to know what was happening, there'd been more for Glory to tell me had we not run out of time, and the overall silence resulting from the proximity of many minds with shuttered thoughts, which was normally a pleasure, was now nothing but a pain. I couldn't pick up anything and the more questions went round in my head the muddier the answers they churned up.

CHAPTER FORTY-SIX

"*Absolutely* not," David said, and I knew the next thing he was going to say was 'I forbid it' but he looked at me, knew I knew and wisely bit his lip.

"Of course I'll do it," I said.

I suppose you could say we were in crisis talks; and if we were a funny combination seated round the table in the dining room that morning, the darkness of the discussion obscured any amusement. I didn't feel particularly well, and it was nothing I could blame on the baby in my arms, it was the all too familiar twisting of apprehension in my gut, plus my guilt over any number of things. At a time when David should have been relaxed and celebrating – he wasn't. And as unruffled as he was trying to remain, the strain of yesterday and now today was showing. This morning when we'd woken, I'd sworn to him this was the last, the very last time I'd put him in this kind of position, but we were where we were and decisions and actions had to be taken of which I had to be a part – and he refused to let me go and discuss that without him.

Rachael was seated opposite me; I hoped but doubted I'd hidden my shock when I saw her. When they'd turned up yesterday on the rescue mission, I wasn't really in a state to take stock of how anyone looked but now, the morning light streaming through the large windows was merciless, she was early fifties but today looked years older. She'd been silver-haired almost as long as I'd known her, but now the uncompromisingly chopped, chin-length bob was dulled to match her drained face. If her appearance told a truth, her manner was as brusque and unbowed as ever. She turned to Boris seated next to her, his face giving nothing away because he looked strained at the best of times.

"Right," she said, "alternatives?"

Cheek swollen with one of the aniseed balls everyone else had refused, he said, "We do have options. Sam?" Sam was running through possibilities in his head, visualising, stacking, organising. I wondered what the tutors and students at Oxford made of him, hoped he was doing well, but it was an irrefutable fact he'd probably been a better diagnostician at six than many of them would be in a lifetime. Seventeen now, he'd shot up to around six foot. There were still elements of teenage gawkiness but many more of the man he would become; unchanged was the watchful deep brown gaze of the six-year-old I'd first met. Across the table, he ducked his head briefly at me and dropped an eyelid in a swift wink, it probably wasn't a move anybody would notice, just something I'd taught a traumatised grubby small boy. To both of us it meant a great deal.

For the purposes of this meeting, shields had been dropped. When I'd raised an eyebrow Glory had said, "Quicker," and of course it was for all of us, well with the exception of David and, I devoutly hoped, Sara snuffling in my arms.

"We're currently keeping him unconscious at a deep level, limiting brain activity to the bare minimum to keep him alive." Sam was speaking aloud for David's benefit, but we all saw and felt Alison flinch. Glory had brought her through in a wheelchair earlier, and a chair the other side of me had been removed to make space for her at the table. She was wearing a silk scarf shaped into a colourful turban; I was surprised to recognise it as one of Laura's. Alison caught my eye and lifted her hand to touch it self-consciously.

"Hermes, no less!" Then she spotted the baby and her face softened, erasing for a moment all the strain. Glancing at me for permission, she put out a cautious finger which Sara obligingly gripped. She'd paled though at mention of Phillip.

"He can't hurt you," Rachael reassured her, "he's in a solid steel reinforced section at the back of the building, safer than a safe and Ed's there monitoring him." Beside me I heard David's instant thought, as did all the others.

'What the hell do they usually use *that* for?'

Boris with a twist of a smile answered obliquely, "I assure you dear boy, only in extremis," and David subsided, somewhere between amused and embarrassed, but still wondering.

Ignoring interruptions, Sam continued, "We have options but each carries its own risks. There's a lot we know and a lot we don't. We presume he's embedded as deeply in others as he is in Ruth?" he looked at Alison who nodded; the copper taint of her guilt felt by everyone. Sam nodded, "We know keeping him under will stop him causing pain, or further draining victims but it won't resolve anything. We believe when he embeds, he leaves something of himself, marks his territory, uses it to find his way back and go straight in. We know he's not particularly strong on his own, he has to utilise Alison to boost him," he looked across at her, "you're positive you've no way of identifying victims?

She shook her head, hearing Sam's clear summary was an unanticipated ordeal, "There was so much pain, - mine and theirs - I never really had any sense of them as individuals," she looked at Rachael, "I didn't know about your sister, I am so sorry."

Rachael nodded briskly, "Not your fault and Ruth would say the same."

Sam turned to me. "We know Stella, that you were specifically targeted and we believe you've also been infected and affected." David's shock was palpable, this was news to him and although it wasn't to me, I'd deliberately filed it away in the 'don't think about it yet' drawer.

"We can," Sam went on, "simply eliminate him," beside me and despite everything David flinched a little, "that's not the problem," he paused, "the problem lies in the unknowns. We don't yet understand how or what he's implanted. We don't know if he's not around, whether what's inside his victims will simply wither away or whether it will rot, in which case it could be a death sentence." He paused, he had a real sense of the dramatic and in other circumstances I'd have told him so. "We don't know how many victims are already as damaged as Ruth, or whether there are others we can help," he paused to let us assimilate and point out anything he'd missed; no-one spoke. "Bottom line is, if he's dead, we'll never know."

The summary was all the more chilling for the evenness with which it had been delivered, although in the midst of all the awfulness, I felt a certain amount of proprictorial pride at what Sam had turned into; I smothered it quickly, before anyone picked up on it.

Boris took over smoothly. "As Sam said, we think there are only two courses of action and we have to move fast with both because we're losing Ruth." The pain of this reverberated as he carried on, seemingly at a tangent and I jumped as he addressed me. "Stella, we must first look at you and Devlin, because it would seem when you pulled him back from wherever the brain injury had taken him, you did the same thing, you left something behind." David knew about Devlin and what I'd done in the hospital, but it must have slipped my mind to fill him in on what had happened since, and his bemusement was clear.

Rachael drew a quick breath, if time was short, so was her patience, so she bridged the information gap. I was apprehensive, I knew how he'd reacted when I'd done a similar brain dump, but under these circumstances he accepted it, maybe it was different because it was Rachael.

He blinked hard. "Blimey."

Boris was still waiting, "Well, Stella?"

"Well, what?"

"Will you let us see if we can work out what happened and how? It could be key to saving Ruth."

"Wouldn't you need Devlin too?"

"He's already here." That shocked me, there was obviously a whole lot of stuff I didn't know either, but I'd ask questions later.

"Is there a risk? I asked.

"There's always an element of risk, you know that."

"Tell me what you need."

"*Absolutely* not," said David.

"Of course, I'll do it," I said.

From my other side Alison asked, although she already knew, "And the second thing?"

Boris smiled at her, "Ah now, with you, Alison we have a different situation. After all your time with him, we can find no trace of him in you," Sam confirmed with a nod, and Boris went on, "we think he understood enough to know that embedding in you, would somehow lessen what you could do; and to be frank he didn't need any extra hold over you. He had you under lock and key and all he ever needed was the pain of others to trigger yours and keep you under control. But we need you to help us track them down. You know this man, probably better than he knows himself. Will you help us?"

"You'd need him conscious?" she said. Boris nodded and we felt the immediate repugnance in her reaction; she could not, absolutely would not, go there again.

I hesitated, I knew what I could do and how much of a risk I was prepared to take but that was my right. Did I have any right to push the frailty of this woman who'd already helped me so much. I decided it was probably as much for her own good as for the good of the many unknown others, Glory caught my eye and nodded.

"Alison Olivia," I said softly, "what was it your parents used to say?"

She grimaced slightly, "That I always knew my own mind." we waited while guilt swamped gut reaction and she sighed, "I'll do my best."

CHAPTER FORTY-SEVEN

I'm sure I've said it before, but as you know, that's not going to stop me saying it again; however crazy a situation gets, I believe we only have the capacity to reach a defined level of stunned. When that level's reached, our brains recalibrate to cope. At no time was this more evident than the couple of days following Sara's birth.

After our morning's planning session, I wasn't sure I was ready to deal with David's entirely justifiable concerns, many and varied as they were. I did try to put any information omissions down to not wanting to worry him, to which he responded a trifle tersely.

"And how's that working out then?" I felt I had to take into account he'd been bearing the brunt when it came to family matters, which was enough to leave anyone tetchy. Last night, at an ungodly hour, David had called his now frantic father to reassure him Laura wasn't really missing; was safe and well with us, and then divert attention with the baby announcement, although Melvyn apparently was still almost as frantic at the end of the call, as at the beginning.

The call to my parents didn't go well either, up till now my Mother had maintained an affectionate yet dignified, Mother-in-law to Son-in-law dynamic, but in the face of what he had to say, I gather that temporarily went out the window and there was a fair amount of sobbing, some of which was joyful, a fair portion recriminatory and the rest; sheer disbelief all this had happened without her knowing. She couldn't quite get her mind around the fact that not only was I not comfortably ensconced at Edgware General in a pink bed jacket, but was snowbound at an unknown school, miles away in 'the country', and that Laura was with me instead of my own Mother! I gathered at this point, and before anyone could say anything they'd regret, my Father had commandeered the phone.

Whilst we'd had our crisis talk in the dining room, Laura, to my surprise and I gathered to hers too, had been press-ganged by Mrs Millsop to lend a hand in the kitchen, providing breakfast for the half dozen kids who were still boarding over the holidays. When I popped down to see her, she was helping clear up and greeted my arrival with some relief. She'd had to borrow some clothes and from the vivid scarlet loose trousers and black and scarlet splashed top, I could see who from.

"I'm a bit worried about phoning Melvyn," she confided, "David said he wasn't happy."

"Just worried," I reassured her, "he'll be fine."

"And your Mother? I hope she doesn't feel I've been treading on her toes."

"Absolutely not," I lied. "Would you like a cuddle with your granddaughter?"

Laura eyed Sara cautiously, "Maybe later, I've been washing up," she leaned in and hissed, "no Marigolds!" then in normal tones, "my hands are a bit slippery; I might drop her."

Mrs Millsop, giving the wooden table a good seeing to with a soapy brush, looked over at me and frowned.

"You, young lady, should have your feet up, not be rushing here, there and everywhere. I'll be finished here in just a mo., I'll take Baby; you go and have a rest."

Laura nodded sagely, "I'd listen to Enid." *Enid,* I was impressed, I'd no idea Mrs Millsop even had a first name and was mighty impressed Laura had been given permission to use it.

"No," I said, "thank you," then because it sounded a bit short, softened it with a laugh, "you're so kind to offer but honestly, I'm fine, don't want to let go of her." Which was the truth, but nothing like the whole truth. I didn't know why, but knew it was essential she was in my arms, and I'd been around me enough years to know a feeling which seemed to carry no logic, proved all too often to make sense at a later date.

"That was sweet," I said to Laura, "you lending Alison your scarf."

"She could hardly go around as she was, could she, she'd frighten the children." But beneath the words, I felt her shock and distress. In the face of experiences so far removed from anything she'd known; she was thinking she had little to offer other than a pretty scarf. She stopped me as I moved towards the door.

"When are we heading home?"

"Soon," I said, "just a couple of things I have to do first."

* * * *

On my way out of the kitchen, I was intercepted by Boris accompanied by a smaller, distinctly truculent figure who stood stock still when he saw me, then retreated a little.

"Hello Devlin," I said.

"You gave me a fright," he said accusingly.

"Boris told you I was here, didn't he?"

"Not *now*," he was impatient, "*before*."

"Ah…" I said, "you were very ill, you know."

"I know."

"It seemed the only way to help you." I wasn't sure whether you told a child just how close to death he'd been.

"You *scared* me." In his indignation he took a step forward.

"I did," I conceded. Boris, watchful behind him was surprised; he and Devlin had talked this through; he thought he'd explained, I gathered though he wasn't accustomed to twelve-year old boys who well knew how to grab a grudge and hang on and there was no arguing, what I'd done that day hadn't been nice. He was still glaring at me, fists clenched and I saw the depth of his outrage. I took another risk. "I'm sorry you're angry," I said crisply, "and I understand how you felt about it; let me show you how I felt."

It wasn't hard to summon from a couple of years back the sounds, the scents and echoes of the critical care equipment; the appalling emptiness in Devlin's head as everything swirled away down an ever-deepening hole and my desperation to stop it. I parcelled all that up, exactly as it had been and put it firmly into his head.

"Ow!" he took a step back. "I didn't know you were scared too, thought it was just me."

"No, not just you." I said. He looked at me thoughtfully and I decided to seize the moment.

"And you've been copying what I did, haven't you Devlin?"

"Huh?"

"You've been giving people bad frights, haven't you?"

"Maybe."

"Poor Jane, what made you pick on her?"

He shrugged, scuffed a sneaker toe-down along the carpet. "Dunno. I just knew her."

"You scared her so much that you made her ill."

"Really?" there was more than a hint of pride.

"And all the others," I said, "in cinemas, theatres, people were injured, did you know that?"

"Wasn't my fault," sulkiness set in, "they all just ran; I didn't make them run."

"Two people died - after the butterflies."

He looked up shocked, bravado abandoned, "Because of me?"

"They were knocked down and killed by a taxi. They didn't see a single one of your butterflies, they ran because everyone else was running." There was another silence. "Everything has consequences Devlin."

"But…"

Boris interrupted, "I'm afraid Devlin, there is no room for a 'but' in such circumstances."

Devlin swung round to face him, "You said, I wasn't in any trouble."

"You're not," I said, "but if you still remember so clearly, how dreadful I made you feel, why would you want to do it to anyone else?" He was crying now, not the quivering lip and forced tears that always melted his mother. I wasn't feeling great, just a big bully, but Boris forestalled me offering comfort.

"Too important for that." He said in my head, then aloud, "Do you understand what we are telling you Devlin?"

Devlin scrubbed his face quickly with a jumper sleeve. "S'pose." Focusing hard on his carpet-raking sneaker he muttered "didn't know…"

"Well, you do now." I thought I was sounding more like Rachael than Rachael and saw from the small twist of the lips that Boris did too. "So, Devlin, you and me, are we OK?"

"S'pose." This was a boy with a lot to take in, "I didn't want to come here you know. Mum made me."

"Did she?"

"Yeah. He," Devlin paused, he'd nicknamed Boris, 'Bones' but didn't feel that ought to be shared aloud, Boris and I exchanged an amused glance, "…came round yesterday, he and Mum talked, then she said I could go with him," he shook his head slightly in wonder, after so many years of being told never to go off with a stranger, his Mother had changed her tune, just like that!

"Boris can be very persuasive," I said. I imagined Susan would have no idea afterwards quite what had possessed her either.

"He said I'd be back by this evening, but now the snow's come I might have to stay longer. Don't mind, I like that Sam. Will you be there? Will it hurt?"

"What?"

"He said I had to have tests."

Boris was impatient to get on with things now, shepherding me and Devlin ahead of him down the hall. "I thought I explained," he said, "we only want you to solve a few puzzles. Nothing will hurt, you have my word."

Devlin sniffed unconvinced, but regaining some of his normal nosiness. "Is everyone here a bit 'funny then?"

"No," Boris was short. He was turning things over in his mind. He was unsure of the outcome and Boris hated to be unsure of anything. If I'd inadvertently passed something to Devlin, then tracing that back, understanding and reversing, would not only be taking a loaded weapon out of the hands of a child, but the key that was needed to try and save Ruth and the unknown others. It would also allow them to break whatever connection there might be between Obnoxious and me. But was it possible what had been put in, could be taken out? Was it reversible?

* * * *

"Down here," Boris said, unlocking a door at the other end of the corridor. There was a well-lit flight of carpeted stairs. Devlin went first, I instinctively drew back, I'd gone down another staircase recently and that hadn't gone well. "Don't be silly," Boris had a hand at my back.

In my arms, Sara murmured and stirred and descending I held tightly to the wall-mounted rail, I thought if I fell on top of young Devlin, it could well ruin our new friendship and it wouldn't get Sara and I off to a great start either.

I needn't have worried. The space Obnoxious had led me to was cold and clinical, this was warm and welcoming. Polished wooden flooring, with soft ceiling lighting reflecting back from mellow wood panelled walls, there were a few groupings of leather easy-chairs, and a couple of tables and chairs for work rather than relaxation.

It was a larger duplicate of the basement in the Peacock's St. John's Wood home. I looked around for the booths and there at the far side of the area were the same type of glass-walled, telephone-box sized constructions, this time there was a row of six, ranged at intervals along the wall. Each held a leather chair facing a shelf on which were a pair of substantial black leather headphones and a mic. To the left of the wall with the booths was a wide corridor with doors opening off. Rachael's sharp peppermint was near, she was with Ruth, or rather the shadow of Ruth, deeply unconscious, totally absent.

I swallowed, but my mouth was dry from talking or maybe apprehension. Sam had already come down and rose from one of the deep leather chairs to pour me a glass of water, I smiled thanks. Devlin meanwhile was turning in entranced circles, "Wowzers gershmowzers, it's like a secret hideout, like in a film. Like MI5 or like maybe the baddie who's going to blow up the world. Cool bananas! What d'you want me to do?"

"A jigsaw puzzle," Sam, pointed to a box on the table, "I warn you, it's a complicated one." Devlin wilted a fair bit, he'd been thinking along the lines of donning a helmet with wires on it and possibly being strapped down in a special chair, and now here he was with a rotten old jigsaw, the purpose of which, although he didn't know, was simply to distract him while Sam and Boris did their stuff.

Sam immediately saw where things were falling short. "Of course, that's not all," he said. Devlin brightened, "While you're doing the puzzle there's going to be something a bit frightening going on. You'll be able to see your own brain."

"Isn't that dangerous?" Devlin was nobody's fool.

"It is," said Sam solemnly, "And if you don't want to look, you don't have to, none of us will think any the less of you, I promise."

"Here Stella," Boris indicated the chair Sam had vacated, "make yourself comfortable, doze if you want." "Devlin, let's have you here at the table; sooner you get going, the sooner we will."

Sam and Boris took a couple of the upright chairs and settled themselves a little way away. They were going to go through my head and Devlin's with a fine-tooth comb, looking for similarities, differences, traces of memory, emotion, anything that might provide explanation and the way forward. I knew it had to be done, but had no intention of dozing while other people tramped through my mind.

I settled Sara more comfortably in my arms, I hadn't had any experience with babies, but she seemed to be remarkably well-behaved, which considering how hectic my life was at the moment, was a blessing. I knew I should be paying her more attention, and made a promise, once we'd got all of this head to head stuff out of the way, I'd do just that. I made a deliberate attempt to relax and did an automatic scan around to check who was where and what they were doing.

Ed wasn't in the building at the moment, I knew he'd taken David and the large van to the nearest shops to restock on essentials. A quiet Christmas had originally been planned and the deluge of guests had been unexpected.

Alison was outside. Ed had wheeled her onto the patio at the back of the building, overlooking the lawns. They'd had a brief but intense disagreement about the weather. Ed, who'd been raised to caution on such matters by the Peacocks, said it was far too cold to sit out. Alison who'd been starved of 'outside' for more years than she could count, was having none of it. They compromised with an extra jacket on top of the one she was wearing, a hat on top of the turban and a pile of blankets firmly tucked in by Mrs Millsop who happened to be passing when they were setting up. I knew how tight a Millsop tucked blanket could be so Alison wouldn't be going anywhere soon, but I also shared what she was feeling, the bliss of breathing in the cold clear air.

Glory was with Phillip; they'd all agreed he needed to be watched, conscious or not while the investigation operation was conducted and it was her couple of hours. She was seated as far away as she could possibly get from him in the small room; beige painted walls, no window and a door which looked as if it wouldn't stand any nonsense. Glory was used to being on an even keel, so pessimism had taken her by surprise and she didn't like it one bit. But whichever way you looked at it, Ruth was not doing well. With a grimace and an effort, Glory pulled her mind back to keeping an eye on Obnoxious.

Rachael and Ruth were nearer to me, in a room along the corridor. Rachael had spent the night sleeping on and off in a chair by her sister's bed, jerking awake every few minutes, full of fear and helplessness. She couldn't remember a time in their lives when Ruth hadn't been there, always instantly reachable. Now, nothing.

Bella, who since Ruth had gone downhill, had refused to leave her side was sleeping, a massive brown weight against one of Rachael's legs which had also consequently gone to sleep, but she didn't want to move away from the warmth and affection. She was automatically shielding but seeping through was her grief, raw and intensely personal. Like Glory, she feared that whatever Sam and Boris came up with, it would be too late for Ruth. I withdraw quickly and guiltily.

Near to where I was sitting, Devlin despite himself, was rising to the challenge of the jigsaw, but was also fascinated with the slowly revolving holographic images Sam had created of our brains, mine and Devlin's. I could feel Boris and Sam in my head, although from the lack of any reaction, I don't think Devlin could. Sam and Boris were outwardly relaxed, leaning back in their chairs. They were working calmly and methodically, thoughts flashing between them. The speed of thought that was the only indication of how worried they were that they wouldn't find what they were looking for.

Despite myself, I must have drifted off. When I woke, it was because death was approaching in the beloved form of Ruth.

CHAPTER FORTY-EIGHT

My first thought was that I was dreaming. My second thought was that first thoughts like that can make the difference between life and death.

I reached out for Rachael and Glory, but got nothing. Sam, Boris and Devlin were on the floor, each lying neatly by the chair on which they'd been sitting, and there was silence there too. The only thing I could hear was the underlying hum of the air-conditioning system. It was accompanying Ruth, who was also humming. I briefly thought, what the hell was I going to say to Devlin's Mother and then I thought maybe I wouldn't be around long enough to say anything to anybody.

It was such a wonderfully familiar sound, Ruth's tuneless hum; she did it when concentrating, although, strenuously denied any such thing if anyone was tactless enough to mention it. Her caved-in cheeks were hectically red, like one of Dottie Lowbell's dolls. Her eyes, usually deep hazel and shining with humour were currently white rimmed, blood-shot and empty; devoid of intelligence or feeling.

Ruth and the air-conditioning weren't the only things humming now. The room was too, an almost inaudible low vibration bouncing off the walls and felt deep in my chest, the massive amount of psychic energy being generated. It was feverishly unnatural and uncomfortable familiar.

It seemed, on balance, retreat might be the better part of valour right now and holding Sara tightly, I started to move towards the stairs, then I paused. This was Ruth, my Ruth. How could I not at least try and get her back, but as I took a breath to speak, so did she. Ruth's mouth, but not her voice, nor her vocabulary; a hoarse torrent of obscenities spat directly at me, venom-filled and hitting me like a fusillade of shots, one after the other after the other.

"Ruth," I yelled, because I needed to reach her wherever she was, "Ruth, it's *me*,"

She stopped abruptly, refocused those empty eyes and tilted her head. "Why Stella dear, so it is. How lovely, nobody told me you were here, now that's naughty isn't it?" she waggled an admonishing finger, paused and smiled, her lips stretching and parting over her teeth. "And the baby, the baby's here."

I started backing away again slowly, this wasn't going as well as could be hoped and it's always good to keep options open. I went into her head and came out quickly; there were an awful lot of minds in there and as far as I could tell, none of them was Ruth. She smiled at me again, a crooked, knowing grimace of a grin, widened her eyes and whispered.

"I wish I wish I wish I knew, exactly what to do with you." And ice slid down my spine as the voice that wasn't Ruth's, blended with another, then another and another, an unholy chorus repeating the chant and no longer whispering. I reached the foot of the stairs, couldn't risk turning my back on her so consequently stumbled, landing painfully on one hip and she moved slowly towards me. Slow and steady.

I knew what had happened and I wondered how it was that a roomful of highly intelligent telepaths had overlooked the 'what ifs'. What if solid steel reinforcements weren't enough to hold Phillip? What if it hadn't been possible to keep him unconscious? What if he didn't need Alison's consent to use her?' Because that's where the enormous power was coming from. I knew we could stop Alison as a group, we'd blended before and we were powerful indeed, but we weren't together now, I didn't even know if the others were still alive. The living energy in the room was cutting off all other sensation and whatever Ruth was now, her intention was clear, she was coming for Sara.

I had one option and only one chance, there wouldn't be a second. I had to stop Ruth and Alison simultaneously, one without the other wouldn't do it. Two colossal but surgically precise hammer blows I couldn't afford to get wrong, the stakes were too high. I was now making a clumsy, seated ascent backwards, step by step. Ruth was still advancing; things weren't great and then they got worse.

From the shadows of the corridor, emerged my old friend Phillip the Obnoxious. Average height, average build and Bugs Bunny pout, he should have looked comical, he didn't. It would have been wonderful at that point to hear something from Glory or Rachael, but I couldn't. I was on my own; solo so to speak. Well, not quite, I had a brand-new baby to protect.

Phillip giggled, licked the pinkness of his lips and I realised, not only was he boosted by Alison's power, he was using Ruth's too, which meant he sliced into my head like a knife through butter, and I instantly felt the draining of energy and ability. In my arms Sara squirmed, catching my panic or maybe I just squeezed her too hard. Ruth was mounting the stairs; one foot on a step, the second brought up alongside. First foot on another step, second brought alongside, it wasn't the quickest way, but who was I to talk, I was going up on my bottom.

I had to act before I had nothing left to act with. I focused and knocked Ruth backwards, she grabbed at the wall rail too late, stepped back into nothingness and toppled clumsily back down the few stairs she'd climbed. I don't think I even touched Alison, certainly didn't feel any flicker in the power levels.

Ruth ponderously got to her feet again, far sooner than she should have been able to, and those empty, empty eyes looked up to where I was now crouched at the top of the stairs, my back against the closed door. And she started moving again.

In those few dreadful seconds, I looked over at him, he had the upper hand now, Alison's power, Ruth's too. He pouted a smile at me and shook his head slowly, had I really thought I could get the better of him? Of course, I could knock Ruth down again, and then again and again, but both he and I knew my strength would give out before theirs did. I reached for the door handle behind me. A door between us would only be an illusion of safety, it certainly wasn't going to stop anyone, but it was better than staying on the stairs like a sitting duck.

Ruth was looking directly at me, ready to attempt the stairs again, those empty eyes met and held mine as she moved and then slowly she turned. And he knew. In that moment he knew, but it was already too late. What leapt across the distance between them was soundless and invisible but swift and terrible. He stayed upright for a riveted few seconds longer, but he was stone dead, way before he hit the floor.

Several other things happened all at once. The door behind me was flung open and as I turned my head, Ed and David both tried to squeeze through at once and from the basement corridor an enormous burnished brown shape crossed the floor in one huge leap and a bound and landed squarely on what had once been Phillip Obnoxious. David put his arms round me and the baby, and Ed, with hitherto unsuspected acrobatic ability, hands braced on the wall either side, vaulted over the top of us, hurled himself down the remaining stairs and caught Ruth before she too hit the floor. Supported by him, she looked up and if her voice was a little hoarse, it was her voice.

"Stella dear," she said, "would you mind?" and she inclined her head towards a furious Bella growling and circling the body.

"I'll do it. Bella, here girl.," Rachael, more the worse for wear than I'd ever seen her, had followed Bella but at a slower pace and close behind was Glory, who also looked as if she'd been pulled through a bush backwards.

If Rachael sounded near enough her normal authoritative self, it didn't mask in any way, the supreme effort she was making to maintain self-control. Bella now obediently at heel, Glory and Rachael, each with an arm round the other crossed the floor, making a wide berth around the late unlamented. I wasn't sure who was supporting who.

Rachael said, "I don't understand." then couldn't seem to say any more.

Ruth, my Ruth now, leaning against Ed, reached one hand to her sister, the other to Glory. "It has all," she admitted, "been a little tricky," and she gave a small dry sob as Ed, enclosed Rachael and Glory with his other arm.

A few feet away, Sam was holding his head with one hand, checking Boris with the other. "He's OK, just taking longer to come round." He turned to Devlin who wasn't at all sure what it was that had happened, but hugely disgruntled that his partially completed puzzle been knocked completely off the table. He was, however, instantly distracted and awe-struck by the body on the floor.

"*Wow!*" he said, "Oh *wow, wow, wow!* Is that a real live dead body?" I vaguely wondered whether Sam and Boris had found what they wanted, before they'd been so rudely interrupted. and was aware David was asking me all sorts of questions I didn't have answers to. I felt sick, lightheaded and shivery and it was only because he was holding on to me that I hadn't tumbled straight down the stairs.

I looked over at Rachael who normally took bossy charge at times like these. But she, Ruth and Glory looked as if they were only upright because Ed was holding them.

Well, this was daft, we couldn't just stay here. Someone needed to take charge of the current not-run-of-the-mill situation, and as no-one else looked in a fit enough state, I stopped shaking and clinging and levered myself up.

"If," I said, "I don't get a cup of coffee soon, there's no telling what I'll do or who I'll do it to. What say we take this upstairs?"

CHAPTER FORTY-NINE

"I do know," said Ruth, "what I've put you all through. I am so sorry." This time round we'd gathered upstairs in Ruth and Rachael's living room, which if it had been crowded before, was now positively packed but it felt like the right place to be, and cosier than downstairs.

We'd emerged from the basement under the horrified gaze of Mrs Millsop who'd commandeered the corridor to lead the children in a *What's the Time Mr Wolf?* assisted by Laura who had the air of a woman landed on a strange planet and told to be nice to the aliens.

"Good Gawd Almighty!" normally fairly unflappable Mrs Millsop had her hand to her chest, "what's happened?" She turned swiftly to the children whose eyes were growing wider by the minute and clapped hands sharply, "Television room. Now. I'll be there in a minute. Yes, course you can turn it on - go!" she didn't have to tell them twice. As the last of the kids disappeared towards the back of the building, she turned and lifted Sara from my arms, thrusting her into the unready arms of her Grandmother, "Laura, sort her out, she's soaking."

"I need to feed her," I protested.

"And she'll be a lot happier if that happens when she's clean and dry."

"Oh no, I really don't think…" said Laura.

"Rubbish." Mrs Millsop didn't have time for nonsense. "You had a baby, didn't you?"

"Years ago!"

"Well, they haven't brought out a new model." Mrs Millsop gave her a small push in the right direction, "chop chop." Beside me, David, who was looking a little grey and leaning against the wall, gave a snort of amusement and Mrs Millsop hastened forward to Ruth and Rachel, neither of whom looked in better nick than the other. Rachael's normally crisp white shirt looked as if it had been slept in, which it had, and her neat hair showed evidence of her having run hands through it more than once. Ruth had put on the track suit she must have been wearing before they put her to bed down there. Orange with black stripes, it would have done nobody any favours at the best of times.

"No, don't fuss Enid," Rachael, rising above her appearance, had pulled herself together, "we're better than we look; nothing to worry about."

"That's as maybe," Mrs Millsop was sceptical; she recognised shock when she saw it, "but I'm getting you hot sweet tea." Then as Boris came up the stairs, supporting Ed who in his leap to catch Ruth had done something to his leg, she added "And ice for that leg." Glory had followed behind the two men with the idea of preventing Ed from falling should he lose balance, although what she could have done was debatable.

Boris looked pretty much untouched on the outside but his ordered mind was badly ruffled, he was appalled at how effectively he'd been knocked out; pride, if nothing else severely dented. Sam was last to emerge, holding the hand of an overexcited Devlin who grabbed the nearest arm, which happened to be Mrs Millsop's as she hurried past.

"There's a dead body down there," he shouted, "a real, dead, dead, dead body, want to see?"

"Don't be ridiculous, young man. I think I'm looking at someone who's had a bit more sugar than's good for him." she glanced briefly over at Rachael. Matron Millsop was a woman with her size eights planted firmly on the ground, but little as she liked to dwell, there was no doubt there were some funny things that went on here from time to time. Rachael had become extremely interested in ridding herself of a random piece of fluff which had attached itself to her cardigan sleeve. Mrs Millsop knew an avoidance tactic when she saw one, but it was her conviction that the Peacocks, whatever they did or did not do, were on the side of the angels. 'Least questions asked', her old mum used to say, 'least damage done' and Mrs Millsop had never seen fit to deviate from that policy.

"Right young fellow, me lad," she lifted Devlin's hand from her arm, turned him smartly in the opposite direction "you need a bit of quiet time; the others are watching some TV rubbish; go on and I'll want to see you sitting down when I come in, mind."

"Oh Lord," Glory suddenly exclaimed, "Alison, where's Alison?" Boris and Sam hastily made a guilty dash and returned pushing the wheelchair. Retrieved from outside she was dreadfully cold, utterly exhausted yet remarkably cheerful.

"Well, yes," she said to extreme concern "I was a little chilly I will admit, my own fault though, I insisted. Anyway, I knew someone at some stage would remember where I was, but I wasn't freezing, this wonderful animal took it upon herself to look after me, bit of a squash, both of us in this chair but honestly, she was better than an electric blanket. Katerina shook herself a little and looked suitably modest. I was amazed, she wasn't that keen on people, rarely attached herself to anyone other than me, and I'd always thought that was more contingency than caring, but maybe she sensed more than I gave her credit for.

Alison looked reproachfully at Rachael, "You did say he wouldn't be able to get to me."

"I was wrong," said Rachael grimly, "I am so sorry."

Alison shrugged, "Perhaps for the best," she looked at Ruth, "we did it, didn't we?"

"We did," said Ruth.

Alison nodded slowly, "I hope he rots in hell," she said, and if the sentiment resounded oddly in the domestic setting of the hall, I don't think any of us felt it was in any way out of place. Mrs Millsop returned at a trot, with a hot water bottle and Alison sat a little straighter in the chair and accepted it with gratitude.

Bella had meanwhile climbed the stairs too and in the narrow confines of the hall, seemed larger than ever, the burnished brown of her coat rippling as she moved. She'd arrived in the downstairs fray a little late only because Rachael, with no clear idea of what was happening had hung onto her for dear life, but I couldn't forget the speed and height she'd reached, then the heft of her landing on what she recognised as the threat to Ruth. She ambled past, giving my hip a gentle nudge, nearly knocking me over. Kat had her back turned but whirled indignantly when her rear end was sniffed, it was not a form of greeting she appreciated, but suddenly eye to eye with the bulk which was Bella, she gave a shriek and a jump which I swear took all four feet simultaneously off the ground, maybe she was channelling Laura. Alison, greeted in turn by Bella placing two enormous paws on her lap to stand upright and be patted, didn't shriek but was taken aback.

"Good God," she said, "what *is* it?"

"Leonberger-Newfoundland cross," said Boris, leaning forward to urge Bella down.

"Is she fully grown?" asked Alison, with interest.

"Hang on one flipping minute," David's patience had run out, "what the heck? We're standing around here chatting like nothing's just happened. In fact, I've no clear idea what has just happened." His voice rose further; if he'd been in a jokey mood I'd have told him it was verging on the petulant, but he wasn't, so I didn't.

"I'd *really, really* like to know," he paused, "but first, I'd better check on Ma and the baby," and off he dashed, leaving me feeling guilty. The baby had rather slipped my mind; I'd have to watch that when I took her out, it would be awful if she ended up in Lost and Found. It was odd though, I didn't feel anywhere near that same desperate urge to hold onto her all the time, what was all that about?

"Not sure," Boris answered my thought aloud "at a guess, I'd say it's not anything you're getting from the baby, but the change she brings about in you." He glanced at Sam, who silently agreed. I wasn't clear what he meant but before I could ask,

"I think," said Rachael, showing signs of getting back to brisk, "you're probably right, but David has a point. This has been a trying time, all round and we need to discuss what happened while it's fresh in our minds."

* * * *

"I would never have known as early as I did, had it not been for Stella," Ruth was sitting next to me on one of the sofas and she placed her hand over mine. "You spotted, in the middle of that dreadful show-down with Jamie, what I should have seen earlier. I hadn't felt right for such a long time before that, drained of energy and fearful - in the true sense of the word - full of fear. I imagined all sorts of medical awfulness going on inside me, but when you said what you did, it instantly made complete and terrible sense. I was…" she paused, and we shared with her the shock of that first appalling realisation; for David, she politely put it into words, "not thrilled! In that instant, I understood there was something within me that shouldn't have been there, and almost as swiftly I understood what it was, what it could do and worst of all, that I wasn't the only one in trouble." She wrapped her hands together in her lap, they were trembling and she wanted to still them, "At that point in time, my dears, I made my decision; I had to buy in, in order to bow out. And I had to do it on my own."

Rachael on her other side, sighed heavily, "Oh, Ruth, how could you?"

"How could I not? The choices were stark, in truth there were no choices and I had no idea if the rest of you were at risk," she looked at me again, "as indeed *you* were."

Rachael shifted against the cushions, her agitation plain, "How *on earth* did you think you could possibly conceal something so dreadful for so long?"

"And yet, Rachael, she did," Boris spoke for the first time since we'd sat down.

"Well, it was no walk in the park," said Ruth, the wryness of the comment not concealing what she'd taken on, "I had to compartmentalise. Shut away my knowledge of his presence. He never knew I knew he was there. At the same time I had to deceive all of you, that was hateful, and harder. But in order to deal with him, with what he was doing to me and to others, I had to know more. Pleasant it was not, but the alternatives were worse, and I watched you all more closely than you can ever imagine," her voice wavered; she covered it, "I watched you like an eagle."

"Hawk," corrected David absently, "sorry, the journalist in me!"

She laughed and we felt her total exhaustion, but she needed to get everything out. "I watched all of you for a sign or sense of infection, infiltration. At the same time I had to learn how he was able to do what he was doing."

Glory leaned forward, "But Ruth, you could have finished him - at any time."

"Of course I could!" Ruth's response had echoes of Rachael's impatience, "he wasn't that strong, I knew that. What I did not understand was how he was able to exponentially increase what he had. I was also aware of the many others and it was their fate I held in my hand too. If I eliminated him, would I damage them, or worse still was he able to simply transfer completely into one of those minds he was already in."

The strain on her face was reflected across the table in Alison's, two women sharing the impossibility of the position they'd found themselves in. Then tension was defused and that was no bad thing, by a token brisk knock on the door as it was flung open by Mrs Millsop with a tray over-burdened with sandwiches, flasks of tea, coffee, several varieties of cake and a fresh hot-water bottle to replenish Alison's current one.

Mrs Millsop was uncharacteristically anxious, didn't know what had been going on and didn't want to, because there was sod all she could do about it. The best thing she could do was make sure nobody went hungry. Laura was close on her heels. She was anxious too, in fact so much out of her depth, she was doubtful she'd ever find solid ground again. Unlike Mrs Millsop, she hadn't picked up on the atmosphere, had assumed these strange friends of mine, who she really wasn't sure about at all, behaved oddly all the time. Problem was, whilst naturally thrilled to bits about the baby, she hadn't expected to be dealing so early in their acquaintance with such basics as nappy changing. In the event, thrust into unexpected and seemingly unavoidable action she'd panicked;

forgotten how to fold the terry square, been traumatised at the lethally large safety pins and was convinced she'd break the baby in the struggle to get her into waterproof plastic pants. You had to feel for the woman, and understand the relief with which she placed Sara in David's arms and beat a hasty retreat. The two dogs had sneaked in along with the sandwiches, adopting laughably similar 'just pretend we're not here' expressions and had quietly positioned themselves either side of the fireplace like a pair of mismatched bookends, but a bit of normality wasn't a bad thing.

CHAPTER FIFTY

Despite, or maybe because of recent events, the sandwiches were as welcome as was the pause while we tucked in. Everyone was quiet - nobody was even thinking hard, although David spent a moment looking from one to the other of us, convinced there was frenzied conversation going on below the surface. I murmured that we wouldn't be that rude and he raised a sceptical eyebrow. Sara meanwhile gave the three small coughs, which we'd already established preceded her becoming vocal, and under cover of my track suit top, I popped her on for a feed before she could take-off. David seized the moment to get some input from the assembled experts. Was she or wasn't she? It was a question important to all of us but one by one heads shook, nobody could hear anything. David did his best to hide his reaction, he wasn't successful but I certainly didn't blame him; roles reversed; I'd have been hugely relieved too.

Fortified by refreshment and patting the side of her mouth to ensure no lingering egg and cress, Ruth continued.

"It was you Stella, who fascinated him, he found you because you found Jamie and then I turned up on the scene and he realised our relationship. But you were a problem."

"And not for the first time," Glory said under her breath. I ignored her.

"Why?"

She shrugged, "For some reason he couldn't seem to get to you in the way he had with the others, myself included. He always went in with stealth," she looked at Alison who confirmed with a nod. "Most didn't feel him, only knew he was there when it was too late, but you Stella dear, he pursued you for a long time." I shivered involuntarily and Ruth, with a look acknowledged this was hard to hear, "He tracked you and I tracked him. Something about you kept him out. Even with Alison's power behind him, he could only touch the surface of your mind. When you became pregnant," she looked at Glory, "I know you tried to keep it from me, you didn't succeed my dear, you should know me better than that, and if I hadn't learnt it from you I would have from him."

I stood abruptly; luckily Sara had finished, burped and dropped off in David's arms. I needed to walk around, couldn't sit still. I felt sick, angry, revolted – a load of emotions, none of them good because I now knew what it was I'd been feeling – not apprehension *about* Ruth, apprehension *because* of Ruth, because of her connection to the sickness that was trying to invade me. And he had, he had got in – the masks, the chant.

"I'm sorry," I said, nausea was rising, I made it to the loo just in time. When I emerged, Rachael was waiting for me.

She eyed my green complexion. "Better out than in." She brushed a strand of hair away from my eye, then unexpectedly pulled me close, arms tight around me. As I put my arms around her too, she sent something through my head. I tried to analyse it later, the best I could come up with was a disinfectant wash. Sharp, pepperminty, cleansing, it made me feel a whole lot better. I smiled in gratitude.

"Come on then, can't stand here all day." she said. "That husband of yours will fuss."

David had handed Sara to Glory and was on his way out, so we met in the doorway. "You OK?" he said, Rachael said to give you a minute." He frowned slightly.

She waved a dismissive hand, "You'd have only mollycoddled her and we have no time for that."

I sat down again, "I'm fine, sorry, just…"

"We know," Glory had Sara sleeping on her shoulder and was patting her back although whose comfort that was for, was a moot question. Over my years of involvement with the Peacock gang, we'd had many a serious discussion, but I couldn't remember anything that had this much weight to it.

Ruth put thought into words, "This has hit us all a little harder than usual, but now there are only loose strings…"

"…ends," said David. She chuckled. This was a woman who knew how to work her audience and I was relieved beyond measure to hear the shakiness going from her voice. Even in the short time that had elapsed, colour was coming back to her cheeks and her eyes were again those I knew so well.

"Loose ends indeed. He wanted the baby, you know."

"Yup, he told me," I said, "back at the house." This was all news to David, but far better, I felt, that he should know after the fact rather than during.

"Getting you to the house was his big final move." Ruth said, "But you coped."

"I wouldn't have done if Alison hadn't chipped in." I pointed out and with that, suddenly realised I'd given no thought to what was to become of her now.

"Sorted," said Rachael, "she's staying here for the time being. We're putting her to work."

"I'm going to be helping this gentleman," Alison smiled across at Boris. "I don't want to; honestly I want nothing more to do with the inside of anybody's head anymore." She shifted her position in the armchair Ed had helped her into, Laura's turbaned scarf still colourfully perky on her head, "But when all's said and done, I have a responsibility, he could never have done what he did to Ruth and all the others, without me."

"Under duress," Boris added.

She nodded, "But I will do everything I can to put things right."

Boris added, "Alison doesn't want to go back to the house."

"Certainly not," Alison agreed, her mouth downturned, "it holds only dreadful memories."

Boris continued smoothly, "We'll help with all the practicalities of selling and after Christmas, Mrs Millsop's organised a physiotherapist, Sam thinks muscle atrophy in her legs can be reversed." I frowned, I had reservations, this was a woman who'd lived for years under the dreadful control of someone else. Whilst all this subsequent stuff was well-intentioned, was her independence again being taken away? She heard, shook her head and smiled.

"Trust me," she said, "Alison Olivia, knows her own mind," and that put mine at rest, although David's was still churning with unanswered queries.

"How did he get out of where you were keeping him? You said there wasn't a chance."

"There wasn't," Ruth answered him. "That was me," she rested her head between her two hands for a moment, "it's all so convoluted," unexpectedly she snorted a laugh without mirth and over her bowed head glances were exchanged, had the whole thing been just too much? "You see, he thought he had me under control. He didn't know I knew he thought that. He told me to knock out Glory, then Rachael and Bella."

Rachael on the opposite sofa frowned. "You didn't have to though."

"Don't be silly, of course I did," said Ruth and the sisters glared at each other for a moment, one determined jaw and expression echoing the other, before she continued. "There was so little time, he was determined to have the baby." She ignored a combined indrawn breath from the baby's parents, "To do that, he knew I had to put you Boris, and Sam out of action, and of course young Devlin too." she shrugged at their expressions, "I had no choice, I had to make him believe in me until the very last second. He'd hi-jacked Alison and was draining Stella as well as me. He had, in those moments, more power than he'd ever dreamt possible; he was superhuman, euphoric!" She coughed, throat dried by talking and Ed sent a glass of water over. She drained it, smiled at him and continued. "I had to be genuine; Stella had to believe she was in fear of her life."

"I was," I said slowly. "Convinced, I mean."

"I took a dreadful gamble," said Ruth, I gambled everybody's lives on just two things; my ability to act within seconds, and my assessment of Alison."

We all looked at Alison whose colourful turban had now slipped to a slightly rakish angle. She closed her eyes briefly, recalling. "All l knew was he was back, despite all your assurances and promises. I trusted you all, yet he was back in my head. I wasn't sure what was happening but I kept getting flashes and as far as I could see, Ruth was on a rampage. And the pain in my head - the worst it had ever been.

Ruth nodded in agreement, "Dreadful pain plus the shrieking of other victims. I had to use all of that as a kind of distraction in the hopes it was enough to obscure my individual thought and Alison's reaction," she paused again, whether for dramatic effect, which I wouldn't put past her, or simply for breath, "I knew I might not be strong enough to do what had to be done, so I used some of the precious few seconds I had and screamed at Alison – **Help Me!** She understood, reacted instantly and…" Ruth looked across and left the grand finale to the damaged woman in the armchair who kept it pragmatic.

"We took him by surprise!" said Alison with quiet satisfaction.

* * * *

After the drama and angst, everything else was a little anticlimactic, but had to be gone through just the same. We had a brief break during which the marvellous Mrs Millsop supplied fresh tea and coffee, and then Sam took over up-dating,

"I'll be quick, we're all tired. First and foremost, we couldn't find any trace of Phillip in your mind Stella, not a whisper, we can only assume, he was able to reach you but unable to get any further." I hadn't realised quite how relieved I'd be as I took that in.

Sam went on, "But, we do know what it was you left in Devlin," I realised from the look David gave me, this might be another something he wasn't abreast of, goodness the surprises were coming thick and fast, I only hoped he'd still be talking to me by the time we left.

"Do you see here?" Sam projected a slowly revolving brain over the centre of the table and opened it up like a halved piece of fruit, "Devlin's brain, see where there's scarring? It's as if it's been burnt, but look just above that point," we all obligingly craned forward but I could tell, as could Sam, we weren't much the wiser. "It's not easy to make out, but where connections have been broken, new ones have developed, similar but not identical to the originals. That's the change Stella made to Devlin, that's why he found he could do what he did."

Boris put in "This is not something any of us had come across before but then we were never looking. However, the knowledge is invaluable - we think this is how Ruth and all the others were affected. The difference is that Stella made changes accidentally. Philip," Boris's normally impassive expression altered only fractionally but spoke volumes, "crawled in, and stayed. But we know what we're looking for now, we're confident we can eliminate any trace of him."

"Hang on," David had been following with fascination, "How will you find them, these other victims?"

"We think we can take memories from Ruth and Alison." said Sam, and grinned, triumphant at the discovery. It made him look like the boy he was.

"And Devlin?" I asked.

Rachael chimed in, "We will do the same for him and when Ed drops him back to his Mother, all Devlin will remember is doing some tests; shapes, colours, the usual sort of thing, but we'll be able to say with complete truthfulness that he's showing no sign of anything untoward.

"No!" said Ed. We looked at him, Ed didn't talk unless he had something to say.

"What?" Glory said.

"Philip created victims, he was about aggression and control, right? But Stella caused a change in Devlin by saving his life."

Boris had popped in another aniseed ball, so was a little muffled, "Correct, but when Devlin used it, he created chaos."

"He didn't know what he was doing," Ed said, "well he did, but not enough to factor in consequences. What Stella did was well intentioned, even if unintentional, but maybe there was something in him in the first place that allowed it to happen. Do we have the right to take that away? Look at Sam, look at what he's achieving."

"Sam was born that way," Rachael pointed out.

"But isn't it possible Devlin was too, Stella might just have kick-started what was there. Do we have a right to change that back? He doesn't need changing, he needs teaching."

Ruth, Rachael and Boris exchanged a flash of thoughts, so fast I couldn't catch them.

Boris looked around the room, "Anyone? Stella?" I hesitated I could see pros and cons. Devlin had family, how was that going to go – 'Your son has extra sensory abilities he caught from Stella. How about letting him come and stay with a group of strangers so he can learn how to handle it?' The others followed my train of thought.

Rachael said thoughtfully, "Devlin's Mother didn't need a lot of persuasion to let him come here. He's been expelled from two schools in the last two years, his parents are running out of options. We run a school for children who've had problems in mainstream education. Ed may have a point."

CHAPTER FIFTY-ONE

As I'd found so often in the past, the more traumatic the event, the more banal and down to earth everything is that follows. Not a bad thing, you couldn't live at that level of fear and tension for too long without going a little bit batty.

Despite the original dire weather warnings, further snow seemed to have held off for a while and David was keen to start for home before it got too dark and possibly started again. He wasn't getting any argument from Laura, who'd had way too much mucking in and was keen to revert to her more normal state of exhausted. As always, I felt the familiar wrench at leaving. I was also uncomfortably aware that a major momentous event, the birth of our baby had been shifted from centre stage for quite a while. I knew parenthood came with its share of guilt; I just hadn't expected it so soon.

Getting ready to go didn't take long because I hadn't arrived with much, other than Katerina and David's sadly mistreated overcoat. Mrs Millsop had helpfully washed everything of Laura's but it was still damp, so Glory insisted she keep the borrowed silk trousers and matching tunic. Perhaps, Glory suggested with a straight face, she might enjoy wearing them in the future and we had to avoid each other's eye as Laura smiled and thanked her profusely whilst thinking, "like that's going to happen!" For my part, I was relieved that David had, in all the panic, remembered to bring my hospital bag which meant I was going home in a track suit that was mine. It was a point that would forever count in his favour.

When we left, only Rachael, Ruth and Glory were there to wave us off. That didn't matter, bonds with Ed and Sam were unshakeably and unbreakably permanent. Boris? Well, perhaps Boris and I would always maintain a warm if wary distance, maybe in time we'd meet in the middle with affection but for now, mutual respect was fine.

It seemed Rachael had used up her cuddle quotient, "Oh, please," she said, "with all this fissy-fussing, you'll still be here next week. Never could make a quick exit, could you Stella?" and she smiled; not her usual, mustn't-scare-the-people smile, but the rarer one that lit her face with all the warmth, humour and affection she didn't show to many. That said it all, I didn't need more.

I turned to Ruth, who for warmth had pulled on an additional orange and green jumper vivid enough to be spotted from space. She held out her arms. I hesitated fractionally before I moved forward, only fractionally but of course she knew I was as afraid of what I might feel as she was; logic can lay out the facts, it can't always make you certain, but as soon as I hugged her I knew; only rich, deep purple lavender Ruthness; nothing more, nothing less.

"You're sure?" she murmured in my ear.

"Never surer."

Glory had been holding Sara until the last possible moment, she planted a kiss which Sara accepted with equanimity, handed her over to David and turned to give me a swift, fierce hug.

"Do me a favour?" she said, "Try and steer clear of trouble, just for a little while. And take care of that baby, poor kid does not know what she's been landed with." We turned at a shout from inside; Mrs Millsop was bowling down the corridor at speed, with the wheelchair and Alison and only narrowly avoided hitting the doorstep and sending chair and passenger flying.

"Here," she thrust a paper bag into my hand, "for the journey," she looked me up and down, "hmm, too much running around," then to David, "you make sure she puts her feet up when you get home." He assured her he would and gave her a bear hug.

"You, Mrs Millsop," he said, "are absobloodylutely wonderful, we couldn't have done it without you." She shoved him away laughing.

"Get away with you. Now do what I say, you hear? And make sure you eat and drink on the drive. I've not made those sandwiches just to fill in the time." I hugged and thanked her too, then bent to Alison in the chair. She rested the back of her hand on my cheek for just a moment.

"You've saved my life Stella, in every possible way. Thank you isn't enough, but it'll have to do for now." Beneath the colours of Laura's donated scarf, her eyes were bright and even in these last fraught hours, freedom had fleshed her face.

"You'll be OK?" I asked.

"Oh, I'll be so much more than that."

"If," said Rachael, "you are actually going, will you please actually go; we're freezing to death here."

CHAPTER FIFTY-TWO

The fallout was huge. Melvyn had been going out of his normally unruffled mind. He kept saying, it was the first time in thirty years of marriage they'd spent nights apart, and with a failure of his usual good humour, didn't take kindly to David joking he was probably well overdue for a break then. I think he was also slightly traumatised by the reappearance of Laura in exotic garb.

Disconcerted by his out of character crossness, Laura pointed out it hadn't exactly been a picnic. The truth was, she couldn't work out quite how everything had happened as it did – and all so fast - and the more thought she gave it, the more uncertain she was. Faced with the sheer impossibility of trying to explain to anyone else what she couldn't explain to herself, and back on home ground, she found it easiest to revert to type and a pill. She was, she explained in a weak voice, utterly exhausted; after all it's not every day one becomes a grandmother. She somehow managed to convey she'd delivered the baby with one hand, catered for a whole host of people with the other and between times dug paths through heavy snowdrifts to secure supplies. By the time she'd recounted this a couple of times, she'd convinced both Melvyn and herself, and marital harmony was restored.

I did feel our relationship had moved forward slightly and that I'd seen, if briefly, another side of her. I was surprised and pleased when she mentioned, in passing, she'd purchased and despatched a couple of silky scarves and a soft cashmere pull-on hat in bright fuchsia for poor Alison – just until her hair grows back, and had thoughtfully included some Marigolds for Enid.

My Mother, having established I was none the worse for haring all over the place like a lunatic, that David wasn't about to leave me due to said haring, and that Sara, thank God, showed no evidence of 'strangeness'; shed tears of relief. She and my Father, able to read a lot more between the lines than Laura, weren't as amazed at how swiftly things had got out of control – they'd seen it happen before. Despite that, my Mother made it clear she'd been more than a little hurt it was Laura who was with me at such a life-changing time. She wouldn't dream of mentioning it again she said, but I suspected that it might remain for all times, the slightly martyred elephant in the room.

Our drive back from the school had been easier than feared, and in fact the predicted fresh snowfall considerably held off until late the next day, which allowed everyone to come and coo, congratulate and head off again. The heavens then opened and Great Britain ground to a complete halt for nearly a week, which suited us rather well and gave us a belated opportunity to get our bearings and give Sara some of the attention she deserved.

She was even to my inexperienced eye, an exceptionally good baby, sleeping through the night after five weeks. Religiously reading *Mother & Baby* magazines, whilst they were careful not to put the fear of God up brand-new parents, they intimated that terminal tiredness, baby brain and breast or bottle issues were likely to loom large. However, this baby proved the exception to the rule sleeping so often, so deeply and for so long, that on occasion I had to shake her, just to make sure she was breathing properly.

David was a man of two opposing parts that he was having trouble reconciling. There was no doubt, even whilst accepting it wasn't entirely my fault, he hated the danger I'd put myself in. On the other hand, he couldn't help but be pleased that Alison had been rescued from certain extinction, and a man who deserved all he got, had the tables turned on him so thoroughly. But he didn't want to talk about it all, in fact, he was trying to forget most of it.

Midwife Mavis, when I eventually got to the clinic for my check-up was reproachful.

"Had it," she said, shaking her head as she completed her notes, "occurred to me, heading off to stay with friends during the worst snow for years, might not be the brightest idea?" Nevertheless, she was delighted to pronounce that Sara and I were both in excellent working order and I seemed to have experienced far fewer issues than she would normally expect from a first-time Mum. Under her approving eye I nodded and smiled a lot, appreciating it wasn't so much an issue of innate ability, more short spells of inattention, because awkward situations such as the ones we'd been in, tend to demand full concentration.

* * * *

It was always planned that I'd go back to work, the only difference being that now I had baskets either side of my chair; Katerina in one, Sara in the other or occasionally both in the same. Kat had taken upon herself a supervisory role and would sit in the Moses basket, accepting the kicking of small feet as just part of the job.

It was no surprise I'd had no luck in pushing through the no-family-visits office rule. If anything, conviviality only increased. I sometimes wondered how we managed to churn out the amount of work we did, with maximum professionalism, minimal error and universal client satisfaction. There was one thing which had been playing massively on my mind, and I put off dealing with it for as long as I could manage, but eventually everything has to be faced.

Trevor had spent a considerable time in hospital, unconscious for the first two weeks, during which Joy had taken time off, before then deciding she was better when at work. She said if she was at home doing nothing, she'd simply go round the bend although, visiting hours permitting, she spent most of the rest of the time at his bedside.

In a quick consultation with Hilary and Brenda, mercifully not in the toilet, they couldn't really tell how she was, other than distressed and worried over Trevor, although Brenda muttered;

"Maybe best if he doesn't come round. A leopard doesn't change its spots," then in answer to Hilary's expression, "Oh, don't give me that look - only saying what we're all thinking." Joy hadn't said a word about what happened 'that day', so we'd all followed her lead and it wasn't mentioned. I knew I ought to spend some time with her, sit down and talk; truth was I didn't know what to say. I'd gone over it often; what I'd done, could it have been done differently? Had my intervention caused the stroke? And then latterly, with my unwelcome new knowledge, could I have affected

Trevor in the same way as Devlin and that didn't bear thinking about. My reflections usually came full circle, there was no doubt at the point in time I took him down, something had snapped in his mind, his intentions were murderous and measuring all the 'ifs' and 'buts' against that certainty, didn't leave much else to say.

Initially when he did come round, it wasn't known how much damage had been done, but with the endless patience and persistence of physio and speech therapists, his improvement was swifter than expected. To Joy's delight (and Brenda's misgivings), at the beginning of April he was allowed home and the grey pall of worry hanging over Joy started to dissipate.

Almost imperceptibly during that time, she'd been gradually slipping back to who she had been. Her hair was bobbed, because it was too time-consuming to dry and style when long. This way, she pointed out, a quick fingers-through did the job and she was ready to go. Prior to Trevor's illness she'd been toning down her bright blonde natural colour with a brown wash, but now said she simply couldn't be bothered to re-apply and so for a time, until it grew out, sported a slightly piebald appearance which didn't look as odd as you'd expect. By the time she was ready to welcome Trevor home, she was back to bright blonde and had reverted to red lipstick because she said it cheered her up, whereas the pale beige gloss she'd been using only reflected what she was feeling - and that wasn't great.

I'd cravenly avoided visiting Trevor in hospital – new baby and all that - then when he came home, put it off until such time as I couldn't put it off anymore. But I went mob-handed, choosing a day I knew I'd be flanked by Brenda and Hilary. I left Sara with my Mother and Aunt Edna, along with a carefully typed out schedule, of which I knew they'd take no notice whatsoever.

During my previous somewhat fraught visit to the house, there hadn't exactly been time for a conducted tour, but I did remember how dark and dated the decorations were and indeed most of the furniture. However, when Joy ushered us into the hall, it was all light, bright and colourful with flocked wallpaper banished.

She laughed when she saw my expression. "Yup, bit of a makeover - Mr Pegneddy, I've had them hard at it and I want to talk to you about something," she was leading the way into the living room. I hadn't been in there before, but there was no mistaking the Joy touch here too. She'd done away with nets and drapes, great heavy green velvet things she said, swagged to kingdom come. Instead, she'd put in thin slatted blinds, matching the off-white walls which were lined with large colourful framed prints. She'd kept the sofa and armchairs, dark brown originally, but now re-covered and with a whole new lease of life.

Trevor rose from an armchair to greet us, he was leaning on a walking stick, but other than that, and an almost imperceptible hesitancy over some words, I thought he was getting back to his old smooth self, but as I shook his hand, and went into his head, I couldn't have been more wrong. He wasn't back to anything like his old self. The constant internal dialogue had stopped and although we were only exchanging small talk, what he was saying was what he meant, there seemed to be no element of control, criticism or impatience running beneath, and when Joy went over to stand behind him and rest a hand on his shoulder, he reached up to cover it with his, and he wasn't doing it for our benefit. I had heard stroke survivors sometimes underwent personality changes, but this was amazing. I relaxed a little then delved deeper and relaxed even further, I couldn't find or feel anything I might have left behind.

"Tea and cake?" said Joy, "hang on while I get it, and Trevor; don't you dare tell anyone anything till I'm back!"

Joy had taken a couple of major life decisions and although it meant she'd be leaving us, that was the only thing we could find fault with. Sipping tea, I nipped into her head. I don't know what I expected, maybe a total blank as to what had happened between them, shock can sometimes mercifully do that, or maybe, I thought she'd have created a sanitised version she could live with.

I was wrong. Joy had complete recollection, remembered every dreadful detail and in fact had made up her mind back there, back then. If he survived the stroke, she'd do her duty, see him through and help him all she could. She hoped he'd get back on his feet, but if he didn't, she would organise and put in place whatever care he needed. Once that was done she was off. She'd made a terrible mistake; she'd chosen not to see what was happening in their relationship because she loved him, genuinely wanted to please him and hated the thought of being out there on her own again. But she was an intelligent woman, had seen how a problem ignored, isn't a problem disappeared. She cared deeply for Trevor but she didn't believe people could change, and she wasn't prepared to take that risk.

Things hadn't turned out as she planned though. During his recovery, he seemed to be a different person. She didn't have what I have, but based on what she could see and hear, he'd changed. She didn't believe it at first and didn't plan to let it impact on her decision, but despite that, it felt as if their relationship had started all over afresh. She was still pretty certain she'd be going, but then she made her second big decision – if there was a chance, just a chance he was changed, did she owe it to him and to herself to see if she could rebuild a future?

"Trevor doesn't want to go back to what he was doing before," she was saying now, "he probably could but we've decided on a different direction. We're selling his practice but we'll still need income so, and don't you dare laugh," she took a breath, "we're setting up a Bed & Breakfast!" She held up a hand as if to forestall protest, although there wasn't any and certainly nobody laughed.

"We're centrally located here, not far from the Tube straight into town. We've five big bedrooms of which we only use one and two big bathrooms. There's another floor above as well, where the maid slept in the days when they had maids, smaller rooms but great view, and another bathroom. We're using the money we get from the practice sale to do up the rooms, one by one. She opened an efficient looking lever arch file on the table in front of her.

"Look, I've got a separate section for each room, they're all going to be different – colour scheme, furniture, style. We're hoping for a couple of permanent long-term lodgers and then a lot of come-and-go stays, business-people, that sort of thing. So, what do you think?" I saw how carefully she'd thought things through and the fine threads of growing optimism and below those, the carefully tamped down fear it could all come to nothing.

I said I thought it was a brilliant idea and as we started talking about how best to get word out, I glanced over at Trevor. If there was anything, anything at all I felt could hurt her, I wanted to know, but all I could see was his pride in her and excitement at their plans. Joy was sitting next to him on the sofa, on impulse I got up and went over to better look at the file with her. I moved his walking stick, so I could sit down. My hand where his hand had been, I didn't have long, so let it flood through me – I got nothing, not a flicker of anything that set alarm bells going and certainly no memory of anything at all prior to the time he'd come round in hospital. Maybe this was one leopard whose spots had changed. All I could do was wait with her; watch and wait.

CHAPTER FIFTY-THREE

To my enormous relief I had no return of the cramping, all pervading apprehension which had coloured my life for such a long time. I'd have liked to talk a bit about it, but I knew David didn't want to and I found the odd phone conversations with Ruth or Glory to be unsatisfactory, compared with the ease of communication when we were together. I hadn't of course spoken to Rachael in ages, but then she didn't do chatting. There had always been two sides of the fence in my life and I'd spent years making it clear to myself and everyone else, on which side I wanted to be. Whilst I'd been happy to use what I had when I needed it, straddling the fence in order to get involved in other things was now, more than ever not on the cards.

Obviously, along with my parents, David and I watched Sara closely and like all families came to the inescapable conclusion that if this wasn't the cleverest, most beautiful baby ever, she was pretty close. Everyone seemed delighted she was normal and showed no signs of anything else and if very occasionally, I might have wished their relief to be a little less enthusiastically expressed, it was only now I had my own child, that I truly appreciated what my parents had to put up with. There was a tiny blip at her six-month check-up.

"Ever noticed these?" Sara was on my lap and I had the task of holding her still so the doctor could check her eyes. With a gentle forefinger and thumb, he opened Sara's right eye wide again, making little clicking noises with his tongue for distraction purposes. "See?" he said. I instantly knew two things; firstly, I was the worst mother in the world for not noticing and secondly, I didn't need to see them, I had the same shadow markings on my eye. He guessed in part what I was thinking and was reassuring, "You wouldn't normally spot them, they're way up under the lid, nothing to worry about, rare but of no concern."

"It won't affect her sight?" I asked, although it had never affected mine.

"No, just a thinning of the sclera, the white outer layer of the eyeball - like a birthmark, sometimes runs in families, anyone else have this?"

"No," I said for no reason other than it felt right. If we were talking about anything being in the family, the less said, the better.

"Right, well, she's a bonny baby all round. Anything else worrying you, anything you want to ask?" There actually were several things I'd like to ask but didn't think that well-trained and highly experienced as he was, he'd have any of the answers. As we spoke, I was trying to get Sara back into her babygro, always a struggle if she didn't want to go.

He finished his notes, looked up and frowned, "Erm, haven't you…?"

"Got it back to front? Yes," I said, "and believe me, it isn't designed for this, but she's learnt how to pull the poppers open and if she wriggles enough, she's out of it."

He laughed, "Right, well let's see you in another six months, anything bothers you in the meantime, have a word with your Health Visitor or pop in and see me."

That visit unsettled me, I knew logically the marks in my eye were nothing to do with anything else and the marks in Sara's were the same, unconnected, but if I hadn't noticed them, was there anything else I hadn't noticed? I was policing myself carefully. At home plates were now carried to the table, cups didn't fly into the sink and if I wanted something, I jolly well got up and got it. There was of course, the odd occasion when acting on instinct couldn't hurt; driving us home from the office one day, just as it was getting dark, a large estate car shot from a side road practically under my wheels. I hooted as soon as I saw him moving but he didn't stop and I had to stamp on the brake to avoid unpleasantness. He must have been in a rush but nevertheless took the time as he drove ahead of us, to open his window and give me two fingers. The subsequent veering of his steering indicated just how disconcerting it must have been, to find he couldn't get them down again for a good long while.

****

By the time Sara's first birthday came round, and despite my protests that she honestly wouldn't know what was going on, plans were in place for a party that kept growing in numbers. We did have something additional to celebrate though. In November, David had been commissioned to do a series of articles which were going to be syndicated and there was the distinct possibility of a book to follow. It did present certain issues, but we'd have to find a way to work round those.

David was approached on the recommendation of a journalist he'd shadowed for work experience, years ago. They'd struck up an unlikely friendship and stayed intermittently in touch, David always relieved to find Roger was still alive.

Roger Simstridd was old-style Fleet Street, having earned his spurs in the days when you couldn't see your hand in front of your face for cigarette smoke, a bottle of whiskey was in every desk drawer and editors ruled with a rod of iron which they weren't afraid to use every time they lost their temper. Simstridd, when David met him, was a man weighed down by three bitter divorces, numerous children all estranged, and the deep cynicism which comes from reporting on the sourer side of human nature.

Back then he was a Fleet Street legend because of his unerring instinct for smelling out scandals however deeply buried. It was probably true to say, in his view, if something wasn't hidden under layers of lies it wasn't worth writing about in the first place. The scoops he garnered on the back of his intransigence, made knees knock at all levels of society, industry and government. He was a great reporter although that same intransigence never made him popular with editors. He was ethical to a fault and refused to exaggerate to enhance a headline, flat out rejected any suggestion of bending the facts and used to say, 'if an effing story, isn't the whole effing truth and nothing but the effing truth, then it's not effing getting Simstridd's by-line.'

One of the many bees in his bonnet, on which he'd been accumulating files for years, was the enormous sums of government money used to fund research into extra sensory perception, not just in this country but the US, Russia and China too. Simstridd's goal was to haul into the light of day, the scandal of what had been spent on crazy, no-hope projects. The problem was, whilst he was able to dig up a lot, the more he dug, the more his views changed. There were things out there, he told David, that simply didn't fit expected parameters. He didn't want to write about some of the things he'd come across because he'd be laughed out of the business, but neither could he bring himself to write the dénouement originally planned.

Recently Simstridd had been approached by a national paper to resuscitate the years-ago, abandoned project. Unfortunately, he wasn't in the best of health, having survived on alcohol, cigarettes and chips for 60 of his 70 years. He said he was way past taking on a big project like this, but he knew a man who might.

The advantages for David were many. He could do a lot of it from home, and that worked out well for both of us. Although there was no shortage of volunteers to keep an eye on Sara when she accompanied me to the office, it did slow up productivity and as she could crawl at a faster rate than most of us could run and yearned only to beat us to the stairs so she could hurl herself down, things could turn a little tiresome.

Finding myself totally overruled on the birthday party, I took the lazy way out and left planning in the hands of my Mother and Mother-in-Law, although apparently things got a little heated when it came to Victoria Plum versus The Munch Bunch and peace was only brokered by David suggesting a half and half arrangement. I did say I'd make the birthday cake, a suggestion which was greeted with so much amusement from all sides, that I felt it verged on the hurtful.

I was touched when a couple of days before her birthday, a parcel arrived addressed to Sara. In it was a set of building bricks from Mrs Millsop with a card, and also a tiny bracelet from Alison, who was back on her feet in every sense of the word. Glory and Ed sent something for me rather than Sara, on the basis I'd appreciate it and she wouldn't. It was a rather gorgeously coloured, thin, pashmina shawl which was surprisingly warm and the brevity of the note - Glory didn't waffle - didn't hide her affection. I left the box which was from Ruth, Rachael and Sam till last, It turned out to hold two carefully tissue-wrapped, beautifully made and painted puppets; a girl in a flower-covered straw hat and her dog. The dog bore more than a passing resemblance to Katerina and I wondered if they'd had the puppets specially made. They were gorgeous items but obviously needed to be put away until Sara was ready to handle them which, judging from the problem we had untangling strings after their journey was probably not going to be until her twenties. With the wooden cross-bar handle and attachment of a multitude of strings, the puppets could be operated in a highly professional manner, elbows and knees, jointed and moving as well as hands, feet and head. David raised his eyes to heaven when he saw them,

"Lovely, but if she gets her hands on them now, those strings are going to be impossible. Maybe we ought to cut a few out?" I was horrified and said so, I thought what we should do is establish them as decorative ornaments for her room, at least for the next few years and David said that sounded more sensible and he'd suspend a couple of hooks from the ceiling, which would hold the T-bars.

* * * *

We had the party on her actual birthday which fell on the weekend, and Laura and my Mother had truly pushed the boat out with mini bridge rolls; egg, cream-cheese and salmon bedecked, as well as enough cakes and pastries to cover next year's birthday too. When I mentioned this to David, he instantly made me feel mean.

"Look at the pleasure they're getting out of it." He said. I had reservations about the amount of pleasure Laura was garnering, but thought it best not to say. I think in her initial enthusiasm for the idea, she'd totally underestimated just how long it took to butter and fill more mini bridge rolls than you could shake a fist at. I also think she probably shot her bolt way before the party started, and as soon as everyone had arrived and lavished praise on the table, she declared herself a wee bit tired and thought she'd sit down with a cup of tea for ten minutes – a break from which she didn't rise until it was time to leave. Nevertheless, I genuinely appreciated everything she'd done and to be honest; sympathised. I knew to my cost that anyone with any sense of self-preservation did well to stay out of the way of my Mother and Aunts Edna and Kitty in serving mode. All three were hot-wired to sense an empty plate or cup from the other side of a room, and the speed with which this was remedied could send you flying if you got in the way.

Other than Sara, there were a few other babies and parents we'd gathered from our NCT class, although it has to be said that as I suspected, all the little ones sat through the party looking puzzled until it came to the cake, candles and Happy Birthday, at which point they all looked positively alarmed.

By the time everyone left and we got Sara to bed, it felt far later than the 7.30 it actually was. We'd put her down in the usual back to front mode because our babygro situation hadn't improved. On the couple of occasions we'd re-attempted the right way round, she'd not only wriggled out of the babygro but her nappy too - I'll say no more.

Collapsed at either end of the sofa, because we really felt we had to hold out until at least 9.00 before we could head for bed, David put the television on and I think I must have drifted off, until he said,

"Stella, don't." I jerked awake; had I been snoring? I hated it when that happened.

"Sorry?"

"You're going to get all the strings tangled again and it took us hours last time to get them sorted." He was looking at the armchair across the room where the girl in a colourful, flower-covered straw hat and her brown and white dog were dancing merrily, one on each of the broad arms of the chair.

"David," I said. "That's not me."

~**end**~

ACKNOWLEDGEMENTS

I'd like to say a heartfelt, thank you to the people who've earned my undying gratitude for their support, both professional and personal, without them, the Strange series would have remained in my head, and I think, on balance, it's probably better out than in!

Thank you to the saintly designer Gail D'almaine who creates all my book covers. She always manages to read my mind as to exactly what I want, then produces it, ten times better than I ever imagined. It is also the long- suffering Gail who takes my publicity head shots, and has to put up with a lot of whining because I hate having them done. We've had many an undignified tussle, last session we headed in through a hotel revolving door and I revolved all the way round and out again, forcing Gail to chase and bring me down with a perfectly timed rugby tackle. She eventually got me in place and posed and I honestly don't think you can tell how firmly I'm roped to that chair. Well done Gail!

I couldn't wish for a more wonderful publisher than Nicky Fitzmaurice of Satin Publishing. This book is a shining example of what patience, expertise and gritted teeth can produce, in the face of some truly daft questions, deadlines to be met and an author with a tendency to rock in a corner when things don't go well. Should you want to get hold of her, you'll find her recuperating in a dark room, in the local rest-home for beleaguered publishing professionals.

The biggest acknowledgements go, of course, to you **Wonderful Readers** who've taken Stella to your hearts – it is so much appreciated and I love getting your letters, emails and social media messages – please don't stop letting me know what you think.

I hope you enjoyed this third outing of Stella's, and should any of you lovely lot feel inclined to write a few words, please know reviews are always welcomed with open arms, small shrieks of delight and a happy dance, unless they're dreadful, in which case just small shrieks.

The Strange series was originally going to be a trilogy, but as time has gone on it seems to me Stella and co. have a lot more to say, so we're heading at least for a quadrilogy and who knows, it might not end there.

If you'd like to be kept up to date with my *Bookish News & Views Newsletter*, which comes out roughly once a month and features, new releases, special offers & introductions to other authors, just drop me an email or make contact through my site.

Finally, as always, love and thanks to my family for putting up with me – and Stella!

* * * *

05..04.20

e: marilyn@marilynmessik.com
w: marilynmessik.co.uk

About the Author

Marilyn was a regular feature and fiction writer for national magazines when her children were small. She set up her first business from home, selling toys, books and party goods, before opening first one shop then another. When she sold both shops, she moved into the world of travel, focusing on B & B's and Country Inns in New England, USA. Her advisory, planning and booking service flourished and she concurrently launched a publishing company, producing annual, full-colour accommodation guides to the areas.

In 2010 she set up a copywriting consultancy, to help businesses shape their messages to optimum effect.

She's blogged for *The Telegraph online,* created and published *The Vintage Ladies Collection,* written for businesses with *Getting it Write* and *The Little Black Business Books* and published four *Paranormal Thrillers.* She's been married to her very patient husband for more years than he deserves. They have two children, five grandchildren and, somewhat to their surprise, several granddogs.

Read more at Marilyn Messik's site.

Printed in Great Britain
by Amazon